T

Marshall Browne was born in Melbourne, where he now lives and writes. An international banker for thirty-eight years, he worked in the Far East and Europe. Banking has taken him to thirty countries, and the banking life and foreign locales have frequently featured in his fiction. He has written three suspense novels, including *City of Masks*. *The Burnt City* is his second novel with an Australian historical setting following the acclaimed *The Gilded Cage*.

THE BURNT CITY

Marshall Browne

ARCADIA

First published 1999 by
Australian Scholarly Publishing
PO Box 299
Kew Victoria 3101

Tel: (03) 9817 5208
Fax:(03) 9817 6431
E-mail: aspic@ozemail.com.au

National Library of Australia
Cataloguing-in-publication entry:

Browne, Marshall.
    The burnt city.

    ISBN 1 875606 59 9.

    I. Title.

    823.914

Designed and typeset by Green Poles Design
Printed by McPherson's Printing Group

The illustration from the front cover entitled
'Carlton Gardens' is taken from
The Picturesque Atlas of Australasia by Andrew Garran,
Melbourne 1888. Courtesy of
La Trobe Picture Collection, State Library of Victoria.

FOR MERELL

My thanks to the following authors for permission to quote from their well-known histories: Michael Cannon, *The Land Boomers*; Keith Dunstan, *The Store on the Hill*; Graeme Davison, *The Rise and Fall of Marvellous Melbourne*; David Dunstan, *Victorian Icon: The Royal Exhibition Building, Melbourne* and *Better Than Pommard! A History of Wine in Victoria*. And to *The Age* for permission to quote from *Melbourne's Great Outdoors Parks, Waterways and Trails*.

PRELUDE

Tonight the fretted Yarra chafes its banks,
And dusks and glistens; while the city shows
A ring of windy light…

Henry Kendall

Voyager

THE BODY floated down the Yarra River embraced by a languorous current. At ten minutes to midnight, on a high-summer February night in 1893, it was travelling in centre-stream about two hundred yards above the Church Street Bridge. The back of its coat had billowed up and the arms trailed in a kind of 'V', however, its progress left barely a ripple on the heavily smooth, effluent-slicked water. In that longish reach it cruised purposefully, as though well set on a voyage. On its right the street-lights of working-class Richmond glimmered, on its left the matching lights of well-to-do South Yarra pricked the darkness; each cast incidental, silvery darts on the pitch-black water.

To an imaginative observer, it might have seemed that the river, and the Southern Hemisphere city of Melbourne, showed each other a mutual disregard, the body, apathy—once the shock of the latter had been absorbed! But there was no-one…

The night was hot and airless. The stinks hovered over the water bad enough to make the gorge rise. In this sultry atmosphere, even the river's usual liquid swish and suck sounded restrained. On St Kilda and other beaches, people were sleeping out, hoping for a breeze. In the distant Dandenong Ranges it appeared a wind might have sprung up; looped across the darkness like an amber necklace, fires burned with a fresh lustre. For days the city had been hazy from the smoke, sickened by it.

That crescent of flame: eye-catching, thought-provoking; but not for this voyager…

At Church Street, in the indigo dark beneath the narrow, enclosed iron bridge a mini-whirlpool twirled it slightly, set it on an

1

oblique course for the northern bank. Perhaps it twirled of its own volition on to the new course, tiring of even this short voyage. It came ashore about half-past midnight to rest under a fallen tree-branch, pretty much hidden.

It was to remain there for several days until the river level, falling daily in that dry season, allowed it to float free and continue its voyage downstream to Princes Bridge and its rendezvous with Constable Thompson, a specialist—with his grappling irons—in landing these voyagers.

1

...573 acres planted with various kinds of pines, and with elm trees in clumps and avenues. It also contains an extensive natural lagoon, deepened and widened...and this is dotted with artificial islands...among the numerous 'lungs' of Melbourne...The surroundings of this fine and capacious pleasure ground have marked it out as the future Hyde Park or Bois de Boulogne of...Melbourne.
Historical Sketch of Victoria (1886).

The Lake

HE STOOD BACK from the parapet of the tower as if wishing to observe without being seen. However, it was midnight and unlikely that he would be seen by anyone. He gazed down, and into the distance between an avenue of well-grown elm trees, fringed by clumps of pines, to the Albert Park Lake. In the becalmed night and the moonlight, the trees stood like statues, the lake like a sheet of ice.

Tonight it seemed near, and from his fifty-foot-high perspective, slightly flattened and elongated—like a tiny Scottish loch he'd seen in '87. He breathed in, drew the sylvan-aqueous serenity into his soul. A substitute for cool air.

On this February night of heat and humidity, the second most populous city south of the Equator appeared abandoned—or, perhaps conquered and under curfew? He smiled one of his ironic smiles; certainly, Albert Road, the wide-set thoroughfare curving between the line of residences and the parkland surrounding the lake, was devoid of humanity: not even the ubiquitous lights of a hansom cab. It struck him that the luminant pools of gas-lamps, stretching away on either side, demarked an empty stage.

He thought: A good metaphor for the way the city's fixed.

His name was Angus Wallace. He was coatless, his shirt open at the neck, the sheen of perspiration on his brow. He didn't often climb the tower of his house but the search for air had brought him up tonight. Not only that: two diverse matters, each complicated, needing a little time, awaited him in the study below.

Space, and air. But not even a breeze from the south; the black expanse of Port Phillip Bay, half a mile away, was as inanimate as the lake: not a single seaborne light. In his hall directly beneath him, the thermometer recorded ninety-one degrees. A native-born man of forty-two, he was as knocked about by the heat as the latest immigrant off a ship from Liverpool. So he told himself.

Next door, a pianist began to play. Mrs Hammond often played at night, not usually this late. The rich sound came up to him, faltered and died—without explanation. Abruptly, he turned to face north. Here, also seeming nearer across the rooftops, was the ghostly grey South Melbourne Town Hall with its fine-boned clock tower—the princess of town halls. It was the direction, also, of the city's heart—the cockpit of the calamity which had struck into it like a dagger.

The faces of men he saw each day in Collins Street came into his mind. Familiar, yet unfamiliar: stony faces with dead eyes; or, faces of tics and grimaces, hands that were dead-cold, or wet and shaking, belonging to men who stalked through the city like spectres—but cunning and desperate spectres—burning records, covering their tracks, muddying the waters.

Conspiracies, and webs of lies. On his desk, yesterday's *Argus* had within its pages the headlines: *The Freehold Investment and Banking Company. Civil Proceedings Against Directors Authorized.* This kind of thing was becoming a daily diet.

Was that a breeze? He faced south. No. The furls of Mrs Hammond's flag on its pole might have been carved from wood. He turned his back on the sultry night.

In his study, insects bonged off the glass shades on the gas wall lamps. The gas hissed. The room was infernally close, and dense with shadows. He poured a glass of water. Tepid—but wet. The two letters lay on his desk. He took up the top one and re-read it.

…As agreed in our discussions, we confirm that you are hereby appointed liquidator of the First Bank of Victoria Limited, pursuant to the decision of the Committee of Shareholders, and so forth, at a remuneration of ten pounds per day, and so forth…

Under the letterhead of Larkin & Larkin, solicitors, signed by his friend Philip Larkin. He dropped it back on the desk.

He was a barrister—admitted to the Victorian bar in 1879—had been a Minister in the Gillies Government during 1888, since then, back at the bar. He'd kept clear of the land boom and the boomers. Now, he was to be thrust into the heart of one of their disasters. And, given the rich weave of vested interests, recriminations, and fierce hatreds which were blooming on all sides, the appointment was not going to improve his popularity; especially with the Premier.

He was his father replicated, they said. The long, serious face with its aquiline nose; almost swarthy complexion; brown eyes, by turns meditative and level; thinning black hair. To that point, a carbon copy. But the lips, fleshy and mobile, were a variation. A worry, some with an interest thought. His father had been pessimistic and nervous. He'd been born, bred, on the English-Scottish border, where history was conducive to nervousness. His son wasn't nervous—merely careful, and calculating.

But not in *all* matters. He took up the other letter and went to a chair. A scented page, a woman's hand, large, rolling—enemies might say—devouring, characters. *My Dear Angus—A week since you have been here! And not a line from you. Are you thinking over what I said to you after the theatre?...With you, who can tell. That is the problem. Well, my dear, you must make up your mind. I feel I have done my part...I have admitted you to my affections—and dare I write this?—to my bed...And I have waited and waited for a sign, or a word. Have I waited, am I waiting, in vain? I am a woman who must know where she stands. You know me well enough to understand that. It cannot go on like this...*

The ink was smudging under his fingers; the night had closed in to sit at his back. What was he going to do? What *could* he do? He had a vision of her in one of her height-of-fashion green gowns, her green eyes, often restless, as often dauntingly steady. As they'd been that recent night. The emerald necklace had been brilliant against her breast. A tall, slim woman, except for that deep breast, who moved through a room with a well-founded air of superiority.

A woman to make your heart suddenly race. An intelligent, quick-witted woman. 'Dangerous, to a wayward bachelor,' a friend had whispered. He'd given a curt response.

His shirt was stuck to his back. And both were stuck to the leather of the chair. Irresolution, he detested, yet not every problem was capable of being solved. He listened. His housekeeper was long abed. Nothing but the faint 'talk' from the house's timbers moving in the heat.

Ten pounds a day! It meant something of a future. A life-raft. He had lost his money—not in the land boom; he'd found another way.

By God! There was a shortage of oxygen tonight. He felt a communality with his 490,000 suffering fellow citizens. He would try to sleep, prepare himself for tomorrow's meeting. It was going to be about as pleasant as rubbing salt into an ulcer.

When the smash came every bank manager showed himself to be a tin man painted to look like iron.

George D. Meudell, The Pleasant Career of a Spendthrift

The Liquidator

AT TEN O'CLOCK, Wallace, his clerk, Mainwearing Binks, and the solicitor, Philip Larkin, were admitted by a side-door to the premises of the First Bank of Victoria. The caretaker led them across the marble-floored banking chamber to the carved marble staircase which had been eulogized, Wallace recollected, by *The Age* on the day in '88 when the building was officially opened, and Sir John Adams had triumphantly strode in at the head of directors and staff.

Dead days, dead dreams.

The temperature was up already, though in here the marble made it cool. Nonetheless, it smelt dusty, was shut tight against its customers and anyone else who might've wished to settle their affairs with it. Payment had been suspended on the 28th October.

Wallace thought: Battened down tight—except against the incoming liquidator appointed to probe its mysteries, write its finis. He'd hardly slept, but cold water, a shave, a change of linen had revived him, and he was ready to deal with this meeting.

'Gentlemen waiting in the boardroom,' said the caretaker.

Reluctantly, they were. The four men rose to their feet from deep and crackling leather chairs in the cedar-panelled room. Peremptory handshakes, introductions not needed, they all knew each other—except for Binks, whose status didn't warrant one.

Wallace surveyed the room. 'This is a sorry business, Sir John, I'm here to look into it for the shareholders—and the depositors. See what can be done.'

Adams nodded, deliberately. He was a giant of a man, six feet six, Wallace understood, and broad to match—muscular, yet a paunch, looped with a gold watch-chain, dropped down heavily. He was fifty-five and life had been rich for the land boomers. Wallace knew him socially; they were members of the same club, which some might have found awkward. He doubted if the commercial potentate did.

'As you say, Wallace. Hard on us all. You'll have our full co-operation.' He stopped, pursed his red, moist lips. His beard was stylishly trimmed, and he'd taken to waxing the ends of his moustache.

Toned down that steam-roller manner of his, Wallace thought.

Larkin wondered if he had a new mistress.

They sat at the table; quite naturally lined up on opposite sides, setting an adversarial note.

The knight had folded his huge, white, soft hands on the gleaming cedar; the diamond rings on them sparkled, no change there.

'I second that...' the full-bearded man with the deadly light-blue eyes said.

Wallace turned. He'd long considered those eyes that. Jonathan Savage, member of the Legislative Assembly, land boomer, promoter of mushroom companies—and director of this failed bank. He'd come up against him before, in '88, when as Minister without Portfolio he'd investigated an imbroglio involving land purchases and a railway line. He'd exposed Savage's dealings, but an attempt to prosecute him had been blocked by the Attorney-General of the day; behind him had been the shadow of the expansionist Premier, who'd run the public debt up to mad heights.

Wallace had come out of it badly.

'...the bank's reputation has been whispered away by rumour-mongers, sabotaged by persons as yet unknown. A sound institution thrown on the scrap-heap.' Savage smiled, as if in due course, he would have the guts of these enemies. 'This, is what we trust you'll find out, Wallace.' The tone of arrogance held them.

Wallace nodded slightly. He shifted his gaze, took in the man next to Savage—Sandhurst, also a member of the lower house, another land boomer linked with Savage in that railway scandal. Not a better prospect: an oiled, olive, pock-marked complexion. Thick, black, curly hair. The essence of smooth urbanity; notorious for it. But dark eyes that speared into you.

Yet, it was Savage who'd silver-tongued the shareholders and depositors meetings, attempted to persuade those confused and desperate assemblies to put the bank into voluntary liquidation with himself and Sandhurst as joint liquidators.

Wallace recalled the lies, the bare-faced attempt to cover up whatever it was that needed to be. Fortunately, it hadn't worked. Now, it was his task to uncover. Knowing these men, it wasn't going to be easy.

Savage said, 'You wouldn't be here, Wallace, except for those damned London depositors, which you, Larkin, were pretty quick to act for.'

Larkin, the court papers under his hands, didn't respond. They'd agreed Wallace would make the running.

With an ironic smile, Wallace said, 'It's unfortunate the Londoners were out of range of your persuasive arguments. But that's history. I don't wish to take up too much of your time at present—nor have mine taken up. Please, listen closely to what I require.'

They flinched at that.

Tersely, he laid it out. The surrender of keys, seals, the assembling of ledgers, account books, letter-books, files, minute books, vouchers...the long list, painstakingly compiled by Binks, went on.

Each item fell into the room like a deadweight, was ticked off by Binks with a flick of his pencil.

'Should I bring in my laundry?' Savage interrupted.

Wallace ignored the sarcasm. 'You won't enter these premises except at my invitation. I'll require your presence, here, at ten o'clock Wednesday week for such examinations as I find necessary.'

Savage gave a low laugh. 'Oh? I'll print it in my diary in red letters.'

'Savage!' Sir John lifted his head from a lengthy study of the table-top, eyed his colleague, re-asserted command.

The parliamentarian rubbed a hand through his thick hair, displacing a pepper and salt shower. '*Really*, Sir John, this is a charade.'

Wallace looked up. 'I suggest it'll be in your interests to be here.' He finished his instructions, smiled coldly.

The fourth man, the chief manager of the bank, Jamison Smith, tall, balding, thin, with streaky sandy hair, and side-whiskers in which droplets of perspiration were set like diamonds, had watched, listened, totally fascinated, out of it. His glance had shifted around his old domain—as if seeing it with new eyes. The expression on his drawn face implied: Is this happening?

Wallace turned to him. 'What staff are still on the strength?'

His head snapped around. He swallowed. 'Douglas, the sub-manager. And Fellows, a senior clerk. And the caretaker.'

Philip Larkin scribbled a note, pushed it in front of Wallace. The liquidator glanced at it.

'The head cashier, Hubble?'

'Dismissed.'

Wallace raised his eyebrows. 'And Harbrace, the accountant?'

'Dismissed with the others, before Christmas.'

The chief manager's voice had creaked with nerves. All were silent. From the street, for the first time the faint rumble of carriages and drays could be heard. A sullenness had fallen on the room—as if the bankers, suddenly, had comprehended the situation. Even Savage's arrogant smile had tightened.

A lack of air…but no-one would open the windows. In this heat, the smells from the old cesspits were doubly bad.

Sir John gathered himself again. 'Wallace, I hope I'm wrong—but I've detected…a certain atmosphere. I'm a plain man and I put it plain. You're not coming in here with a notion that there've been acts of dishonesty, are you?'

Wallace regarded them for a long moment.

'Sir John, I'm here to do my duty. I have no preconceptions.'

It was a lie, but he was dealing with liars.

Keys clanked on the table—a sizeable bunch from the chief manager. Binks had retrieved the key register from a heap of books on a side-table. Signatures were required. Savage was last to sit forward to this. He signed swiftly, negligently, muttering to himself. Suddenly, with an oath he flung the steel-nibbed pen into the cedar table where it stuck vibrating with a whirring sound.

'Savage!' Sir John exclaimed.

But the mad blue eyes challenged them all.

The chief manager looked appalled; a slight smile played on Sandhurst's lips; no surprise to him.

Wallace sat still, ignoring the still quivering shaft. He said, 'I believe that concludes our business for the present.'

No parting handshakes, the ex-board and ex-chief manager filed out like the accused leaving the dock at a court recess.

'You were hard on them,' Larkin said. He reached out and plucked out that pen. 'It may be fanciful, but did I catch the taint of secret compositions?'

They had relaxed back in their chairs. Binks had gone out.

Wallace said, 'Not fanciful, quite probable, I'd say. If you were their lawyer, Philip, what would you advise?'

'Thank God, I'm not!'

'Cut and run—that's the advice they'll be getting. Do the secret deals with their creditors, keep out of bankruptcy.'

'Sir John…?'

Wallace glanced at Larkin. The solicitor was a close friend of the knight. Was it going to make matters awkward?

'In that, he'll be no different from the rest.'

Larkin stood up, went to the windows, looked down at Collins Street, squinted against the sunlight blazing back from stone facades. A mile-long horror stretch. He turned and looked at Wallace. Where did he get that dark face from? Almost saturnine, the thin black hair brushed back from the broad forehead. The eyes which bored into you. He was the man for *this* job. In the law, even politics, he'd proved himself as straight as they came. Had the enemies to testify to it. His mistakes lay in other directions.

Yet, in making the appointment, had he given enough weight to that old enmity? He'd felt the liquidator's collision of will with Savage and Sandhurst.

He said, 'God knows what you're going to find here, Angus, what we might be able to do about it.'

The liquidator raised his hands. 'After their performances at the Athenaeum Hall?…Let's wait and see. Ah, Binks. Got them off the premises? Let's get down to work. We'll need to keep a close watch on the rear-guard—Douglas and Fellows, isn't it? No doubt they're in the pockets of this board.'

In the street, Sir John merely raised his be-ringed hand in farewell to his colleagues, and immense with his stove-pipe hat on, walked up Collins Street hill amid swirling dust-clouds, his gaze straight ahead.

Savage watched him go with a calculating eye. 'Slash and burn, that's the kind of job we've got ahead,' he said to Sandhurst. 'Already, I've been doing a bit.'

He didn't elaborate and Sandhurst, his eyes also on the knight's receding back, looked thoughtful.

He said, 'Deuced bad luck to strike Wallace.'

'He didn't sink us in '89. We sank him. And he's not going to sink us now,' Savage growled.

'A sardonic smiler,' Sandhurst mused. 'But he's got a brain.'

They had ignored the chief manager. He stood by, listening to the exchange, rivulets of perspiration streaking his sallow face, his eyes moving from one to the other. They turned to him as though a trigger had been pulled in each of their brains.

'Buck up, Smith,' Sandhurst said, his urbanity back.

Critically, they examined the banker. Here, it seemed, was a weak and dangerous link.

3

*So George & George Ltd fought back with keenly priced items.
There were striped Surah silks at 1s 3 1/2d a yard in brown,
black, green, grey, ruby and cardinal. In the hosiery department
there was a black lisle thread hose with rich silk embroidery at 1s
11d a pair, and worth 'double the money'.*

Keith Dunstan, The Store on the Hill

Edinburgh Gardens

AT SEVEN O'CLOCK, William Boyd crossed the road from his house and
entered the Edinburgh Gardens. The light had a pearly lustre, the air
a transient coolness which would soon evaporate. In an hour,
Katherine and their maid would be closing windows, lowering blinds
against the expected north wind with its scalding heat and dust.

Direct from the continent's dead-heart, he thought.

The path through the gardens was his usual route to the tram-stop
in St George's Road. One of the city's 'lungs', the Edinburgh Gardens
covered thirty-four acres; was spartan and plebeian in character—
compared to say the verdant and venerable Fitzroy Gardens. But good
enough.

Sometimes this walk, when he felt optimistic, was a pleasant pre-
amble. Not this morning. He was keyed up, already entering the store's
substantial doors in Flinders Street, confronting the problems which
awaited him; which had been queued up since the summer of '90.

In his last phase, Tom Montrose had taken to referring to the store
as a ship; had even designed an emblem for it reminiscent of the coat-
of-arms of Paris with its ship and its island. 'I'm the captain,' he'd say,
'you're the first officer; the staff, crew, the customers, the first-class
passengers.' He'd been half-serious. Tom had died in '89, and he'd
been left to steer it through rocks and shoals, trickier by the month.
Dead-reckoning—and luck, had kept them afloat. For how much
longer?

He walked quickly beneath the rustling foliage, ignoring the glades of burnt-brown grassland on either side, a man of thirty-four, in a light-grey suit, wearing one of the new Panama hats recently imported by the Men's Clothing Department; thinner than he'd been twelve months ago; a touch of grey already at the temples. Lines of strain cut from the long, thin nose to a wide mouth. He had the look of a businessman up against it; his old easy smoothness had dropped away, though, he was still capable of it. Katherine accepted that he was a more earnest man than the one she'd married.

The tram from North Fitzroy glided along Brunswick Street, then Collins Street. He alighted at Swanston Street in the heart of the city. Another walk, past the scores of new buildings, mainly untenanted—exuberant facades, each square yard compacted with bits of every architectural style known to man—columned, fluted, dripping with a rich variety of stucco ornament. They reminded him of celebratory cakes. Baked too late!

The few people about were care-worn, shabby, unconfident. A drastic change from the swaggering eighties; the confidence of individuals, of society at large, was blown to smithereens.

He entered the impressive doors. Since 1890, Boyd, Montrose & Co. had occupied this wide-fronted, four-storey building in Flinders Street. He passed Miss Pettifer's burnished show-cases of finest gloves, filmiest laces, delicate embroideries...which weren't selling, skirted the elaborate staircase, navigated gentlemen's imported clothing...a similar drug on the market, to take the rear stairs to the office. Dust covers were still over the counters, floor-walkers and assistants, not yet arrived. On the landing, he turned to survey the full sweep of the ground floor. As artful an arrangement as a stage-set, but motionless, airless—and hangdog.

In his office, he removed his hat and coat, put on a light office coat, and went to the desk with the air of a man putting himself in danger.

The store hadn't made a profit since '90, had survived by using up its reserves, a large portion of its capital, and by increasing its overdraft with the Commercial Bank. He took up a document: the profit and loss statement for the previous month, began to scrutinize the columns...

He was manager, had been half-owner with Tom Montrose until, in '88–'89, the Machiavellian conspiracy of a dangerous individual had forced him into the county court where he'd been convicted on a criminal charge. The other consequence was his near insolvency, and the sale of his interest to an old family friend, Hilda Wilberforce. With

Tom Montrose's nieces, Mrs Wilberforce now owned the firm.

At speed, his eye and index finger ran down the handwritten figures. Bad news. Like castor oil, to be taken quickly. He looked up, a tiny, close-shaven man, with brown gimlet eyes, a snowy handkerchief drooping from his sleeve stood in the door. He appeared alert, yet weary. Isaacs, the accountant.

William leaned back. 'Another bad month.'

'Bad across the board, I regret to say, Mr Boyd. Wine and Spirits, Menswear, and Ladies' Fashions, the worst.'

'It can't go on like this.'

Isaacs, pursed his lips. How many times had he heard that?

William regarded the Jew who had come to them in '90, when they'd moved to Flinders Street and expanded their retailing activities: the start of the rot. He'd not yet looked at the list of creditors due for payment, knew that picture. Some were pressing, more would be soon. The bank was the key to the future—and given the shocks the banks had been taking…

'How does the overdraft stand?'

'High. £13,250. I've kept a margin for the payroll this Thursday.'

Isaacs moved into the room. A large room, full of heavy furniture, cracked leather chairs, framed testimonials on the walls from his father's and Tom's days. He had occupied this room for nearly three years, but had added nothing. Portraits of his father and Tom hung side-by-side: neat, prosperous-looking Irishmen in three-inch-high collars, out from Galway in '67. They were also buried side-by-side in the St Kilda Cemetery.

He thought: Each fortnight that payroll hangs over my head like the Sword of Damocles.

He said, 'And in this weather the customers won't be coming in.' He felt the trickle of perspiration on his brow. They couldn't afford the new electrical fans. 'Tell Mr Maybury the men may remove their coats.'

Isaacs nodded, but lingered.

William folded his arms, gazed at the statement. 'I suppose I must go and see Stevens. Find out what might be done.'

The accountant nodded at the broad, cedar partners' desk with its worn leather inset. 'Letter there from Mr Stevens, hand-delivered last evening.'

William lifted the financial statement, found an envelope, tore it open, read: *Dear Mr Boyd, I should be obliged if you would call on me at your earliest convenience…*

He put it aside. 'Two birds with one stone,' he said grimly.

As he turned to go, Isaacs gave him a look. It was his guess that the interview would encompass a single issue—the parties merely coming from opposite directions. He had an ear to the ground, knew what was happening in the bank managerial world—but then, so did Mr Boyd.

Katherine Boyd and her maid, Mary, had shut up the house. Behind the drawn blinds and shutters, they worked in a twilight. The dining room felt as salt-sticky as the St Kilda sea-water baths. This evening, come what may, they would throw the house open.

'Mary, pray for a cool change otherwise it'll be insufferable tonight.'

Thirty were coming. Katherine had even thought of setting up tables and chairs under the elms in the gardens. A radical step, to meet the extreme conditions. But yesterday's paper predicted a southerly change this evening.

'Prayin' is somethin', I suppose, but one of those electrical fans is what'd suit me down to the ground,' the maid said dourly. She had stayed with them from the beginning.

'Can't afford that,' Katherine said cheerily.

It was to be a buffet. Katherine, her darkish auburn hair loose on her shoulders, her arms bare, quickly and efficiently set out aunt Fiona's sterling silver cutlery from the Dublin maker. The table was covered with an Irish linen cloth: embroidered in silk thread, a hundred evenings work, she'd calculated. Exquisite work. From the age of six, aunt Fiona had sent her to the best teacher in Westport, ruthlessly criticized her efforts—though she hadn't sewn a stitch herself—demanding perfection from the earnest, trying-hard, orphaned child. She brought the tureen for the cold soup to the table, her thoughts moving independently of the preparations…

Why were they doing this? She sighed, in a mood, despite her brightness. She'd accepted with fortitude the social stigma of William's trial and conviction. So had he. As far as she could determine there were two schools of thought on it: one considered he'd come out of it with honour, a stronger character; the other excluded them from social life, 'cut' them in the streets.

It *had* died down. They never discussed it. They were well content to revolve within their small circle of friends.

'This 'ere?' Mary asked.

14

'Yes.'

Mary was setting out stacks of turquoise and white dinner plates, arranging the damask serviettes, wiping her brow frequently, but humming softly...

Katherine placed the silver pheasant as a centre-piece on the table; it was the only silver William had saved from his father's house. She swept her eyes over table, side-board. Everything looked fine, but she was uneasy...

Three years of marriage had changed her appearance only slightly. Her fine complexion remained untouched by the Antipodean sun; self-protection from that element had been Hilda Wilberforce's first lesson; the same slim and lithesome figure—and graceful carriage, which her height accentuated. At thirty, her pale blue eyes most often looked on people and events with sympathetic humour—accurately portrayed her goodwill. Her fine, sculpted lips, the long, thin-bridged nose made a first impression of delicacy. Closer acquaintance enabled the perceptive to detect a well-intentioned toughness. A kind of: What can I do to help you?

But for all that, a seasoning process had been going on. A change that William, and a few close friends, had picked up. She had known bereavement and anxiety in her own and William's affairs. However, in the past twelve months she'd discovered tragedies of a different kind, and the shadow of this sadness had entered her.

She carried in a tray of Waterford glasses—more of aunt Fiona—placed them on a table...

There was starvation in the suburbs. There'd been deaths. Three mornings a week she worked at a Collingwood refuge for the distressed—hard physical work, there was nothing of the table-sitting committee woman in her; harder even was the emotional strain. No miracles were in sight, nor should she expect any.

And now, on this day of her third wedding anniversary, she was to give a party. Not a lavish party—but nonetheless the food and drink would be adequate—and therein was the source of her unease. She hadn't wanted it, he had. She shook her head in exasperation. From what William said, it would be their last. Good!

Carefully she filled the decanters in the pantry with claret and hock. Carried them to the dining room...

The city *should* be awash with guilt, the civic leaders should be the most contrite people in the Southern Hemisphere! But, generally, it wasn't so. They'd abdicated their responsibilities—were burrowing around to save themselves. The pity of it all! Some men were emerg-

15

ing from the ruck intent on justice—and salvage; some women…

Her interior monologues! She smiled grimly at herself. Her mind had turned, unexpectedly, in another sadhearted direction. They were in the hands of Dr MacKenzie. In her heart, she believed no miracles could be expected in this case, either.

'We like to see a current account "in the black" now and again, Mr Boyd. Yours has been "in the red" for two years. What we have, I'm afraid, is a "hard core" of debt.'

Stevens, the manager of the Commercial Bank's main office at 30 Collins Street, sat back, his hands together on his blotter. 'Not a good sign, I fear—for us, for you.'

William was silent. The banker's predecessor had practically shovelled the money down their throats. But he was gone, sacked by an unnerved board, who, he suspected, should also have sacked themselves. They'd unearthed Stevens from a backroom to 'hold the fort'.

This room is hotter than mine, he thought. His Panama hat was on the desk together with the glass of water which the banker had offered. He stirred, drew on his energy, said: 'To be straight, we need another two thousand—pending a reorganization.'

An expression akin to pain flickered on the banker's face. 'Good Heavens, Mr Boyd! I've the board's instructions to *reduce* your limit.'

They regarded each other, as though across a chasm, into which one of them—or both—was in danger of falling.

'You've our last balance sheet—we're solvent. And you've first mortgage on the store—which we paid £30,000 for…'

'And which, my dear sir, is now worth £17,000 at best. *And*, which carries a second mortgage of £7,500 to the First Bank of Victoria where the liquidator's gone in and will be calling up overdrafts! So, *there's* a problem ahead.'

William considered that, said, 'You've a bill of sale over our stock-in-trade.'

'In today's conditions, in a forced sale, what's that worth?…I see you continue to run at a loss. Extremely worrying…What's this reorganization?'

William flinched, and steeled himself to articulate what he'd been sleepless over for weeks. There was no help for it. And, it might not be enough.

'We've been making cuts, economizing…I now propose to dismiss staff…twenty persons at least. Also, to reduce each employee's wage.'

At first, he didn't say that he'd reduced his own salary in the two preceding years. From nine hundred, down to five. Then, he did—the case needed everything he could muster.

'But if sales continue to be down?'

'We'll cut expenses to the bone, reorganize departments…reconsider our stock lines.'

In one sense, William was fortunate. Unlike many of the city's bank managers, Stevens was trying to distinguish between customers who had a fighting chance, those who were doomed. His directors were in a state of panic, and panicking more at each fortnightly board meeting.

'Could you provide additional security?'

The nub of it. William had known it must come to this. He put his chin into his hand, and studied the leather desk-top. He was not the owner, and yet he was carrying the full weight. Could he do this to Katherine—to himself? There was no other honourable choice. It was the tortuous way matters had evolved. He still felt the connection of proprietorship—of his father's inheritance. Faces bloomed in his mind's eye, Tom's nieces, Hilda Wilberforce, his senior employees. His determination, his energy rose.

'My house at Fitzroy—it's worth £1,500. Nothing else.'

The banker rubbed his damp face with a handkerchief, shot a sympathetic look.

'This is what I'll do—all I can do…'

With a sense of temporary reprieve, William walked up a scalding Collins Street, squinting against the flying dust. Tonight, after the party, he would tell Katherine. A pang of bitterness came: he knew exactly how she would take it.

4

I know she is fair as the angels are fair,
For have I not caught a faint glimpse of her there;
A glimpse of her face, and her glittering hair,
And a hand with the Harp of Australia?
Henry Kendall, *'The Muse of Australia'*

The Anniversary Party

A FEW MINUTES after eight, a happenstance convoy came with jinking lights, rattle of wheels and discordant jingle of harness, around the half-moon of road that looped off St George's Road to border the Edinburgh Gardens, heading for the Boyds' house which, with its Mogul-like dome, every window wide-open for air and illuminated, stood like a beacon on a benighted headland.

Watching from the portico, William counted seven lights approaching. Considering the diverse geographic origins of the journeys, it was remarkably good timing. Behind him, Katherine and Mary were rushing through the rooms. In the kitchen, Mrs Johnson was organized down to the last sauce-boat.

'William, my dear—all well?' Mrs Wilberforce, in an ivory silk gown trimmed with seed-pearl embroidery, swept up the steps to take his hand. All wasn't, but he smiled and kissed her warmly. She gave him a look, passed into the house.

'Our congratulations, William,' Lady Adams said, extending a white-gloved hand, shaking hands concisely—but, with as much warmth as she ever mustered, while Sir John's great figure towered over her in the half-dark, muttering something inaudible as he fumbled with hat and stick.

Ear-splitting, the shrill of cicadas came like a tidal wave from the heat of the dark parkland...

'My dear Hanna...so glad...' William kissed her... 'And this is the famous Miss Fairfax?' He'd turned to look at the woman at Hanna Dewhurst's side.

'Exceedingly famous, William. Susan this is William Boyd.'

Exceedingly *beautiful*, William thought, taken off-guard on this day of tribulation. His choice of 'famous' had been light-hearted—as had Hanna's response. Now he stood frozen in the gas-light thrown from the hall, arrested by a rush of potent impressions: as to blonde-ness, a glowing luminosity of skin...She had the most delicate and perfect features. Eyes—which were unwavering, of indeterminate colour in this light, but clearly intelligent, clearly sizing him up. A mouth—perhaps slightly quizzical. An intoxicating perfume...A woman to stand and stare at, and he was.

'My brainy friend,' Hanna had said with a laugh. He wasn't look-ing at a porcelain figure: he sensed the same efficient air of business as in Hanna. He thought: Is this the new breed of woman?

They shook hands. She was out from Preston, Hanna's life-long friend, and the bookseller had been excitedly extolling her accom-plishments for months. Obviously, Hanna considered it a major coup to have lured her to the southern city.

Hanna was a fine-figured, rose-cheeked, vital woman, but Miss Fairfax, in the department of looks, was another thing altogether.

'I'm so pleased to be here, Mr Boyd. I look forward to meeting your wife. Hanna has talked and written so much of you both.' A no-nonsense, Lancashire voice with a soft, rhythmical stress. And now, a warm, estimating smile.

They passed into the interior in a swirl of silk, the tempting fra-grance. He stared after them.

Moths made clumsy fluttering circuits in the portico...

Philip Larkin had arrived. The friends and contemporaries shook hands.

'What a day!' Philip said, spreading his hands. The ruddy-faced solicitor looked wrung out.

'I've had one of my own.'

'Is Sir John here?'

William nodded.

'This *is* going to be pleasant,' Larkin said, turning to contemplate the gardens, now dark, now mysterious. Then he shrugged at his host. 'Who was that with Hanna?'

'Miss Fairfax.'

'Oh, so she's arrived.' He entered the house.

In this fashion, William continued to greet their friends as they disembarked, climbed the steps, and passed into the house, the ladies' long-tailed satin gowns swishing, each arrival immediately bringing a

19

new peak of animation, as Mary with a tray of glasses of cooled hock, claret, and mineral water, picked them up and Katherine, despite her earlier mood, in her natural way, rejoiced at seeing old friends. No presents were brought; the invitations had forbidden them.

From that convoy all had entered—all, in fact, had arrived, if his recollection was correct. Except Angus Wallace, and Mrs Spencer. Would they come? He checked the street, went in to join the party, reflecting that all present were their oldest friends; it was a pity that some of them were no longer friends of each other.

The evening proceeded, as directed by Katherine. Drinks were had, plates loaded from the dining-table and sideboard, and conveyed to chairs arranged in the two front rooms which were connected by the hall. The ladies, lightly attired in summer silks, and satins, in which the colour red seemed to predominate, when not actually eating, adroitly fanned themselves with delicate fans; the men had been invited to remove their coats, none had.

At nine o'clock, there was a stir at the door. Mary was taking a dark-green lace-trimmed, satin mantle, a hat and stick. Angus Wallace and Mrs Spencer had arrived. They came into the drawing-room, each making apologies. He was perspiring, otherwise calm. She was her usual cool, aloof self. Her carriage had done in a wheel…These suburban roads! It took ages to find a hansom…

This injected a ripple of excitement—not because of the mishap, but due to them having shared a conveyance, having arrived *together*. Heads turned. Eyes met other eyes. Are they a couple? Then, plates were got for them, and they were absorbed into the gathering as grated cheese melts into hot food.

Katherine, having seized her first free moment, sat down with a plate in the bay window next to Hilda Wilberforce and Lady Adams who, she quickly found out, were not so much in conversation as engaged in a running commentary.

'The usual vision in green,' Lady Adams said, her sharpshooter's eyes levelled at Mrs Spencer.

'It's well-suited to those eyes, that complexion—and those emeralds,' Hilda Wilberforce responded easily.

'And, to her personality.'

Hilda laughed. 'She's one of the most elegant persons in town—and she won't give a fig for our opinions.'

'I wonder if she *is* with that man—or if it's an accident?'

Katherine, eating, listened to this exchange; they'd been invited together, but she didn't enlighten the commentators. She loved Mrs

Wilberforce who had been her mentor in the Colony, was less fond of Lady Adams—though she understood the social leader, and got on well enough with her. At least, the Adams had never rebuffed them. But that was Hilda's doing.

Laura Adams persisted. 'If she is. For her, it may well prove to be an *accident*. He's had woman after woman. We all know…Look at him. Takes the high-ground, a man of principle, they say. But what of his *morals*? Hilda, are you listening?'

Katherine looked down at her plate, hoped they would lower their voices.

Mrs Wilberforce's attention had drifted—in the direction of Hanna, and that fascinating young woman. Lady Adams leaned closer, did lower her voice.

'And now he's after John and his directors. It's scandalous!'

With a slightly strained smile, Katherine rose, and went to the next room. All around her fans were aflutter like trapped birds.

John Adams, seated slightly apart, was giving his attention to his food. No-one approached him. His brooding mood discouraged it. He'd seen Wallace come in with the Spencer woman, but they hadn't come around the company so he ignored their presence. He'd exchanged a cool nod with Larkin. The same as he would've given Wallace, if he had come around. It suited him to sit incommunicado. Different from the old days, he thought. Probably, he should make more of an effort. A man didn't want to be seen as lying low. But his spirits, his energy were not up to it…at present. Taking a sabbatical, as those academic fellows say.

He cogitated as he chewed his food. He'd been accustomed to the occasional setback in the past, but these days shocks were coming thick and fast, and the credo on which he'd built his business life seemed to be cracking up. He raised his eyes from his plate, stared morosely down the room. Everything was in a state of flux…

What a striking woman! His attention arrested in mid-conversation, glass held aloft, Wallace stared at the blonde woman around whom several persons of both sexes were clustered. He hadn't been introduced. She must have been in the other room. He stood beside Helena and Philip, who seated, were chatting.

Helena Spencer, her eyes ever alert noted his gaze, smiled slightly. Was he a hopeless case? Before the night was over, she was determined to have the answer. With her height, gracious carriage, dark handsome looks, monumental bosom—and vivacity—she was usually the centre of attention. But not tonight. Was it a sign? She was no stranger to small flashes of irony against herself; no-one would have guessed that.

Philip Larkin was talking about the Panama scandals in Paris reported that morning in *The Argus*. It was a topic which fascinated him.

Her eyes found William in the hall, momentarily disengaged. She considered him with the air of one who's discovered a once-coveted painting, on the wall of a friend's house. In his bachelor days, she'd run her eyes over him, been tempted. There'd been something which had held her back. A different man now…but safely married.

'Are you seeing wonderful visions, Angus?' she said.

Wallace glanced down at her, but, the barb released, she'd turned back to a nonplussed Larkin.

Mrs Wilberforce thought: William is so tense. It must be worse at the store. *Is* it a lost cause? How terrible to think that. These wretched times! Are they going to drag down even the most prudent of us?… As for Katherine…

Hilda Wilberforce was disturbed: these were the two persons she was fondest of in the world. She must sit down tomorrow, really devote some thought to it.

With her dark eyes, she scanned the room. John and Laura. A crisis was coming there…Did Laura understand what was happening? Was she prepared? It appeared John hadn't been frank with her. What fools these men had been! Still were.

She shuddered, her shrewd mind had grasped that, in John's case, the disaster might not be confined to his solvency. She would need to stand ready for Laura.

'Delightful party, Hilda,' a man said. Judge Mountain. He didn't enjoy parties.

Reluctantly, she surfaced and saw the slight, grey-haired judge giving her one of his white-lipped, acerbic smiles.

Come closer, she motioned with her fan. He did. The pale, aesthetic face now floated attentively above her. Much to the surprise of her circle, the dry-as-dust judge had succeeded her previous companion—Tom Montrose—who'd died three years ago, who'd succeeded William's father. In her case, no-one quite understood what 'companion' signified. It did mean sitting at the head of her dining table on occasion, escorting her to functions.

William had never been able to work it out. One thing was clear—his father and Tom had had the highest regard for the chatelaine of the big house on the Fitzroy Gardens—which seemed also to be the case with the judge. And why not? At fifty-four, statuesque, full-figured, with those striking black eyes which could smile or blaze with equal power, an unblemished face delineated with common sense and good humour, of independent means—and with egalitarian ideas which were a breath of fresh air—she was a catch for any discerning, liberal-minded man who was available.

'Are you being serious, Edgar?'

'I am. Some currents are adrift here tonight which interest me.'

'Yes? Perhaps you'll tell me later.'

'My dear, I think everything here's an open book to you.'

Not everything, she thought.

The judge tended to pay her compliments—something she'd not seen him do to anyone else. As always, she took compliments in her stride. Before inviting him into her circle, she had followed his cases in the papers, had decided then, and since, that professionally he was clear-minded and unprejudiced. And, unafraid. The fact that he was sometimes quite boring she could put up with.

At last, she smiled at him.

Across the road in the gardens, avenued and bunched, the elms stood deep-rooted and heat-struck, the dusty leaves might've been fashioned from metal…

And someone was banging metal—a large spoon—on a silver tray. Philip Larkin. Mary and Mrs Johnson were handing around glasses of champagne. The solicitor, fair-haired and nuggetty, stood side-on in the hall between the two rooms, waiting for silence. Katherine perceived his sadness, but he was intent on what he was doing. He made a short speech, proposed the toast. William responded very briefly. After all, a third wedding anniversary…Why had he wanted the party, Katherine wondered again.

Outside, there was a distant, rushing sound like an on-coming steam-train. Katherine tilted her head. The cool change struck the house. The pushed-back curtains went flying, the flowers waving. The men cheered as if they were at the races. The ladies waved their fans in celebration. After four days of unremitting heat, the southerly had arrived!

The party had gained a second lease on life—conversation enlivened, second glasses of champagne were taken. Katherine headed for Hanna and Miss Fairfax with whom she had had only the briefest of conversations as yet.

Lady Adams had rejoined Mrs Wilberforce.

'What is going on with Hanna and Philip, Hilda?'

'It's moving forward, I think.'

Lady Adams looked doubtful. The matrons were adept match-makers and they'd had the young spinster and the young widower in their sights for twelve months, had made a pact on it. Tonight, though, Laura Adams was ambivalent about Larkin. She produced a lorgnette from her bag, and turned in another direction with the air of having saved the most interesting topic till last.

'That girl from Lancashire is quite stunning. So assured. Now—if she had a suitable gown, a fashionable hair-style. Of course, not *very* young…'

Hilda said drily, 'Like Hanna, I suspect her mind is on other matters. Really, I find it quite refreshing. Hanna says she's brilliant. She was the right-hand to Sir Somebody Or Other, a department store magnate in the north.'

Lady Adams showed exasperation. 'I'll never get used to these girls being in business. Doubtless, *that* knight has one of those titles they're handing out to the *nouveaux riches*. I expect he's a barbarian with his knife and fork.'

Mrs Wilberforce smiled. Sir John had received his in '89, following a donation of £10,000 to the Imperial Institute. She said: 'At any rate, after Lancashire, this must seem very strange. Hanna is bringing her to me for tea next Thursday. Are you free?'

'I believe so…I see it's eleven, well past John's time to retire. Will you break this up, Hilda, or will I?'

The guests had gone and the house was filled with the blessed, billowing breeze. William had taken out the empty bottles, re-arranged the furniture, turned off the lamps, while the three women washed and cleaned up. Now, he and Katherine were in their bedroom at the top of their house—level with the garden's tree-tops now buoyant with the noise and movement of foliage seemingly fleeing through the night. They seemed in an eyrie, in a gale.

He gathered himself: the moment he'd been dreading. He sat on their bed and very deliberately told her of his visit to the Commercial Bank, of his agreement to mortgage this eyrie-like house. His voice was heavy, yet he spoke with determination.

'I should've made changes earlier. I've been putting off the evil day. Stupid, really. We'll have to let twenty or more go—and you know what that means. There're no other jobs. But, it'll buy us time…perhaps save the rest. If I can find the right strategy—and trading conditions don't worsen. There are obvious things to do. But a radical re-organization must be attempted…I'll take it all to Hilda.'

She stood at the window, an arm extended to hold back a whipping, snapping curtain.

He added: 'This house is really all we have. Tom's attempt to give us a fresh start.' He smiled tensely. She turned back into the room, serious, but reassuring.

'Dearest, if it must be done, it must.' She looked directly into his eyes. 'There's no need to discuss it further.'

But their thoughts dwelt on it, as they prepared for bed. In the past, she had offered to sell the small estate which aunt Fiona had left her in Ireland. It would bring in little enough, earned practically no income. He'd refused to even consider it. Something occurred to her now: Did he see it as a kind of bolt-hole?

That Katherine had taken the disastrous news as he'd anticipated, didn't ease William's feelings. On the contrary, he felt his responsibilities aggregating. They seemed to tower above him like one of the city's dark and empty skyscrapers—dramatized by the wind streaming through the trees.

In a surprising turn, he found himself thinking of Miss Fairfax. What had she thought of tonight?

———

Wallace and Mrs Spencer travelled home at a brisk pace through Fitzroy and Carlton, skirting the city's heart. The streets were depopulated, other traffic non-existent. What lay between them had not been spoken of, but would be shortly. It seemed as if each were waiting for the other to make the move. In reality, the delicacy of the subject, the mishap on the journey out, and the whole evening being ahead of them, had conspired to a postponement.

Asking her permission, Wallace had lowered the window, removed his hat, and his thin hair was ruffled by the breeze. Thank God for it. At his side, her uncovered *décolletage* put a pale, fleshly glow into the hansom's interior. Into his mind.

He turned to her. 'I've had your letter.'

'Of course. Why didn't you respond?…Did it slip your mind?'

'It required thought.' He didn't wish to say that almost all his waking moments had been consumed by the bank; that there was a chasm between their immediate priorities. Now he was facing it; he sensed her coolness—anger.

'I see. As with one of your legal briefs?…I may not have put my feelings in precise words, but I believe the *fact* of the letter—and the tone—must've let you know where I stand.'

'Yes.' It was as clear an ultimatum as he'd ever received.

'I've taken more risks for you than I would normally choose to take. It can't go on. *You* must say where you stand. Forgive me, your reputation with women has not been very well concealed.' She paused, probably it was exaggerated, these things usually were. However…'I observe the way you look at attractive members of my sex. For me to linger any longer, without an understanding…would not be prudent, not in my interests.'

He reflected that others had, and had paid a price. He regretted that, but it was water under the bridge. She was of different mettle— that was becoming clear.

She said, 'My dear, you have said you love me.'

He had. The subtle shaking of her body in the well-sprung hansom, the fading fragrance of her perfume over the odour of their bodies which had been heated, now were cooled, vividly brought back to him the circumstances of that declaration.

Her hands rested on the small evening bag on her lap. 'I have money enough—so it is not that.'

No, it wasn't—though, he was strapped himself.

It was thirty minutes since they'd left Fitzroy, and they were entering her street in South Melbourne. Too soon for him. The hansom drew up at her house, he helped her down, motioned the cab-driver to wait. The street, prodigiously wide, wanly illuminated by the gas-lamps, seemed like a desert, they, two travellers conferring on the direction to take.

Inconsequentially, he thought: The town surveyor, who ran amok.

They stood in her portico. He was not going to be invited in to a candle-lit supper, the soft bed…and still he'd not resolved his position…

To her, it was a great puzzle. He'd the reputation of being articulate in the courts. That he'd left a trail of women behind him, some of them deceived, she didn't doubt, though not, she thought, having come to know him, by design. In her case, she felt strongly and instinctively that his manner, when she'd at last pressed him, didn't infer *that* kind of exit. So, what was it?

Her steady gaze was on his face. She was only slightly shorter than he. 'Do you wish it to end like this? You are a free man, aren't you? Or, is there something I should know? Should have known?'

She'd found the nub of it. He said suddenly, 'Helena, I don't wish it to end at all. There *is* something…Something exceedingly hard for me to deal with. One day, I may have its measure…'

She emitted a drawn-out sigh. He heard it with deep regret. Not a message of hope. 'We are a lost cause.'

'I wouldn't say so.'

'I can't wait. Too many mistakes are made of that kind. I don't wish to look ridiculous—or worse. Will you say nothing more?'

He was silent.

She pressed her lips against his. 'Goodbye, my love.'

She went in, leaving him standing, hat in hand in the street, with the after-taste of a new experience. The magnificent door had closed as softly, as irrevocably, as that final kiss. But it was to take him a while to understand that.

5

SHOCKING DISCOVERY IN THE YARRA
A SUPPOSED SUICIDE

The body of a young man was found…opposite the Sir Henry Barkly Hotel, Punt-road, Richmond, yesterday afternoon. The body was lying partly in the river, which was discoloured…by blood…from a gaping wound in the forehead. Near the right hand, which was outstretched, was a six-chambered revolver, with two of its chambers recently discharged…The clothing consisted of a suit of heavy dark tweed, white shirt and collar, and lavender tie and elastic-side boots.

The Argus, *24.2.1893*

Conspiracy of Silence

'HERE'S SOMETHING,' Binks said with a direct, cryptic look. His eyes, blinking quickly, signalled a certain tension. It was five after eight, and Wallace had just arrived at the boardroom. He went to his assistant's side, and looked down to where Binks' finger had come to rest on page six of *The Age*.

DROWNING AT JOLIMONT

A body, identified as James Robert Hubble, was found floating in the Yarra, upstream of the Princes Bridge, at about 4:00 o'clock yesterday afternoon. The deceased was formerly Head Cashier of the First Bank of Victoria. The police confirm that the deceased had been missing from his lodgings since Tuesday last. The matter is in the hands of the Coroner.

The liquidator read it twice. He felt a surge of apprehension. 'Mmm, that's a turn-up.'

Binks, staring at his ink-stained finger, still marking the spot, thought it an understatement. They pondered the development.

'Did he get our letter?' Binks said.

Wallace discarded his hat, began to unpack his brief case. 'We might well wonder about that—and a few other things.'

Having found out his latest address they'd planned to interview

Hubble at the earliest opportunity. They'd not yet tracked down Harbrace, the bank's former accountant.

Except for the caretaker they were alone on the premises. The two remaining officials had been questioned the first day, and dismissed. A week had passed since Wallace had taken up his appointment—since the first tense meeting with the directors. It would be interesting to see what effect a week's reflection had had on them. The chairman had promised their co-operation. In Wallace's opinion, Sir John might not carry the others with him on that point.

Binks said, 'Mr Larkin's coming at half-past nine. The rest at ten—if they turn up. I've got the auditor, Moore, this time.'

Wallace nodded, and ran his eye down the notes he'd spread out before him. 'Floating in the Yarra,' he murmured.

Despite Binks' pessimism, they arrived promptly. Led by Sir John Adams they filed in and occupied the five chairs across the polished cedar table—one of the few assets he was, as yet, sure of, Wallace reflected drily. No hand-shakes today, they'd gone past that.

Wallace said, 'Good morning. Have you heard about Hubble?'

Obviously they had. Each, in his own way, indicated it, though none spoke. The silence lengthened, and Wallace let it.

'A sad and tragic event,' Sir John said.

'One might say in tune with the times,' Wallace suggested. He'd wanted to put this on the table first up. In a new silence, they evaluated that possibility. Jonathan Savage broke it.

'Nothing to do with our business—which I suggest we get down to. I've got pressing matters to attend to in town.' His eyes flicked to the scar on the cedar.

Wallace glanced at the parliamentarian's sardonic face, looked down at his notes. If Savage had more pressing business than this…The liquidator looked at Sir John. 'It's early days yet, but already we've turned up certain interesting situations. For example, the bank's books don't balance! Didn't balance on the date of its closure. May not've balanced for some time. An extremely basic point, I'm sure you'll agree. Nonetheless, one that's giving us some difficulty.'

'Accountants' work,' Savage growled.

'Do you think so? But then Harbrace has disappeared. At least, we haven't found him yet. But we do have the chief manager with us— and the auditor. One might think they're qualified to comment.'

Wallace had been studying his notes as he spoke. Now he lifted his eyes to Jamison Smith. The chief manager appeared perpetually awash with perspiration: his fingerprints smudged the glittering table-top. He reddened at the hint of sarcasm, but kept quiet. A nervy kind of recalcitrance, Wallace judged. The liquidator raised his eyebrows, looked at Thomas Moore, the auditor, who hadn't been present at the earlier meeting. A dark, narrow-faced man, black circles under his eyes, a fancy and fastidious dresser, a yellow waistcoat. A trace of scent? Definitely, a worried expression.

The auditor said, 'I assure you, they balanced at the last audit.'

'Which was?'

'The 30th of September last.'

'Of course they did,' Savage sneered. 'Always have.'

Wallace smoothed his hand over his notes as if to put it aside for the moment—a mannerism from his time at the bar.

'Always have?' He smiled his equally confident doubt. 'Let me give you another interesting example. Gentlemen, I'm just throwing these up as pointers from a rather rich lode to give you our drift. The bank suspended payment on the 28th October, and the board paid itself fees amounting to a thousand pounds two days later. Fairly surprising?'

The silences were accumulating—becoming a deadweight. Wallace turned back to Sir John.

'The fees were properly due,' the knight said.

Wallace smiled, shrugged. 'Do you think so, Sir John? Payment was suspended! I believe you'll find some contrary opinions on it. No matter.'

He turned to Moore. 'Our schedule of loans shows your name on the books as a debtor—overdraft of £5,200. The bank's external auditor?'

The liquidator raised his hands a little, to illustrate his surprise, or, perhaps, his lack of it.

'Don't answer,' Savage said.

Wallace smiled. He wasn't expecting explanations at this stage. Nor was it his intention to give these men 'the drift' of his investigation, despite what he'd said. Already he and Binks, in a week of fourteen-hour days, with Larkin present at some sessions, had found out much more than he was laying on the table here.

The fog of negligence and mismanagement was one thing, but he'd smelt the stench of criminality. There was more to be mined at deeper levels. Much as a geologist sizes up terrain, he and Binks had surveyed the scene, dug into the books. Today, he was putting up some thought-starters; he suspected he'd be putting up the heart-stoppers later. He wished to concentrate their minds, drive in a few wedges, explore who might crack.

It wouldn't be Savage. You didn't often see men with eyes like that. As for Sandhurst, the Legislative Assembly member had hardly moved a muscle. Not spoken a word, had a skin as toughened as rawhide; a mind as cold as ice coming out of the Federal Coffee Palace's new plant. He was watching with his snake-like urbanity. His oiled, olive face seemed impervious to all influences. Wallace remembered him in the witness-box in '88.

Nor Sir John. He seemed to be miles away. If the rumours in the city about his affairs in general had a smidgen of truth, the preoccupation was understandable. Even so, it seemed exaggerated…The signs pointed to the chief manager, to a lesser extent, the auditor.

He studied their faces, one by one. A row of masks, not yielding anything definitive on what was being processed in their brains. Even the chief manager, Smith, was unreadable on that count.

He said, 'We'll continue our work. The position of depositors and shareholders should be pretty clear in a fortnight or so. In the meantime, I feel sure a meeting with Mr Smith will throw light on certain questions.'

He paused, deliberately putting the weight of the moment on to the chief manager. 'Please make yourself available this Friday, Smith. Ten o'clock.'

The chief manager's eyes had widened. The eyes of those on his side of the table were now fixed on him in an accusative gaze. 'Of course…at your service,' he muttered.

Savage brooded on the banker's face; he might have been watching the outbreak of a spot fire in dry country.

After the visitors, escorted by Binks, had left, Philip Larkin rose from his chair and paced to the window. By agreement, he'd kept quiet during the meeting. Wallace was determined to do it his way.

The solicitor said, 'As I said before—you're riding them hard, aren't you? I mean, laying on the sarcasm. Do you think that's productive?'

Wallace laughed. 'Smith's the weak link. If we can get him going, it will save us a tremendous amount of work. Without it we mightn't get near the heart of what they've been up to. In fact, as individuals *none* of 'em might have the full picture. I'm guessing there's been several plays afoot. *They* know Smith's the weak point…Divide and conquer, my dear fellow!'

Larkin remained doubtful.

Wallace was back with his papers, turning them over. 'Look, you could bounce questions all day off the likes of Savage and Sandhurst and not get a straight answer—if that was their mind. And Sir John would close up like a clam—if that was his mind. So we'll go for Smith. Meanwhile, we'll keep mining away.' He brought out a small cigar, lit up.

After a moment, Larkin said, 'Don't be surprised if Smith turns up on Friday with a lawyer in tow.'

Binks had returned to the room.

'When you know about that Coroner's hearing you might slip along to it,' Wallace said to his clerk.

To Larkin, he said, 'Why would it surprise me?'

6

The report of the Charities Commission weighs heavy on the conscience of the Government.

Table Talk, *24.2.1893*

Holding the Line

KATHERINE WORE a plain cotton dress, an unadorned, wide-brimmed straw hat as she went to her work on this fine, warm morning.

She arrived at the Collingwood Presbyterian Church hall at eleven o'clock, and took her place at the copper in which the soup was heated. Some ladies on the roster were cutting bread. The queue had already formed in the bare, echoing hall. A silent line of women and children, a few men, from the backstreets of Fitzroy and Collingwood; a line of humanity, concentrated in its need and misery; a line of stunned, pinched faces, indescribable eyes…The stench of unwashed bodies, soiled clothes, hung over it, like a cloud of gas leaking from a street main.

A line to break the heart, Katherine had thought the first time she'd seen it, but no longer had time to. So quiet you could hear the floor-boards creak. The odd coughs and sniffles, a few querulous infants—even the committee apparently voiceless, as they worked.

Mrs Napier didn't like it. 'Come on, ladies,' she said, 'a few smiles, some chatter, please.'

Crisply efficient, they called her the sergeant-major. Some lady from East Melbourne—'the Melbourne Belgravia'—had thought of that. Five feet of military personality. Faces to feed, she said, get them through, get it done. But with more humanity than she showed. She kept the line under her critical eye. Today, three hundred had turned up. Numbers rising. She'd let them know when it was start-time with an instruction bellowed out to the far corners of the hall. None of your drop-the-handkerchief kind of starts for her. She was scrutinizing for 'fainters'. Get 'em before they go down, she instructed her colleagues. But they did only half the time.

And, for the sick. Already one wagon-load had gone off to Dr Singleton's.

'Ready, ladies? *Dinner is served!*' Mrs Napier roared. 'Roll up, roll up, ladies and gents, misses and masters.'

It raised wan smiles, from those capable of them. No sanctimonious clap-trap, she instructed her ladies. Fast and friendly. That's the ticket.

Katherine was ladling and passing as fast as she could. Hat removed, sleeves rolled up, perspiring freely. The queue shuffled past, a blur of white faces. She managed a smile, a bright remark for each, and for a moment that face stood out for her: a contact of eyes, an exchange of humanity. Some were up to it, some too cast down.

'Get that one!' Mrs Napier cried. Two of her colleagues rushed forward to support a woman, take her out of the line to a chair. Then one went down with a sickening crash on the bare-boards.

'O God!' Mrs Napier intoned. 'Missed her. Up with her.' Four of them carried a young woman, hardly a weight, to a trestle table, laid her out, shepherded the small wide-eyed, panicked ones to her side, applied smelling salts. 'Is she hurt?' She was bleeding from the nose.

Katherine hardly looked up, the queue kept coming.

The women and the children were the worst nourished; fragile, in their disintegrating clothing. The windows were opened wide, but the oppressive steaming breath came at you in a deadly wave. They'd done what they could about the cesspool but you couldn't kill the smell in this weather.

Half an hour. Nearly finished—so was the soup and bread. A lull.

'Well done, Mrs Boyd, Mrs Dawson. We'll do the joints shortly.'

The worst for Katherine. They'd only twenty joints of mutton today—sent from the Federal Butchering Co., Richmond. They'd attempt to get them into the most desperate hands—an exhausting and heart-rending operation. At least, tomorrow was sugar-bag day.

'Dropped dead from starvation,' one of the lady helpers was saying to a colleague.

'Enough of that,' Mrs Napier boomed.

'God bless you,' a clerkly looking man said on his way back to the streets.

'And you,' Mrs Napier responded. A two-way benediction.

Katherine left at two, walked half a mile, into the familiar, dead-end Collingwood street. A woman, about thirty, met her at the door of a cottage, a child on her hip, another at her skirts. She'd made an effort to pin back her hair, made another to smile.

Katherine entered the single room which served as bed- and living-room. Window tight shut, she observed, and looked to the man slumped in a chair, face turned aside, eyes half-closed, skin yellowish and translucent; expressive of a desperate internal battle. She thought: Though he's not fighting now, just enduring…So hot in here, but not for him. She looked inquiringly at the woman.

'He's been poorly. A little worse.'

Katherine went into the other room, lifted her heavy basket on to the table. At least they still had their furniture. A fortnight since they'd come here from Elsternwick at two in the morning. In a last surge of energy, the husband had found this place—got them away with the help of a man who was donating himself, his horse and cart to such desperate nocturnal city transits. A few days more and the landlord might have had everything but the clothes they stood in, had them in the street for four pounds back-rent. Then again, he might've let them be. Who could tell? An empty house was a magnet to the 'strippers'.

She unpacked the joint, loaf of bread, the bag of vegetables, and the smaller packages she'd brought from home. The women of her group, each had a family to tend to.

'He's taking the medicine?'

'Yes.'

He was doomed. She had taken him to Dr Singleton. Galloping consumption. He wasn't coughing today, or struggling for breath. Katherine turned and looked critically at each child. The baby was asleep on the woman's shoulder now. The boy, seven, was watching her closely. He was thin and stringy, but not like many she'd just seen. She turned to the three-year-old girl who'd left her mother's skirts to stand by her father.

'How are you, Jean?' Katherine said holding out her hand. The child smiled shyly at the sound of her name, went to a bed and brought a rag-doll to Katherine, held it up.

'What a beautiful baby,' Katherine breathed, meant the child.

The man began to cough, had been trying not to. She had already made her assessment of the woman. Bearing up. Only my age, she thought. From their fund, Katherine had paid the rent four weeks ahead. A weight off their minds.

'Can you put on the dinner?'

'Of course, thank you.'

The boy had begun to carry kindling into a lean-to at the back where the stove was.

Katherine went to the man. His eyes had opened. On his better days they'd exchanged a few words. He knew he was dying. What desperate thoughts was he having for his family? Perhaps he was beyond thinking along those lines, just waiting for oblivion. She knew he was an educated man, had worked in a bank.

She leaned close, said softly, 'These are sad, hard times. I want you to know I will do my very best for your family. Do you understand me, Mr Harbrace?'

He understood, she saw.

———•———

'This is the hardest thing I've had to do,' William said tersely. He stared down at the list of names—the employees to be dismissed this coming Friday. Floor-walkers, to packing and shipping hands, to cleaners.

Deputy Manager Maybury and Isaacs remained silent, watched him across the desk. Sympathetically, he thought, but who could tell where their thoughts were on this. Maybury was sixty, tall, upright and silver-haired. Had never had a beard or a moustache that William remembered, was the living repository of the firm's history since its start in 1870.

'However, there's no other way.'

No other way. His last words seemed to vibrate in the dusty, dun-coloured office. It was going to crash on the store like a thunder-bolt. Though, for months there had been an atmosphere of apprehension. Fear—if you got down to it. He couldn't dwell on it. Had to put it firmly aside, and go on.

'You'll have the letters prepared, the four weeks extra pay in the packets. I'll see each one, starting at four o'clock.' He was going to see every employee—those being dismissed, those staying. Those staying were to have their pay cut by a quarter.

Isaacs nodded.

Most of the previous week they'd been closeted in this room working on a survival plan. The Commercial Bank had granted them three months—an impossibly short time to turn their fortunes around, even if sales had been buoyant. However, if an improving trend could be demonstrated perhaps more time might be negotiated.

The Cyclorama Department was to be closed down. Over two years it had racked up nothing but losses. Competition was fierce: every suburb had its bicycle shops. For the briefest of periods, it had looked a winner. The Wine and Spirits Department, also—and an attempt would be made to sell its licence; therein lay a story which was going to unfold this day, William reflected.

Every department was scrutinizing its stock, pricing it for a store-wide sale to commence next week, compiling advertisements for *The Age*. Isaacs was preparing his budgets, carefully setting priorities for the payment of creditors. Duties were being reorganized.

The room had been awhirl with paper and plans. Each of the seven nights since the anniversary party he had taken it all back to Edinburgh Gardens in his head. The heat-wave which had broken the night of the party had brought a few days of cool. Now the mercury was rising again, and the city was bracing itself to withstand more above-century heat.

'It'll be a stinker by Friday,' Maybury said gruffly.

At five o'clock, William was standing behind his desk when Maybury and Isaacs brought in the head of the Wine and Spirits Department. They all remained standing.

O'Riley had been with the firm for six years. Now that they knew the score, six disastrous years. But why had it taken so long to find out? That was something their auditors would have to answer to.

Maybury and Isaacs had laid the situation before William the previous evening. He'd been astonished, then angered that they'd delayed. Obviously, it was a keen embarrassment to them. But he'd said nothing. The crux of it was that O'Riley had been faking the closing stock figures for years, had got away with hundreds of pounds. The mystery of the chronic losses of the Wine and Spirits Department had been solved!

Isaacs believed it would be hard to prove the defalcations—Maybury worried about the adverse publicity. So William had had his advice.

And now he was confronting the tall, stringy Irishman getting a full dose of the arrogance which for years he'd caught undercurrents of. O'Riley had a high complexion, even higher at the moment. He had clear blue eyes that slipped elsewhere when he was talking to you.

'You know why we're here, what have you to say?'

'Are allegations being made, Mr Boyd?'

'You're being given a chance to explain your actions.'

'Nothing to explain. It's all fair and square. I've done my job.'

'Not in the interests of this firm you haven't.'

'So you're making allegations?'

William rubbed his chin, found his hand was shaking. He was rarely angry—a cool customer, too much detached, some thought—but he could feel a white heat rising in him. He fought against it. Something like this on top of all the rest! This man had taken them for fools.

'Do you want the police in?'

'You could try it. Providing you take the consequences.' The Irishman smiled a tight sneering smile making it clear he knew his number was up.

By God! William could feel his control slipping beyond his grasp—as irrevocably as a tidal race. His breathing was audible. He continued to fight it.

'This firm has treated you well...'

O'Riley laughed softly, bitterly. 'We Catholics on the staff have always been on the outer. Now they say you're going to sack us all. Catholics out first.'

William found that he'd clenched his fists. He found himself directly in front of the Irishman who stepped back a pace.

'You're a blackguard!'

'Mr Boyd!' Maybury said.

'Take care who you call that. There's witnesses here.' The Irishman's eyes had narrowed, changed from taunting to hard.

William turned to Maybury. 'Get him off the premises immediately.' He looked the Irishman up and down. 'Get out!' He turned his back, and walked back to his desk. He was shaking all over. Maybury and Isaacs had taken the man by the arms and were escorting him out.

'Hands off!' he snarled. 'We'll see about this.'

William did not take it in: he had fallen into wonder at how a man like this had come to be employed at Boyd & Montrose. He cooled down. Put it behind you, he admonished himself. Maybe they should look again at whether the Wine and Spirits Department should close.

Isaacs came back in. 'He's gone. Uttering a lot of threats, but we know how these Irish are.'

William had opened a letter book. 'It seems rumours are out...I'd like to know how many Catholics *are* on the list for Friday.'

7

Some of the information obviously came from the early court cases, some from company liquidators, some from angry shareholders. Some…could only have come from bank officials who must have taken copies of overdraft lists and unlawfully passed them on to Brodzky.

Michael Cannon, The Land Boomers

Out of the Silence

THE DAY HAD DONE its best—or worst—when Wallace rode home to Albert Park. The thought came as he sat in a slow-moving hansom submerged in a cloud of drifting dust. It was after seven, and dusk, bleary with gas-light, heavy with humidity, ripe with the stinks of horse manure and urine, had got the city by its throat. Got him, too. He felt dead-tired, sticky, dry in the mouth, was looking forward to a good wash.

It was the first night off. Eye-strain, and mental exhaustion from the intensity they were applying to the bank's records, slabs of recently petrified history, were taking their toll. Fourteen-hour days. Binks was skilled and indefatigable; he wanted him kept at his sharpest. Likewise, himself.

It was curious—and salutary—that this bank so vigorous if wrong-headed a few weeks past, was now a corpse under his hands. He smiled: The coroner of finance. However, the *consequences* from its demise were still very much alive and kicking. Late this afternoon he'd seen a microcosm of that.

What had happened was this: three men had called on him. Against Binks' doubtful look, he'd decided to see them. The spokesman for the trio, a full-bearded individual of sixty or so who he'd seen before in the streets, came straight to the point—they represented seventy shareholders and depositors from the suburb of Camberwell.

'Seventy-eight,' a desiccated man with a tic-active face corrected.

'All of whom are in extreme difficulty due to the bank's failure…'

'He means we're ruined.'

The spokesman shrugged irritably. 'I won't burden you with actual cases…'

'I will,' the nervy man interjected again. 'My wife and I are living with my sister. We're charity cases. There'd be no roof over our heads, no food, if we weren't. And, there's little enough of the last. I had £15,000 on term deposit, and a nice little business. Now I've got neither. And, my wife and my sister've *never* got on.'

He released this last comment as if it were the crux of his misfortune. He was close to tears; did produce a handkerchief, brusquely wiped his eyes. They were well-dressed, the remains of better days.

The third man, hitherto silent, said, 'I'm a widower. My daughter's been the slave of our family. She'll never marry. I put £10,000 on deposit to provide for her future…' His eyes had become appalled. Stories were common that honest women were resorting to the street to feed their children. He couldn't continue.

'Gentlemen, we *agreed*…' the spokesman said wearily. He turned to the liquidator. 'Sir, you mightn't be able to tell us much yet, but, we wish to make it clear how many of us are depending on you. There's more heartbreak and misery amongst us than honest people should have to bear. Already, there's been tragedies. It's life and death.'

'Get us justice,' the nervy man said fiercely, thrusting a clenched fist forward.

After they'd gone, he'd gazed at the splendidly appointed boardroom: an extravagant, now dead illusion.

Their eyes!

The Camberwell conclave. There were another three thousand depositors, and five hundred-odd shareholders out there, many of them in the same straits. The pity of it was that he didn't see relief ahead for them. Day-by-day, gazing into the affairs of the First Bank of Victoria was like gazing into a black hole. As for getting them justice!

He ate his dinner. Mrs Beattie had been surprised to see him home at this hour, but she was always prepared. He'd opened a bottle of wine: a heady hermitage from South Australia. Probably, he'd regret it in the morning.

Helena Spencer had been in the shadows of his mind. Now she seemed to step forward with a swirl of pleated gown. In full-flood. A vibrant presence in his mind's eye, driven by her aspirations—her character. Did he still feature in those aspirations? Despite all his experience gleaned in facing parliamentary and legal opponents, witnesses, judges—and women—he'd no idea. Whether the confrontation outside her house had been final, or a tactic, was a mystery.

The red wine was heavy on his palate, sinking into his mind, like into blotting paper. Mrs Beattie glanced at him as she cleared the table. Sometimes he talked, but not tonight.

Did it matter?...It was hopeless. Marriage, a commitment without the full revelation of *that* chapter in his life would be grossly imprudent. Yet, opening that Pandora's Box on what he and a few others had conspired to conceal, would be madness. The thought deadened him. He was as far away as ever from resolving it, stranded a long way from Helena.

Is it moral cowardice? he asked himself. Or, a kind of psychological barrier? No answer. He could only alleviate the depression through work. That's how it had been. He stared at the wall of his dining room, and slowly the intractability merged into it.

He went to his study carrying the wine glass. The house was warming up again, though still cool downstairs. These thick-set, brick houses took three or four days to heat up on the ground floor, nearly as long to cool down. He stood, contemplating another trip up the tower. He might hear a sad sonata from Mrs Hammond. He dismissed the idea. Anyway, she played much better in the winter months. Instead, he lit a cigar.

The portrait of his father stared down, done when he was fifty. I hardly knew you, he thought. On his desk was a pile of unopened post—he'd had no time for it. Tonight, he had.

What first took his eye was a buff envelope inscribed in a clerkly, if shaky, hand. It was quite heavy—he picked up a pearl-handled paper-knife (his father's) and slit it open. Out fell a sheaf of papers pinned together. Puzzled, he retrieved it: twenty or so pages, closely written—names and amounts. He looked in the envelope: nothing else. He flicked over to the last page: a kind of certificate. *Abstract of Overdrafts of First Bank of Victoria as at close of business Wednesday, 26th October, 1892.*

He stared, put down the cigar. What was this? Who'd sent it? Suddenly his heart was beating quicker, his brain was working. The certificate was unsigned. The date was exactly two days prior to the date the bank had ceased payment. This raced through his mind. He stood, head on one side, as if listening.

The city was thick with aggrieved parties, outraged or frightened insiders, and anonymous information was emerging from the woodwork, falling into the laps of liquidators, investigators, the newspapers.

Look at the revelations in *Table Talk*. He knew it was of that nature.

At the end of the last column was a total. A new starting point? Perhaps now they'd be able to balance the books!

Who are you?...He laid it on his desk, took up the wine glass and drained it. This'd light up Binks' eyes.

He climbed the stairs to his bedroom. The windows were open wide and a slender breeze teased at the curtains, didn't even ruffle his hair. He stood gazing towards the invisible bay reviewing the matters which had been in his mind this off-duty evening, as though ruling off their status, carrying forward a balance.

In respect of Helena, he could've saved himself the effort; there was nothing to carry forward. Her character alone should have been evidence enough for that. An avid bridge-player she had worked out her hand, her next bid, and it was unrelated to Angus Wallace.

He mused: A lonely life, in the interstices of his struggles over the years. Tonight, meditations of the kind he was having were coming and going—encouraged by his semi-leisured interlude, the heavy hermitage. Doors opening and shutting. And now this communication! He went to bed.

The face, the figure of Miss Fairfax filled his mind—dominating the Boyds' drawing-room with her beauty, her calm assurance. A new star in the southern city's firmament? He smiled at the banality of the thought. But, it was the last before he slept.

8

The P and O Company's new steamship Himalaya arrived...from London, having been delayed...by the extremely hazy weather prevailing along the coast...caused by the smoke from bush fires raging inland.

The Argus, *14.2.1893*

The Brilliant Career

THAT AFTERNOON, Mrs Wilberforce's Italianate, white-stuccoed mansion, on the east side of the verdant Fitzroy Gardens, resembled a ship afloat on a hazy, dreamy sea.

In reality, William thought edgily, it was a solid product of the boom and its concepts. As prepossessing as its chatelaine could be, when she chose. And, a frequent port of call for him throughout his life, in good times and bad. Bad, this afternoon. He was coming to report on the crisis.

As he'd passed the gardens, he'd eyed the bucolic mass of towering, dark-green foliage, and browned grass glades, amongst which glistened marble, masquerading as flesh. His mind had slipped back. Four years ago, he'd walked often in this 'lung' where the air did have a fresher tang. Here, he'd fallen in love with Katherine. Here, before that, events on another matter of the heart had been enacted, were still in his mind like a locked-up room. He never walked here these days before those eyeless statues.

Mrs Wilberforce received him in the small drawing-room. The room was closed up, the wooden-slatted venetian blinds lowered.

They kissed with affection. 'I'm glad you've come,' she said. 'These days, I don't see enough of you or Katherine.'

'I wish it were a happier occasion.'

'Well, we had better sit down. I won't interrupt.'

Fully, though succinctly, he laid out the store's situation, telling of his arrangement with the bank, the re-organization, the staff dismissals which were to come on Friday. He told it without pulling any punches; his manner was edgy, yet pragmatic.

'It can't be counted on that we'll win through.'

Mrs Wilberforce listened. She had £15,000 invested, and a loan of £10,000 put in in '92. She'd not had a dividend since '90. As an investment, it had been a mistake. However, her motives had not been of an economic nature.

She pursed her lips, gazed down at her hands folded on her lap. After a difficult start, William had proved himself capable. It was the times which were beating him. Beating them all. She had term deposits at two of the Associated banks, but not money at present to help…and, there was a point beyond which it would be imprudent to go.

'I can cut costs till I'm blue in the face, but what's needed is cash coming across the counters. We're starting a store-wide sale next week.'

She studied him. 'Don't take the dismissals to heart, William.'

He didn't respond, hadn't mentioned that he was mortgaging their house, had agreed with Katherine that he wouldn't.

She frowned. 'The city's awash with troubles. I hope and trust those rogues and charlatans of company directors posing as upright men, are going to be found out.'

William smiled, grimly. How had she squared this with what Sir John had been up to? The rumours were that the knight had made a secret composition, walked out on his creditors. But perhaps she saw him merely as a fool.

In one of her quicksilver changes, she said, 'Watch Katherine. She's doing hard work at Collingwood. *Depressing* work. She's always been on the lookout for those who are down. Too much so.'

That made him think. His wife appeared to take it in her stride. But Hilda was right. He should lift himself above his own troubles.

She thought to say more on Katherine. Three years and no child. What was going forward—or *not* going forward? However, the subject was too delicate, even for her. Katherine was coming for tea—as William knew—perhaps there'd be an opportunity.

A maid entered. Lady Adams had arrived. William's business was done and he excused himself. He bowed to Laura Adams. She acknowledged him with a shadow of a smile. She looked striking—if severe—in a moss-green tweed costume, high-necked, narrow-waist-ed, edged with plaited black braid; had on a matching velvet hat trimmed with ostrich feathers. But her face was white and drawn.

Coming down the steps he reflected that Hilda was right about the city. It *was* awash with troubles. These days, he imagined he could hear mournful music over it—a kind of menacing requiem. All our nerves are shot, he told himself.

'William looks worried,' Laura Adams said, embracing Hilda, seating herself in her usual chair.

So do you, Hilda thought, said, 'It's the store.'

'Oh, the store. *I'm* worried about Katherine.'

'She'll be here shortly…you can tell her.'

They'd spoken to Katherine about her work at Collingwood. Linked by a kind of telepathy as they often were, each was thinking of Sonia Larkin—Philip's wife—who had died of typhoid contracted during her hospital work.

Mrs Wilberforce studied her friend's face. She didn't look at all well.

'Laura, what is happening with John?'

Lady Adams' grey eyes flicked down, became fixed, contemplating a mystery.

'I wish I knew. He won't tell me a thing. He goes out, returns. Spends hours brooding in his study. I don't understand any of it. I do know he's not paying bills, has a drawer full of them.' She would never have revealed this to anyone else. 'Why? We own so much property.'

Property for which there's no buyer, Hilda Wilberforce reflected. Worth a fraction of its purchase price. How could she not understand that?

'He hardly goes to his club…'

She had tears in her eyes. In twenty years, Hilda had seen this only once before. She felt a pain in her own heart.

'He's never been communicative. There's always been so much going on. So many boards, so many committees. So connected to the Government. Now, he's plunged into total silence.'

Hilda thought: It's been coming since '88. With grave disquiet, she'd observed his depressed air at the Boyds' party.

Lady Adams went on: 'And now, this business at the bank. That *womanizer*, sitting in judgment on a man like John! My God! The other night, with that Spencer woman!' 'Womanizer' was a word she used with reluctance and distaste.

Hilda Wilberforce nodded. What to tell her friend, how to comfort her?

She said quietly, 'You *must* talk to him, Laura, tell him you've a right to know the full story. He *must* end this suspense.'

Yes, she would try again. And keep on trying. Lady Adams' world had been shaken to its foundations. She was full of apprehension—rattled even—and that didn't happen easily. However, she turned to her friend with a changed expression.

'Hilda, what are we to do about Hanna? It's just drifting, you know.'

Their unfruitful match-making! The fact Larkin had appointed 'that womanizer' as liquidator to her husband's bank had, finally, not raised Lady Adams' ire. It was purely legal process, and, he wasn't the one firing the shots.

On Hanna's side, Mrs Wilberforce knew the lay of the land. Philip's feelings were more elusive. This was serious though light relief from the Adams' affairs. They discussed it until they heard the sound of voices coming up the stairs.

Katherine, Hanna, and Susan Fairfax, entered in a rush of energy and chatter which made the older women smile.

Such attractive young women, Hilda thought. This was the occasion they were to get to know Miss Fairfax. On that first meeting, Laura had pronounced her 'stunning'—with certain reservations about her hair and dress. Hilda had observed the looks she'd got from the men that hot and airless night. Now, with a searching look she reaffirmed that opinion. Without speaking a word, with her assured glances, her bearing, the Lancashire woman had a special aura. Obviously, Hanna was very proud of her.

As for Hanna…her brisk, no-nonsense manner had become accentuated. She'd never had the feminine wiles of her competitors in the marriage stakes. And, there was no escaping it, that was the cut of society. An admirable girl, but such a pity not to have a little of that.

Katherine had come there directly from Collingwood, had not changed from the cotton dress, which showed signs of her labour. They noted this.

'William was just here,' Hilda said to her.

Katherine smiled, wondered how it had gone.

'Katherine has been on duty at Collingwood,' Hilda announced.

'Doing too much, risking her health,' Lady Adams said rigorously.

Miss Fairfax appraised Katherine. 'Is it very bad?'

In turn, Katherine examined the Lancashire woman. 'Yes. I fear it'll be much worse. Unless the Government acts.'

'Expect nothing,' Hilda Wilberforce said flatly. 'Most of those men have been too busy making money, and now it's crashed they're taken up with keeping out of bankruptcy. But let's not spoil our afternoon. We want to hear what's going on at home. All about Miss Fairfax's life.'

She rang for tea, and a trolley was wheeled in by two maids who'd been waiting in the passage.

Susan Fairfax's eyes met Mrs Wilberforce's, slipped away. Yes, but she'd need to be careful—though her hostess seemed more friend than foe. Pleasant women—except for her ladyship. And Hanna was a darling—but what did any of them know? She was confident, but cautious. She'd learned that both sexes were prone to look askance at her business acumen, unique career—and her opinions.

'The *Himalaya* is a fine ship. We were delayed. Off-shore, it was so hazy. The fires raging inland, they said.'

It was a fiddling beginning. She glanced at the expectant faces, then, with a light touch, embarked on an account of her 'history'. She outlined her career as the protege and right-hand of Sir Joshua Sadler, the expansionist retailing legend of the Midlands.

Listening intently, Hanna noted how skilfully the past was edited, how everything was understated. Several crucial matters were omitted. The reason for leaving Manchester, for one. The pleasant Lancashire accents captivated her listeners.

'An uneventful life,' Susan finished with a smile.

Over the delicate rim of her porcelain tea-cup, Lady Adams sent one of her rifle-shot looks which seemed to say: We will find out about that.

'Isn't she marvellous?' Hanna asked. She knew very well Lady Adams' feelings.

'Hanna, please…you're making me blush.' No blush was visible.

Hilda Wilberforce had become thoughtful. An idea had come to her, and she looked up to see Hanna watching her, as if it had struck them both simultaneously.

The conversation became general, partly a briefing to the new arrival on the ins and outs of colonial life. Lady Adams said, 'My dear, you'll find it the best policy not to ask those you're introduced to about their *early* life in the Colony.'

Across the road, the Fitzroy Gardens burst into life under a breeze: a long, airy sigh, repeated by Mrs Wilberforce. She rang for her maids to open the windows.

Hanna said to her hostess, 'I trust Judge Mountain is well.'

Hilda turned her dark, perceptive eyes on the young bookseller, observed the hint of a smile, felt the hint of her own. She was being teased; knew her young friends thought the judge as boring 'as a block of wood'.

'I believe the judge is on the bench today, judging away.'

Lady Adams pursed her lips, glanced at her friend. Why did she take these men up? First William's father, then Tom Montrose. She wondered if she'd ever be admitted to this inner sanctum of her best friend's life.

'Have you seen Philip lately? If not, why not?' Mrs Wilberforce riposted.

Hanna smiled, gave one of her characteristic shrugs.

Nothing to report, Hilda thought.

The Sevres clock on the marble mantle-piece chimed four o'clock. They went out to the landing, passed the closed-up main drawing-room. The vast room, with its carefully positioned pieces of cedar and mahogany furniture, reminded Katherine of a museum. She knew that Hilda had twice postponed its re-decoration. The times. The days of the soirées seemed lost to the past. Her thoughts moved ahead to home and the evening with William—and the latest news from the store.

Hilda and Laura Adams, standing in the portico, watched the younger women depart.

'There's something not quite right about that young woman. Something to be found out,' Lady Adams said.

Hilda Wilberforce glanced at her friend; the remarks mirrored her own conclusion.

'Hanna knows more than she's said, but I don't think we'll have a word from her of *that* nature.'

Lady Adams turned her cool grey eyes on Mrs Wilberforce. 'I've a cousin in Manchester. Perhaps a discreet letter…'

She left. Mrs Wilberforce watched the elegant carriage drive off along Clarendon Street, and went inside. At least, the afternoon had given Laura some relief from her problems. Now she had to go home to them. However, tonight she would have her 'discreet' letter to write.

There'd been no opportunity to talk to Katherine about that intensely private matter. But her thoughts had returned instantly to Miss Fairfax. Here was promise indeed. So why this vague disquiet? Something she couldn't put her finger on. Perhaps, it was more a slow pulse of excitement and expectation; whatever it was, it sang softly to her like a kettle on the hob.

9

The colony seems just now to have nothing else but bank boom directors, rogues, swindlers, and, lastly of all, Parliament is becoming a hot bed of useless talk, extravagance and shame.

Table Talk, 24.2.1893

Razor's Edge

'HAVE A LOOK at this,' Wallace said. He passed the communication which had lain overnight on his desk, which had figured in a dream he'd had, to his clerk. It was half-past seven. He'd come through the deserted banking chamber, resonant with echoes—seemingly more so each day.

Binks, his coat slung over the back of his chair, was already ferreting into untied packets of vouchers, surrounded by neat stacks of cheques, deposit forms, office entries, totally absorbed in the arcane work. Already the room stank of dust. He surfaced, took it, scanned the pages, read the note on the last, and looked up at his employer. 'An insider,' he said.

'Yes. Came in the post—out of the blue.'

'An axe to grind?' Binks studied the first page. The clerk was imprecise with his razor, each morning did havoc with it. Blood speckled his pale cheeks, but Wallace no longer noticed.

'Or a troubled conscience.'

They considered the possibilities.

Binks said, 'A schedule of overdrafts. What's the implication? Something here that isn't in the books? I'll start on it immediately...' He turned away. 'This came for you. Delivered five minutes ago.' He passed a white envelope to the liquidator.

Someone's up early, Wallace thought. He sat down at his place and opened it. No clerkly writing here—a dashed off but readable script. Wallace read the few sentences, and frowned. He tossed it to Binks, who read: *Dear Mr Wallace, You will be familiar, we believe, with the work of our paper in exposing certain unsavoury situations pertaining to*

*the land-booming fiasco and its financial manipulations. We have informa-
tion which we consider relevant to your current investigation. May I suggest
you meet our Mr Murdoch, this day, if possible…I assure you we will not
be wasting your time. Yours faithfully, Maurice Brodzky.*

'Fiasco,' Wallace murmured. Thoughtfully, he lit one of his small
cigars. He'd never met Brodzky but read his paper, *Table Talk*, with
considerable interest. Since '91, Brodzky had been printing meticulous
reports on company manipulations—taking the lid off frauds which
otherwise would have remained covered up. His informants were one
of the city's multitude of mysteries, though assuredly, some would
come from sources akin to the communication which he'd received
last night.

According to the standpoint of the commentator, the journal was
'scurrilous, defamatory and sensational'—or, 'razor-sharp, public-
spirited and courageous'. Wallace knew which camp he was in.
Already court cases were proving up the veracity of the articles to a
remarkable degree.

Binks had finished reading.

'What do you think?' Wallace asked.

'Nothing to be lost. Maybe something to gain. You'd have to be
careful. He may be looking for a fair exchange of information.'

Wallace brushed a shred of tobacco from his lips. 'They've never
revealed their sources.' He was thinking ahead. Brodzky was pushing
fear into quarters where a bit of fear sometimes did some good. The
publisher had suggested four o'clock at a rather peculiar location. For
the moment, Wallace put it aside.

'The vouchers during the last week…' Binks began. The liquidator glanced at him, he'd caught a whiff of brandy. On the job early,
too, but he hardly noticed that any more, either.

The day before yesterday's meeting with the directors, chief manager, and auditor, they'd examined the book entries passed during the
last frantic days of the bank's existence. It had been a rich prospect.
Wallace had not chosen to question the directors on what they'd discovered—he was keeping his powder dry, as he'd told Larkin.

The main substance was: at a meeting on the eve of the closure,
the board had written off as irrecoverable six overdrafts in the names
of companies controlled by Sir John Adams, aggregating £322,000,
and one each in the names of Savage and Sandhurst for £57,000 and
£33,000 respectively; all written off against the bank's reserve
account.

After this discovery, they'd sat in silence contemplating the directors' last-minute, personally productive work. Wallace had said, 'No wonder they wanted a voluntary liquidation. They didn't want *this* out in the open.'

'Well, it's as plain as day in the books, and they must know we're on to it.'

'I'd like to know what's in their minds,' Wallace had mused.

Binks had shrugged.

Now, Wallace reflected that the directors hadn't written off any other overdrafts from the bank's loan portfolio, and clearly it was riddled with bad debts. That was going to be left to him. Suddenly he thought of something. 'That accountant—whatshisname—Harbrace? We're going to need help to find him. Larkin knows a man—a detective. I'll speak to him about it tonight.'

Binks nodded, absorbed again. He'd taken up the schedule of overdrafts. He'd deconstruct it line by line, if necessary. He knew there was a message in it—if he could find it out.

10

From 1891 onwards the columns of Table Talk *were increasingly filled with the most detailed and sensational evidence of company manipulations…Most of the frauds of the boom period would have been successfully covered up had it not been for Brodzky's work.*

Michael Cannon, The Land Boomers

Brodzky

AT TEN TO FOUR, Wallace arrived at the All Nations Hotel for his rendezvous with the reporter. The Richmond hostelry was a half-hour's drive from town and he regretted this time lost to a mission of unknown value; on the other hand, it was a relief to escape for a bit from the defunct bank. For the first time in days, he could see the Dandenong Ranges; the smoke-haze had cleared.

He entered the bar by a side-door. With a look of inquiry, a man rose from a corner table and came to meet him. A miniature man, moving fast…

'Mr Wallace? I'm Murdoch. I'm glad to see you here, sir.'

They shook hands. It was immediately clear that the reporter's lack of inches was overshadowed by a combination of outfitting—and energy. Perfect black suit, red rose in the button hole, snowy white shirt and cuffs, ebonized stick, sharp, high-crowned bowler; his hands, shoulders, were shedding a wealth of gestures. In contrast, his face was as still and serious as an undertaker arriving to collect the deceased.

He went rapidly back to the table, pulled out a chair for the liquidator, took the other. He removed his bowler, joined his hands as if to impose control, and leaned the serious face confidentially across the table.

'Mr Brodzky thought somewhere off the beaten track the best policy. People know you, sir, and what you're engaged in. And certain people know me, and what I'm engaged in. *Table Talk* is very careful to protect its contacts.'

His voice was low and persuasive.

Wallace removed his hat, wondered what quagmire he might be stepping into. He studied the white, axe-featured face clean-shaven between the brown whiskers rimming it. An inch of white chin separated the encirclement. Everything was sharp, especially the eyes. He'd not spoken a word. The paper's brilliant political and finance pages were the reason why he was sitting here. A thought came: Was it the source of the schedule of overdrafts which Binks was working on at this moment?

'What will you drink?' The press-man rapped on the table, and the barman appeared from the next room. He ordered the white wine for Wallace, a whisky for himself. He watched the liquidator add water to the wine.

'Very wise, sir. Makes it a wholesome drink…Now, I know your time's valuable.' He took out a sheet of paper, unfolded it, and pushed it across the table. 'Mr Brodzky thinks you'll be interested to see this.'

A column of newsprint, smudged from the warmth of the press-man's breast pocket. Wallace read:

Knight Dumps Creditors
Manoeuvres Under Cover of Voluntary Liquidation
Act to Escape the Insolvency Court

He looked up into the reporter's piercing eyes.

'Of course, not published yet,' Murdoch said. 'Please read on, sir.'

The liquidator did, scanning the close-printed lines; phrases leapt up at him: *Sir John Adams, who achieved his knighthood in 1890, following a donation of £10,000 to the Imperial Institute, has been engaged in another somewhat more remarkable case of cause and effect…This well-known figurehead and paragon of Melbourne Commerce has been secretly liquidating some fifteen boomer companies, of which he is the principal…aided and abetted by the unsavoury Voluntary Liquidation Act 1891, which was rushed through both houses in the dead of night, with only one dissenting voice, by our self-serving parliamentarians, led by then Premier Munro…which abolished the rights of minority depositors in banks and other companies, to send a business into compulsory liquidation, or obtain a court investigation… Interestingly, six of the knight's companies owed £322,000 to the First Bank of Victoria, of which Sir John also happened to be chairman…one of those co-incidences which abound in Victoria…This nefarious circle of events does not end there…the indefatigable knight, sweeping more under the carpet, has secretly resorted to that other piece of shoddy legislation—Composition by Arrangement—whereby he will pay his creditors one-shilling in the pound, and escape the bankruptcy court…His small creditors will be left lamenting…As for the larger, what can one say?...Nothing of this was intended to see the light of day...We await with bated breath the liquidator's report on the ill-fated bank...What else will be discovered?...Is the character of Victoria's commercial morality to be sunk in the slime of such events...The British investor and creditor must shrink from the very mention of our Colony...As for our own unfortunate thousands...*

Wallace felt that Murdoch's gaze had not deviated one inch from his face. The reporter smiled slightly, sipped his whisky.

'Well, Mr Wallace, what do you think of that?'

The liquidator pushed the sheet back, regarded Murdoch thoughtfully. It startled him to see all this in print; but the nature of it didn't surprise him. Some of it he knew already. From the beginning, the liquidation had had the atmosphere of corruption and fraud; that was virtually guaranteed with Savage and Sandhurst involved.

He'd had dealings with the press in the past. He should move cautiously. Murdoch positively exuded the seasoned journalist. Show him a crack of daylight and he'd go through it like a Carlton wingman, or a smart colt up the rails in the Flemington straight.

Wallace said, 'Would it stand up in court?'

The reporter patted his hands on his pockets, as though looking for a pipe, but came up with nothing. 'Mr Brodzky stands by what he prints. That's our record. You'll have seen the official investigations and the courts bear us out. We've been wrong once or twice, have promptly printed corrections. Ninety per cent, we've been right.'

'I suppose it's asking too much to know your source?'

The tiny, fine-boned hands fluttered. 'Mr Brodzky's firm on that. But it doesn't close the door. Once the facts are out in the public domain, doors open. We've seen it often enough.'

'When will you publish?'

'Not decided. You've seen our side. Mr Brodzky's hoping for something from *yours*—to round it out. Give it even more bite. Not attributed, of course...That's why I'm here. Though, Mr Brodzky thought it might help your work.'

Wallace contemplated the bantamweight, dandified man who he didn't doubt matched him in intelligence. He said, 'I can't give you anything as yet. It's early days. If I see the possibility of it, I'll be in touch.'

'Fair enough,' Murdoch said, disappointed but pragmatic.

Dusk had submerged the city's work-a-day structures, given it a softer, shadowed persona, when they parted outside the hotel. The evening resounded with the song of crickets which had taken over from the cicadas. The heat-drugged noon was a memory. The sky was an indigo blue, littered with stars. Wallace walked two streets in the quiet neighbourhood, past oil-lit interiors of workmen's cottages, past a silent atmosphere of deprivation. However, clattering homeward in a hansom he felt a peacefulness that his day was done. He now had a picture of the other side of the board's extraordinary write-offs in the bank's dying days; it might build up to evidence. And, in Brodzky and his paper he might have a useful ally.

As for the schedule of overdrafts which had turned up, his mind now focussed on the missing Harbrace. He'd dismissed his earlier conjecture that it might've been from Brodzky. He wondered what Binks was making of it.

In moments of respite, Helena came floating into his thoughts. What entertainment was she gracing tonight? Wherever it was, he was excluded. Then, his thoughts went to the old perplexity, like a tongue to an impacted tooth.

11

PRETTY MILLINERY AT MRS WHITE'S
(COLLINS-STREET)
*A perfect hat is a green beaver, lined with black velvet, the
trimming…perfectly lovely tinted roses…A chic model has a rather
full crown of mouse colour velvet with an edge of sap green velvet
finished with a wing and a bunch of violets…little gem of violet
velvet with gold passementerie edged all round with black ostrich
feathers…*

Table Talk, *21.4.1893*

The Dropped Glove

MRS SPENCER was in the ante-room asking to see him. Philip Larkin
was surprised when his clerk announced this. He consulted his watch.
At the behest of Angus Wallace, he was expecting to shortly interview
a private detective. Uneasily, he wondered if it was Wallace she had
come about. The prospect of a case of breach of promise winged into
his head.

Though their connection was a slim one—they'd met at the houses of mutual friends—he felt an obligation to see her, and a curiosity;
he'd heard rumours about her, discreetly circulated in drawing-rooms;
though, that was bound to happen if you were a single woman seen in
the company of the likes of Angus Wallace.

In a prism of fragrance, a sensuous rustle of fabric, she entered
before he was ready, the tap-tap of her parasol on the bare-boards
injecting a confident note, and stood before his desk regarding him
with a smile and an appraising look.

He rose hurriedly, and came around to take her hand. 'Mrs
Spencer…a pleasure.' He thought: What *is* this? And: Curiosity on
both sides.

'Mr Larkin. So good of you to see me without notice.'

He settled her in a chair. She was dressed from head to ankle in
white silk, but he caught a discreet flash of black stockings above the

stylish black patent leather shoes. A sweeping straw hat, dressed with a single red rose, completed her toilette. He had never seen her before in anything other than green, and it made a strong impression on him. He quickly judged there was nothing in her manner or her dress which depicted the discarded lover, or the pining widow...but then who had discarded who, and, it had been five years since Spencer had died suddenly.

He was looking at a very fine figure of a woman indeed. All his senses told him so. As she adjusted her dress, her green eyes never left his. *Still* measuring, green eyes. He shifted in his seat. Such narrow-waisted slimness...such tall grace...and that bosom! Seduced by her fragrance, he was fascinated, amazed at this twist to his day.

'You must be overrun with work, so I won't delay.' She dropped her eyes for the first time, pulled at the tip of each gloved finger of her right hand, deftly removed it. 'I'm too much troubled with financial affairs. My dear husband left me well off and I've been attending to matters myself—with help from my bank manager. But the times are so worrying, and I'm losing confidence in bank managers.

'A woman alone in today's world, Mr Larkin, is not in an enviable situation. I feel in need of support and guidance. But where to turn? Friends tell me to be wary of business agents—apparently most are either fools or knaves.'

Her eyes flicked up, levelled on him. 'But not all. I've heard you act in such a capacity. Are *you* an honest and competent man, Mr Larkin?'

This was a small shock. Then he absorbed the teasing undercurrent, smiled slightly.

'Would you take me on?'

The picture, suddenly, had become clear—so he thought. The business and legal side of his brain was now engaged. He smiled across his desk at this vision, this luminous presence in his drab office.

'If I may say so, we act for several prominent persons. You're wise to be concerned. There *are* great worries and problems in the city.'

Abruptly, he'd sensed other matters beneath the surface. So?...He jumped in (as he was to do again in a more literal sense a few weeks later).

'I'd be honoured to act for you, Mrs Spencer.'

'Marvellous! I'm so relieved. I escaped from the City of Melbourne Bank, just in time. Now I'm with the National.'

Mrs Spencer might have felt herself, and her fortune, in peril, but she did not show any signs of it. She appeared totally in command of her life. This did occur to Larkin, as he asked some questions, and they made certain arrangements.

With another handshake, and a look which is so level and penetrating that it causes him to hold his breath, she rises from the bentwood chair. In doing that, she drops her glove. He retrieves it. She smiles, bobs her dark, coiffured head, with that striking hat, that burning-bright rose, and sweeps out of the dry-as-dust surroundings, which are instantly dimmer.

He stands, rooted to the spot, almost knocked out. Ten minutes, precisely, have gone by since she entered. Suddenly, mind-bendingly, the realization, of which he'd had that pale preview, sheets home that more might've been on the table than her financial affairs. He stared at the door which had closed behind her. And, how would Wallace take this?

Mrs Spencer's exit aroused the interest of the ruddy-faced, short, solid, tradesman-like man sitting in the ante-room, dressed in hard-worn colonial tweed, a silver watch chain looped over his pot belly, highly polished brown boots planted neatly on the boards.

Nice type of client, he adjudged.

He suggested a man who was about to face an interview pertaining to employment—though, with equanimity. That, on both counts, was the case.

12

THE MERCANTILE BANK PROSECUTIONS
RETURN OF MR MILLIDGE

Mr Millidge, the late manager…who is to be prosecuted…for having issued a false written statement with intent to defraud the shareholders of the bank, arrived in Melbourne yesterday on board the RMS Himalaya…Detective Coleman, of Port Melbourne, boarded…and informed Mr Millidge that though a warrant for his arrest was still in force it would not be executed unless he failed to attend at the City Court on the 8th of March…

The Argus, *13.2.1893*

Into Thin Air

INTO THE HEART OF IT, Wallace told himself on the ride in. Overnight, the reporter Murdoch's revelations had been working on him, and he was eager to learn what his clerk had turned up from the mysterious schedule.

He found Binks sitting in a half-circle of ledgers, lists, and packets of vouchers. He had on a green eye-shade and the liquidator wondered if he'd stayed all night; then he noted the bloody scraps of paper stuck on his cheeks.

'We've balanced the loans outstanding.'

Wallace froze on the tract of floral carpet.

'Take a look at page six.' The clerk passed over the schedule from the anonymous informant.

Wallace gazed at two names which his clerk had underlined in red ink: Jonathan Savage No. 2 Account, £7,200 and Edward Sandhurst No. 2 Account, £6,700. Neither account appeared in the bank's records. He knew that. He looked up. 'What kind of sleight of hand have we here?'

Binks grinned sourly. 'That's about what it is. Look at this. *Someone's* torn out two leaves from the overdraft ledger.' He showed the liquidator where the pages had been extracted. Slight traces of their presence remained in the binding, though only the closest scrutiny detected them. Each had been in strict alphabetical order behind the parliamentarians' written-off ordinary overdrafts.

'So.' Wallace stared at his clerk. 'But, how does it make sense? They formally wrote off their other accounts at that death-knock board meeting, why not these?'

Phlegmatically, the clerk shrugged his thin shoulders. 'Who knows. Second thoughts after they'd done that write-off? A last minute panic? They might've had the chairman to worry about. Did he know about these *extra* loans? When a bank goes down so fast it's like a ship sinking. There's a rush for the life-boats. It's not your neat and clean finish.'

Wallace rubbed his chin. 'Sir John wouldn't have had much of an argument against it...Getting down to more detail, though, without the co-operation of a third party'll be nigh impossible. Co-operation's a notion as foreign to these people as paying their creditors is.'

Binks agreed with that.

Wallace smiled grimly. 'Harbrace. He'll be our man.'

He'd briefed Philip Larkin, asked him to put a private detective on to it.

Binks said, 'I reckon *he's* gone to ground—and for a good reason.'

The clerk had had a sudden vision of the bloated body of the head cashier, Hubble, being taken with grappling irons from the Yarra. He said, 'That inquest comes up on the 28th.'

Wallace nodded slowly. He had his own vision: Savage and Sandhurst, moving in the city's halls of influence, as familiar to them as the hairs and freckles on the backs of their hands, adept at the counter-attack. All that white-waistcoat brigade were the same. They wouldn't be sitting quiet. The railway manipulations, his defeat in parliament and the courts in '87–'88, were as fresh as yesterday.

Binks had been coming to it. He said tersely, but with a note of triumph, 'The files on those two accounts have disappeared. But the *vouchers* haven't.' Fan-like, he spread several cheques on the table. At a glance, Wallace took in Savage's flourishing signature, Sandhurst's more complicated one—each with No. 2 Account appended.

Binks said, 'They had the money, all right. As I said, panic might've set in. They didn't think it right through—or those who acted for them, didn't.'

Wallace felt a flood of confirmation. He sat down, dropped his hands on the table with a soft thud.

'We've got 'em!'

Binks thought: Don't bet on it. But his employer had released a momentary excitement. Wallace knew better than anyone that they were in for a long, tortuous haul.

'All right, now listen to this…' Wallace said. He outlined last evening's interview with the reporter.

Binks gazed at him.

'When *Table Talk* brings out that report!' Wallace concluded.

'That'll be the day,' his clerk agreed.

The liquidator dropped it for the present. Thoughtfully, he took out a cigar and lit it. More heat on the way. The air seemed thin and sour in expectation. He'd noted from a glance at the paper that there were blizzards in the United States, and a strike on the Chicago railways. Out in the wide-world, plenty of other problems were in play.

Like a jig-saw, they were putting together the extent of the disaster. Valuations were coming in on the properties held as security, and the picture emerging was grimmer even than he'd expected. It seemed the valuators had gone from one extreme to the other. There'd be nothing for shareholders—they'd have to pay in more—and not much for the depositors, unless the directors could be brought to account and funds recovered. The desperate faces of the delegation from Camberwell came back to him.

Binks reminded him: 'The chief manager'll be here tomorrow.'

Could that nerve-racked man be worked on? Be brought to bear as a witness against the directors? Unless he was a total fool, he must know the footings of it all. Or, was he too much in their pockets? It struck him that Jamison Smith might also be in fear of more than exposure.

But he put this aside, too. 'If all else fails, we've done enough work to show the balance sheet they signed and put before the shareholders on the 30th September last, was false. The bank was insolvent, and it was in '91, too. A criminal offence, Binks.'

The clerk stared into space. '*If* we can get it into court,' he growled.

13

The sensation of the month has been the legal proceedings taken by Mr Templeton, the liquidator appointed by the Supreme Court for winding up the affairs of the Premier Permanent Building Society, against the directors and officers of the society on various charges, all more or less of a very serious nature.

Illustrated Australian News, 2.6.1890

On the Case

OTTO RUDD, Private Detective of Rudd's Inquiry Office, Queen Street, was on the case. He'd arrived at Elsternwick by train, now was outside the house which was the last known address of the ex-chief accountant of the First Bank of Victoria. He'd made a few casts up and down the street; so far he'd drawn a blank. No-one was talking, everyone was sticking together.

The detective meditated on the row of houses: Rock-solid against the landlord. Not surprising. He'd interviewed that individual an hour since. The man was bitter. 'Crept away like criminals in the dead of night,' he'd said. 'Five pounds owing. Must've had a horse and cart, and I've got suspicions about that.'

Landlord talk. Beat a seizure in distraint of rent by a whisker, Rudd surmised. Not much of a house for a bank accountant. The fugitive family had his sympathy, still Harbrace had to be found; his instructions were that it'd be to the man's financial advantage if he was.

He'd been surprised to be summoned to Messrs Larkin & Larkin. The last time he'd come up against that firm, nearly four years ago, he'd been on the other side. And the other side had been a bitter opponent of Larkins' client. Plainly, it was water under the bridge so far as Mr Philip Larkin was concerned. Rudd congratulated himself: dealing with a firm of this reputation was satisfying, and work, these days, was hard to get.

Time for dinner. During his long widower-hood, he'd become a connoisseur of street-food. He found a good vendor in Glenhuntly Road and lunched on a gigantic meat pie thickly covered with salt.

'Horse and cart,' he muttered to himself brushing piecrust crumbs from his waist-coat. He knew a man five minutes walk away who might have some information on that particular. He removed his bowler, wiped his lips, brow, with a red handkerchief, replaced the bowler, tipped it forward slightly to shade his eyes against the afternoon sun, and set off in that direction.

———•———

By evening, Wallace felt himself flagging. For the second time in a week he dined at home, which pleased Mrs Beattie who believed that his diet of her sandwiches, eaten at the bank while he worked, was not enough sustenance, though they were filled with meat and pickles. Two years ago he'd bought her one of the new nickel-plated Douglas gas stoves seen in a catalogue. One of his impulses, she'd thought. She'd doubted he could afford it. He was a man of impulses, and of up-and-down moods. One day full of conversation, the next, of silence—and depression. But, generally, not hard to live with.

She had an occasional nocturnal fantasy about him: he appeared at the foot of her bed in his night-shirt. In her waking hours, it wasn't something she had any hope of.

After dinner, he sat in his study, a brandy in hand, and thought over the investigation. He'd soon be under pressure to report to shareholders and depositors. But he wasn't ready yet. Loose ends were fluttering in the breeze, as enigmatic as those Buddhist prayer-flags in illustrated books.

They were framing up a set of charges against Adams and his colleagues, but needed more evidence on certain aspects. And witnesses. Larkin was cautious, as he was himself. They didn't want to go off half-cocked. What to bring forward, what to let pass? Give these men an inch…Whether they could get a case even to preliminary committal proceedings, depended on the Attorney-General—and the Premier. A double enigma! He found himself tense thinking of it. However, he'd some weapons in reserve. For instance, Brodzky.

It had arrived by the afternoon post, lay on his desk. Another clandestine communication! He'd read it and tossed it aside. Over the years, as a parliamentarian, as a barrister, he'd received a few such. They'd been anonymous—the usual trademark. He'd never reported them, and nothing had happened. This one wasn't hand-written. It appeared that letters had been cut from a newspaper and pasted on to a blank sheet of paper.

BE SURe YOuR SiN wiLL FiND yOU OuT

He smile thinly. This communicator wasn't a stranger to the Old Testament. So it appeared.

The windows of his study were open wide to receive whatever breeze might be on the move. What flowed into the room was the immense stillness of the night. It seemed to sing in the high-ceilinged room, in his ears. He glanced up at his father's portrait, varnished with the gas-light. Almost raised his glass, did begin one of his monologues.

*What do you think? What's it connect with? I've had one or two problems since you cut the painter…Quite a few possibilities…*His father's brown eyes, in his pale face, didn't deviate from his.

He'd failed as a parliamentarian, as a Minister in the Gillies Government. That was the general opinion, and his own. He'd gone into politics in '86 with a certain viewpoint on the Colony's affairs, the zeal to be an agent of change in particular areas. For example, the Colony's woeful Companies Act. Nothing had come off. At every turn, he'd found himself opposed by colleagues in the lower house, finally, blocked by the conservative self-interests of the upper. That council was about as rotten and corrupt a crew as one could envisage. A boatload of damned privateers, someone had said.

But they were in your time, too, weren't they?…

One of his enemies in the house had scornfully dubbed him 'The Crusader'. He'd worn it, a badge of contempt in the eyes of the boomers and their hangers-on in that boom year of '88. Since the crash, many saw what he'd been after, and some hated him for it—or feared the kind of platform he might've now found.

He sipped brandy. This morning's thought returned: The case of Savage and Sandhurst. It had written finis to his parliamentary career. On the back of privileged information, the duo had been fecund in private deals, their speciality the location of new railway lines. They'd bought up land in advance for subdivision, selling it at great profit. In one case, even persuaded the Government where a station should be built. That was what he'd unearthed.

I went into bat…

They'd sold five acres to the Government for the station—at thirty times cost. The Premier had opposed an inquiry, hadn't wanted members of his party tarred with that brush.

So, I resigned. Right or wrong?…

He did raise his glass. These 'talks' were a rarity; sprang into being on the back of a few brandies.

He'd made a statement in the house on this 'plundering of Government finances,' had written to the papers. Savage and Sandhurst had sued him, and won. Nearly bankrupted him. He'd found out what he should've known: anyone who stood between them and money, was on dangerous ground. The Attorney-General, and the Crown Law Department, had sat on their hands.

Were those men the authors of the missive on his desk? Would they telegraph their punches like this? More like some prankster. Yes…

He spoke aloud: 'I won't go into that other matter. Maybe you know about it…'

A night for grim reminiscences—and for gazing at the future. Thoughts on that 'other matter' had been too frequent to need taking up tonight. He let this lie as a 'given'.

Mrs Beattie had long gone to bed. He poured another glass from the decanter. His father's, brought out from Scotland. They said his father had been 'straight'. Too much so to make money, though he'd always been trying to cut deals. He'd left him this house and contents.

Savage and Sandhurst had also exacted revenge on his career at the bar. Briefs, suddenly, had become hard to come by. And the class that he'd brought under attack had made sure he got none of the plums that were around these days. The liquidator's appointment had come in the nick of time. He stood, glass in hand, shedding these thoughts; one by one they were absorbed by the silence.

He turned the gas off, and climbed the stairs to his bedroom. Before he slept, his mind turned, yet again, in a grand sweep, to Helena Spencer, pictured her regal, resplendent in her bed among the many small, embroidered pillows she affected, incense in the air, the green eyes mirroring the keen thoughts weaving in her brain.

Goodbye, Helena. At last, he'd realized that.

When he slept, it was fitfully. All the paraphernalia on the board-room table seemed tossed up by a wind, was floating in the air. A woman in white was walking in his house, floating, in turn, on the stairs. It was a recurring dream.

14

The Governor held a cloth continually soaked in water over the open window against the fierce north wind, to try if by evaporation he could freshen the airs but it remained oven-like for all his efforts.
Ada Cambridge, Thirty Years in Australia (1903)

Night Talk

'BY GOD, THEIR FACES—the eyes! Worse than that, the way they crept off the premises into the evening.'

Re-living it, William halted in mid-stride, and stared along the shadowy, leafy tunnel of the Edinburgh Gardens' east–west walk, as if a horrific manifestation had appeared there.

Throughout dinner, he'd been so tense that rather than have coffee, Katherine had suggested a walk. At four o'clock, he'd commenced the dismissals. One by one he'd said his piece to each of twenty-seven employees, and they'd left. The atmosphere in the store had been indescribable.

'A terrible day,' Katherine said.

'Disastrous for them.'

Arm-in-arm, they resumed their walk. The air felt heavy and warm to the skin, was torpid beneath the thick foliage. This city lung was hardly breathing. In the far distance thunder muttered, lightning flickered as rapid as eye-blinks on the western horizon. To their right, a hundred yards distant, a line of houses, faintly illuminated, straggled off into the darkness resembling esplanade lights going out to a point. Katherine picked out the high silhouette of their house, with its distinctive cupola; it seemed to beckon them home.

He would come to terms with it, she knew, though not forget. There was more of the businessman in him than anyone of their circle could have imagined four years ago.

He said, 'It's eased my feelings to talk about it. I'll put it behind me. I must.'

She was silent. Yes, eyes to the future, and the struggle ahead. She wondered if Tom Montrose might be looking down, watching his 'ship' trying to outrun the storm. In the darkness, she compressed her lips.

William had also reported his interview with Hilda, and now recalled his brief encounter with Lady Adams as he'd left the East Melbourne house, the deep worry in her eyes.

'I've never seen Laura like that.'

It had been concealed by the time Katherine had arrived. She wasn't interested in the gossip which circulated, wasn't exposed to much of it because of their restricted social life. Anyway, society was a shadow of its former self. William hadn't said much, but she'd sensed trouble.

She said, 'Hilda's worried about them.'

'Be prepared for bad news. Sir John owes us £200 for wine and spirits and the account's long overdue. That'll be the tip of the iceberg.'

'It hardly seems possible.'

'It's his bank,' he said grimly.

They walked on, leaving the path and turning back over the dead-dry grass. They were alone in the gardens. After a moment, Katherine said, 'Hilda and Laura are unhappy there've been no developments between Philip and Hanna. I think they're making a new plan.' She'd lightened her voice.

William grunted. His thoughts had moved on to something Hilda had said. He glanced at his wife.

'Your work at the Benevolent Society...I know it's important...but the risk...'

He faded into silence. A vision of Sonia Larkin's face had come to him. Dead at thirty-one; of Philip's grief, the night she'd died. He'd never been to the Collingwood centre, never seen the family she visited. It was a gap which, tonight, he was acutely aware of.

Katherine smiled. *Hilda* was worried. She said, 'Don't worry, my love. I'm not running any risks. It *is* something I must do.' She recalled a blur of faces from this morning...out of it materialized those of the Harbraces, little Jean.

He wasn't satisfied. However, he put it aside, turned to a painful subject which she'd held close in her heart these past two years. It was the delicate subject which Hilda Wilberforce had not yet found or created an opportunity to discuss with her. Childless herself, Hilda remembered with a still heart-felt poignancy, her own sadness—her retrospective doubts as to whether all avenues had been explored.

They didn't know where the point of failure was. Dr MacKenzie had made certain suggestions, recommended a text for study. Intent now on his wife, and her silences as they walked, William said, 'Tonight, should we put into practice Chapter 10 of the good Dr Neff's book?' He'd tried to lighten *his* voice.

She laughed quietly. 'If you like.'

They were coming back to the house. As they crossed the road, Katherine wondered how serious that impasse was to him; she felt it was mainly on her shoulders. All her life she'd been open and forthright, but early in their marriage she'd realized that his character was different. He had corners which, probably, would remain unknown to her; not necessarily dark corners.

As they went up the steps, she remembered the gilded bird-cage hanging in a corner of their conservatory, empty. It was one of the few possessions that he'd brought with him. Instinctively, she'd felt a story attached to it, but something had held her back from asking. She wondered if he remembered its existence.

———————

Surprising Hanna, distantly but clearly the clock on the Fitzroy Town Hall had just struck eleven. She put aside a catalogue from Messrs John Murray, the London publishers, and glanced across at her friend who was reading that morning's *Table Talk* with strict attention.

Susan Fairfax looked up. 'What fascinating reports. I've never come across anything like it: "The Colony seems…to have nothing else but bank-boom directors, rogues, swindlers…" She let the paper drop. 'I don't know if I'm ready for Melbourne!'

'I don't know whether Melbourne's ready for you!' Hanna replied.

Smiling, the Lancashire woman retrieved the paper. They'd been having a quiet evening. In the three weeks since she'd arrived they'd almost exhausted themselves talking—catching up on 'home', family, old friends, the events in their lives since they'd be young girls at school together. Also, Hanna had been giving her friend a quick introduction to the Melbourne topography, and to her friends.

It was this last point which Susan took up now. She had enjoyed her visit to the Italianate mansion at East Melbourne.

'Mrs Wilberforce has a strong character, yet she's delicate in her perceptions. They rarely go together, you know.'

Hanna laughed. 'She's quite modern in her outlook. She's an excellent head for business. I think you'll find much in common. The men respect her, but are wary. Some, downright nervous. She calls a spade a spade. They aren't used to it.'

'You teased her—about the judge.'

'He's the most recent in a long line. The poor men all seem to die. They've all been much older than she.' She paused, said thoughtfully, '*He* gives me the shivers. Those pale staring eyes. The way he just appears from nowhere.' She shrugged expressively. 'Of course, she's trying to marry me off to Philip Larkin. Aided and abetted by Lady Adams.'

Susan Fairfax's eyes widened. 'Hanna! Why haven't you mentioned it?'

'Because, I don't think anything like that has crossed his mind.'

Hanna had blushed, now was frowning. Susan saw this, didn't say more. But, what a surprise! Hanna was frowning, really, for another reason. The idea she'd had that afternoon, which she'd thought might've come also to Hilda Wilberforce, had returned. She'd listened to Susan's account (she almost knew it by heart) of the marvellous Sir Joshua, of his ground-breaking emporia—selling everything from drapery to pots and pans, of her own work in actually *managing* one of the vast stores. It was the latest experience.

When she'd made her remark about Melbourne being ready for Susan she'd had in mind her luminous beauty—*and* the managerial situation she'd had in England. The intention had been for Susan to come into the book store, take over its administration. However, a task much more worthy of her mettle was to hand.

She lifted her head to meet her friend's gaze.

'Susan, William Boyd's emporium's in trouble. William is capable, has a good staff, but he's had to learn the business quickly. If I could arrange it, would you go in to see what might be done?'

For the second time that night, Susan's eyes widened. She'd become super-alert.

15

When selfish greed becomes a social sin
The world's regeneration will begin.
Ada Cambridge, 'Fashion'

Helping Hands

THE ENIGMATIC, anonymous threat was in Wallace's mind when he awoke the next morning. It was the least consequential of the matters on his mind, but the brain was often fickle with priorities. By the time he reached the bank, he'd forgotten it.

Binks was at work in the boardroom, and Philip Larkin arrived straight away.

'Any news of Harbrace?' the liquidator asked.

The solicitor shook his head. 'If he's still in Melbourne, my man'll find him.'

Then Wallace told Larkin of the expunged No. 2 Accounts they'd discovered in Savage's and Sandhurst's names. As he listened attentively, Larkin thought that Wallace's heart must have been delighted by this.

'Harbrace *must* know what went on. If we can get his evidence...Or, the chief manager's.'

'The more we have to nail it down the better,' Binks growled.

'And Harbrace might have other information to spill,' Wallace said. He consulted his watch, then told Larkin of his meeting with Murdoch, of the impending exposure in *Table Talk* concerning Sir John's affairs.

The solicitor thought: It's opening up. He said, 'That'll test his mettle.'

Larkin's caution about the chief manager had been well-founded. Jamison Smith turned up escorted by a lawyer known slightly to the three men waiting in the boardroom.

'Sorry to bring you out on a Saturday,' Wallace began. He glanced at Jamison Smith who, already, was perspiring profusely. It'd been unpleasant to shake his hand.

'We've reached a stage where we have a number of questions to put to you. Which we hope'll throw light.'

Under his hand was a list of them. He put the first. Immediately it was clear they weren't going to hear responses of substance. The lawyer, a Mr Billings, wasn't a bluff, tricks-of-the-trade practitioner—he was more effective; a bone-thin, older man, his head and face overrun with wiry grey hair, humourless features, level eyes, and a pointed way of speaking. He was extremely proficient in tactics of obstruction. Clearly, he'd been hand-picked.

After five minutes of listening to the lawyer's flat interventions, Wallace looked at Larkin, and leaned back in his chair. 'Why don't you keep quiet for a moment, Billings? Co-operation from your client at this point, might stand him in good stead later on. I presume it is *his* interests you have at heart?'

In the subsequent silence, Jamison Smith turned agitated eyes on the lawyer; Larkin glanced at Wallace, questioning his tone.

'Of course, we can wait to hear his story in the criminal court. Under oath. If you think *that's* in his interests.'

Billings smiled thinly. 'Oh, you think you'll get to court, do you? I wouldn't count on it, Wallace.'

It was pointless to continue this charade, and Wallace terminated it. The lawyer left, taking away his client, intact. He'd made no incriminating statements, in fact, no statements at all.

'That's a setback,' Larkin said.

Wallace brooded on the failed interview. 'Time will sort it out. Show us which cards to play.'

Larkin considered this. 'What about this *Table Talk* farrago on Sir John?'

'They hope for information from our end to round it off, I've promised nothing.'

'Another case of wait and see,' Larkin suggested. He found himself ambivalent about it; his long friendship with the Adams was troubling him.

Wallace glanced at him, reached in his brief case and took out the anonymous pasted-up communication, put it on the table. Larkin and Binks looked surprised, examined it.

'Mmm,'—thoughtfully, from Philip.

'Uhuh,'—warily, from Binks.

'I don't take it too seriously,' Wallace said. 'Look at it. Reeks of the prankster. I've had 'em before—more virulent. It'd be of interest, though, to know what it connects with.'

Philip Larkin thought: That'll be complicated. A wide field to canvass. He wondered if his friend knew Helena Spencer was putting her business affairs into his hands.

Binks said, 'Have you noticed how the sender's got his letters? He's cut 'em from the mastheads of Melbourne papers.'

'He?' Larkin said.

'Just a manner of speaking.'

'These things shouldn't be taken lightly,' Philip said. 'The police?'

Wallace laughed. 'No.'

Larkin frowned. 'This is right up the alley of that detective.'

'Let it rest where it is,' the liquidator said.

———•———

Hanna believed in striking while the iron was hot. She entered Boyd, Montrose & Co.'s emporium at a minute to ten. Few customers were present as she walked through departments festooned with SALES signs. The ground floor resembled a tableau. Tense assistants stood behind their counters; floor-walkers in poses. No discreet chit-chat. Serious faces, and a kind of hush, prevailed. *Not* an inviting atmosphere. A consummate businesswoman, she frowned as she made her way to William's office hearing her own quiet footfalls. Her mission was going to be every bit as delicate as Susan Fairfax had predicted when she'd agreed to it.

After they'd kissed, and he'd sat her down in front of his desk, William regarded this old friend expectantly. She identified the same tense atmosphere in this room—in him.

'William, I'll come straight to the point. *Susan Fairfax.* It might be useful to spell out what kind of woman she is.'

He showed his surprise, said nothing.

In her no-nonsense way, with which he was well familiar, sitting strictly upright, wearing a little tip-tilted straw Saturday hat adorned with flowers and ribbons, she proceeded, succinctly, to outline her friend's character and experience in the world of retailing. Quite remarkable experience, which spoke for itself; worth its weight in gold. Her eyes never left his face.

After five minutes, she drew breath, straightened the gloves which she'd removed and laid on his desk. 'Sir Joshua Sadler's emporia are the most advanced in the Midlands. Susan's been his right hand for five years. In difficult times, she successfully managed the Manchester store with a staff of 350.' She paused. 'Suddenly, this unique person is in Melbourne!'

She gazed at him. If she'd been another type, she might have said that Fate had brought Susan Fairfax to his doorstep. Instead, she gave one of her expressive shrugs which was emphasis enough.

After the first moments, William had realized why she was here. He'd great respect for Hanna's business judgment. She'd had a sound apprenticeship under her father, and since his death, had run the business successfully. He thought: A lovely woman. He'd taken in Katherine's remark about Hilda's match-making plans. If Philip had a mind to marry again, he wouldn't do better.

He smiled. 'Hanna, with your unerring eye you've seen how we're fixed here. I hope it isn't as obvious to the city at large.'

Earnestly, she said, 'Every business in Melbourne is in difficulty. We've never seen such times.' Looking at his youngish, but haggard face, she was conscious of the feelings which four years ago she'd had for him. Perhaps still had. But, he'd married Katherine.

He didn't want this. How to decline it? He didn't waste words either. 'I can't afford her. It's as simple as that. I dismissed twenty-seven staff on Friday. I'm cutting expenses to the bone. As Tom Montrose might've said, it's all hands to the pumps. And frankly, for your ears only, the future's bleak…Hilda knows.'

Hanna gazed at him.

'It's as bad as that?'

He spread his hands in a restrained despair.

'Then, William, you *must* have Susan.' She leaned forward. 'Forget about "affording her", I'll look to that.'

Otto Rudd waited patiently in a dark doorway in the unlit street. He knew it was after three. Acting on information received, it was the second night he'd stationed himself in an Elsternwick street. Yesterday, he'd gone home as a dirty-pink, airless dawn had appeared. He was used to such boring and indifferent daybreaks, but he was getting older. It might take a few more nights. The rough with the smooth, Rudd, he reminded himself.

He didn't hear the cart until it was right on top of him. Its bulk just materialized from the darkness. Only then did he hear the soft squeaking of well-greased wheels and axle, the gentle thud of the horse's hoofs. With a sense of judgment confirmed, he stepped out of the doorway.

'Hold up there,' he said in a low, authoritative voice.

A touch of the reins, and the monstrous, heavy-breathing, odorous animal veered away.

'Hold it right there, Mr Harris,' Rudd repeated, louder.

The dark silhouette of the driver was craning towards him, detached from the bulk of piled-up goods.

'Keep going, Mr Harris,' a male voice whispered urgently from up in the dark cargo.

'Do you want me to raise a ruckus?' Rudd said, pacing beside the cart. It eased to a stop. He could make out that the horse's hoofs were wrapped in hessian.

'What do you want?' the driver whispered harshly.

'I'm nothing to do with landlords.' Rudd came forward and peered up. There were several people on board, he now discerned. He sensed their agitation. 'I'm a detective on the trail of Mr Harbrace. For his own good. Pure and simple, I want to know where he was taken.'

Silence above. The arrested equipage with its packed-up lives, seemed poised on a hair-trigger.

'Nothing to say about that.'

Rudd put his foot on the step and hauled himself up so that his face was a few feet from the driver's. They could each now make out the other's features. 'On my oath, it'll be to Harbrace's financial advantage. Those are my instructions from reputable lawyers...No-one with any brains pays for a private detective to chase after a few pounds rent, do they?'

Rudd impressed those that he met as a moderately prosperous, honest tradesman, and the silent Harris was absorbing this. He was reasoning also, that the odds were against him getting away with tonight's flit, if this man chose to raise an alarm. The practicality of his future work would be on the chopping block. He had to get moving.

'All right,' he said. He gave an address.

'Got that,' Rudd said. He stepped down, and immediately the reins flapped and the cart was on its way.

'Good luck,' the detective called up to the indistinguishable persons as they went into the night, and some kind of temporary sanctuary.

16

*The Carlton Gardens with their grand Royal Exhibition Building
are a special place…the gardens might be said to constitute a fine
example of white man's dreaming. It seems especially so in the
afternoon light…when the sun sparkles on the waters of the
fountains and filtered light streams through leaves and branches of
century-old plane and elm trees on to the lawns and ornamental
garden beds…the building itself…A cement-rendered Victorian-
period giant, it glistens brightly with its arches, parapets, urns and
towers…Rising above it all is the dome, a mighty antipodean echo
of the Florentine Renaissance.*

David Dunstan, Victorian Icon: The Royal Exhibition
Building Melbourne

Black to Move

'SHOULD I BE DOING THIS?' Wallace asked himself. In a hansom cab, he
was rapidly passing the southern edge of the Carlton Gardens. It was
a breezy Sunday, a God-given respite from the summer now grinding
grittily to an end. A crowd was strolling or loitering in the gardens:
colour from women's dresses, from twirling parasols, flashed amid the
greenery, like tropical birds in flight. Voices, laughter, wafted to him.
The ice-cream men were out. The atmosphere was of ease and relax-
ation and enjoyment. The depressed southern city had given itself a
holiday—a transient but genuine breather.

That was how he'd felt, when he'd opened the venetian blinds,
and seen the speckless azure sky, felt the cool breeze on his face. He'd
breakfasted on his balcony fussed over by Mrs Beattie, later had
worked on his papers for two hours, then dined at one, on roast mutton and roast vegetables, taking two glasses of claret. Mrs Beattie had
been delighted.

Now, he was headed for the residence of Hanna Dewhurst, temporarily also the residence of Miss Susan Fairfax.

He answered himself: '*An open question.*' But the exchange was academic—he *was* doing it. That first eye-contact with the day had crystallized something.

Impulsive—Mrs Beattie's opinion of him. It was more in the appearance than the reality; an ingredient of 'evidence', was always mixed with the emotion which sparked the impulse. In this case: two pieces. That it was finished with Helena, had come like a delayed reaction to an accident. He'd had his run. In cricketers' parlance, he'd taken his eye off the ball—for her character had always been on view.

The other? Different country altogether. Twelve days ago when he'd set eyes on the Lancashire woman in the Boyds' drawing-room, another subtle and tricky run had begun in him. Silent, deep—like the delicate mind-weaving intonations of a cello playing late at night. He'd been electrified, in a way new and remarkable. He'd broken out of it quickly, but Helena had picked it up, and perhaps the moment had been the catalyst for *her*.

He didn't notice they'd turned left into Nicholson Street. He'd fallen into this muse, received a jolt when they drew up outside an imposing terrace of three-storey houses. He blinked at them, was back in the present. A brass plate on the house said: *Carlton Gardens*. The cast iron palisade-barred fence said: *1850s*.

Hanna was surprised when her maid announced that Mr Angus Wallace had called, was waiting below. That man, here? She glanced across the room to where Susan was turning the pages of an issue of *Sylvia*—the first Indian and colonial edition of the London magazine of women's fashions—accommodating the Antipodean seasons.

Susan looked up, curiously. 'Mr Wallace? The man at the Boyds—with the lady in green?'

Hanna nodded, and rose from her chair. Her friend had remembered the salient point. The day had been uneventful thus far—church, a walk in the gardens, and lunch. She wondered if the pattern was to be disturbed, suspected it might be. She had a good idea why he was here.

One had to admit he has presence, she thought, as the barrister, minus hat and stick, left in the hall, briskly entered the first-floor sitting room—gained in the courts, and on the floor of the Legislative Assembly. She'd seen him in several drawing-rooms, around several dining tables, sometimes articulate, sometimes silent. He'd never tried to be the star turn, which had impressed her. Where was Mrs Spencer today?

'Miss Dewhurst, I trust this isn't inconvenient?'

'Of course not, Mr Wallace, though, we're hardly dressed to

receive visitors.' She spread her hands to indicate the simple, loose, white linen neck-to-ankle dresses they each wore. 'Look at us. You might think we are twin sisters. Will you sit down?'

He smiled, and abruptly stepped forward to shake hands. He'd put on a newish cutaway black coat, and his grey trousers were pressed with a crease in the latest fashion. A yellow silk cravat gave him the air of a gentleman of leisure. His manner spoke for it as being leisure gained at a price. He sat down, glanced at the wide-open windows.

'You've a fine view of the Exhibition Building.'

From the first floor, they looked straight across to the immense Florentine dome, glistening in the bright sunlight, encompassed by that azure sky; almost a painting, except the Union Jacks flapped in the breeze.

'The gardens are pleasant to walk in, we've just been there. *You* must have a splendid view of the Albert Park Lake.'

'A distant one.' He smiled, at her slight irony.

To this point, he'd concentrated his gaze on Hanna. Now he turned to Miss Fairfax. He was surprised that her hair had been cut. Its soft blondeness was shaped close to her head. She looked a new woman to the one in the Boyds' drawing-room. But the fine features, the flawless delicacy of her complexion, the easy grace with which she sat—that steady, pleasant blue gaze—on his face, instantly reinstated that vision. The same *essence*.

What had she heard about him?

He said, 'This heat must've been hard on you, Miss Fairfax. Not a good time of the year to arrive.'

She looked as cool and airy as his drive here had been—the antithesis of his remark, he realized. Polite discourse was such a damned effort. Led you round in circles. Though, sometimes his cross examinations did that—until he found an entry point.

Susan was accustomed to male scrutiny; admiring, naturally enough. After the Boyds' party, Hanna had sketched small biographies, she'd heard a snippet on Wallace—and Mrs Spencer. In Manchester, there'd always been legal matters afoot with the store. Legal men were not strangers to her. One in particular...

'It'll be bitter and snowy at home. I think I've a fair exchange, Mr Wallace.' She easily understood his dilemma of the moment.

He'd moved a black pawn forward, and she'd responded with a white. He wanted to ask her what her plans were for staying in the Colony, but that would have been a knight's move. As for plans, he'd come with the one which had sprung into his mind with the first sight of the morning.

'Mr Wallace is delving into the affairs of one of our failed banks,' Hanna said. 'He's the liquidator, trying to put together the pieces from a smash.' She had been watching him, a curious frown on her brow.

He nodded.

'I see from the papers…' Susan began.

'They report only the tip of the iceberg,' Hanna, the business-woman, interrupted.

And I'm chipping steadily into that submerged ice, he thought.

'I see from the papers,' Susan repeated, 'that business conditions are similar to what we've had at home. Very hard times.'

Hanna said, 'The story here's been stupidity and greed. And crookedness.' She turned to Susan. 'Hilda Wilberforce has followed it all. She can tell you. Just as Katherine Boyd can about the despair and misery among the poor.'

Not to speak of what's in the eyes of men in the street, Wallace thought.

'*Are* you putting the pieces of this bank together, Mr Wallace?' Susan asked.

He smiled. 'It's a slow process.'

'Will more fail?'

He paused. 'The signs aren't good.'

'Which?' Hanna asked.

The liquidator considered. He'd been enjoying his holiday. 'I don't wish to make guesses.'

'We business people are having to. Who's insolvent, who's not. Who it's safe to extend credit to.'

He was studying her. 'The Insolvency Act's a rotten piece of legislation,' he said. Hanna saw that she had hit a nerve.

In the silence which ensued, to Hanna, the sun-filled room scattered with the pieces of Georgian furniture brought by her father from Lancashire in '73, seemed to have become sterile, dispirited. She rose to ring a bell.

Wallace said, 'I should tell you the reason for my visit…Would you come to a dinner at my house? Philip Larkin will be present, among others.'

Hanna blinked with surprise; Susan looked interested.

His dark face flushed slightly.

Hanna exchanged a glance with Susan. 'We're delighted to accept.'

Tea was brought in, and a date arranged. The conversation moved to what Miss Fairfax should see and do. It was premature to talk of what she might be engaged in at Boyd & Montrose's. William had agreed to show her over the store, discuss its predicament, have her there for a week or two as an observer. That was all. But Hanna felt she'd prevailed. Once Susan was in…she was quietly confident about the outcome. It wasn't often that you had the chance to help two friends with one action. Despite their deep friendship, Susan kept certain matters absolutely private. However, Hanna had sensed that her friend was virtually in mourning for her lost position in Manchester. She did know how painful that exit had been. There was something else which she found exasperating…not its nature, but Susan's reticence about it.

She said, with a meaningful look at her, 'Susan has already visited Mrs Dugdale.'

A flicker of annoyance passed over Susan's face, but she said nothing.

Hanna continued. 'What do you think of these suffragettes, Mr Wallace?'

He shrugged slightly. He knew that Henrietta Dugdale was a Melbourne leader in that field, but he had nothing to say, either.

'I'm sure Mr Wallace is used to difficult questions, but that is hardly a fair one,' Susan said pleasantly, smiling at Hanna. Why was she opening this up before a stranger?

Half an hour later, Wallace stood in the street. This had been an 'experience'. These young women were extraordinary. A distinctly different breed from the usual run. That last expression wouldn't have won their favour, he instantly realized. He would have to watch himself.

However, as he rode homeward it was the face, figure and aura of Susan Fairfax which rode with him—as breezy and delicious in his head as this day had been. He hadn't once thought of the anonymous, threatening communication lying on his desk—or of Savage and Sandhurst.

17

Mr Hill, the liquidator of the Land Credit Bank, has been threat-
ened with an action for libel by Mr Fuller, who holds a power of
attorney from Sir M. H. Davies.

Table Talk, 8.6.1892

Witness

'HARBRACE IS FOUND.' That was the scrawled message Wallace had
received from Philip Larkin on Sunday evening. It was Monday morning, and he was headed for the address at Collingwood, accompanied
by Binks. Already, smoke from factories smeared the sky.

When they arrived at the workman's cottage in the grim street
with its stagnant drains, rubbish heaps, and stink of cesspits, neither
of them noticed the short, thick-set man in the bowler standing in a
doorway. The street was paved with bluestone pitchers. Hard and
uncompromising as life here, Wallace thought. Breezy yesterday
seemed a dream, a rarefied existence.

What would this interview yield?

In one respect, more than he calculated. He knocked on the door,
it opened immediately, and he was face-to-face with Katherine Boyd.
Astonishment froze on their faces.

'Katherine! What are you doing here?' Wallace burst out.

'Angus!…I might ask the same of you.'

He removed his hat. Binks was watching with interest.

'I'm hoping to interview a Mr Harbrace concerning the bank…'
He stopped. The sound of children's voices had come from the
interior.

Katherine opened the door wide. She'd removed her hat and her
darkish auburn hair was up, secured with a small tortoise-shell comb.
Her face was without a trace of make-up. Her complexion appeared so
pale as to be transparent, but her face was purposeful. Her sleeves were
rolled up, her hands hastily dried. Her pale blue eyes flicked to Binks,
flicked across the street to where Otto Rudd stood in his doorway.

'He's here. Very ill. Angus, this is my "family" from the Ladies' Benevolent Society. I don't know whether he'll be able to receive you…I'll go and see.'

She went down the passage, thinking: How things connect.

Wallace waited on the doorstep, looked across the street, noticed the bowler-hatted man. He thought: Ah, the detective.

Katherine was back, beckoning him in. 'You should be quiet with him, Angus.'

Wallace glanced at Binks. 'Better wait here.'

The liquidator was shocked to see the condition of his potential witness. He drew up a chair close to where the ex-chief accountant sat, covered by a rug, head fallen forward. He leaned close. 'I'm Wallace, the bank's liquidator,' he said quietly. 'I presume, Mr Harbrace, that you sent me that abstract of overdrafts?'

Harbrace raised his head, looked at the liquidator who was relieved to see the almost imperceptible nod. Wallace began to speak slowly and concisely, and from the other room Katherine heard the murmur of talk, punctuated by Harbrace's coughing, faint responses.

She continued to bath the children in the small tin bath. Mrs Harbrace sat at a table chopping up vegetables for a soup. Katherine glanced at her. She'd found out that she was again 'in the family way'. Could the timing be worse?—she thought grimly, pouring a dipper of water over Jean's small, patient head. The doll was in sight nearby on a stool. She plucked the child out of the bath, began to dry her.

Otto Rudd consulted his watch, tilted his hat forward, and with a nod in the direction of the watching Binks, ambled off. This job was done. He'd been standing guard until the parties had turned up, and now they had. He'd go and put in his account to Messrs Larkin & Larkin. On the way, he'd have a spot of breakfast; he knew where a good saveloy-man had set up a stand.

Wallace reached for the ill man's hand to shake it, went to the door of the adjoining room, surveyed the scene. At the front door, he said to Katherine, 'Is he seeing a doctor?'

'Dr Singleton's been several times. There's nothing to be done. You can see for yourself…though he has better days.'

Wallace took out a note-case, produced a banknote. 'I'd be very much obliged, Katherine, if you'd put that towards the family's needs.' She gave him a look which he couldn't interpret. Curiosity?

And Binks looked at him, inquiringly, when he came out to the street. 'He's the one that sent it. I've got the story behind Savage's and Sandhurst's No. 2 Accounts.' The liquidator sounded excited. 'He's desperately ill. I don't think he'd make it into the witness-box—though, he's willing to try. I think we had better look to an affidavit. It might count for something, if the judge is so minded.'

'If we get into court,' Binks growled.

'What happened to that detective?'

Binks shrugged. 'Just drifted off like those fellows do.' He'd had more than enough dealings with that profession over the years. He was curious about Mrs Boyd being here, but didn't put the question. He looked forward to hearing the story concerning the No. 2 Accounts.

In one of the habitual twists in his thinking, his mind had turned back to Savage and Sandhurst. He reckoned they were lying out there like brown snakes in the sun—ready to make a move. But his employer would know that.

18

Like one who sees
  A rebel light
  In the thick of the night,
As he stumbles and staggers on summits afar—
          Henry Kendall, 'Euroclydon'

Mirrors

THAT EVENING, Philip Larkin came to Wallace's house, was shown into the study by Mrs Beattie. Wallace and Binks were waiting for the solicitor. This was to be a crucial meeting.

Seated at his desk, Wallace reported on the Harbrace interview, the details of which made Philip blink. Then he summarized the status of their work. It was the most dismal picture. The capital and reserves were gone; the shareholders would have to face up to a call of three pounds per share. With bankruptcy in the air everywhere, probably not a great deal of this would be collected. The other obscurity was what could be realized on the properties held as security; here, again, they were checkmated: no-one had money, or if they did, the courage to buy real estate.

'The depositors are going to be left pretty much stranded,' he finished.

'What a short and bitter life,' Larkin said quietly. The doom-struck bank had shot across the Melbourne scene, with the transience of a shooting star.

'All I see is losers,' Binks said morosely.

'*And* criminals,' the liquidator said.

He switched to this aspect. 'There's no doubt in my mind we've a case against them for issuing a false balance sheet. A criminal offence, even under this rotten Companies Act. Whether there's a case of conspiracy to defraud over the writing-off of their own loans, needs more looking into. As to the brazen frauds perpetrated by Savage and Sandhurst re their No. 2 Accounts, I reckon we've got them cold. A cert, if we can get Harbrace's evidence up.'

'They've milked it dry,' Larkin mused. 'Hard to believe it of Sir John.'

Wallace looked at him narrowly. 'It might go further. Was the bank formed with the *intention* of bleeding it dry?'

Larkin was astonished. 'That's hard to believe. Be impossible to prove.'

Wallace shrugged. 'We'll see.'

They were silent. The wooden-slatted blinds stirring, the bonging of insects against the lamps, the sibilant flaring of the gas-lights, sounded in the room. Wallace said, 'I want 'em in prison.'

Philip Larkin glanced up. There'd been something in the tone …A wrong note? Binks heard it, too, brooded on the carpet's pattern.

'*If* it serves the best interests of the depositors and shareholders,' Larkin said concisely. 'That's what we're here for, is it not?' He shifted uneasily in his chair; it was becoming clear Wallace might be hard to rein in.

The liquidator smiled slightly. What about the public good? he thought. He said, 'The Crown Law Office should take it off our hands. I'll make an appointment to see the Attorney-General. Do you agree?'

Larkin relaxed slightly. This was the ticket. 'Yes.'

Wallace frowned. He rose and paced across the room. He stopped, looked at Philip. 'I hear Boyd & Montrose have their problems.'

'I've heard it.'

'They're a debtor to the bank for £7,500, and we'll be serving demand on borrowers, shortly.'

They considered the predicament of William Boyd.

'There's not much we can do about it,' Larkin said, 'if we're not to be tarred with the same brush as the Savages of the world.'

Larkin and Binks departed. For a moment, Wallace stood with the former on his portico. A velvet, dark-blue night. Next door, Mrs Hammond had begun to play.

'Mozart,' Larkin said and stepped off into the shadowy street, but not towards home, which made Wallace wonder. But he forgot it and went in. His ex-politician's mind had turned to the Attorney-General, another shadowy direction.

———•———

Philip Larkin did have another destination. Fifteen minutes after leaving Wallace he was in Cecil Street, South Melbourne, gazing at a fine,

Italianate house. Behind a narrow space demarked by cast iron pal-
isade railings, it stood close to the street alignment; a tower, which
enclosed and soared up above a portico, did so stand. The grey-stuccoed facade was illumined from the street-light. Mrs Spencer's house.
He perceived that it wasn't on the grand scale, but was extremely elegant; didn't yet know that she described it as 'a poem of a house'.

His thoughts had transferred from the bank's affairs to those of his
new client. He was to receive the records and paraphernalia of her
financial empire. 'Empire' might be an exaggeration, but he'd made
inquiries and it wasn't too far off the mark. The late Mr Spencer had
been both astute and fortunate. Only in his longevity had he been
short-changed.

Larkin had several widows and maiden ladies for whom he acted,
and they sent him social invitations. He'd reminded himself of this
when the note had arrived from Mrs Spencer 'summoning' him—that
was the tone—to her house at eight o'clock. 'Nearby to Wallace's, two
birds with one stone,' he'd told himself.

However, an awakening had come the morning she'd visited his
office. It was as if a bell had chimed. What it signified, where it might
take him, he didn't know.

He peered at his watch. The night air was as tepid as that in the
bank's vault. He faced the house. The front rooms were brightly illuminated. Electric light. He removed his hat, set his shoulders, went up
the steps, stood on the tessellated floor of the portico. Perspiration
filmed his body. That was the walk.

A youngish maid, spic-and-span, opened the door.

Philip found himself walking on marble, pink and black squares of
it, past French furniture, being announced into a drawing-room. He
stepped through the door, and a Parisian world broke over his head
with the force of a translucent-green Southern Ocean roller.

And, Mrs Spencer was coming to him, a splendid figure against
the glistening, electric-lit background.

In public or private, Mrs Spencer made a point of being perfectly
groomed, and this evening she'd made certain of it. She wore a striking emerald-green gown in material with the latest 'looking glass'
surface. Her hair was swept up, pinned with a diamond ornament. A
crescent of diamonds glittered on her bosom. She moved in her long-
legged, languorous, and confident walk—familiar to many, of both
sexes, in the city's best drawing-rooms, the Block Arcade, the Princess
Theatre. She was a regular performer on all those stages. Her toilette,
the magnetism of her personality, the fluidity of her carriage, seemed

to announce: 'I am Mrs Helena Spencer.'

Philip took the extended hand, absorbing all this—and a Parisian fragrance.

'Mr Larkin! You've come to my rescue! What an hour for you to be still working! Though, I hope you don't see it in that light entirely. After all, we've met often in the houses of friends.'

He took in the undercurrent of amusement, was being overloaded with impressions.

'My pleasure…' he said. He turned, spread his hands. A reaction was called for. 'What a fine room you've created, Mrs Spencer.'

He stood, frozen in a chamber of mirrors; momentarily, he'd felt imperilled. Mirrors—huge, ornate, gilt-framed, bevelled and glittering, covered two of the walls. The decorative magnificence was multiplied. He and she were. From the turgid considerations on the failed bank, the airless street, to this!

'Thank you. I'm a devotee of Paris. Do sit here. Have you heard of my salons?'

He had. He'd heard that most of Melbourne's art, literary and musical luminaries—and those visiting—had shown themselves to these mirrors. They sat side-by-side on a settee. At hand was a leather case. In it were Mrs Spencer's deeds, certificates, bank statements, private ledger and account books, all carefully arranged for him to take away. He was invited to look them over, and did so quickly.

'All perfectly sorted and noted,' he said glancing at her.

'Of course. However, I look forward to your guidance.'

There was something of bravado in the way she conducted herself. He had that thought, as the maid came in.

'Now…' Mrs Spencer said. 'That's done. I've champagne here to celebrate our union,' she smiled brilliantly, 'and sandwiches.' Her green-eyed gaze hadn't left his face.

Delicious chicken sandwiches, and he took refuge in them from those eyes. He'd not eaten. He'd gone from the office directly to Wallace's, and there'd been nothing on offer there.

Mrs Spencer sipped her champagne, watched his attack on the sandwiches with concerned and smiling interest. 'I do hope your servants look after you, Mr Larkin?'

'They do. Tonight I had to miss my dinner.' Suddenly, he wondered what her reaction would be if he told her he'd been at Wallace's.

'You men should put your health *first*.' The voice of experience.

While he ate and drank, she launched into a vivacious commentary on the events of the day. She did it with little stabs of wit which kept arresting his attention. In this kind of talk, her voice was low and melodic. She said, sipping champagne, 'I see a committee of investigation into the English and Australian Mortgage Bank's been appointed. First the smoke, then the flames? One by one they fall. But you're very familiar with it.'

The thought came to him that she could be a junior version of Hilda Wilberforce. For years, Hilda had run her soirées—which he supposed were interchangeable with 'salons'...

He looked at her. Her bare arms, delicately but emphatically slicing this rarefied air; her flawless white bosom plunging down, captured by superior corsetry, moving subtly and delightfully with the gentle heaving of an ocean swell; the fragrance of her hair and body—all of it, wafting in the room, had suddenly knocked him sideways. All of it, a few inches away.

Suddenly, she was calling him Philip; clearly, he was to respond with Helena. Two electrical fans swished high above their heads. Cooling, conspiratorial, but not cooling him.

He heard himself saying, 'The bachelors of the Melbourne Club are to give a ball...Might I presume?'

Indeed, he might. Mrs Spencer was well aware of the occasion—her mind was sign-posted with the dates of such events. She would be *delighted*.

Shortly after, not quite certain of the circumstances of his exit, he descended the steps, walked along the street, the champagne lingering on his palate, in his head.

A hansom loomed out of the dark; like everything tonight.

Rattling homewards to St Kilda, going along the Esplanade, the bay darkly ambiguous to his right, he tried to get another ambiguity straight in his head.

'Bravado', he'd thought, but that wasn't it. It was more as if at one moment she was a slightly over-the-top actress, the next, superimposed in a blink, that persona of penetrative, amused green eyes. As if the second was mocking the first, and inviting you to share in it. However, he judged that was only one agenda of those green stares.

He alighted from the hansom, the leather case, the new stewardship, firmly in hand, and a new prospect, illuminated as brightly as her house, in his mind.

19

Important Announcement: George & George Ltd beg to advise…they will commence their 27th Half-Year Clearing Sale on Monday next…Reducing all Surplus and Seasonable Stock to prices that will Force Sale even in the present depressed state of trade…Goods of the Latest Fashion at Great Sacrifices…less than Half the Original Cost.

Table Talk, 8.6.1892

Sea Lanes

WITH A SENSE of mission, and keen expectation, Susan Fairfax arrived at Boyd, Montrose & Co. at nine o'clock on a Tuesday morning. As she entered the main door, the emporia-world washed over her. Melbourne's retailing market was an enigma, but, instantly, she felt on home-ground. She smiled at a memory of Sir Joshua entering one of his stores, sniffing the air like an old war horse, instantly in command, fawned over by staff.

A young woman waited for her. 'Miss Fairfax? Would you come this way, please.'

A nervous smile, a curious glance, and the slight, dark-haired woman from the Ladies' Department led the tall, blonde vision who might have been a model stepped straight out of the latest *Harper's Bazaar* from America, to Mr Boyd's office. The speculative glances of floor-walkers and sales assistants followed them. As they walked through the departments, Susan had begun.

Outside William Boyd's office, she considered the nervy atmosphere she'd passed through. Definitely, home-ground.

William was smiling, his hand extended.

She thought: Controlled nerves, in this case. She turned to the young woman. 'Thank you.'

William guided her to a bentwood chair before his desk, and sat down on another so that they were opposite each other. She noted this touch of informality.

'May I call you Susan? Hanna is such a great friend to us both.'

She smiled. 'I'd welcome it.' She thought: What can I do for you? What will you *let* me do?

Despite his good intentions, she felt his restraint. He might be as liberal-thinking as Hanna had said, nonetheless it would be exceedingly hard to accept a woman as an expert—and difficult to put it on his staff. She could make it work, but *he* must make the first move.

He said, 'Hanna's spoken of your experience in glowing terms. I won't beat about the bush—I'd be very glad to have the benefit of it. We're up against it. Every business in Melbourne is. It's a matter of cutting our cloth right to survive. No margin for error. We're putting everything under close scrutiny. On Friday, I dismissed twenty-seven of our people.'

He sat back in his chair. 'A terrible business.'

He was clear-eyed, she observed, but the dark circles under them contradicted that. And, his clipped speech. But no panic; he was straightforward and determined. It was much more encouraging than she'd expected.

'Perhaps, if I start with how we began, how we've been changing.'

At the end of the hour, William had called in Maybury and Isaacs to introduce them. Quiet, watchful men, respectful of her sex, her association with their employer, reserving judgment on anything else. He'd already told them of Miss Fairfax, formerly of Sadler's Emporia of Manchester.

He took her over the store from top to bottom: four floors, introducing the department heads, giving a running commentary on each department's recent trading experience. It became obvious to her that he was well-versed in the intricacies of the drapery side, less well so on other facets. It became obvious to him that she was quickly on top of all that he said.

Large SALE placards, suspended by cotton thread, twirled in the air like dancers performing in a near-empty theatre. Even the customers who were providing the thin patronage that morning sent curious glances at the tall, graceful beauty with the efficient aura, the all-seeing look, clearly moving 'behind the scenes'—in close attendance, Mr William Boyd, its respected manager, though memory of his criminal conviction still lingered in a few minds.

Susan did nothing to attract attention, yet everywhere, she did. Her peacock blue hat with its lone feather added 'dash' to the air of efficiency, the statuesque presence.

They reached the basement. It was dim and stacked with stock—much of it obsolescent. 'We're looking at this,' he said. 'Tom Montrose likened the store to a ship. I think of this as the bilges—necessary, but…'

They returned to his office. He indicated a small room next to his own. A stack of journals and ledgers and reports and stock-taking lists waited on a desk.

'You might like to settle in here,' he said.

'Thank you, William.'

'Don't hesitate to call on me.'

'I won't.'

He left. He had another ship on his mind. It was a week overdue ex-London with autumn and winter stock, and the summer days were ebbing away. But he admitted to himself, he was pleased with how this morning had gone. Now, they'd have to see.

She sat behind the desk, removed her hat. She hadn't worn gloves. She was to have a clear run at it. So much better than she'd expected. She told herself that it showed the measure of William Boyd. A thought she had once before in Manchester re-surfaced. How had it gone precisely?…She'd equated herself with a specialist physician called in to a desperate case. In the silent room, her own pulse seemed to whisper in her ears.

She touched nothing, sat back to think. Sir Joshua's words came into her head: You need a plan, girl. The business must be run to a plan. Get the strengths and weaknesses out on the table, and make a plan…Then, 'Shoulder to the wheel!'—said almost as a benediction.

Unexpectedly, something totally unrelated came: the person of Angus Wallace, sitting in Hanna's drawing-room, dark, intense, reticent; making polite conversation as though swallowing ground glass. She'd looked at him, the intriguing snippets she'd heard about him in mind. It had struck her that on a sunny, breezy Sunday afternoon, something was beginning.

And, here she was this morning, on the threshold of another conundrum. It struck her, again, that her transference to the Antipodes might yield challenges and opportunities well beyond the expectations she'd sailed with. That a door she'd thought closed forever had sprung open. In fact, that *her* ship might be coming in.

20

Dr Youl, the Melbourne City Coroner for 40 years, takes his compulsory retirement very much to heart...Where will they find another coroner who will put so much enthusiasm into his work as Dr Youl did? Where will they discover one as able and willing as he was to make an inquest as funny as an Irish wake? I am afraid that in him we have seen the last of the fine old Deadhouse Humorists...

Table Talk, 7.4.1893

Inquests

THE ATTORNEY-GENERAL disliked Wallace, but he put on an affable enough front at their infrequent meetings in the courts, the club, or the street. Wallace knew it, and regretted the man's recent appointment to his office; it was a stroke of bad luck for the liquidator. He'd been surprised when his request for an interview was promptly granted. However, they'd been colleagues and Ministers in the Gillies Government, and he supposed that counted for something.

At four o'clock, he entered this man's domain to find him standing off from a desk piled high with files and papers, eyeing it like someone trying to decide if a dog is dangerous.

'Look at that, Wallace. How can a man deal with it? More than in your time, eh?' He winked, as if to emphasize a witticism.

The liquidator glanced that way, admitted the possibility. 'I've brought some more.'

The Attorney-General spread his hands. Only the Almighty could stop the deluge. 'Let's sit down over here—away from all *that*—and you can tell me about it.'

He strode away, round-shouldered, weighty with responsibility and power, an ex-Premier riding the political winds like an unwieldy seabird, the interests of himself, his intimates, and up to a point his constituents, rigidly ordered in his brain. They sat in capacious leather armchairs facing each other. The large grin appeared in his neatly trimmed whiskers. 'Let's hear it.'

Wallace kept it short—as succinct as the paper he'd brought to hand to him. He was giving away nothing more than necessary to achieve his objective. He released the bare bones of the bank's disastrous story; outlined the alleged transgressions of Adams, Savage, and Sandhurst. Detailed the charges they'd framed against them. As he did, he watched the Attorney as though he had him in the witness-box. Watched him fiddle with his watch-chain, stroke his beard.

This man was partial to land boomers, had been up to his armpits in that fray. More to the point, Savage and Sandhurst were of the same political party. The Attorney's grin had vanished; his eyes had turned cold and resolute. He brooded on the liquidator's face as the tale was told.

Wallace said, 'We believe the Crown Law Department should take over the investigation and prosecute. All the evidence would be placed at their disposal.' Deliberately, he'd said 'the Crown Law Department' rather than 'the Government'. Men like this needed their muffins buttered.

'You've been busy, old man.'

Wallace was silent.

'You had a run-in with Savage and Sandhurst before. Stirred up a lot of mud. Didn't do you—or anyone—much good.'

Wallace kept quiet, left the inference of a vendetta in the air. A trace of annoyance showed on the Attorney's face.

'In fact, they took money off you in court. How does that look?'

'It has nothing to do with this case.'

The Attorney shrugged elaborately. 'Appearances, old man.' He sucked at his teeth.

Eyes narrowed, Wallace watched the parade of mannerisms.

'Wallace, the exuberance of the land boom saw a lot of i's undotted, a lot of t's uncrossed. People got carried away with the spirit of the times. They call it a laissez-faire economy—and the experts swear it's the thing.' He studied the liquidator.

Wallace said, 'Here, we're talking about fraud and theft, not economics.'

The Attorney-General leaned back, gazed above the liquidator's head out the window as though checking the weather, or allowing his irritation to pass. He'd laced his bulbous fingers over his stomach; they sparkled with diamond rings, reminded Wallace of Sir John. Mellow blocks of afternoon sunlight lay on the floriated carpet.

'So you say. I'll look at it. Perhaps I'll take it to the Premier. Before we turn the Crown Law fellows loose on it. *If* we do.'

Wallace nodded slowly. 'I have a shareholders and depositors meeting coming up. We'd be well advised to have it settled by then.'

The Attorney lowered his eyes to Wallace's face, wondered if there'd been a threat, couldn't decide. He smiled censoriously. 'You were never one of us, were you? Never a party man. Some people here haven't forgotten that, find it hard to forgive, though I suppose that doesn't surprise you.'

On that note, Wallace departed. As he walked out into Spring Street he speculated what wheels and pulleys might begin to whirr in the cabinet room. He wished he could feel confident about the outcome—wasn't carrying so much nervy baggage into the situation. Would Philip Larkin soon be regretting his choice of liquidator?

———•———

The Melbourne City Coroner, Dr Youl, a veteran of forty years in the job, did this kind of hearing almost by rote. From where the parties sat, it was obviously a case of suicide 'while the balance of the deceased's mind was disturbed'. The evidence given by the few parties involved was straightforward enough, and predictable.

The body of James Robert Hubble, former head cashier of the First Bank of Victoria, had been taken from the Yarra near Jolimont on the afternoon of the 21st February. It had been in the water for some time. There were no signs of violence on the body, though it was partially decomposed, and fifty pounds in water-logged Commercial Bank five-pound notes were found in the pockets. For two months he'd been living at a Richmond hotel, not engaged in any work since his discharge from the bank. Apparently, his days had been spent either mooching along the river or in the public bar. He'd no family, friends or companions in evidence.

With one possible exception. The Coroner's attention was held, momentarily, by a piece of information elicited from the licensee of the hotel.

Coroner: So in the two months he was at your hotel, he spent most of his days drinking in your public bar?

Licensee: He did. Nights, too.

Coroner: Drowning his sorrows? And, finally, he did so. (Dr Youl was noted for his deadhouse humour.)

Licensee: He never talked to anyone. Took the odd meal, paid his board on time.

Coroner: He had plenty of funds?

Licensee: No shortage on that front.

Coroner: Was the bank's trouble preying on his mind?

Licensee: I don't know what was on his mind.

Coroner: But no visitors?

Licensee: No…though, now I think on it, I did see a man on the backstairs late one night going up to his room. Might've come more often.

Coroner: Could you describe this nocturnal backstairs individual?

Licensee: No. No lights there…A man in dark clothes, stove-pipe hat. I'd the impression he didn't want to be seen…But none of my business.

Coroner: You weren't worried about burglars then?

Licensee: Nothing back there to steal. Nothing much up front, either. (Laughter.)

'Very well, you can step down,' Dr Youl said.

Constable Thompson had given evidence.

Coroner: Did you notice anything unusual about the body?

Constable: He had his coat on.

Coroner: Had his coat on?

Constable: They usually takes their coat off.

A short silence.

Coroner: I don't think we can read anything into that.

Shortly afterwards, Dr Youl closed the case, and went on to the next matter.

From where he sat, at the rear, Binks listened to the exchange with the publican, a small bell ringing in his head. The Coroner had paused at the information on the night visitor, considering whether it might be consequential. Then he'd passed on. To him, it was an occupational hazard: the dead-end. To Binks, with his wider perspective, it was an item for more concentrated speculation. However, he, too, for the moment, left it at that.

Thirty minutes later he was walking up the path of a neat bungalow close to the Victoria Gardens, Prahran. He knocked briefly, and was admitted by a pale, slim woman, fortyish, her hair drawn back in a severe bun accentuating her sharp facial features. Not a hint of make-up. She'd allowed herself a slight, unreadable smile at the sight of the clerk. The house was spic-and-span, smelt of floor polish.

Seated at the parlour table, Binks took a sealed envelope out and laid it down. 'He wants to know if the doctor's been this month.'

'Yes, as usual. They're both well.'

'And you? He particularly asked that.'

'Thank him—quite well.'

The sound of childish voices came suddenly, faintly, from the next room. The door was shut.

'He'll be coming on the usual dates.'

'We will look forward to it. Tell him the children are always asking for him.'

'I will.'

It seemed to Binks that he'd had this exact conversation innumerable times. It always left him with a feeling of *déjà vu*. As usual, a cup of tea was offered, and accepted. He wondered how much company she had. She'd been good-looking, still was.

As he walked back to the station he reflected that while he was at the centre of his employer's affairs in other matters, in this case, he was merely a courier. It was an extremely puzzling case, and if his guesses about it were on the mark—and, he was a good guesser about obscurities—even on those terms, hard to understand.

But then, didn't everybody have their secret corners?

21

If the general managers of the twelve banks that burst in 1891 and 1893 had kept paid clowns to make fun of the valuations of city and suburban land, made by the old-established auctioneers and valuators...in the land boom days, their banks would never have closed...Every bank should keep a laughing department where absurd valuations...could be laughed off the premises.

George D. Meudell, The Pleasant Career of a Spendthrift

An Absence of Clowns

ON FRIDAY MORNING of that week, the *Table Talk* exposé of Sir John Adams' financial affairs crashed down on the city's business circles and polite society, like the toppling facade of a fire-ravaged building. The southern city, still in shock from Thursday's heat wave, which had seen the temperature jump twenty degrees to reach 105.5 in the shade between one and two o'clock in the afternoon, when the air had been like a blast from a furnace, had, however, absorbed this latest accusative litany with a battered fortitude.

In a light, cotton dressing-gown, seated at an untouched breakfast, Mrs Wilberforce read:

Knight Dumps Creditors
Manoeuvres Under Cover of Voluntary Liquidation
Act to Escape the Insolvency Court

A sense of amazement ran through her—like red wine spilling across a damask table-cloth. Then she quickly scanned the article, absorbed the references to the extraordinary actions by the bank's board, the taint of criminality. 'Good Heavens!' she murmured. This is a disaster. Far, far worse than I expected. But how *much* of it's true?...I must go to Laura.'

At Fitzroy, grimly, William showed it to Katherine, and they stood side-by-side taking in the several columns. 'Poor Laura,' Katherine said. 'And poor John...so hard.'

William was about to leave for the store. 'The bills are coming in for the '80s. Sir John was one of the big gamblers at that table. We've seen some brought down already, and there'll be more. Which is surprising. If it wasn't for this man Brodzky, most of it would've been covered up.'

'Is it *all* true?'

William looked at her acutely. He'd warned her to be ready for something like this. Was it another matter she was going to take to heart? He noticed, suddenly, how much thinner she'd become. 'Probably, close enough. I don't envy men like Angus Wallace.'

'I'll call on Laura—this morning.'

He hesitated. 'Yes.'

In Collins Street, Wallace and Binks had read the article, and the journal lay on the boardroom table; an incongruity, Wallace felt. This was the table at which so much that was revealed had been transacted.

He said, 'Brodzky didn't wait.'

'No skin off our nose,' Binks growled.

The liquidator smiled slightly. 'You're right.' It was going to work in their favour—publicly put pressure on the Attorney-General, and the Premier.

'What'll it mean for the shareholders and depositors, though, in pounds shillings and pence?' Binks asked.

'We'll see. Sir John's still sitting in his mansion; doubtless there's other assets salted away.'

Binks stroked his jowls, soothingly. There'd been the usual morning massacre with the razor.

Wallace lit a cigar. 'Wait till we get the chief manager in the witness-box. He'll crack.'

'If we do, and if he does. I reckon there's others stalking him besides us.'

The liquidator ignored this, paced up the room gazing into the future. 'By God! We must *make* it happen! All this villainy must be sheeted home.'

Binks frowned at the papers under his hands, thought of a response, abandoned it. His employer was getting bound up in it more and more. But then, that was the cut of the man.

'One thing,' Wallace said, turning, 'it's going to give the meeting a real edge.'

They looked at the notice, also lying on the table, which had been sent out for the meeting in ten days time. Wallace had his report to deliver, but the way he'd deliver it would depend on the decision taken in the cabinet room up in Spring Street. Presuming they didn't sit on their hands. Either way, the meeting was going to be a testing experience; he could feel the storm clouds heaping up.

At Kew, Lady Adams sat in the drawing-room of the forty-roomed, grey-stuccoed Italianate mansion, with its high tower and soaring flagpole—from which a Union Jack fluttered in the suburb's famous sweet air. Her vision had alternatively blurred and sharpened, like a scene being wiped out then reinstated between scudding showers, as she'd read the vicious and damning paragraphs, the vile, insulting words adeptly honed to a razor's edge by Murdoch—a man whose existence had been unknown to her fifteen minutes before, and whose identity still was, for the journal used no by-lines.

Laura Adams had a strong character—was resilient—but this bombshell had numbed her mind. Dimly, however, she was conscious of her marriage, of thirty years of life in the Colony, of a glittering social position, swiftly receding to the horizon with the inevitability of the sun's rays at eventide. Similarly, she was conscious of Sir John, pacing up and down the terrace outside the drawing-room windows.

He had risen from the table without a word; had seemed to have an urge immediately to seek that famous sweet air. Now he went ponderously back and forth, a man over-fed, overweight for his fifty-five years, his brow dark and considering. High above his head, the flag snapped in the breeze which had strengthened.

A tradesman was at the door—his third such call. A flustered maid brought the account into her mistress. It lay before Lady Adams on the breakfast table: an antidote for inertia. Suddenly she was seeing the hand-writing, the figures. She took it up, and went out to the terrace. She arrested the knight in his progress.

'For God's sake, John! Stand still for a moment. The butcher's here again. One hundred and ten pounds. What am I to do?'

Adams looked at her as though hardly seeing her. But he reached in his pocket, brought out a thick roll of banknotes, peeled off a few and handed them to her, then, without a word, went back to his beat.

Twenty minutes later, Mrs Wilberforce's carriage came up the drive. Her parasol open in an instant, even for such a brief exposure to the sun's rising power, she crossed the drive and swept up the steps and into the dim, huge, marble-floored hall. Lady Adams hastened in. She had been expecting Hilda, she realized.

In the few moments before she enfolded her oldest friend in her arms, Hilda Wilberforce was shocked by her appearance. The set, whitened face, the gazing eyes. In a flash, she recalled the other time she'd seen her like this, the morning she'd come following the sudden death of the Adams' daughter.

'Dearest Laura, we must sit down and talk…Where is he?'

For half an hour, Hilda Wilberforce sat beside Lady Adams on a sofa, her arm around her, holding one of her hands, talking to her quietly, while Sir John, visible to them both through the windows, continued his unnerving sentry-walk.

Lady Adams shed no tears, but she had been unable to speak to her friend. Suddenly, her voice returned, a whispery shadow of its usual self. 'A secret composition?…"Sunk in the slime of such events."…It must be lies! Though he won't speak, hasn't once since all this has been in the wind. Will *you* speak to him, Hilda? He respects you…might listen.' She tapped her forehead. 'I must know what is going on in here.'

Sir John came in at the french door and stood filling it, blinking after the blinding sunlight. Like a stag brought to bay, Hilda thought. The knight had convinced himself about certain matters.

He burst out: 'I must *fight*. And I will! I owe—owed—money to the banks only. Now, according to the law, I owe them nothing. They've agreed on a composition. Good God! It's the way business has been done in this city. It's the ebb and flow of the marketplace. As for the bank, it's the valuators who've brought us down.' The remoteness had gone from his face. 'My dear, I am sorry this falls on you.'

Hilda Wilberforce had not been greeted with his usual courtesy. It didn't concern her. She considered what he'd said. Had he lost touch to this extent? She said matter-of-factly, 'You had better take legal advice, John. I understand that is what people do in this situation.'

He looked at her, as if registering her presence. 'That is what I've decided to do. I will go to Chadwick. He did well enough by William in that business four years ago, didn't he?'

Hilda stared at him. Yes, Chadwick…But this time the barrister's instructing solicitors would not be Larkin & Larkin. The thought came to her that their lives were moving in giant circles, revolving to past events, adding new tribulations to the old.

'Yes, I'll fight.' Sir John was informing the room at large. 'I've got friends in high places. People I've looked after. Now, by God, they're going to have to look after me.'

22

But the best thing that ever happened to Melbourne Society, as I have known it, was the snuffing out of the lights of that feast, the coming of that cold daylight to the revellers. A better example of the vulgarising effects of wealth, and of the refining effects of being without it, was never packed in a neater compass.

Ada Cambridge, Thirty Years in Australia (1903)

All Saints took a diploma at Vienna in 1873, gold at London in the same year (the first Australian winery to be awarded a gold medal), first class (silver) at Philadelphia in 1876, and gold at Paris in 1878 (the only Victorian vineyard so honoured).

David Dunstan, Better Than Pommard!
A History of Wine In Victoria

Table Talk

THIS SATURDAY NIGHT Wallace was giving his dinner party: black, was pushing another piece forward.

From the moment she'd stepped into the hall, Hanna had kept her eyes on him. She'd no doubt that Susan was fully capable of protecting her own interests, but she was in new territory, and, apart from their host's reputation as a philanderer, he was something of a mystery man. For instance, where was Mrs Spencer tonight?

Seven guests, including Susan Fairfax, had assembled in the liquidator's house with only a modest expectation of enjoyment on their faces. Too much vexation was in their lives, in the city's atmosphere. Yesterday's *Table Talk* had come like a thunderclap. But, it had been an eventful week all told: the directors and chief officers of the Anglo-Australian Banking Co. were on trial; Sir Matthew Davies, business leader and parliamentarian, was embroiled in committal proceedings connected with the collapse of the Mercantile Bank, also looked like being brought to trial to face damaging charges. And, they'd had the hottest weather for eleven years!

Thus, across a string of elite suburbs nerves were stretched tight, apprehension of further disasters in the air. And, the dinner party was under another pressure: loyalties were divided on the Adams.

However, Mrs Beattie, who considered her talents were being kept under wraps, was in her element. Wallace's mahogany table was artistically set with distinguished silver pieces and the fine china and glassware he'd inherited from his father. A gay centre-piece of yellow roses drew admiration. It all shone in the gas-light, lifted the drab room out of itself.

He, at the centre of the events which threatened Sir John, seemed oblivious to the undercurrents. He'd had eyes only for Susan Fairfax since he'd greeted her at the door, taken her hand and looked into her eyes—as if to transmit a message. It had made her thoughtful.

Mrs Wilberforce could be relied on for many things and conversation was one. Breaking the silence after they were seated, she said, 'What a charming idea, Angus, to have this party. My first time here.' She was seated on Wallace's right, Susan Fairfax on his left.

'I've been remiss.'

Judge Mountain was studying the colour of his wine, holding his glass up, twirling it. A pleasant hermitage from All Saints at Wahgunyah. A prize-winner. Worth coming out for. He said, 'We bachelors don't find this kind of thing easy, Hilda, though Wallace's lucky to have Mrs…'

'Beattie.'

'She's a treasure,' said Katherine, more familiar with this household.

Overhearing this as she helped the maid engaged for the night, Mrs Beattie took a bow on the move in the passage.

Hilda Wilberforce said, 'Indubitably…I see the *bachelors* of the Melbourne Club are to give their ball.' She turned to Larkin, said pointedly, 'You're a member, Philip.'

She was also making moves tonight: had created an opening. Larkin started. He was here reluctantly. Wallace had told him that he wouldn't be let down. He stared at his plate. Trust Hilda!

She watched his lowered head. Turning the screw, she said, 'There're ladies present whom I'm sure would welcome an invitation.'

'Ladies all over town,' Hanna said with a laugh, but she'd blushed deeply.

'We're waiting, Philip,' Mrs Wilberforce said, amused, insistent.

Larkin snapped his head up. He needed to be quick and careful. 'Oh, is it? Thanks for the reminder. I'm afraid work's been keeping my head down.'

He looked hot, wasn't going to say another word. He'd realized the thin ice he was on. He was going to the ball all right. But tonight wasn't the time to disclose that. He wasn't blind to Hilda's motives, felt a pang of guilt.

Examining him, as though auditing his sins, she thought: What's going on? Something…

I hope she'll stop, Katherine thought. Dear Hilda, she can't help herself. But, she could and did. She'd sensed to push further would be unprofitable.

'I'll take *you*, Hilda,' the judge said. 'Perhaps we could make a party.' He'd swiftly eaten every bit of his entrée.

'We'll see.'

At this point, the entrée plates were removed and the main course was served by Mrs Beattie with an appropriate flourish. Katherine had immediately spoken to Hanna. The bookseller responded, smiling, but her heart had become heavy. She felt a pain there, prayed it didn't show on her face. She'd never had the wiles, the flirtatious skills of the young women of the smart set; hadn't been able to capitalize on her few chances of a husband. But, by now, she was experienced at interpreting certain signs. The evasion, the look on his face! It seemed she'd run into another dead-end. Another woman? Was that the story? Or, just plain indifference? Not the saddest of stories, she thought. Why does it hurt so? Katherine was looking at her keenly.

The inevitable questions were asked of Miss Fairfax. She responded with grace and assurance. To a calculated question from Judge Mountain on the Irish Home Rule Bill, she gave a lucid opinion. The judge's question was a 'tester'—he would never, normally, have asked it of a woman. He was sceptical of reputations he heard of, and he'd heard of Miss Fairfax's *ad nauseam*. The calibre of the answer surprised him—charmed the rest of the company. However, he wasn't finished.

He glanced at her shrewdly. 'What about this women's suffrage movement at home? Will they gain their objective?' Both Mrs Wilberforce and Hanna looked at him sharply, then at Susan.

'It's a world-wide movement now. At home, I think they'll win through. They have already in New Zealand.' She examined him with her steady blue gaze.

Mrs Wilberforce said, 'We've our own movement here, Edgar.'

'Ah, the Women's Suffrage Society,' he murmured, as if intoning amen. He would stop here, the atmosphere suggested that he did. But, his mind was tending to a conclusion which went beyond the issue.

Philip jumped in. 'Surely sensible women don't want the vote? After all, men must run affairs.'

The judge smiled, studiously regarded his wine.

God, Philip thought, what have I said.

'And, you've all certainly made a mess of it in this city,' Hilda Wilberforce said.

And that did finish it. The conversation split up. Wallace, tête-à-tête, said to Susan, 'This is a rare night for me. Normally, I'm dining alone, thinking over the week's work. About as dull as ditchwater. So, tonight is grand.' He thought: Do I have a chance with you? How can I impress you?

She smiled. 'I suppose you've a choice.'

The judge took bird-like sips of his wine, neatly sliced his duck, let his eyes roam over the company. It looked like Wallace had a job of work on his hands. Was he up to it? He seemed sound enough in most ways. Bar one, according to the rumour mills. He smiled one of his thin, white-lipped smiles. He could smell work for the courts coming out of the First Bank of Victoria farrago—if the politicians didn't sink it.

He touched Mrs Wilberforce lightly on her bare arm. 'Delightful gown, that.'

Eating his meal, Philip Larkin remembered chicken sandwiches, champagne, and the Parisian ambience just five minutes away by hansom. What was she doing this evening? Why was he here, not there? By the look of things, it'd be no skin off Wallace's nose.

William was talking to Hanna. They'd been discussing Susan's presence at the store. He'd seen her going on missions into the departments, surrounded by paper at her desk. So far, they'd not talked. She'd been there each day from eight till six. He watched her listening to Wallace, a slight smile on her lips, eyes lowered to the table.

With perfect timing, Mrs Wilberforce took the ladies from the room, and the four men sat with port and cigars. For fifteen minutes they discussed politics. Philip castigated both houses, said they needed cleaning out. William supported him. The judge and Wallace, closer to the fire, kept their own counsel. A lengthy silence ensued.

William broke it. 'This is a sad fix Sir John is in.' He glanced at Wallace. Nothing had been said about the Adams and he regretted it.

'Same thing could be said of the depositors and shareholders who trusted him,' Wallace said drily.

The judge examined his cigar. 'That's true, but I suspect Sir John sees himself as a builder. Sees you, Wallace, as a destroyer. You know, while the actions of men like this've been disastrous, it doesn't necessarily follow there's been an intention of criminality.'

'You sound sympathetic, judge,' Wallace said.

The judge smiled. 'No, that's not an accurate representation of my feelings.'

Larkin stirred himself. 'I expect the judge feels we shouldn't lose sight of the overall picture.'

Judge Mountain raised his eyebrows, drew on his cigar.

Wallace had noted his colleague's barb. Philip *was* getting worried. He said, brusquely, 'Too many scoundrels are getting clear. Surely you'd agree they should be brought to account? Facts, evidence, and hopefully, justice. I don't look further than that.'

Judge Mountain smiled again—letting these stabs go past.

The liquidator drew on his cigar, regarded him speculatively. A few of the worst scandals had come before the courts. But it was the tip of the iceberg. The judiciary was going to be busier and would have the chance to make or break its reputation. Judge Molesworth at the Insolvency Court had taken a stand against the charades in his court. The position of Judge Mountain remained to be tested.

'It's not all bad news, you know,' the judge said, casting an assessing eye at the port which he thought wasn't up to much. 'I understand eighty-four gold and silver mines have stayed on the dividend list. That's keeping quite a few in bread and butter.'

'But no circuses,' William muttered.

The door-bell sounded shrilly, and Wallace turned his head. Surprising…He heard Mrs Beattie's footsteps in the hall.

In the drawing-room, Mrs Wilberforce, said, 'Who could that be?' No-one essayed a guess, and the moment passed. She fanned herself and inspected the dark, dense-patterned, heavily embossed William Morris wall paper, the huge old landscape paintings shimmering with varnish. Everything was spotless, yet so drab. In his household arrangements, Wallace had accepted the status quo of his father.

Tonight, she knew that beneath the flow of conversation the thoughts of those present had been running at tangents. Dinner parties were few enough these days, and had such undercurrents of worry and preoccupation. She sighed to herself. Even she wasn't free of it.

Her eyes rested on Miss Fairfax. She thought: Watch out, my girl. Angus Wallace is no knight in shining armour. However…What was it about the girl. Unassailable? Edgar had been after something. Had Laura sent that letter off to Manchester?

The men appeared, smiling faces obliterating the skirmish. A half-hour later, with a flash of gaiety in the hall, the party broke up.

As her carriage rattled homewards along St Kilda Road, Mrs Wilberforce said to the judge, 'You know, Angus Wallace is in pursuit of Miss Fairfax. *That* is what tonight was all about.'

'Oh?' He'd been thinking of the liquidator on another hunting trail. The man seemed to have smelt blood. Men brought to bay could be as dangerous as any other animal. Could circle back to pick up the hunter's trail. Had he reckoned on that? He smiled at his imagery.

'You don't say? She'd be better off finding one of those tea merchants. That's where the money is.'

But Mrs Wilberforce had relapsed into her thoughts. The slight breeze from their brisk pace was pleasant on her face. But her steel and whalebone corseting was threatening to cut her in two. She sighed...Her match-making plans for Hanna and Philip, which had seemed stalled, now appeared to have disintegrated. Something there to be found out, plans to be re-cast. The stricken, but bearing-up face of Laura came into her mind's eye. For Lady Adams had decided to bear up. The issue had never been in doubt, Mrs Wilberforce decided.

For the moment, she'd put aside the judge's leading questions...

'Not a bad dinner,' he was saying to the night.

Wallace had watched them away. His farewell of Susan Fairfax had been as attentive as his greeting. Intense, she'd thought.

The evening had met his expectations. He was putting down footings in a systematic way which he'd never bothered about before. Though it didn't occur to him, he was moving in a very similar fashion to the liquidation. He'd had no opportunity to be alone with her, had expected none. It would've been premature.

He went in, complimented Mrs Beattie on the dinner as she and the maid cleared up. He said, 'Did someone call?'

She pointed to the envelope on a salver on the hall table. 'I didn't wish to interrupt you. No-one there when I went to the door. Just that, slipped under.'

With surprise, he noticed the envelope was blank. He tore it open.

HEll AnD DeSTRUcTioN aRE NeVER FuLL.

A helter-skelter of letters. He let his hand, and the message, drop to his side. *Another.* What the deuce was this? Then, he was imagining the perpetrator, listening a moment, ringing the bell, slipping back into the shadowy street with his malignant, or prankster's, thoughts.

23

*The settlement of the land boom took place in an inferno of dis-
honesty and ruthlessness. Those who had compiled the biggest
schedules…got off scot free…concealing assets of all sorts from
their creditors. A complete list of the alleged honourable men who
made shameful insolvencies would startle their descendants and
amuse the rest of the community.*

George D. Meudell, The Pleasant Career of a Spendthrift

Slash and Burn

WHEN THE MERCANTILE agent returned before noon from the Scots'
Church to his house at South Yarra, he found the parliamentarians
waiting in his drawing-room. Ensconced, he thought. Serious as a peti-
tioning committee, he added. This was a surprise, and he paused for a
moment, before removing his hat and coming forward.

'Well, well, Mr Savage, and you too, Mr Sandhurst, this is pleasant.'

The parliamentarians rose from armchairs to shake hands with
the moon-faced, strikingly bald man.

Savage said, 'I hope this isn't inconvenient?'

'Not at all. A drop of claret?'

The politicians thought this a good idea, and the agent rang the
bell. When they were seated, glasses in hand, the door shut, the agent
studied them with his pale, sceptical eyes which hinted at a tricky
amusement, said, 'Gentlemen, what can I do for you?'

'We're looking for a bit of advice,' Savage said.

'Something more in the way of information,' Sandhurst amended.

Sebastian Low smiled his slow smile, laid his small, soft hand on
his watch-chain. What else would they be here for?

'We've run into a bit of a problem at the First Bank,' Savage said.
'Doubtless, its demise hasn't escaped your attention.'

Low nodded, it hadn't.

'The liquidator's stirring up mud.'

'Ah…Wallace,' Low said.

'Yes. He's running true to form,' Sandhurst said.

'Just another damned lawyer,' Savage sneered.

Sandhurst frowned. Savage had had to do some hard-talking to bring him here. This plump, slightly condescending individual who looked like butter wouldn't melt in his mouth could be expected to run true to form, too: straight down the track of his own interests. He was as devious a runner in the mercantile stakes as existed. Sandhurst thought in such flights of metaphor. He wasn't happy, but an urbane smile lit his dark, oiled face.

'What kind of mud'll come up, we don't know,' Savage growled.

Low smiled. Any kind would be inconvenient, specially with your name already up there in lights as the director of a failed bank. The moment Wallace's name had been mentioned, he'd recalled their previous run-in with him. *That* had been a bitter wrangle. And, ruinous for Wallace.

'He went for us once before—the railway business. We saw him off then and will again. However, a bit of insurance won't go amiss.'

'Quite.' Low nodded his nude, pinkish head.

'Whatever he might try to lay on us, won't stand up,' Savage continued. 'In the heat of the boom, things were done which were the business that should've been done in those times. Today, maybe they wouldn't be.'

Sagely, Low acknowledged these reasonable propositions. Savage had always had those mad blue eyes. An unquiet spirit, he concluded, not in touch with the Almighty. Sandhurst was more stable. In his case, a touch of the Levant? He'd done business with them once before, mutually profitable business.

'Insurance?' he prompted.

'We need a plan to stop him dead,' Savage said. He put down his empty glass, and took out a cheroot. He exuded body odour.

'Dead,' Low mused.

'We need to get some dirt on him. The right dirt.'

'Aha!'

'That's what it comes down to,' Sandhurst said. 'You've got your ear to the ground. Your spies out. We know we can trust you.'

This last was a lie.

Low became thoughtful, turned his pale eyes up to the ceiling, stroked the thick roll of flesh under his chin as though absently smoothing a collar. Savage lit his cheroot, glanced at his colleague, who shrugged. Better not disturb this sifting of the agent's brain. Time was money—and this was going to cost them plenty.

Low was visualizing the kind of problems that might lurk in the bank's past. He was curious about one facet.

'Where does Sir John stand in this?' Last Friday's paper had smoked out a few rabbits, though most of it hadn't been news to him.

Savage hesitated, looked again at his colleague. 'Seems he's going his own way. At least, he won't be talking against us.'

'That's a mercy.'

'Brodzky should be dealt with.'

'Dealt with? Best stick to the main game,' Low suggested. He admired the proprietor of *Table Talk*. He, also, was a dealer in information; in the market for it.

Savage was getting impatient. 'If Wallace does bring up some matters, there's no guarantee he'll get to court.'

'Ah, the Premier?' Low essayed.

Savage ignored the question. 'Even so, who wants mud flying around the market? What d'you think?'

Low smiled omnisciently. He had in his possession a piece of information that would extend beyond these men's most ambitious hopes. An outstanding item, even in the great collection of secrets which it had been his passion to glean these past thirty years. A store which was disbursed in documentation and papers in safe-custody boxes around the city, in the secret compartments of his old, ink-scarred desk. A trove of librettos to comedies of error. Yes, a real collector's item. How fortuitous! But, he'd sit on it.

'I'll think on it,' he said. 'Might I suggest we meet again.'

An arrangement was made. At the door, Savage said, 'I've got something else running which might get a result. If it comes to it.'

'More insurance?' Low smiled.

'Slash and burn,' Savage said coldly.

'Yes, I can see the case might benefit from a scorched earth policy.'

The politicians walked down the drive. 'You didn't have to tell him that,' Sandhurst said.

Savage grunted. 'Sarcastic, hairless bastard. He should know who he's dealing with.'

'He does,' Sandhurst said drily.

Sebastian Low went into his dining-room. His servants were busy in the kitchen. A superior bottle of claret, uncorked, waited on the side-board.

How fascinating were the convolutions of business and politics—

of life! Everywhere you turned! And, marvellous how pieces of information fitted in. He smiled one of his most winning smiles to the empty room. The smile, which a considerable number of ladies in the Scots' Church congregation understood. He had a wonderful rapport with the ladies. He still prowled through his club. It had been a trifle sticky there for a few years, but the passage of time solved most human problems, faded most memories. Out of property, silver shares, and bank deposits long since, into gold sovereigns. That was the strategy. There wasn't a bank in this city you could say was safe and sound.

His man poured the claret, and he tasted it, head to one side as though listening for the first church bell. He'd sung his hymns today. He thought: Boyd & Montrose are in trouble. Now, *that's* fascinating...He was a specialist in looking out unfinished business, and William Boyd was a case close to his heart.

24

Thus the whole of the State's political power was riddled...by the activities and offshoots of the land speculators. Only a rare voice in Parliament, that of a Robert Reid or an Isaac Isaacs, was raised against the scandals of the day. Newspaper criticism caused the fall of government after government at the polls, yet the position did not really improve until after the grim lessons of 1893, when half of Melbourne was out of work and starving.

Michael Cannon, The Land Boomers

Old Testament

THE FOLLOWING MORNING Wallace made his next move on that figurative chessboard: the invitation to Susan Fairfax to the Melbourne Club ball rested on the mantel-piece, enveloped and stamped. But he felt restless and irritated. The house had a moribund atmosphere, though last night, after his guests had departed, he'd been pleased enough. Even the usually equable Mrs Beattie was downcast as she served breakfast.

Of course, this fading of spirit was bound up with the fabulous Miss Fairfax. Fabulous in his eyes, and a good many others, he suspected. In the scraps of time he'd had free, his mind had been turning it over. What had been more or less under control, had begun to burn like a fever. Three occasions he'd feasted his eyes on her. A novelistic phrase, yet presumably taken from life. *Not* moribund, simmering with frustration! He roamed through the house. In his mind's eye, he could see the future unfolding—but, at a dream-like pace, tinted with a rosy glow of unreality. And uncertainty, he thought grimly.

There was *one* certainty: the particular barrier which stood on any road to his future; which, latterly, Helena Spencer had run up against. At odd moments of euphoria he forgot it, then came crashing back to earth.

He paced past the heaps of books and papers; he should have been mining away in them. His mind turned to the communication, delivered late last night by the mysterious hand. The second one. Undoubtedly, both were from the same source…

He climbed the tower and, shading his eyes, gazed towards the lake, hazy in the mid-morning heat. The fronds of the palm trees were as motionless as the folded wings of sculpted birds. A hoax? A warning? If not? Jonathan Savage was the first perpetrator he'd thought of. But the cryptic notes weren't his style, nor that urbane snake Sandhurst's. From them, any blow would fall without warning. Yet, mightn't they use it to unnerve him? It wasn't blackmail—so far. No complaint or grievance stated. Suddenly, it all seemed like a fish-bone stuck in his throat. He turned to gaze towards the bay, a distant blue shimmer. The heavy air trembled with the sound of church bells coming from all quarters: over-laden, like end-of-summer fruit abundant on the bough. Ten o'clock.

He went into his bath-room, turned on a tap, and immersed his face in the filled basin. Thank God for cold water. He towelled his face dry.

<hr>

'Hell and destruction are never full,' Binks read aloud. A new day. They were in the boardroom. The clerk laid it down on the table. He said, 'Might be something, might be nothing. The territory we're headed into, we should take account of all the landmarks. Why don't you get hold of that detective? Have him look into it. Mr Larkin's in touch. Why wait for two to become three—or something else to happen?'

Wallace said he would think about it.

At ten o'clock, a summons to Spring Street came.

The liquidator was back within the hour. He walked into the boardroom, stopped and stared at the expectant Binks.

Hullo, his clerk thought.

Wallace's face was set. 'They won't take it over. The cabinet won't wear it, according to the Attorney. Of course, it's the Premier. He's decided he can't move against two of their own.'

'Fairly predictable,' Binks said cautiously.

Wallace swore quietly. 'I'd better hopes of it. The evidence is water-tight, after all. Whether we'd win, whether we'd get anything back for the creditors—other questions.'

Their thoughts had turned to the meeting advertised for two o'clock a week tomorrow.

'Send a message to Larkin, will you. We'll have to cut ourselves a new strategy.'

When Binks went out, he moved to the windows and meditated on the sun-blasted facade of the building opposite—a bewildering mixture of Corinthian, Ionic, Doric columns, patterned brick and stucco, plaster ornaments of shells and flora—put up in '88. A metaphor for the convoluted situation he was trying to bring out into the light of day?

He shook his head. He was blocking in the blanks of the way ahead. With the Government prepared to sit on its hands—in the opposing camp, for that's what this meant—it was going to be immeasurably harder. His eyes had narrowed; he was going to have to go out on a tight-rope.

25

Craig, Williamson & Thomas's
Enormous
Summer Clearing Sale
...Less Than English Cost
Buyers are assured that the value
we offer cannot be touched by any
firm in the city.
    Advertisement, Table Talk, 6.1.1893

Dry Dock

HALF A MILE from where Wallace gazed at hybrid architecture, and into the liquidation's murky future, Susan was putting finishing touches to her report. More accurately, thinking it through. As each faced their challenge, a connective thread might have linked them. Certainly, he'd been in her thoughts these past days—an enigma—not in respect of his intentions, but as to his character.

At Carlton Gardens, subtle disapproval had been coming. In the air had been his liaison with Mrs Spencer, for she'd gleaned it was that. The trouble was she had mere snippets of information, and hadn't seen fit to ask any direct questions about him. So, she found him an enigma. Condemnation often fell on persons of unique qualities. Was it the case with him?

She smiled perplexedly. Wait long enough, and information was shaken loose from most situations. They wrote of the solar and lunar influences on the tide, attractive forces. Something of this kind seemed to happen between human beings. Back in Manchester, there'd been *another* lawyer...

However, this, though quite enough, wasn't the totality of the situation; in her own nature was embedded another enigma; something else not quite defined. Or, a nettle waiting to be grasped...Her blonde head was lowered in thought.

At ten, she would present her findings to William. How he took them, what he did with them, were going to test him both as man and manager. She shut a ledger with a bang, and went downstairs.

Near the front door, she frowned at Miss Pettifer's show-cases of black-stitched, four-buttoned Italian kid gloves, delicate Belgian laces. 'Miss Pettifer, how many pairs of gloves have we sold this month?'

'Why, miss, I don't know.' The middle-aged woman buried her face, under its swirl of blonde hair, in a docket book, turned pages. 'Three, miss.'

'Thank you.'

Susan walked on. The gloves would have to go—and the lace. As would Miss Pettifer. The London buyer needed some straight instructions, too.

Mr Isaacs slipped through the ground-floor like a shadow.

'Would you come to the basement with me, please.'

He looked surprised.

They regarded the dusty, murkily lit space.

'How much would it cost to clean this up, re-open the stairs. Set up a bargain basement?'

He looked at her appraisingly. 'Not much, Miss Fairfax. Our house-staff could attend to it.'

She was thinking.

'There's enough cases of Jewish lightning around to stock it,' he said in his soft lisp.

She stared at him inquiringly.

'Fires. Breaking out in all quarters. All kinds of businesses. Frauds on insurers.' His brown eyes flickered humorously.

'I see.'

'Are we this bad? Am I this deficient as a manager?' William leaned back in the leather chair, and stared across the desk at the woman from Lancashire who had fallen into their midst like an act of divine intervention. He was beginning to look at it like that. He'd been reading for half an hour. Susan had watched and waited. She was dressed in a long-sleeved, high-collared 'Henley shirt', with a straight grey tweed skirt, a short, mannish tie. The effect was as severe and efficient as that beautiful face would allow.

'Not deficient, William. You've had the most difficult trading conditions to deal with throughout your entire period of management. You've made changes, you're considering others. However, you refer to the store as a ship, and it isn't easy to slow a modern ship to change course.'

She smiled encouragingly. 'I've dwelt on the negative aspects first, the opportunities not yet grasped, because that's where the main remedies might be effected. If you read on, the positives are enumerated—with my recommendations for a business plan.'

He gave her a look, and did read on.

She sat forward slightly, as though in harmony with the graceful line of the bentwood chair. The investigation had accelerated her knowledge of the Colony. She'd gained insights into its mercantile practices, the fabric of its social life, which otherwise might have taken months. It was clearer to her than her own life.

Her legible handwriting flowed away under his eyes. Phrases—ideas—seemed to lift off the pages to enter his brain. He was keyed up to receive it all. It was a startling experience. *Lists of slow-moving and dead stock, calculations of slow-paying creditors and bad debts, sales and cost of sales figures, redundant departments, staff sales training, department heads' responsibilities, their buyer in London…*

It went on and on—based on her Manchester experience, on the natural ability identified and fostered by Sir Joshua. She had put her finger on the critical points. He finished reading, continued to gaze at the last page.

'So we're carrying the wrong class of stock—in most departments?'

'For these times, yes. You've a bias towards luxury goods. In the foreseeable future, it's hard to see a recovery there. Those still in employment are facing salary and wage reductions. I've looked at your competitors. Buckley & Nunn is full of luxury and high-grade stock—and depressingly empty of customers, too. Georges', the same. As for Alston and Brown's! None has adjusted to what the market now is. The exception might be Foy & Gibson.

'I've attached lists of drapery and clothing which have gone on selling at home in the hardest conditions. Ready-to-wear clothes have found their niche—a growing one. You have none. Everything is made up.'

She sat graceful, relaxed, assured, telling him these things without prevarication in her pleasant Lancashire accents, keenly watching his reactions.

Like a skilled equestrian schooling a horse over the jumps, he thought. But he was eager to know it all.

'Similarly, with manchester there are less expensive lines of reasonable quality which go on selling. As for display, the prime positions are taken with show-cases of fine gloves, expensive lace, etc. The basement. It's ideal for the continuous sale of bargains. And stocking it shouldn't be a problem.'

She was bringing out selected points.

Gradually, William spoke up, and for the next two hours they talked earnestly. At the end, they sat in silence regarding each other until he said, 'It'll make or break us. Save us, or kill us off.'

She was silent, then said, 'If *nothing* is done, it is going to fail. The arrangement with the Commercial Bank…If there isn't a decided turnaround I'd expect the overdraft to be called up.'

He nodded slowly. 'Will you talk to Maybury and Isaacs? Much is going to fall on their shoulders.'

'Of course.' She smiled, rose to go.

'Susan, I know how much energy you've devoted to this. Whatever the outcome, my thanks.'

Her steady blue gaze met his. 'I did not expect to be able to resume my career. It's a great thing for me.'

A boy came in with an envelope. William glanced at the printing on its flap, frowned. She was turning to leave. He gestured to her to stay. He'd torn it open, was scanning a document. With a look, he put it into her hand.

It was a formal demand from the liquidator of the First Bank of Victoria calling up the £7,500. She handed it back. He had changed in an instant. His face had lost its colour. He said bitterly, the first time she'd heard him use that tone, 'It seems we may be finished before we've even begun your plan.'

She laid a reassuring hand on his arm. 'These matters take time. We could still be talking about it at Christmas.'

However, as she returned to her office she felt less sanguine. In connection with that wretched bank, Angus Wallace seemed to be a man on an unremitting mission.

26

The Commercial Bank is well trimmed to weather the severest financial gale.

Table Talk, *10.2.1893*

Circling the Wagons

MELBOURNE'S LOST its confidence, Mrs Wilberforce concluded.

Seated in an east-facing room, she'd been thinking over recent events while she looked down at her carriage, which was being brushed and polished by her coachman in the rear court-yard. The carriage was from Pickles. Its brass work glinted, its coachwork with its twelve coats of paint, hand-rubbed between each, shone like a mirror. Twice a week she was lending it to the Ladies' Benevolent Society. Should she relieve herself of the extravagance? She smiled, wondering who in the social milieu might drop her from their calling list, if she did.

She *had* decided to remove her £10,000 fixed deposit from the Commercial Bank. When it matured, she would take it in sovereigns and lodge them in the Melbourne Safe Deposit. She'd confirmed from the paper that the Commercial's shares had again fallen sharply. Trouble at a bank of this stature seemed unlikely. But where there was smoke...and the fall in the shares was definitely smoke to her.

She was expecting Lady Adams. On Friday, she had spent the day at Kew comforting and advising her friend. In the afternoon, Katherine had come out. Barnaby, Sir John's solicitor, had turned up, mid-afternoon, in a disreputable-looking buggy to spend an hour closeted with the knight, before putting on an equally battered hat and going off to call on Chadwick QC. The solicitor hadn't seemed at all like the knight's style.

Sir John had kept to his study. Laura had asked her to go in to him, but she'd demurred—'now it was in the hands of the professionals.' Also, she considered it probable that in view of the day's drama,

Laura would be 'put in the picture' by her husband.

Sitting in a room with blood-red walls and a Pompeian frieze, they had arranged a party to go to the Melbourne Club ball. Hilda considered the arranging, the attendance, as a much-needed diversion for Laura. In these vexatious times, it would probably be a sombre occasion, and it might be an uneasy one for the Adams, but it was a justifiable risk. That Philip hadn't invited Hanna was very unsatisfactory; however, the young bookseller would come in their party.

When Lady Adams arrived for luncheon her lips were compressed, spots of coloured flared on each cheek-bone. There was a note of triumph about her, Hilda decided instantly. They kissed, she removed her hat and gloves, and arm-in-arm they went into the dining-room. When the maids had withdrawn, Laura Adams said, 'Well, Hilda, he's told me everything!'

***

Sir John had not told Lady Adams 'everything', and deep in her heart she doubted that he had. Nor had he revealed all to Chadwick in whose chambers he'd been for some two hours, Barnaby beside him. However, in his weighty, deliberate way, he'd given out enough for the Queen's Counsel to be going on with.

Barnaby, who had been engaged in the wholesale and secretive liquidation of the reckless knight's companies, who had guided him through a secret composition with his personal creditors which would see him pay them a shilling in the pound, sat quietly, nodding sagely, as Sir John told his story to the short, broad man, with a dead-white complexion, the touch of subtle humour in the full lips, the wide mouth. Barnaby was surprised at the knight's command of the detail.

Richard Chadwick QC was one of the most experienced and successful barristers at the Victorian bar. He had the pick of the briefs; there were plenty to select from and he saw a ground-swell of new work in the offing. He'd listened without taking a note, never taking his eyes off Sir John's face.

Gigantic on a hard-backed chair, the knight finished, produced a handkerchief to mop his brow, and began to sneeze. The room reeked of dust. God Almighty, he thought, mopping up, why do these legal birds live like this? A fellow felt wary of moving. Somewhere, an avalanche of books and papers had begun, to finish up in this room. The dome of the Law Courts, looming up in the chamber's unwashed window, compounded the claustrophobia.

Chadwick was in counterpoint to this squalor. He was debonair. Sir John thought: The singer. He was a well-known amateur tenor. He sang at Government House, the South Yarra Musical Society, numerous drawing-rooms. Once he'd performed at their house for some charitable cause. Hopefully, he could perform as effectively in that other channel of his abilities—if needed. During his discourse, Sir John's eyes hadn't deviated from Chadwick's face either. In the subsequent silence, he continued this scrutiny.

An amiable rogue, Chadwick was thinking, but less amiable than he was. Reckless with the money of others. Unscrupulous as any in the '80s scramble for fame and fortune. And now the music's stopped. It hadn't stopped for Chadwick. In describing his secret composition, Sir John had been at pains to emphasize that his unpaid creditors had been mainly the banks—that he'd paid off the 'little people'. The plight of the little people who were depositors in the First Bank of Victoria, appeared to have slipped his mind.

The QC said, 'I take it the *Table Talk* allegations are not necessarily the main issue.'

'That's correct…' Barnaby began.

'Though, a horse-whip, or a writ, might well be applied to that fellow Brodzky,' Sir John growled.

Chadwick relaxed back, smiled broadly. Sir John's stare was iron-hard, but the QC had caught the hint of humour. 'I'd advise against the first. As for the second, Brodzky's been threatened with writs. Nothing's come off. Such cases tend to wash *more* dirty linen in public—if it exists.'

Barnaby tried again. 'The bank liquidation's the problem. The word's about that Wallace is trying to get the Government to prosecute the directors in connection with the balance sheet, and maybe other charges. He's playing it close to the chest—even in his dealings with the Attorney-General. Seems he might have Savage and Sandhurst in his sights on a separate matter.'

'Ah, Wallace…' Chadwick said quietly, much as Sebastian Low had on Sunday.

'Yes. Not in favour with the Premier, or anyone else in Spring Street. And, Savage and Sandhurst are of the Government party. There's a rumour the Attorney-General's turned him down.'

'What next then?'

'Maybe nothing—if there's no prosecution.'

Chadwick swivelled his chair and stared down the room. 'Wallace's not a man to be put off easily.'

'He's called a meeting of the shareholders and depositors Tuesday week. I reckon we'll see the lay of the land then.'

Chadwick was thinking over what he knew of Wallace. If he couldn't get the Government to act he'd a good idea what the liquidator would do next. This had the makings of an interesting case; he didn't share these thoughts with the silent knight, or his solicitor.

He said, consulting his diary, 'It might be an idea for me to be at that meeting.' He smiled. 'A watching brief.'

'We'd be obliged,' Barnaby said.

As they walked away from the cameo-sized, Italian Gothic building, dominated by the heavy-set Law Courts—a pansy beside a sunflower—the two men were a similar incongruous duo: Sir John, with his polished stove-pipe hat squarely in place looking immense, dwarfing the solicitor, hurrying beside him on his short legs. Even more incongruous were the disparate shadows they cast in the late afternoon.

The knight said, 'We're going to need Chadwick, all right. Wallace's like a Red Indian who's smelt blood. He was a damned failure in parliament at getting his way. This is his chance to make up lost ground. I know men like that. Cut off their legs, and they'll pull themselves down the street by their arms. And, the Premier's as weak as piss.'

Barnaby had never before heard a vulgar word from this esteemed client. He was not shocked, but stared ahead solemnly. It was as serious as that. Sir John's verbal shots had put the Future into the frame—got its range.

27

Leave behind the bats and balls,
Leave the racers in the stalls,
Leave the cards for ever shuffled,
Leave the yacht on seas unruffled,
Leave the haunts of pampered ease,
Leave your dull festivities—
Better far the savage glen,
Fitter school for earnest men.
Sir Henry Parkes, 'Solitude'

Loggerheads

'I'VE NO CHOICE but to put the charges to the meeting—the criminal information we consider should be laid, naming the names.' Wallace spoke flatly, nonetheless the declaration reverberated uncannily in the panelled boardroom, as if he'd put some special bias on it.

His colleagues certainly picked that up. They were having their council-of-war. Also uncanny was the atmosphere. The bank seemed to have sunk into oblivion; it was as silent, as irrevocably closed off, as its customers' accounts. The silence from Spring Street was just as definitive: the Attorney-General hadn't responded to a letter Wallace had fired off following the Government's refusal to take over the case.

This morning when Wallace had arrived, he'd felt a comparable silence within himself—and a tightening of his nerves. The meeting at the Athenaeum Hall was going to take all his mental and physical powers; it was now the key to getting the directors and the chief manager before the courts, and it had to be handled just right.

Philip Larkin looked worried. 'Wait a minute. At this stage, I don't think you should give their names.'

Wallace's eyes narrowed. 'At what stage then? It's going to appear half-hearted, look downright strange, if I give the crimes and not the alleged perpetrators.'

'You could report on what we've found, state the onus is on the

Government to investigate further, lay charges…'

'This rotten Government? Milk and water,' the liquidator said tersely. Binks flinched, and stared at the table. 'That's half-baked,' Wallace added.

Larkin had flushed. 'Nonetheless, I advise it.'

'No, my friend. The meeting will be looking for more, you'll see.' He rose from the table and paced to the window. 'And I doubt now the Government will move—unless some kind of bomb's put under it.'

'Good God!' Larkin muttered, shaking his head.

'If I judge the feeling is right, I'm going to announce that I'll lay the charges myself. As liquidator.'

Binks thought: There's the bomb, and, that's courageous.

Larkin swung around in his chair. '*That* is deuced foolhardy! Who's going to pay for such a prosecution? Even if it were successful, what dividends would it bring for the shareholder, the depositor? Wallace, it's one thing for the Government to prosecute, quite another for the liquidator to do it. I don't agree to this at all.'

Larkin staring hard at Wallace, reinforcing his words, thought: By God, his blood's up. Is he totally carried away by this vendetta with Savage and Sandhurst? I can't believe it—I thought him a thorough-going professional. I'm sure he is. Yet, it's running out of control.

'I'm sorry, Philip, but I see no other way to discharge my responsibilities.'

Larkin stood up also. 'Which are primarily to the shareholders and depositors. *Not* to do the Government's work.'

'It goes deeper than that,' Wallace said calmly. 'You know that.'

For a long moment, Larkin stood tense and obdurate. 'All right. I'll agree only if it has a mandate from the meeting.'

Wallace smiled. 'The meeting's going to be swirling with tricky currents. I'll have to see what I can do on that score.'

Larkin said nothing more. He understood that with or without a mandate, Wallace was going to lay the charges. He left the bank, grim-faced, nervy with worry. The currents were as likely to take Wallace and the liquidation straight on to a bottom-ripping reef, as anywhere else.

Despite his outward resolution, Wallace had the same worry. After dinner that evening, he paced his study. Events were quickening. At one point, he sat down at his desk and dashed off a note to Murdoch at *Table Talk*, drawing his attention to next Tuesday's meeting. He guessed it was already in the journalist's diary, but he wished to make sure.

The note from Susan Fairfax lay on the desk. She had accepted his invitation to the ball, and in a straightforward way suggested they join the party which Judge Mountain and Mrs Wilberforce were putting together at short notice. Further, would he escort herself *and* Hanna Dewhurst? Even on these terms, it brought a ray of light into a perplexed day.

He'd relegated the two mysterious, threatening communications to the back of his mind. At the instigation of Binks, the strange detective had come, been briefed in a peremptory fashion, and gone off. Wallace had not the time to spare, nor the inclination to open up passages in his past, therefore the detective had slim grounds to work on.

He stared at his father's face, the watchfulness, caught by the competent artist. In the late, quiet hours, he had to husband his confidence. At these times, all of his life appeared threadbare. The most grievous of his problems came sliding into his mind like a snake.

At eleven, he went upstairs to bed, without much hope of sleeping.

At Carlton Gardens, a disagreement of another kind had arisen between Susan Fairfax and Hanna, fortunately, a much slighter one. It concerned the invitation to the ball.

Hanna was glad for her friend to have the opportunity of attending this gala event, but regretted that Angus Wallace was the provider of it. She felt a growing misgiving about him. Grimly, with her bookseller's facility, she quoted to herself some lines from Longfellow: *The world loves a spice of wickedness.*

She did not wish to attend the ball. Philip's evasion in the face of Hilda Wilberforce's direct intervention had embarrassed—and, disquieted her. Previously, he'd been amenable to such suggestions, though it had never led to anything. After what had happened at the dinner, she judged the situation to be entirely different. However, the combined efforts of Susan and Hilda Wilberforce had persuaded her. Having to be conveyed there, partnerless, by Angus Wallace, was the last straw!

She'd said an early goodnight to Susan, and taken herself off to bed, upset at having allowed herself to be overborne.

In the drawing-room, Susan gazed out the open window towards the blacked-out Carlton Gardens, the vaguely distinguishable mass of the Exhibition Building. She tilted her head listening to the silence. Not even the sound of a hansom.

There was something else between Hanna and she. It had surfaced, briefly, during Angus Wallace's call that breezy Sunday. Hanna knew she'd been to visit Mrs Dugdale carrying a letter of introduction from a famous London suffragette. They'd talked for an hour, and were to meet again. Hanna had some knowledge of her Manchester past in that sphere, and she did intend to bring her fully into her confidence.

However, at present, she was carefully, and cautiously, trying to put in place the footings of her life in this convoluted city. With men and women like Judge Mountain and Lady Adams watching you, with their cold eyes, care and caution were needed.

Via the agency of the trees, was summer sighing farewell? Lancashire would be still steeped in winter, but there'd be the incipient feeling of spring. Before leaving home she'd had no real conception of this city; no accurate notion of this land deep in the Southern Hemisphere; no idea of the existence of Boyd, Montrose & Co.!

She was surrounded by foreignness, with at its heart, a man seemingly poised to become an ardent suitor. How the world turns! And now she was marvelling at how, against all her expectations, it had turned her back to her career.

28

The only man who could frame a workable system of philosophy would be a lawyer who had been a land shark and who had been a company promoter and had gone insolvent.
George D. Meudell, The Pleasant Career of a Spendthrift

> *the quiet silver lights*
> *Dropping from the starry heavens through the*
> *soft Australian nights...*
>
> Henry Kendall

Starlight and Mud

ON A STILL, starry evening they called on Sebastian Low. The parliamentarians were shown into the great barn of a house, sparsely lit by oil lamps; it presented as forbidding territory—echoing floors, shadowed rooms, dark stairways and mysterious passages—entirely appropriate to the character of its owner. Sandhurst thought this, then: Why don't he put in gas-light?

Low awaited them in the drawing-room.

After they'd dealt with the courtesies, seated themselves, his visitors looked expectantly at the business agent. He appeared in good spirits. The politicians exchanged glances.

'I've got a rather tasty morsel for you. I think it'll suit your book.'

Savage sat forward. 'Well, let's have it.'

The agent smiled engagingly. He *was* in good spirits. He enjoyed these opportunities to cull his resources; to isolate information, shape it for tactical deployment on life's battlefield. Apart from that, he'd had a good dinner, a glass or two of claret. He suffered from constipation, but today his bowels were open. So, all in all...

He said, 'Information has its price, and, I think you'll agree, we should settle that. Three hundred in sovereigns.'

In unison, the parliamentarians' eyes narrowed.

'That's *deuced* pricey,' Savage said. His yellow teeth flashed mirthlessly in his beard. Low didn't respond, nor did the pleasant expression on his luminant moon-face change; it was all of a pinkish smooth piece with his nude cranium.

Moon-faced bastard, Savage thought. He said, 'It'll have to be worth it.' He'd reconciled himself to it. In the mercantile jungle of this city, nefarious payments put the sauce on many a dish.

Low lifted his soft hand. 'Very well, you'll be the judge.'

He paused, ordering this expensive information into concise sentences in his head. Where two words would do, he never used three. Beyond the open windows, the expansive grounds were a dark otherworld from which the thrum of crickets rose and fell unchallenged in their dominion.

'A woman and two children. Living in a bungalow at Prahran. Whose existence your friend Wallace has been concealing from the world these past five years. Has taken a great deal of trouble to conceal. That's the nub of it.'

Savage's staring blue eyes had opened wider. His lips worked over his teeth. A spasm crossed his face, as he seemed to repeat the agent's turgid phrases to himself.

'Got him!' Shifting abruptly, he turned to his colleague.

Sandhurst gazed thoughtfully at the agent. 'What else?' His eyes had become hooded.

'The births don't appear to have been registered. The children go by their mother's name—Ellis. No evidence of marriage. The freehold of the bungalow's in the name of Ellis. Wallace's man visits each month. Wallace himself, apparently, goes there several times each year. For instance, on Christmas Day.'

Savage had stood up, and, his hands clenched on his hips, stared down at Low. 'By God! Think of it! At the time he was pontificating in the Assembly, handing out his morality, trying to nail us, and others, he was shafting this woman, spawning his bastards. *And*, hiding it away!' His face was working with excitement.

'Could there be another explanation?' Sandhurst asked calmly.

Low meditated. 'I believe the worst construction can be put on it.' He smiled. 'The best, for your purposes.' His instinct in matters of this nature was usually infallible.

'Could you find out more? Nail it down?'

'We've got enough to be going on with,' Savage said. More work was more money. Damn that. He sat down with a thump.

Low added, 'The woman appears respectable—but of the lower class.'

'Respectable!' Savage said contemptuously. 'It stinks like rotten fish. The hypocrite has been protecting his parliamentary and legal careers. That's as clear as glass. *And*, posing as a bachelor around town. Imagine that! He's had a succession of women, squired them here and there. Doubtless, kept 'em all in the dark.' He laughed venomously. 'The fellow should be on the stage.' He pulled out a cheroot, lit it with a celebratory gesture.

Low examined his perfect fingernails. With private amusement, he thought that where women of a certain type were concerned, parliamentarians led the push. He mused. It was shocking, but apparently factual: above ten thousand women were following the oldest profession in the southern city. Many of them new entrants due to the catastrophic times.

'So you've got your mud,' he said. 'Good value?'

Savage nodded emphatically. 'Granted.'

'How we use it is the next consideration,' Sandhurst said. 'But that's our problem.'

Savage grinned. 'Used the right way, it'll make a stir.' They were thinking that through.

Low would have enjoyed consulting on this also, but once they had the wherewithal these men knew how to run with it. In a way, he admired Wallace. He was a tough and unswerving type. Unfortunately, he was an opponent of the laissez-faire and *caveat emptor* principles the agent found so productive. He agreed, totally, that he should be destroyed.

He listened to the music of the night flowing into the house, heard it almost as the sombre cadences of a hymn played on the organ of the Scots' Church. Blessed instrument. He'd helped finance its acquisition.

Beneath the starry sky vaulting this speck of the Southern Hemisphere, infiltrating the shrubbery of Low's grounds, Otto Rudd worked with practised steps towards the house. This was the type of situation he didn't like: coming on to private property. He'd followed them here, had no time to familiarize himself with the ownership of the South Yarra mansion, the lay of the land. However, if he was careful, and there were no dogs…

When Binks had shown him out from the interview with Wallace, the clerk had given him the names of Savage and Sandhurst, and a bit of the background, as an addition to the slim-pickings Wallace had provided. It was some sort of starting point, though these men didn't seem right as authors of the missives which, he'd worked out, had been pasted together from the typography of *Table Talk*.

He paused in the shadow of a large pine, looked up quickly at the sound of wings. In the half-lit zone between the starry heavens and the dark ground, an owl went by on a mission. You and me, he thought, on the job.

The house was ten yards away across a strip of grass. Four large windows were open on the ground floor, and the room was lit with pools of amber light—oil lamps, obviously. A garden-bed with dense shrubs was before the windows. He could hear voices, not what was being said. Getting across that grass, a problem…He listened, just the monotone of voices; the crickets had subsided as if listening to his stealthy progress.

He'd made it. He stood in the garden-bed behind a rhododendron bush, moved foliage a fraction and was looking into the room: looking squarely at the unmistakable face and figure of his client of five years ago—Sebastian Low. Even for the stoic detective this was a shock. He felt the breath go silently whistling from his lungs.

29

The bachelors of the Melbourne Club have issued invitations for a ball to take place in the Masonic Hall, Collins-street, on Friday, March 10.

Table Talk, *24.2.1893*

Bachelors and Spinsters

WALLACE ARRIVED at Carlton Gardens at half-past seven. He looked debonair in his evening clothes, freshly ironed by Mrs Beattie. Late afternoon, he'd visited a barber for a shave and a trimming of his side-whiskers. His thin black hair was wet and brushed back. He carried a silk top-hat. All of this contrasted with the rough, bluish patches under his eyes, cheekbones which had become pronounced, the deepening lines from eye to mouth. He appeared off-duty, yet on-call.

In a fantastic whispering of silk, Hanna and Susan swept down the stairs; they'd been watching from the drawing-room window.

'What a marvellous sight you both are!' He was smiling at the two ravishing examples of femininity who he was to escort to the ball, though his eyes lingered on one.

'Thank you, sir,' Susan Fairfax said giving him an interested look in his new manifestation. Hanna gave him a sceptical one, as he handed her into the hansom. Ah, how the past weighs us down, he thought.

They set off at a brisk pace for Collins Street. The evening was noticeably cooler, as though the bachelors of the Melbourne Club had had a prayer said in the right place, at the crucial moment. The sky was clear and starry as the previous night, the streets glimmered in dusky-gold corridors.

'A lovely breeze,' Susan said.

The Masonic Hall, with its twin cupolas, blazed with electric light. A line of carriages and hansoms were pulling in, pulling out, keeping a brilliant crowd flowing up the steps. Horses backed, played up, farted lengthily, copiously evacuated dollops of steaming manure, sprayed urine. Behind two rows of constables, a small crowd, perhaps the tail-end of a street march of the unemployed, had assembled. Pinched faces, gazed into another world.

Disembarking, handing the ladies down, Wallace swept it with a cursory glance. Glitter, and short rations. The southern city could still put on a show, though now the atmosphere was counterfeit.

They proceeded down the long corridor festooned with greenery. Delighted feminine cries came, as the head of the procession entered the ballroom which had been converted into a scene of Oriental splendour. Hanna and Susan surveyed the immense mirrors festooned with garlands of greenery, sprouting from banks of moss and pot plants. Emblazoned in the centre of the balcony was the club's crest.

'It's rather fine,' Susan said.

'A fairyland!' a lady beside them enthused.

'Ridiculous extravagance,' Hanna murmured.

Mrs Wilberforce, at one end of the long room, was gesturing elaborately to them with her fan. They joined their party, walking carefully on the sprung, chalked floor.

Hilda Wilberforce was in full flood. She'd decided that the trials and tribulations among her friends made such an effort imperative. With her statuesque figure, flashing black eyes, darts of conversation, she commanded them. At her side, Judge Mountain, eyeing her, soliloquized: Delightful!

Her robe of azure satin, brocaded with shades of brown, draped with lovely old lace, was magnificent. Diamonds sparkled at her neck. Judge Mountain enthused further: Impact!

The ladies greeted each other affectionately—Hilda, Lady Adams, Katherine, and Hanna—all the oldest of friends. And Susan, Hanna's friend, and thus *almost* one of them.

Wallace and Sir John bowed coldly to each other—the extent of their communication that evening. Emphatically, Lady Adams turned her back on the liquidator.

Judge Mountain, who had slipped quite easily from his wig and robes into this other form of fancy dress, observed these by-plays. The night might not be a write-off, though, no evening spent with Hilda could be described thus. His pale blue gaze shifted direction. There was a razor-edged quality in today's world. On an occasion like this, a party was a loose arrangement, so no-one would be trapped. He blinked, became severe. The usual mashers were present, ogling the fine female figures. Here at the club? Why didn't they stick to the Block?

William shook hands with Wallace, the liquidator's demand for the £7,500 was in the air. They chatted for a few moments. As he turned to join the ladies, Wallace said, 'About that communication you received. Ask a solicitor how to attend to it. Not Larkin, of course. There're ways and means of delaying the issue.' It was as much as he could say.

Mrs Wilberforce gave Katherine a sharp look. 'Dearest girl, you're fading away before our eyes. You and I must sit down and have a long talk, soon.' *Very* soon, she thought. Why do I keep putting it off? Even for her, too much seemed to be going on amongst her friends.

Katherine nodded. Today had been tragic. Too late their attention had been drawn to a woman and her two children in Collingwood. They'd arrived to find the woman dying, one child dead, the other hovering on the brink. All of them wrapped in rags, lying on newspapers. Dead of starvation in Melbourne! The horror of it was shadowed in her eyes, the images now before her, unreal. Why was she here?

Yet, despite this horror, and her pallor and thinner appearance, she looked lovely. Her dark auburn hair, swept up, transfused a red-gold sheen to the skin of her shoulders and arms. She'd noticed William look at her twice when she'd descended the stairs at home. He'd been remembering the way she'd looked a day nearly five years ago when they lunched at Menzies Hotel. A day of aggravation and tension between them; the day that, unconsciously, he'd fallen in love with her.

Neither had wanted to come tonight. William was an ex-member of the club, and chose to steer clear of its members. They'd come out of solidarity with Hilda.

'Good gracious, some of these men *smell*,' Lady Adams said loudly. 'At least, I get John into his bath twice a week. All that absolute rubbish about the skin's natural oils they go on with.'

She had stopped the conversation. The judge grinned.

The Acting Governor and his lady arrived amid a fanfare. The dancing was about to commence. Herr Plock's full band, almost buried in the greenery, was tuning up afresh. A stir: a leader of society, resplendent in a toilet of white brocaded satin, the bodice adorned with a zouave trimming of gold and heliotrope embroidery, the edge of the bodice being finished with velvet, lovely diamond tiara—*swept* up the room.

At the main door, another stir.

'Good Lord!' Hilda Wilberforce had turned, could not believe her eyes, but her generous lips tightened. Her ivory-sticked, ostrich-feathered fan froze against her throat.

Hanna's face had become as pale and cold as the marble on the Masonic Hall's steps.

Wallace's eyes narrowed.

Philip Larkin and Mrs Spencer had entered the room—at the precise moment that the floor was cleared, and the band was poised under Herr Plock's raised baton. They stood together, in full view of the assemblage now congregating around the edges of the room.

Transfixed in the public eye by this quirk of fate, Mrs Spencer displayed her usual air of indifference to scrutiny. Here she was, resplendent in green satin, her emeralds, her reputation, and, what did anything else signify?—the carriage of her head, the movement of her eyes said. She'd laid a hand on her partner's arm, perhaps in reassurance. He, fair-haired and ruddy faced looked surprised, resentfully cautious.

It would be inaccurate to say that a general silence fell. To Philip, it only seemed that it had. More potently, he was conscious of the mesmerized gaze from the group at the eastern end of the room: his oldest friends. The gaze had, to him, a single optic force.

The band began a waltz and couples were coming out to the floor, providing a blessed screen. Helena looked at him, took his hand. 'Will you dance with me, Philip?'

He came out of his daze, looked into her green, amused eyes. Damn them all! 'Of course,' he said.

Hilda Wilberforce was thunderstruck. She turned to Laura Adams and said, 'This is amazing.' His evasiveness at Wallace's dinner party had been abruptly, and unpleasantly, explained.

'Unforgivable!' Lady Adams replied, her eyes steely, her face formidable. 'That woman!' Then they both turned to Hanna, to find Katherine talking to her.

The ball proceeded with sufficient *joie de vivre*, organized to the last 'T' by the bachelors' committee, which at least put a veneer over the anxieties and afflictions of most of those present. Ironically, Wallace reflected that many of them were only a step away from the situation of those street-watchers. Supper was taken at eleven o'clock in the large supper-room upstairs.

At the supper table, Hanna had given one of her brief shrugs and smiled at Katherine. 'Oh Katherine, I remember once when you…'

Katherine saw she was smiling through tears, could not continue, but knew the occasion referred to. She took Hanna's hand under the table, and whispered, 'Don't think the worst. Who knows what may be ahead?'

Nothing of this escaped Hilda Wilberforce.

Wallace had danced with Susan twice, once with Hanna, who was a silent, pale presence in his arms—seemingly on another plane. He knew full well the effect of 'that entrance' on these women. Such inter-personal intrigues were always in play, often coming to ends which they dramatized as disastrous. It wasn't his place to offer comfort. He had to admit it had shaken him up, to see Helena like that.

After supper, he danced a waltz with Susan. She was light in his arms. All night, he'd hardly taken his eyes off her. He'd absorbed each change of expression, gesture, voice intonation. Her fragrance…She was fully aware of his scrutiny, as were others. He knew it, didn't care; he was following his plan.

They stood out at the side. She said, 'I suppose you know, Hanna is very sad tonight?'

'I know.'

'It can seem like the saddest thing of all.'

He nodded. He wondered if Larkin had given her cause to have expectations. If so, he was playing with fire. If not…he was playing with it, anyway. Helena wasn't the kind of woman for him.

Finery glittering, a line of dancers advanced down the room to the skirl of music, feet stamping, long white gloves flashing, faces dead serious…

'You men have a great capacity to disappoint us.' He glanced at her, could not tell whether she was serious.

The dancers whirled by, a few feet from them. Behind them, groups of women sat furiously fanning themselves. The older brigade were getting a little tired. A few consumptive, bright-eyed faces from home watched the dancing hungrily. A rare night out.

'Disappointment's all around us,' he said. 'And worse. You may think this ball well attended. It's down on last year, as is the club membership. A lot of others are hanging on by the skin of their teeth. A night like this is a bit of a charade.'

'Yes, I'm coming to understand the circumstances here.'

He looked at her, wondered what she was doing at Boyd & Montrose, what she *could* do there.

At the eastern end, Sir John, monumental in height and presence, stared at the whirling figures, the passing parade, as though they had nothing to do with him. He had not danced, had a horror of it and never did. In fact, he'd not moved from this spot except to go to supper. His eyes were alert, but brooding. He had recorded in his brain those who had come up to him with good wishes, those who had not.

His wife had ignored him, knowing his mood.

Like a prize-fighter weighing up an opponent soon to be faced in the ring, he'd observed Wallace. As he'd told Barnaby: A tough one, and, in action with the passion of an evangelist. But straight. Except, he appeared set to again make a fool of himself over a woman. Gone on this one. It was the chink in his armour...If you could get a dagger into it. Well, they'd see how he performed next Tuesday.

Stamping their patent-leather shoes in thunderous time to Herr Plock's exuberant playing, the bachelors of the Melbourne Club advanced down the room in an extended line, amid a chorus of delighted exclamations from the young spinsters, sceptical gazes from the older, led by a short, rotund, pink-cheeked, butter-haired man (the son of an iron-hearted, strike-breaking ship owner) his white-gloved hands shedding febrile in-time gestures at every hard-won step.

'For God's sake,' Wallace muttered. He looked aside to find Philip Larkin there. The two men regarded each other, eye to eye.

'This is a turn-up,' Wallace said. The subject didn't need elaboration.

Larkin shrugged. 'It's wonderful how people think they can run your life for you. But a word on something *important*...' He checked they couldn't be overheard. 'Last night, our detective followed Savage and Sandhurst to a house at South Yarra. As it turns out, the house of Sebastian Low.' He let this sink in. 'He couldn't hear what was said, but we know that man's character. William Boyd surely does, to his cost.' The criminal trial of four years back still cast a shadow over their circle. 'It may not be connected to what we're engaged in, but anything touching Low calls for caution.'

Wallace stared at him, nodded.

Larkin paused. 'Anything more from the Attorney?'

'No.'

The solicitor frowned. 'So you're determined to go ahead as you said?'

'Yes.'

'You're wrong, you know.' Larkin shrugged, nodded a terse good-night, and blended into the crowd.

The bachelors were dispersing amid mutual congratulations and back-slapping. That had been the finale. Herr Plock consulted his watch. The band had played that afternoon at Albert Park Lake.

The return journey to Carlton Gardens, even allowing for the fatigue of the passengers, was a silent affair. Hanna, who except for a few critical moments had kept up a reasonable front, did not speak. In the dim confines of the cab all their faces were shadowed, which was a good thing Susan thought. Late as it was, she hoped that Hanna would open up her heart when they were alone; that she might be of help.

Hanna was thinking: I'm such a fool. Why did I build up hopes? He never said a word...The obvious manoeuvring of Hilda and Laura had seemed to have an inevitable drift. A conspiracy to raise false hopes, she now judged sadly. Her heart did so hurt.

Wallace had hoped to have a few minutes alone with Susan Fairfax, now doubted it would happen. However, when they arrived, Hanna, out of her silence, said, 'Won't you come in for coffee, Mr Wallace?'

He said he would. The Fitzroy Town Hall clock had just chimed the quarter hour past two.

In the hall, Hanna made her apologies, gave her thanks, and retired. He shook her hand before she vanished up the stairs. Wallace saw that Susan Fairfax wished to follow her friend.

'It's late. You're both tired. I won't have coffee.'

She smiled. 'It's been a memorable evening. Another insight for me.'

Gazing into her eyes, he perceived—a shadow of passing sadness? Quite acute. More a flash of horror?

'What is it?' He felt they'd reached this level of intimacy.

In truth, her mind had moved away from this night, from the present moment. She'd thought of home—and her brother. She smiled again, shook her head slightly.

Not yet, he thought. He considered ways and means. His hat was clenched in his hands. His heart was beating faster. He felt on the edge of a boundless future. If only...

'There's something I wish to say to you.' He'd spoken impulsively, but drew back. On the edge, but not tonight. He said, 'I hope we can meet again soon.'

A handshake, out the door, down the steps to the waiting hansom. He glanced at the sky. It had darkened. Clouds blowing up from the south had cut off the glittering view of the heavens. Helena and Philip! Who would have thought it? He could picture what Helena had been up to.

———•———

Helena Spencer's barouche arrived at her house, also at a quarter past two. South Melbourne seemed as empty as a desert; the gas-lamps lighting the way for no-one but them. Dogs had signalled their progress across the sleeping suburb.

They had danced only with each other; had sat close together at supper, deep in conversation. A few of her friends had approached to exchange brief greetings; a few of his male acquaintances and clients had done likewise. He was sure most of them had wished for a closer look at Helena's fine figure, plunging *décolletage*. They had been bound up in each other, and, immersed in her charms, he'd soon forgotten his unease and annoyance. To feel any guilt concerning Hanna was ridiculous, he'd told himself. But it did not quite settle the question.

As they'd left Collins Street, Helena had said, 'I'm sorry if tonight was awkward for you. Some people have a certain idea of me. Mainly some women. It seems to bring on atmospheres.'

'It wasn't,' Larkin had said, taking her hand.

The night was still young for people like them, she said when the equipage drew up, and he agreed. For people like them. He felt more awake tonight than he'd felt for years. Her house was lit up, the servants had retired to their quarters.

She'd seen him talking to Wallace, wondered what had been said. If Angus had been cast down by their breaking-off, it had been of the briefest duration. He was back at his old games. Drily, she thought she'd never seen him give such ardent attention. The Lancashire woman was a classic beauty. Perhaps she weaved spells as well! She doubted if he would have been to bed with her yet. She felt a pang of jealousy, which made her smile.

Champagne and sandwiches waited on a tray in the drawing-room. The Parisian ambience which had swamped Larkin on his first visit rolled over him again. The mirrors were amazing him with their tricks. Different angles of her, different angles of him. Evening dress, and green gown, over here, over there. He realized he was a little drunk; that he was full to the brim with sexual ardour.

Helena had poured the champagne. She looked as fresh as the moment they'd walked into the ballroom. She came close, then he smelt faintly the energy expended in their dancing. The ardour seemed to rise in his throat, stick there.

His dancing shoes also seemed stuck to the mellow parquet floor. Hazily, he considered how to proceed. Their glasses had clinked. He had not had sexual relations for nearly four years. He'd had no heart to visit Madame Brussells' establishment, or any similar. His friends had looked at him sympathetically, wondering what he did. His business. He worked at his practice night and day, drifted around an abbreviated social circuit. Hilda Wilberforce had not only had Hanna's interests in mind when she'd laid down her survey lines.

He became conscious that the green eyes regarding him had turned cloudy. A trick of this light?…A chemical reaction? Her breath was coming into his face. Inert as he was, slightly under the influence of alcohol as he was, he felt on fire. Helena Spencer comprehended his situation, as well as she did her own.

He was alone. He understood that he was to go upstairs, after a decent interval. A touch of hands, a steady look stripped of all artifice had informed him so. He could have put down his glass, walked out to the hall, let himself out into Cecil Street and the early morning air. Possibly, he should have done it. But it was the furthest thing from his mind.

In this house, the electric lights burned all night. Tonight, at any rate. He no longer felt the influence of alcohol. The curving stairs, polished cedar balustrade, ascended before him with splendid conviction. But he had a compulsion to creep up it as though, if he were not silent, the line of closed doors in view might spring open. One door was open, the interior of the room lit dimly.

Mrs Spencer—Helena—was a pale, night-gowned blur on the sheets of a four-poster bed, four paces from where he stood undressing, laying each item of clothing on a chair. He knew she was watching him. His fingers were swift but clumsy with the dress clothes, studs rolled on the floor, the white tie fluttered down. In what seemed like an eternity, but was something less than two minutes, he stood in his boiled shirt. A revelation came to him as to what its stiffened texture would do to that skin. He stripped it off.

He went to the bed, a nuggetty, white-skinned man, with a growth of soft fair hair on his chest, and a neatly formed erection.

Their first kiss was like drinking from a mountain pool—he had never known one like it. It drew him into her soul. So he thought. His mind was racing like a belt on factory machinery, but missing notches…An overload of sensations…The *décolletage* which had fascinated him with its mystery and promise became breasts free and abundant under his hands.

But he couldn't wait. His member found the spot. It was firmly held and engaged. God Almighty! he gasped. Then they were lost to the entwining, the rhythmic undulation, the creaking of the giant bed, the smell and sound of ardent lubricity. It encapsulated them, then swung the capsule out into a looping orbit…

An image of the new worlds of Monsieur Jules Verne might have

137

flashed in the back of their minds, though Philip would have found it impossible to describe his passion, no words could catch it; later, in odd dreaming moments, he was hazily to re-live it.

Her passion was equally consuming, yet she *had* the full picture in her mind—even saw the future clearly sign-posted. Of course, she'd had it in view already.

In a moment of satiation, she said with a quiet laugh, 'They tell lies about me. The worthy matrons of this city have remarkable imagination. I've been mistress to every captain of commerce, every Government Minister...Nine-tenths of it is lies.'

The one-tenth? But their limbs are entwining again, the French bed has begun to shudder and creak again. For Philip, a kind of drought has broken.

30

*There was a severe depression in Commercial Bank shares last
Saturday partly in consequence of an enigmatic cablegram that the
'opinion' in London was that two unnamed Australian banks were
'shaky'.*

Table Talk, 10.3.1893

After the Ball

THE NEXT MORNING was eye-blinking bright with a vigorous southerly
blowing, and showers forecast. As she moved through the East
Melbourne mansion, images from the Masonic Hall re-played in Mrs
Wilberforce's mind. They fell mainly into the vexatious category.

Her nerves were on edge. Negative events were accumulating to
overshadow the lives of her friends, options were narrowing. And,
she'd just seen in yesterday's *Table Talk* that there'd been another
sharp fall in the Commercial Bank's shares! She felt the peril of her
locked-in £10,000.

At eleven, this was the frame of mind in which she received Lady
Adams. The two old friends had long ago given up the protocol of the
'morning call', capriciously undertaken in the afternoon. They visited
each other without notice.

Hilda Wilberforce took a long look at Laura. Strain and worry
were plain in her friend's pale severity, but so was her determination.
They embraced. 'Laura, what did Chadwick say?'

'Heaven knows!' Lady Adams moved a few paces away, stopped,
and gazed at her friend. She peeled off each glove, maintaining the eye
contact. Her face had become animated with her thoughts, a small
pulse throbbed in her throat.

'What is it, my dear?' Mrs Wilberforce said quietly.

'I don't think John *has* told me the entire truth. I suspect he can
no longer *distinguish* between truth or falsity. I trusted him. I fear the
trust has been misplaced. I've hardly slept these past nights
remembering events and matters. What I should've asked questions

about. My eyes have been opened. I've been a fool.'

Behind her smooth, perceptive face, Hilda Wilberforce was surprised. By what tortuous process Laura, who had been the knight's unquestioning supporter, his proud, devoted wife, had arrived at her realization, she didn't know. She did know that the short speech had sprung from the deepest mental anguish; that behind it, her friend's heart was breaking.

Lady Adams' slender, white, be-ringed hand *had* gone to her heart. 'He needs my support for the present—and I will give it. After it's decided, I don't know what I will do.'

Hilda came forward, her hands out. Lady Adams put a forefinger to her lips. 'Hush! Not another word. We must let the cards fall where they may.' And she meant it.

After this, it was not easy to turn the conversation in a new direction—but Hilda managed it, though for a moment, she'd stood gazing into her friend's eyes. Then she'd broken her gaze away, glanced out the window to the Fitzroy Gardens. The high branches were in a commotion. Twigs with leaves attached were fluttering away across the sky. On high, birds were circling and sailing. Another autumn.

She said with conviction, 'Hanna! How I felt for the girl. But what's to be done?'

Lady Adams relaxed: the tension visibly flowed from her.

'We've made a mess of it.'

Mrs Wilberforce couldn't conceal her surprise this time. Until this morning, she'd never heard her friend admit to making a mess of anything. Today, change *was* in the wind.

'You may be right...But Helena Spencer! They've been moving in the same circles for years. Why now?'

'Doubtless, because that woman's decided *now*. I'd suppose she found herself at a dead-end with Wallace. What else, with his reputation! So she cast out her net again.' Lady Adams compressed her lips. 'I'd thought better of Philip. It seems he's no different from those British officers who come out and play with the hearts of our girls.'

She was now in her element, and Hilda was relieved to see it. However, she said, 'I think that might be a *little* hard. It's unfortunate but I don't think he's said anything to her. There's no understanding.'

'In some cases, Hilda, nothing *needs* to be said. I think *Hanna* understood it as so.'

'She's too level-headed.'

Lady Adams shook her head adamantly. 'We can both remember how susceptible one is at certain times.'

Hilda thought for a moment. What *could* be done? She said, 'I don't think it would be wise for either of us to speak to him.'

'Someone must! He can't be permitted…It should be a man. William Boyd. They've always been close.'

Hilda looked doubtful. From a past experience, she knew how much William would resist such a commission.

With energy, Lady Adams said, 'His feelings for *her* surely can't be of the lasting kind. Let him have his fling. As long as it works out in the end. *You* must speak to William.'

Having dealt with this matter, the friends parted. Lady Adams went home to her doom-laden house where the servants now whispered to each other around corners, and her mysterious husband sat in his study contemplating God knows what. She went home in her carriage. At least, that commonplace in her life was still intact.

———◆———

When she awoke to the bright, windy Saturday, Hanna at first thought that the ball had been a nightmare. Then she remembered the long talk she'd had until three with Susan, her weeping…

In the cold light of day, she felt embarrassed at this weakness. Her face flushed. O God! She, a woman of thirty, proprietor of a well-established business, had behaved like a love-lorn schoolgirl. What must Susan think! But then, she told herself, Susan was her dearest friend.

Today was a business day and she was running late. The real world awaited. The end-of-summer sale began today. The phantoms of the night, of the inner life, were back in their boxes. Thank Heavens! So she told herself as she left to take the tram into town.

They were, and they weren't. As she directed her assistants that morning, images from the ball came and went in her mind. Even in the light of day they seemed dark and unreal.

She'd been sorry for him when his wife had died, had come to care for him over the past year or two. But did she love him? There'd been no flash of such a realization, just a steadily accumulating affection. Hardly romantic! Hardly to be relied on. Hardly to make a tragedian of her! However, her heart had frozen as he'd entered the ballroom with Mrs Spencer on his arm. And, now it ached as she imagined him, intimate, with her. Therein, possibly, lay the answer to everything.

Poor Philip. He was being blamed! That thought stood out.

Referring to a catalogue, the shadow of a smile on her face for a regular customer, she thought: One thing is certain, all this will pass.

31

The flame that feeds upon my heart
fades or flares, by wild winds controll'd:
my heart still walks a thing apart,
my heart is restless as of old.

Christopher Brennan,
'My Heart Was Wandering in the Sands'

Preludes

TOO GOOD A SATURDAY to be indoors, but Wallace was losing track of the days. 'What are you going to do about these?' Binks was asking. Since the *Table Talk* revelations on Sir John's affairs, worried and angry missives had flooded in demanding the liquidator's comment.

'Nothing,' he said. 'They'll have their answers on Tuesday.' Grimly, he reflected that what they would hear wouldn't allay their fears. They had worked most of the day on the report. It was cut and dried.

'They'll be out in force,' Binks growled contemptuously. He was referring to the directors' supporters.

Wallace nodded. He'd caught a whiff of brandy from his clerk. Where did he keep it?... Yes, attempts at disruption and white-washing could be anticipated. Probably, Savage and Sandhurst's parliamentary colleagues would be up on their hind-legs barking out bromides, laying down false trails. Trained obstructionists. They'd seen such tactics when the committee of investigation into the Mercantile Bank had reported. He could count on ridicule, animosity, and challenges being shovelled at him. He hoped Larkin wasn't going to wilt under the pressure.

But he was going to go for them, and, he wouldn't spare the Government either.

They'd gone over it all one last time, and he'd walked out with a feeling of release into Collins Street steeped in late-afternoon sunshine. Whatever Tuesday might bring, he'd done all he could to be ready.

The following afternoon he felt considerably less relaxed, as he waited in the splendid entrance hall of the Federal Coffee Palace for Susan Fairfax. His eyes darted to each face coming through the doors. It seemed to him that he was a juggler, giving attention to each component of his life—just in time to keep each in play.

After the ball, as they'd said goodnight he'd sensed a thread of intimacy between them. A pulse of interest had come faintly to him. A flicker. In marked contrast to his own, right now!

He began to pace across the black, white and red-paved marble floor. He grinned tensely at the thought that he was making another move on a chessboard. The staccato sounds from his steps echoed stagily in the spacious chamber. Actor's steps? In his opinion, the arcaded loggia with its fourteen Ionic columns did resemble a stage-set— except it had the reality of hard and expensive materials. It depicted the extravagance, had been a triumphant icon of the era of Marvellous Melbourne. Dead as ashes.

For a moment, he stopped and stared at this 'set'.

Would she come? Yesterday, he'd sent a note inviting her to meet him here. For tea, he'd said. If she was free, he'd said. If she found the idea of a visit to the 'icon', of interest. *If* she found the idea of his company convivial—he'd thought, but not written. He consulted his watch: four o'clock…

For Wallace, one of those rare experiences in life is about to occur.

She has entered the inner hall. He draws in his breath. She pauses in the filtered, refined light. *Impact!*—the accolade Judge Mountain would have bestowed. She is wearing ivory silk, the smallest of straw hats with a single yellow rose aglow like a light in this cool gloom, looks as fresh as a bay breeze, as assured as someone entering their own house. He releases his breath.

He steps forward. 'Susan, I'm so glad.'

Her quick look to his face is kind, but shaded with caution—even sceptical. He has that in a flash. But she *is* smiling—and, the upturned perfect face, the clear eyes, are projecting at him an image of the women of north Britain. It strikes him thus. It's a poetic, but sobering moment for him—an Australian Native; clear away from politics, the law, bank crashes and liquidations. Momentarily, he even forgets the darkest reality in his life.

But *this* existence has its shoals and its rips. He conducts her through the great hall to the dining-room, passing the six Waygood High Speed Patent Safety elevators. She scans the tracts of plaster decoration, not with admiration, nor with indifference, but with neutrality—he thinks. He points out innovations, mentions the 500 rooms, the six miles of gas piping, the ice-plant. They move through a majestic tract of lounging, smoking, writing and billiard rooms. He's functioning in a blur.

Not until they're seated at a table with the waitresses bustling about does he begin to regain equilibrium.

When the electroplated silver tea service was at last set out, the tea poured, he said, 'Miss Fairfax, I'm going to be heavily engaged this coming week with the First Bank of Victoria. I'm afraid it may be something of a sensation. A lot of mud and nastiness stirred up. Men in a corner strike out, accusations are let fly. I expect to hear hard words about myself.'

He smiled tensely. 'My parliamentary days left me with a good crop of enemies.'

She watched him with the closest attention. Neither had touched their tea. They were eye-to-eye: brown to blue.

'My motives in speaking to you about it are selfish. I hope you might allow me the benefit of the doubt. Allow me the opportunity to explain—should it be necessary.'

She regarded him with sympathy, and puzzlement.

He said, 'This must mystify you, but it's by way of a prelude.' He paused. He was approaching the hard part, but not the *hardest*. She seemed to be staring into his soul.

Before he could continue, she said, 'I'm honoured to think my opinion counts for so much.'

He nodded slightly.

She went on: 'At home, many men are unjustly accused of this or that. Women, too. Rumours circulate. I take no interest.'

He shot her a look. 'I'm speaking of stronger stuff than rumours.'

'Very well. I doubt if we don't have it at home.'

'You may find Melbourne breaks new ground.'

She smiled faintly. 'What I wish to say is, I'm not unaccustomed to this side of life.'

She had observed that many men who'd been in public life glided around like skaters on thin ice concerning their private lives. But accidents were rare. It seemed that only if matters got into court did they go through the ice. Probably that was what he was apprehending. And, she did have a very good idea of the direction he was heading.

The attention he'd shown her at the ball had been crystal clear—to herself, and others. At thirty, a woman of her calibre knew the effect she had on some men.

However, she'd never encountered anything like this. Hanna, certainly, was tight-lipped about him, his 'history' with women. Was there something else?

A whisper came in her brain: What have I touched in him to bring him to this state? And, what were her feelings for him? She hardly knew him…yet, she felt that tidal pull…and the caution. She studied his face, and waited.

He was silent, had arrived at the sticking-point. Was she the woman who could take in, absorb, accept, the revelations he would have to make? Who might understand what he could imperfectly comprehend himself? Instinctively, he'd known that Helena Spencer had not been, nor any of the others.

He leaned forward suddenly, tensely, said, quietly, meaning much more even than the words spoken, 'Susan, I have fallen in love with you.'

For the first time she lowered her eyes—seemed to study the black-stitched seams of her gloves lying on the table.

Ah, there it is, she thought.

32

Benevolent Societies. Fifty-five benevolent or philanthropic societies furnished returns for the year ended 30th June, 1893. These associations are for the relief of indigent persons, and are generally managed by ladies. The persons relieved during the year numbered about 45,553; the receipts amounted to £26,087 of which £5,984 was from Government and £20,103 from private sources.

Night Shelters. At Dr Singleton's Night Shelters, Collingwood, 26,689 cases were accommodated during the year 1893–4…

Victorian Year Book, 1894

The Blackmailers

KATHERINE WAS SURPRISED to see a hansom cab standing outside the Harbrace house when she arrived about one, having come straight from her Collingwood duties. As she looked back at the driver, she felt apprehension come down on her.

Mrs Harbrace answered the door immediately. Katherine saw that she was distraught.

'Who is here, Mrs Harbrace?'

'A Mr Savage. He insisted on seeing James. Pushed past me…He's been talking to him for a half-hour. He's not well enough for it.'

Katherine walked past the woman. The boy, Tom, and little Jean were sitting at the table, silent and wide-eyed. She went into the other room.

The parliamentarian, one hand splayed on his hip, under his frock-coat, was seated beside Harbrace's bed leaning over the ex-bank accountant, speaking. His attitude was arrogant and overbearing, though he was keeping his voice down. He'd put his stove-pipe hat on the floor. His beard seemed inches from the sick man's face. The room was rich with body odour.

Harbrace's unquiet eyes shifted to Katherine as she walked in. Savage turned his head. Katherine had never seen Jonathan Savage before, but she knew who he was. She still held the basket she'd brought.

'I'm Mrs Boyd. Mr Harbrace is far too ill to be receiving visitors. I must ask you to leave.'

Savage rose to his feet. 'Ah, Mrs Boyd. A pleasure…No harm done I hope. A matter of business had to be discussed. Has been. I'll take my leave.'

He retrieved his hat, turned back to the bed. 'Good luck to you, Harbrace. Don't forget what I said.'

He bowed to Katherine, the sick man's wife, and walked out. Katherine went to Harbrace's side, looked into his eyes. He nodded slightly. In the next room, she said, 'Do you know what that was about?'

'Not me. I couldn't hear anything, and I don't think James said a word.' The pregnant woman was still anxious. 'I didn't care for his manner.'

Katherine hadn't cared for it, either. It spoke of threat and trouble. And those eyes! As they prepared soup, the girl brought the rag doll to her. 'How is Jean, today?' she asked the child.

'Good,' she whispered shyly.

Mrs Harbace said, 'I *think* he's from the bank.' But Katherine knew that.

<hr>

Savage was having a busy day. At two o'clock, he met Sandhurst outside the bank. 'What's the news?' the later said laconically.

'I've seen him. He's in a bad way. Didn't, or couldn't, say a word. I reckon it was his information all right that started Wallace nosing around. If it ever gets into court, he might do us some damage.'

'Warned him off?'

'You could say that.'

'And?'

'Hard to say…but he won't last long. They'd have Buckley's chance of getting him into the witness-box. He's set for another kind of box.' The mirthless smile flashed in his beard. It had taken them awhile to track down the chief accountant; they'd found him through another ex-employee.

'They could take the court to him,' Sandhurst said.

Savage glanced at his colleague. 'The fellow we're going to see now, is the worry.'

Wallace was surprised when Binks said the parliamentarians were outside asking to see him on urgent business. He glanced at his clerk. 'What now?'

Binks shrugged. 'Look their usual confident selves.'

Wallace thought: Well, we might shake them up a bit tomorrow. Binks waited. 'Urgent business? All right.'

They came easily into their old stamping ground. The ink mightn't have dried on the last defalcation they'd committed here. They took the seats they'd been used to sitting in, and stared across the now dusty expanse of cedar at the liquidator. Sandhurst's eyes slid to the scar; he smiled faintly as if at a pleasant reminiscence.

Savage said, 'We'd like a word with you, before tomorrow's meeting. In our mutual interests.'

Wallace watched them, his face unreadable.

'In private,' Sandhurst suggested, looking at Binks. The olive complexion of his face had its usual oily sheen, the pockmarks stood out.

Wallace smiled coldly. 'Nothing's private from Mr Binks.'

Sandhurst shrugged, glanced at his colleague, who nodded. 'Up to you. The word is, you're trying to get up a case against us. Trying to get the Government to prosecute,' Savage said. He took out a cheroot, and eyeing the liquidator, lit it. 'From where we stand, there's no case to answer. You can allege this, you can allege that, but it won't wash.'

Wallace kept them in a level gaze. He was surprised at such a barefaced approach—even from them.

'And, it won't get the depositors an extra pound.'

'It'll use up their funds to no good purpose. Get *you* a black mark,' Sandhurst added smoothly.

Savage was enjoying himself. His thick lips were working over his yellow teeth. He dropped ash on the floor, stared at Wallace with his mad blue eyes, gestured. 'So, why not be reasonable? The disputation between us in the past shouldn't come into this. We don't care what you say about the balance sheet—it won't stick anyway. But that little fiction about those No. 2 Accounts is mud that *might* stick. We suggest you drop it.'

'Kill it stone dead,' Sandhurst said. His long white hands were mottled with brown marks. Strangler's hands, Binks thought, watching them with interest. Wallace hadn't moved a muscle. Each of them measured the silence.

'Nothing to say, Wallace?'

To Binks, on the side-line, the Coroner's Court was back in his mind…he was re-hearing the evidence of the mysterious man seen on the hotel's backstairs the night before the ex-head cashier had died.

The liquidator smiled thinly, disdainfully. 'Gentlemen, you'll hear me tomorrow. What needs to be said, I'll say then. In the meantime, we're wasting each other's time.'

The parliamentarians were silent.

'In that case,' Savage said, 'we're going to have to take off the velvet glove.' He made a theatrical motion of pulling off a glove. He paused.

'Douglas Street, Prahran.' The utterance was spoken as if it were a password. That was Wallace's first thought. A password into a new phase. Beside him, he'd felt Binks stiffen.

The two ex-directors, though they still lounged in their seats, were watching him now with an ironclad intensity. It's always been a matter of time, he thought.

Sandhurst said, 'I doubt if there's a man in this city who isn't hiding something. Understandable, that's life. Let 'em keep their secrets, I say. In the normal way.'

Savage straightened in his chair, took the cheroot from between his lips. 'A smart man like you doesn't need any more said, does he?'

Wallace's face had darkened. He brooded on the two men. On Savage's eyes. Mad, or evil? He wasn't considering consequences, they'd have to take care of themselves. Some matters were becoming relatively clear. He turned to Binks. 'Show these gentlemen out.'

A mixture of consternation and amusement appeared on their faces. Then Savage said with a hard look, 'Don't take the high ground with us, Wallace. When you think of it, it's a nasty little story. A rotten piece of deception, against a lot of people. For instance, your string of women friends. The gay bachelor with a family stuck in the suburbs? It'll float around town like a poison gas. Kill your reputation, your credibility.'

'You've taken a deal of trouble to keep it under wraps,' Sandhurst said, at his most fluid and snake-like. 'Why lose the plot now?'

'Get out!' Wallace said.

'What does the world think of a man who abandons his children?' Savage sneered.

Wallace stood up. Binks did, too.

'Come on, Savage,' Sandhurst said contemptuously, 'or we might have violence done on us.'

'Have a good hard think, and sleep on it,' Savage said.

They sauntered out, and were let out to Collins Street by the caretaker. Savage lit up another cheroot. 'What d'you think he'll do?'

'Better get ready for a hot time tomorrow, I'd say.'

In the boardroom, Wallace had resumed his seat, was staring across the room. Binks stood watching him, thinking: He's been on a razor's edge with this for what—six years? Eating away at him. Perhaps better in the long run if it's out. If he's got the character to survive it. And, he might have. He said, 'They've got a good idea of the charges we might be laying.'

'The Attorney-General,' Wallace murmured. Suddenly, he swore brutally. 'Blackmail! By God, I might crash, but I'll take those scum with me.'

Cool down, Binks thought, we want a cool head now.

33

I am sorry to say that in this community it is not considered a disgraceful thing for a man to enter into contracts which he cannot pay when called upon;…to offer his creditors one farthing in the pound, even when those creditors include tradesmen from whom he obtained…groceries, meat, clothing and the like. I believe that the morality of the Insolvency Court is in some respects worse than that of the racecourse. If a gambler at the races who contracted to pay £1,000 in the event of a certain horse winning were, on being called to pay, to offer 1,000 farthings, his conduct would be described in language more forcible than elegant.

Judge Hickman Molesworth

The Breaker

ANOTHER SCORCHER. Like a butcher slicing choice cuts from the ribs of a bullock, the north wind had been stripping top-soil from the Wimmera and Mallee for days, bearing it south in broiling, black clouds. On an airless and torpid Tuesday afternoon in March, the city's citizens were drained and irritable. They sleep-walked the streets, breathing the stifling, gritty air, yearning for rain or even a steady cooling breeze.

In that atmosphere, at two o'clock, Wallace rose to his feet on the stage of the Athenaeum Hall. Eight hundred shareholders and depositors filled the hall to over-flowing, and he stood for a moment in the expectant hush, looking down on the serried crowd, whose arms were locked in a metronome movement of papers and fans before perspiring faces.

Every eye was upturned. He felt their anger—and despair. It was going to be a scorcher of another kind.

'Good afternoon, ladies and gentlemen. My name is Angus Wallace, the liquidator. It's my duty to report to you the progress of the liquidation to date…'

In short order, he summarized the facts relating to the dates of the suspension of payment, his own appointment.

'With profound regret, I'm bound to advise you my investigation confirms the bank is in a very serious situation. The position I'll lay before you, can only be described as disastrous.'

The assemblage was a giant lung, *en masse* it breathed in. A deeper, straining-to-listen silence fell; even the restless fanning died out.

He plunged into it. He gave them the liabilities item by item, the assets line by line with estimated realizations. He said that the shareholders' funds and reserves had been lost, told them that on current estimates the deficiency in the bank's books was one million pounds. That shareholders would face a call of three pounds on each share held. That depositors, at best, could expect three shillings in the pound.

In stunned silence, they heard it.

Then, like a wind rushing into a pine forest—the lung exhaled. Riding on that gale, he told them that his estimates depended on the prices obtained for real estate or shares held as security. That the real estate market was in a terrible situation. That the values of shares were severely depressed, or non-existent. He painted it as black as it was.

Beside him, nerves wire-tight, Philip Larkin and Binks stared over the heads like firemen watching bushland for a first puff of smoke. Larkin thought: Any moment now.

Sir John, Savage, Sandhurst, Jamison Smith, the auditor, Moore, were sitting in the front row.

Binks thought: A stiff-faced, and sullen crew. Behind them sat their legal advisers, serious as men listening to a funeral oration.

'How did the bank get into this situation? Doubtless, that's *one* of the questions on your lips…' He brushed perspiration from his forehead. He was quite calm, but every man there, whatever his emotional state, was boiling in his suit. The ladies were in better condition. Yes, the ladies. A surprising number present.

'*Ladies* and gentlemen. We sit here, in the dark shadow of the land boom. I'm afraid all the factors we've seen, case after case in the aftermath of that disaster, are present in your bank. I hardly need enumerate them. Foolish, incompetent directors and management—engaged in the most reckless lending imaginable. Stupid, blind, greedy men. That is bad enough. In the case of this bank, it's only half the story.

'Regrettably I must…'

'The loans—to Sir John Adams' companies? Tell us about them, sir.' The question came looping up from the assembly, shouted by a tall man who held aloft his top-hat to gain attention. The muscles in his lean face had set into a rictus from which those nearby turned their eyes away.

'We've all read *Table Talk*,' another cried.

'By God, we have!'—from someone else.

A wave of movement flowed across the close-packed rows—as though the prayed-for breeze had arrived—but the majority sensed they'd had only the entrée, that the main course was still to be served.

'*What's the other half?*'

'*Quiet!*'

'Bear with me. I'm coming to that matter, among others…'

His gaze fell on Chadwick QC, sitting apart from the directors, picked up a faint smile curving his singer's mouth.

'The other half?…There's been crookedness and fraud and misfeasance in your bank.' The turgid words, the rapid-fire delivery, hit hard. The corpus below seemed to rock back. Could he get this part done? Beside him, Larkin had flinched.

'What I say next, I'm fully prepared to substantiate in a court of law.'

Again, he felt it slipping to the edge. 'Hear me out, please!'

He informed them, reading from his report, that all the balance sheets back to 1890 were false, that eight loans to directors or their interests totalling £412,000 had been written off by those same directors as irrecoverable, that records pertaining to loans to two directors totalling £13,990 had been fraudulently removed from the books, that…

Amazed and angry ejaculations punctuated his speech. But he kept going, raising his voice progressively.

'The suspension of payment on the 28th October legally meant the stoppage of *all* payments—but these directors, in the succeeding days, paid themselves the sum of £1,000 for fees…'

A roar of ironical laughter shook the hall.

'These are facts. And I'm afraid there's more, but you'll have my report to read for yourselves.'

He had been too occupied to see the effect of his speech on those in the front row, now he glanced there, saw a frozen tableau gazing at him as though at the devil. Not Sir John; he was contemplating a private vista. Savage's face was twisted, glaring; Sandhurst leant back, his, a stony mask.

He thought: They *must* be dealt with. He'd also have to deal with the hatred which blazed at him; the counter-attack which must come from the floor of the meeting.

With the ear-stopping whiz-bang of a ship's rocket going up, the meeting exploded. Uproar washed over the Athenaeum Hall like a giant Southern Ocean roller crashing on a headland. The whole auditorium swayed. A score of men were on their feet, shouting, gesticulating.

He didn't care that he'd lost control. He'd said his piece—or most of it—let it run where it might, hopefully, all the way to the courts.

He sat down.

'By God! The tiger's out of the cage now,' Larkin shouted into his ear. The solicitor looked shocked.

'Christ Almighty!' Binks muttered.

In his seat at the side of the hall, Murdoch had been rapidly recording in his shorthand. By Jove, a warm afternoon's work! If his journalistic instinct was worth anything, the temperature hadn't risen to its maximum yet either! Brodzky and he would be burning the midnight oil tonight. His dancing pencil recorded: *The shock waves from Mr Wallace's announcement shook the Athenaeum Hall, ran like wildfire into Collins-street...*

'I've never seen anything like this,' Susan said into Hanna's ear. 'Has he lost control?' They were at the rear, under the balcony, which thundered above them from stamping feet.

Hanna replied, 'It'll quieten down in a minute. They'll want to hear him out.'

'What an ordeal for him. He seems calm enough.'

'He's doing his job.' Hanna had not wanted to come.

It *was* ebbing. Wallace got to his feet again.

'*Ladies and gentlemen! Pray silence!* I'm prepared to take questions.'

'You've had mine, one of 'em'—the tall, hat-waving man had sprung up again. His heat-struck face was lobster red, twitching all the more.

'I have, sir. *Table Talk* was quite correct. Six loans were made to the chairman's companies. All of those companies have been liquidated under the Voluntary Liquidation Act 1891. The subject loans were written off by the board at its meeting on the 26th October...'

'Two days before the bank closed its doors?'

'That's correct.'

A sigh of regret from that common lung. In the wings, an elderly man with a great mane of white hair, was banging on the floor with a stick. 'My name is Duncan. By Heavens! If we take the charitable view...'

'*Why should we?*'

'It's hard to.'

'...that these loans were made in the normal course of business, how extremely unlucky our chairman's been in his private business ventures. How *deuced* unlucky! Six loans, six projects, six failures! *And* according to the report, he's made a secret composition for his personal affairs as well. This paragon of civic life, this master of commerce? Words fail me. God forgive us that we've put our affairs into the hands of the likes of him.' He desisted with his stick, sank down on his chair.

Others took up the running. Questions and assertions flew at the stage like sparks off a whetstone.

'We were fools.'

'The city's awash with trusting fools.'

'And with rogues and tricksters.'

In his place, Chadwick thought: A disorganized rabble, they're not going to get far like this. But Wallace seems happy to let it run. What's his game?

A small, greyish man, immaculate in a frock-coat, walked with quick precise steps down the aisle, turned to face the meeting. In a 'V', he raised and spread his arms, each hand of which supported his ebony-topped stick, and waited.

Like a bloody band-master bringing the band to the ready—Binks thought. The man's face, framed by silky side-whiskers, was flushed and amused. The dramatic pose worked, the lull came. Here was the voice of reason, of getting forward, come to their aid. A very English voice.

'Edwards is my name. Listen, my friends, if we keep our heads the liquidator can tell us a good deal more. It'll save you some reading. *And*, let's hear from the architects of this mess. Especially, Sir John...The liquidator used the words 'crookedness', 'fraud' and 'misfeasance'. That's strong stuff. I'm a lawyer, and I know it is. So let's hear about that, too. *I'll* say one thing. It seems the directors've funnelled our money into their own ill-conceived projects. They've got clear with loans equivalent to about fifty per cent of the total loans made. They've treated the bank like a personal slush-fund. Apart from any crookedness which we may hear of, what kind of morality is that?' He walked back up the aisle to his seat, twirling his stick.

Chadwick decided: He's not attempting to control it at present. He's letting it work for him.

The solicitor, Barnaby, had risen to his feet from behind Sir John still confronting his personal vista. 'Ladies and Gentlemen. Sir John has authorized me to speak for him at this juncture…' (Uproar.)

'*Has he lost his voice?*'

'*Get him up!*'

'…He is distraught at the bank's situation…' Barnaby was shouting above the ironical laughter, groans, and hisses… 'Following advice given to him, he'll respond, make his explanations in an atmosphere more conducive to getting the truth out…'

'*He's funking it.*'

'*He's frightened of the courts.*'

Binks thought: The *truth*? That'll be the day.

Barnaby had to resume his seat.

Throughout these past minutes, Wallace had stood, a silent adjudicator. Now it was time to come back into it. He raised his arms, much as the elegant Edwards had done.

'For the moment, I'll pass over the false balance sheets and go to two loans, made to Director Savage for £7,213 and Director Sandhurst for £6,777. These particular loans have neither been repaid, nor written off. By some mysterious process, they've been expunged from the bank's books. Have disappeared into thin air! But they existed all right. Why they weren't written off with the other directors' loans I can't say…'

'Aha,' Chadwick muttered to himself. The men each side of him were bumping him in their excitement.

'Steady on,' Larkin said into Wallace's ear. 'That's far enough.'

'Why aren't these matters before the courts?' Up in the gallery, a man had climbed precariously on a chair to shout this.

'What does the Government say about it?'—from someone else.

Wallace had been waiting for this. He slipped into a crack in the pandemonium. 'The Government's washed their hands of it. The Premier, the Attorney-General, don't see it's their business.' (Fresh uproar.)

Cool as a cucumber, veteran of a score of similar meetings, Murdoch's pencil went on: *Pointed questions were asked about the Government's failure to act…*

Larkin stared stonily down at the crowd. The course Wallace was plotting through the meeting was the one that had drawn his disquiet and remonstrance. The solicitor understood that his colleague was gambling that publicity and public opinion would force the Government to act. If it didn't, the liquidator would lay the charges himself. It was a plan fraught with uncertainty and peril. Suddenly he seized Wallace's arm.

Savage had got to his feet, was crossing to the steps of the stage. He shook with passion, his fists were clenched. His customary arrogant, devil-take-you orbs were reddened and blazing. And locked on the liquidator.

'Watch out!' Larkin warned.

Wallace, his face expressionless did watch the parliamentarian bound up the steps. In the distance, Susan gripped Hanna's arm.

Barnaby and Sandhurst came rushing after him. They caught him when he was a few paces from Wallace, gripped his arms, pulled him away. Spittle was flying from his mouth. The liquidator thought that once grabbed, he had given up too easily.

Most of the eight hundred had leapt to their feet, were cheering ironically or booing. A lady was being carried out, a number of others were obviously distressed.

'What an actor,' Wallace said to Larkin.

'He's mad enough for anything.'

His colleague under restraint, Sandhurst had turned back, was cleaving the air with his long white hand. His urbanity had been blown to smithereens. 'You can look forward to a writ. Your slanderous conduct will have to be answered for,' he shouted at Wallace.

That'll be the day, Binks thought.

'Sit down!'—a chorus of contempt.

Murdoch his racing pencil poised, gazed in fascination at this incident, then wrote: *Mr Wallace's remarks caused a sensation. Mr Savage rushed at the stage amidst great excitement. His friends interposed and dragged him back...*

A statuesque figure had risen in the second row. Here was the former Speaker of the Legislative Assembly—a household name in the Colony.

'No-one wants to hear from you,' someone yelled.

'I will be heard,' he shouted. 'As I always am. Nobody is on trial here. Why are you baying after this board like blood-hounds? It's a nasty fact that the bank has gone down, but so have a lot of others. The times have been treacherous. Many a good board's been tripped up. Many a good man's been caught out. You and I are among 'em. But we've got to take our medicine like men. Like Britons! You've heard this liquidator make his charges. What of them? Nothing is substantiated...'

'Let's get them into court, then we'll find out,' someone advised.

'Get them into court, you say. My advice to you, sir, is to keep out of the clutches of the lawyers. That would be putting good money after bad.' (Loud laughter.) I've known this man, Wallace, for a long time. Another *lawyer*. Aren't they like bees around a honey-pot? I've known him as a wrecker. A *breaker*. Men of the calibre of this board are *builders*. He's a man who destroys. Forget about his wild accusations. They're not worth the paper they're written on. That's why the Government won't listen to him. Your directors are honourable men. We should turn our back on the past. Make a fresh start.'

In a kind of sudden, eerie, puzzled silence, he sat down.

For a moment, to Murdoch, it seemed that the Athenaeum Hall had imposed a correctional silence. In the past three years, it had seen drama enough as institutions had writhed in their toils. Its walls had soaked up torrents of accusations, abuse, lies—all the off-cuts of disaster. They'd made a patina. That was it. He grinned to himself. He could work that in.

Wallace ignored the famous man's intercession. He looked further afield. 'Yes, sir. Do you wish to speak?'

He'd recognized the leader of the Camberwell group. The man was pale and nervous. A paper shook uncontrollably in his hands. 'I do, sir. I do.' He stepped out into the aisle. 'We haven't heard a word from the small shareholder or depositor. The people who are facing ruin—and bankruptcy isn't the worst of that. Some of us are at our wits' end to know how to keep a roof over the heads of our families, to put food on the table. We've been fools, no doubt. But who can blame us? The directors of this bank are prominent citizens. They've been puffed up by the papers as brilliant men of business, paragons of virtue… We've seen them heading up civic committees. Now we hear that our money's gone, of false balance sheets, and all the rest of it. We've been blinded—or deceived—or swindled. I don't know which. I don't take kindly to the remarks of the previous speaker. A fresh start, he says. With what? I say. My family is on bread and dripping. His speech was a load of rubbish—another tissue of deception from a land boomer.'

'Why don't you keep quiet, you know nothing,' the household name said contemptuously.

'You would like that. I don't know what can be done, but something must.' He sat down amidst the Camberwell delegation's plaudits, and general acclamation.

'Our friend is quite right. Something must be done.' It was the debonair solicitor, Edwards, again, nodding his head, smiling, holding aloft his stick. 'We must make the Government act. What do you intend to do, Mr Wallace?'

Wallace gazed at Edwards.

'If they won't act, I will lay criminal information myself against these directors.' (Cheers.)

I don't like his chances, Chadwick thought, but you've got to give it to him for courage.

Edwards was in his element. 'Sir, I would like to claim that honour myself. If you agree and will co-operate with me. They've made their compositions, yet they sit in their Toorak mansions, ride around in carriages, go to their clubs, for them not much seems to have changed. We must find the way to shake them free of these assets. That money belongs to us.' (Uproar, cries of 'It does!')

'What would a johnny-come-lately like you know?' the household name sneered.

'As much as a colonial swindler, sir,' Edwards replied, to a roar of approval.

Off-stage in Collins Street, long bluish shadows were climbing up the hill. Dust hung in the air. The meeting had been in progress for over three hours. It seemed no-one had left. It had begun in an atmosphere of sweltering discomfort and expectancy. Individuals had shouted themselves hoarse, worn themselves and their neighbours to a frazzle; were saturated with perspiration. It broke up in a final acrimonious frenzy as the board were shepherded out the back door by their advisers and friends, and Wallace, Larkin and Binks followed.

In Little Collins Street, the directors' party piled into several hansom cabs and headed off. Wallace found out later that they were bound for a private room at White's Hotel, and a council-of-war.

Chadwick came out, nodded smilingly to Wallace and Larkin—as though they were all conspirators together—and glided into the homeward-bound crowd in the fluid walk which fascinated juries.

'What part is he playing in this?' Larkin muttered.

Wallace shrugged. 'After today, we'll see how everyone lines up.'

He was satisfied. They would lay the information against the board tomorrow. Edwards had approached them at the back of the stage to honour his promise, but he'd declined with thanks. Larkin had remonstrated with him in vain; he wanted the prosecution under his own hand.

They walked away into the dusk. He now had a moment of respite, to consider what price he was going to have to pay for his afternoon's work.

Susan and Hanna, feeling wrung out, went home by hansom instead of tram. Each had solid business experience at the managerial level, and thus an informed outlook far beyond most of their sex, however, the sensational histrionics, the mass hysteria, the malignant spectre of business-gone-wrong, had drained them.

Yesterday, Susan had decided to attend the meeting. She had heard it spoken of in their circle for the past fortnight, and it hadn't seemed important. After the meeting at the Federal Coffee Palace, it had. She'd persuaded Hanna to go with her. She wished to see for herself what Angus Wallace was up to, and how he conducted himself. She wished to begin to try to sort out fact and rumour about him. It was a kind of reconnaissance. She'd felt *impelled* to attend.

A pregnant silence had followed his abrupt declaration to her over the electroplated tea-service. In the following moments, she wondered if, having spoken, he regretted it. His silence seemed unnatural. It was as if a horse had been whipped up, and then the brakes jammed on. Then, she'd wondered if she'd heard him right.

She had. He'd said, 'I've surprised you. We've known each other such a short time. However, what I've said I mean with all my heart.'

So there it was. And she had no idea at all about the condition of her own heart! He'd said nothing of marriage, though, palpably, it was in the air. And, it had seemed plain he wasn't going to say anything more at the moment…How strange, she'd found herself thinking.

He'd handed her into a hansom, and in a bemused state she had returned to Hanna's. She'd asked herself, with a flash of humour: 'Is it a colonial way of conducting it?'

They were nearly home. Ahead, the Exhibition Building's dome touched by a last glow of sunset resembled an Indian palace engraved in an illustrated periodical.

Hanna shook her head. 'I know what you're thinking of,' she said with a look.

34

His Honour (Judge Molesworth): You are like the Irishman who, when asked whether he was guilty or not guilty, wanted to know how he could tell until he heard the evidence. (Laughter.)

The Argus, 24.5.1890

Flashpoints

Startling Disclosures
Bank Directors Face Grave Allegations

ON WEDNESDAY, these headlines appeared in *The Age* above a graphic report of the meeting. The directors were named as were their questioners where they'd been identified. *The Argus* had similar.

'They're having a field day,' Wallace said. He, Larkin and Binks were poring over the papers. They'd met in the boardroom at eight. Murdoch's report was expected out on Friday.

The liquidator had slept nine hours, but the black circles under his eyes, the lines of strain now appeared indelible, though Philip Larkin decided he was fully in control of himself. He thought: More than I am.

'It'll stir things up in Spring Street,' the liquidator added with a sardonic smile.

Larkin sucked at his teeth, Binks looked ambivalent about that. Wallace frowned. 'Maybe they'll close ranks.'

'That's what *I'm* afraid of,' Larkin said. All last evening he had mulled over Edwards' offer to lay the charges—and Wallace's refusal.

The liquidator said tersely, 'The Government's abrogated its duty so it falls on my shoulders. If we can get 'em committed for trial, then they *must* take it over.'

Larkin considered this in sceptical silence.

Wallace said quietly, 'I want their personal assets, Philip. I want them thrown out of their houses, all their possessions up for auction. And, if we can swing it, I want 'em in prison. And you should, too.'

Larkin felt his colleague's critical gaze.

Binks, staring at his papers, was inclined to agree with Larkin, but wild horses wouldn't change his employer's mind. If Larkin knew of the sword that Savage and Sandhurst held poised over the liquidator's head...And, he might know soon.

Wallace accompanied Philip Larkin down the marble stairs. He wanted a word in private. When they stood in the desolate banking chamber he said, 'This is a rather delicate matter. We've been friends for years, and I hope you won't take it amiss...Helena Spencer.'

Larkin stiffened, and a slow flush came to his face. 'Wallace, I don't think you should go on.'

'Old man, I must. I've some experience in these matters—and forgive me, with the lady in question.' He paused, 'Look, a word of caution...'

Philip Larkin was flabbergasted, staring. For a moment, he couldn't find his voice. 'Stop! By God! What right have you...?' He'd spoken in an intense whisper. His shoulders were flexing in an outbreak of nerves. He felt his face burning. Suddenly, he laughed bitterly. 'Oh, I can see how it is.'

Wallace saw it was useless to go on. 'I doubt it. I speak only out of friendship.'

The solicitor glared at the liquidator. 'You've stepped over a line.' He turned his back and walked out.

Wallace watched him go. To provoke a reaction like that, he probably had. The advice he'd been about to give was well-intentioned; he knew it was well-founded. Better to have kept silent? He'd never seen this side of Philip. And, he thought he'd picked up a flash of guilt. He wondered if he'd bedded her yet—or, if she'd bedded him. He shook his head, and went back upstairs. You continue to learn, he told himself.

It was clear to Hilda Wilberforce that a climax was near in her friends' affairs. Her lorgnette held close to her eyes, she'd scanned each line in *The Age* report. The allegations confirmed her worst fears—and Laura's. She guessed there would be more to come. They were *only* allegations, but she remembered the ebullient knight's multifarious schemes spawned in his ever-fertile mind. Numberless times, in this house she'd heard him pronounce on 'progress', on the 'survival of the fittest'. He was no longer ebullient. 'Progress' was a notion which had crashed from the pinnacle the southern city had raised it to in '89, and, it appeared 'the fittest' no longer included himself.

Her mind came, full-circle, back to Laura. Her social situation would now be extremely difficult. In future, her third-Thursday 'At Homes' would be sparsely attended. Since the bank's crash, and the *Table Talk* revelations, society had put the Adams into a twilight region. That would now change.

She found herself thinking about Angus Wallace. He couldn't be blamed. Whatever else might be said of him, in his public life he'd never shirked anything. Her eye caught a paragraph in *The Age* which she'd missed before: *Mr Wallace appears intent on laying charges and a number of people expect him to be touched with something hard, one of these dark nights.*

'My God,' she breathed, 'we haven't fallen to this, have we?'

That afternoon Binks went out to Prahran on 'the milk run'. However, there was something extra to attend to today. He was always discreet on these journeys, and today took more precautions. As he walked from Prahran station, several times he turned and studied the street behind. He took a good look at the house's environs. He couldn't spot anyone. But, the fact that *they* knew the address was ominous.

All this vigilance made matters difficult for Otto Rudd. He solved the problem by taking a tram up High Street, passing Binks, and getting out two stops on. Then he went into a public house and watched the clerk approach. What's he playing at, he wondered.

His observation of Savage and Sandhurst at Sebastian Low's had given him a shock. Anyone who'd had dealings with Low had that kind of reaction when they came across him again. Instinctively, however, he felt the clandestine communications didn't have the trademark of these men. He'd made a cast in a new direction. It was ironical to be following your own client but, with investigations, you never ruled anything out. So, after Binks had entered the house he went past for a hundred yards and took up a watching position.

In this interregnum, the detective brooded on his last night's reading of the papers. Two headlines appeared in his mind. *Death of a Confederate General. Suicide of a London Banker.* Meat and drink. There'd be more reports on the suicide to look forward to. Each night, in his sitting-room, via the marvel of the overseas telegraph, the wide-world came to him. He relished keeping an eye on it all, just as he relished this city's street life.

Binks' business took him half an hour. He had delivered the letter Wallace had written that morning, and it had certainly shocked the woman. She had looked at him with grave disquiet.

'Not to worry too much,' he'd said—gently for him. 'He just wants to prepare you—in case.'

'It's a pity...*Will* be such a pity, if the children are dragged in,' she said with a faraway look which Binks perceived gazed back into a past unknown to him. The clerk nodded slowly, and left. He returned the way he'd come.

The detective watched him go, then moved to an iron street-bench closer to the house. He examined in a leisurely but practised way every window on the facade of the house. What was this house all about? He tipped his bowler over his forehead, and settled down to find out.

35

Doubtless it is the duty of a liquidator to realise assets as quickly as possible, but then that is no reason why he should not prosecute offenders also...No more shirk one task than the other.

The Age, *22.5.1890*

Forewarned and Forearmed

ON THE POINT of departure, Wallace lingered as if trying to recall something. His eyes moved to the Gothic oak hall-stand with its crop of hats and sticks. He went to it, and selected a stick with an ebony handle. It looked decorative, precision-made, and functional. His father's. And, functional in a capacity beyond the normal. He drew out the long blade of Birmingham steel. It came out with what sounded to him like a whisper of regret—or anticipation.

At that moment, Mrs Beattie appeared. She gave a stifled cry. 'We're not back to those days, are we?'

Wallace glanced at her, then continued to admire the blade which had a slight smear of oil on it. He slid it back, fixed the catch. 'Don't concern yourself. I think my father would like the idea of its having an airing.'

She wasn't reassured; she'd also read that paragraph in *The Age*.

At the bank, he picked up Binks and the paperwork.

'No news from Spring Street?'

The clerk shook his head.

'Very well, let's go and do this job.'

They walked up to the Central Police Station to lay their criminal information. When their mission became known in the station there was a buzz. An inspector came out to the counter to supervise the proceedings. The serious-faced officer knew he was on delicate ground, and was meticulous with the formalities. However, it was dealt with expeditiously, and they walked out of the station an hour later.

Alone, Wallace went to the Crown Law Office, and asked for the Chief Crown Prosecutor. He waited in an ante-room, seated on a cracked leather bench. No-one came or went. No sound came from the inner rooms. It seemed that humanity might have abandoned the place. Faintly, he heard the street traffic.

He was taking a step into the dark here, but one which could be advantageous if it came off. He could imagine the Attorney-General's reaction—if and when he heard of it.

Chief Prosecutor Danby came out himself. The men knew each other. Danby was forty-seven, a slight man with a lined, brown face, clean-shaven, and short grey hair. He moved as if he were narrowly evading danger; had always looked like this.

'Well, Wallace, what can I do for you?'

'I've laid criminal information against the directors and an officer of the First Bank of Victoria.'

Danby raised his eyebrows expressively, studied his visitor. He indicated armchairs. They sat down.

'You've gone out on a limb.' Danby smiled slightly. It wasn't the first time. He was familiar with the liquidator's assignment as Wallace knew he would be, had scanned the newspaper reports. The Attorney-General had sent Wallace's original submission to him for an opinion. He'd advised that it was justifiable to start proceedings against the directors. His advice had been ignored. But he couldn't tell Wallace this, shouldn't even have him in his office on the matter.

Wallace said, 'We'll get them into the Police Court—and, I think, committed for trial. In which case…'

'You might find it harder than you think.'

'You mean, it'll be hard to find a strong magistrate, and a per-suadable bench of JPs?'

'You know I can't discuss it with you.'

Wallace grinned. 'We've got additional evidence to what you've seen.' He'd guessed the fate of his submission.

Danby stroked his chin. 'If you obtain a committal, the Crown must take over the prosecution. If you don't…' He spread his hands.

Wallace nodded. 'Would you take it yourself? It's a case to get your teeth into.' In asking this question, he knew his man. Danby had a reputation as a reformer, as an opponent of the excesses of the land boom; against the odds he'd had two noteworthy successes—and had hung on to his job.

Danby thought for a moment. 'I'd look at it closely. There might be pressures against me.'

'Fair enough.'

That was all. They shook hands and Wallace stepped out into a

Spring Street steeped in noon-day sun. Some days this summer the bitumen had felt molten under his shoes. Not today, the summer was surely on the wane.

Danby would lead the prosecution—if they got to trial.

Having for the moment done all he could on one front, he turned his mind to the other: Savage's and Sandhurst's threat. He categorized it as a blunt instrument; but, it'd be subtle enough and unexpected when they swung it. He felt himself powerless to avoid it. It was a question of where and when, and how he might survive. Various fragments drifted through his mind. That paragraph in *The Age*, the two mysterious communications which he hadn't thought of for several days. What had the detective found out? Suddenly, he realized that he didn't feel well. Too much on his plate? A delayed reaction to Tuesday?

He returned to his house at half-past four. For half an hour he paced his study—the other vexed matter had taken over. By God, this was hard. His head was pounding. He went upstairs, splashed water over his face, gazed at himself in the mirror.

He'd go over to Carlton Gardens! Whether he'd tell her tonight, he did not honestly know. It was the one sector of his life where he was irresolute. The obstacle seemed so immense. But, if he didn't deal with it before Savage and Sandhurst released their poison…

He came downstairs. Amongst the post on the hall table was a letter addressed in a female hand. He tore it open. He was surprised to see it was from Katherine Boyd. His eyes raced over the lines. *Dear Angus, When I arrived at the Harbraces' on Monday I found Mr Savage there talking to Mr Harbrace in a most serious and confidential way. I asked him to leave, in view of Harbrace's condition. Poor Harbrace was quite distressed when he'd gone, and quite unable or unwilling to speak of it. Mrs Harbrace was also extremely agitated. I thought you should know. Yours sincerely, Katherine.*

Savage! He stared at the letter. They had the cheques and the teller's book entries to substantiate the fraudulent No. 2 Accounts, but the ex-chief accountant's evidence in the witness-box—if it could be obtained—would clinch it. *If* the man survived that long. What had Savage said to him? More to the point, how far would the parliamentarian go?

He took up the stick again, and went out to hail a hansom.

Susan was not home when he arrived before five o'clock. He asked to wait, and was shown upstairs to the drawing-room by the maid. Half an hour later Hanna entered, obviously surprised to see him. In truth, she had a momentary problem in juxtaposing the man sitting quietly in her drawing-room with Tuesday's man on the embattled stage of the Athenaeum Hall.

'Mr Wallace!'

'Miss Dewhurst.' He rose to his feet. 'I trust this isn't inconvenient. I was hoping to see Miss Fairfax to have a few words. I won't delay her long.'

Hanna cast him an ambivalent look. She thought she could understand what he was up to in his professional life, and she had a certain idea what he might be up to with her friend. All the same, she wondered if she was being too hard on him.

Hanna ordered tea; Susan was expected home by six. 'We were at the Athenaeum Hall,' she said.

Wallace gazed at her. 'I'm surprised.'

'What a performance the whole thing was! We both thought you remarkably calm and in control.'

He bowed slightly in his chair.

'Of course, it's a great sadness to see Sir John—and Laura Adams—so brought down.'

He nodded, absorbed her serious gaze. There was nothing he could do to help the Adams. He wanted their mansion and their possessions down to the last sterling silver sauce-boat, if he could get them.

'That paragraph in *The Age*?'

'Newspaper talk,' he said.

Wallace's mind was not in tune for small talk. He had stepped into this drawing-room and the hoped-for interview with a good deal more trepidation than he'd stepped on to the Athenaeum's stage. En route, in the hansom, he'd steeled himself to reveal what he'd been keeping from the world these six years. In a practical sense, it had to be done; in an honourable sense it had. This evening he *would* do it. It was his only chance of a future with her.

However, it occurred to him that this might be an opportunity to take another matter forward. He put aside his preoccupations, looked at Hanna in a new light.

He could imagine what was going on behind the scenes concerning Philip's liaison with Helena; had witnessed the impact at the ball, the aftermath in the cab returning home. It was an extremely delicate topic. All personal relations seemed an unforgiving quagmire for misunderstandings! Nonetheless…

168

'I hope you might allow me to say something of a personal nature to you...It concerns Philip Larkin.'

With a heightened look, she put down her tea-cup. Points of colour had appeared instantly on her cheeks.

'Philip and I are old friends. Our fathers did gold business together in the '50s. We're both Australian Natives. I was in Scotland when he lost Sonia, couldn't give him the support I would've wished, though I know William Boyd came through with that.'

She had lowered her eyes to stare at her hands folded on her lap, was listening intently. He studied the top of her fair head, framing his words. 'Helena Spencer is a much maligned woman. Unfairly, in my view. Fortunately, it doesn't worry her overmuch. She has many sound qualities. She is not, however, the right woman for Philip.'

Hanna lifted her head and stared at him. How could anyone know that?

'I don't propose to explain my opinion. I've known Helena; I know Philip. And, I've spoken to him on it.' He let the ensuing silence speak for Larkin's reaction. 'I can't say what he'll do. Which of the parties may wake up first. He's not the right man for her, either.'

He was startled to see that Hanna's eyes were brimming with tears. This self-contained, matter-of-fact woman. He thought that they weren't tears of distress.

At that moment, there were sounds on the stairs and Susan swept into the room. Her eyes were cautious yet welcoming. She took in Hanna's unwiped eyes. She hesitated. 'Mr Wallace...What a pleasant surprise. One would have thought you buried under legal papers at this stage.'

He stood up quickly. His head had gone into a whirl; his heart was racing. He'd been so calm talking to Hanna. The law and its history has romance in it, and some lawyers have it in them. He'd found the niche years ago. He'd realized that he'd entered another dimension of it.

She'd come in, a be-ribboned hat flying in her hand, resembling some blonde Grecian goddess, lifting like foam off the Aegean Sea. His impression, his fantasy.

'Mr Wallace wishes to have a talk with you, Susan,' Hanna said smiling, at last briefly wiping her eyes. 'He's already had one with me.'

36

I HAVE toiled in the light
  Of a disastrous day;
Now in dark night
  I fling my heart away.

Like a dead man empty,
  His grief done,
I walk beyond the mountains,
  I lie beyond the sun.
                    Robert Crawford,
                    'Frustration'

Hochgurtel's Fountain

THEY WALKED ACROSS the street to the gardens. The distant GPO, and Fitzroy Town Hall clocks, not quite with unison, were sounding six o'clock. They took the main path towards the Exhibition Building. The great dome was ablush with the rays of the retreating sun, the dome's cupola winked like a golden eye; in the slanting light, other pedestrians had a blurry, luminous appearance which made identification tricky.

Susan noticed that the leaves had begun to turn. The first breath of autumn—though, for her, the Southern Hemisphere summer had been tolerable. Her complexion was as fresh and fine as the day she'd embarked at Tilbury. Of course, several mentors, alarmed to see the danger she'd be in, had counselled her on precautions.

To Wallace, her face might have been modelled from the most delicate porcelain, charmingly animated with small changes of expression and the quicksilver shadows, dominated by her clear-sighted eyes. She walked firmly, resigned to waiting. What was he going to say now? And, those tears from Hanna?…He'd suggested they walk in the gardens for a half-hour. She'd agreed, and they'd come this far in silence. It seemed nothing was to be said until they were beneath the trees.

Was he staging this as carefully as he had the meeting at the Athenaeum Hall?

Susan had come away from that meeting with her spirits lifted. She'd divined that his conduct was being impelled by a moral attitude—as well as the requirements of the liquidation; that he would've taken the job without pay. It had helped her with the picture she was building up. She thought: Yes, Mr Wallace, I'm attracted to you—interested in your life—beyond that?

He glanced aside at her, at last spoke. 'Larkin and Mrs Spencer are not suited. I don't think it'll last. I told Miss Dewhurst—Hanna—as much.'

Immediately, she knew the nature of Hanna's tears.

'Sometimes it's clear some relations are just plain wrong. I've spoken to him.'

She'd received a small jolt of surprise. That must've been an interesting interview, as would be Mrs Spencer's reaction if she ever got to hear of it. How strange that he'd been prepared to intervene. He'd watched at the ball, in the hansom afterwards, reflected on it, and taken action. In the midst of his other cares. Some might think it presumptuous, she didn't.

'I see you intended a kindness to Hanna.'

He made a slight, dismissive gesture. They continued on, side-by-side, this woman who turned all heads, dressed in her day clothes, a brown costume, this man in a crumpled grey suit, a Panama hat, with a drawn face, a staring-into-the-future look, an ebony-handled stick.

He said, 'However, that's not what I came here for. On Sunday, I spoke of my feelings…' He thought, with a quickening heart-beat: It seems an age away. '…I'm afraid, I left it suspended in thin air.'

She was gazing ahead at the dome whose pinkish blush had transformed into a crimson glaze—as though the sun had waited till the last, to sacrifice all. He smiled tensely, wondering if she was listening.

She was. She turned her head towards him.

He shook his head grimly. 'You must think me a fool. My impulse was to go on, make a formal declaration. But I couldn't do that. There's something which stands in the way. A great difficulty for me. I fear it may ruin my very faint hopes. But I must disclose it.'

She wondered: What, in God's name, has he to tell me? In contrast to his staccato utterances, they seemed to be pacing in a slow-march to the edge of a chasm. Suddenly, she was remembering the long, agonized talks she'd had with the Manchester lawyer. A cold, hopeless thought came: Was it history repeating itself?

He wasn't quite to it yet. He was assembling each preliminary remark with care; when the structure was right he'd make his revelation, his plea in mitigation. Bleakly, he felt he was building a house of cards.

They had arrived at an open court which led to the building's main entrance. To their right, Hochgurtel's fountain disported wavering, sunset-tinted curtains of water. He'd stopped—was staring at colossal cement figures, half-human, half-fish, entwining, posturing, small boys dancing—as though mesmerized by the fantasy. It might have been that he was seeing it, suddenly, as a metaphor for his convoluted predicament.

She stopped, her eyes on his face in profile.

He was staring at Binks' face. Ten yards away, coming from the fountain as if he'd materialized from those curtains of water. His clerk was hurrying towards him. For a moment, Wallace was shocked, thought he was waking from a dream. Such was his feeling of unreality at this smashing of his peak of emotional concentration.

It was certainly Binks. 'Excuse me,' the clerk said, coming up, removing his hat, quickly nodding to Susan. 'Thank Heavens, I've tracked you down.'

Wallace stared, shook his mind clear. 'What's wrong?'

'Murdoch's at your house. Been waiting there this past hour. Something big's broken. That's all I know. I've got a hansom at Miss Dewhurst's.'

Wallace remained frozen, except his hand gripping the stick had risen, involuntarily, to point at his clerk's midriff. He shook his head. 'Wait five minutes.'

He turned on his heel to find Susan watching. The point of the stick was back in the gravel. Binks moved away.

'My apologies, I'll have to be more expeditious than I intended.'

Her restraining hand was light on his arm. 'Please go to your business. I can wait.'

He stared into her eyes, irresolute. Already it was going to pieces in his head. He took her hand, and smiled tightly.

'Very well.'

She smiled in turn, warmly, and wondered if Fate, which she believed was always standing in the wings of their lives, had, in the arrival of his clerk, just stepped forward with a sly smile.

They reached Albert Park at a quarter to seven. Murdoch rose from his chair in the study, and shook hands with Wallace. The press-man's appearance was immaculate, showed no signs of haste. 'I'm sorry, but I've got something urgent,' he said. 'This is to be published tomorrow morning in the *Melbourne Punch*.' He handed the liquidator a galley proof of two columns of newsprint.

Wallace took in at a glance:

Never The Twain Shall Meet—Lawyer's Public
And Very Private Lives

His face had become as set as those of the cavorting cement figures he'd gazed on within the last half-hour. He stood in the room and scanned the article. His heart turned to ice at the insulting levity of its tone. The paper was a propaganda organ of the conservative Legislative Council, venomous against opponents.

They remained silent when he'd finished. He let his arm fall. Murdoch was watching his face; Binks contemplated the carpet.

'It's accurate enough,' he said. 'The children are my own. I've kept that part of my life very private these six years.'

He regarded the journalist. 'How did you...?'

Murdoch shook himself out of his thoughts. 'A friend at *Punch*. This is going to cause a stir, you know, specially on the heels of Tuesday's meeting. And ridicule, I'm afraid.'

Wallace nodded. 'That's the intention. They're after my credibility. Were you told the source?'

'Yes.'

'Well, you'll see how it fits in. Off the record, they threatened blackmail.'

The journalist's eyes narrowed, and he nodded to himself.

'Now they've delivered...but we'll keep our powder dry on that.'

'There's time to get something in Friday's *Table Talk*—in explanation, in mitigation. I'd recommend it.'

Binks looked up at this.

'No. I'll not respond.'

Binks turned his eyes down to the carpet again. Yes, the less said the better. It would be *hard* to explain. Harder still to understand!

Murdoch said, 'Our court reporter tells me you've laid the charges. That'll be featured tomorrow, too.'

'Yes. This might sink me in one way, not in another. I reckon they've got it wrong. I don't believe it'll hurt the liquidation or the prosecution. The facts in the latter stand alone.'

He shook himself into movement. 'Could I offer you gentlemen a drink?' Murdoch nodded. Binks was always on.

They sat down, each with a brandy, each face in shadow. Murdoch gazed across the room, visualizing editorials and stories to come. 'I can't speak for the effect of this on your private life, but I don't think you can ignore the impact it might have in court. These barristers love mud. Wallow in it like pigs. Sir John's got Chadwick QC in his corner, so there you are.'

'I expect them to throw mud,' Wallace said. He thought: Larkin is not going to like this. He'll be shocked. It didn't sit well with the gratuitous advice he'd handed out to his friend about his own life. 'But, we've got a strong case.' He shrugged, hiding his tension.

The press-man took a sip of his brandy.

'You'll still testify on Sir John's secret liquidations?'

'I stand by for that.'

'Well, Binks, you've been pretty quiet. Are we going to be able to go through with it?'

The clerk smiled one of his problematic-under-duress smiles. 'It's always been a can of worms, still is. I'd say watch out for the Government. It's been too quiet there.'

Murdoch left, slipping away into the street, the red bloom on his lapel flaring in the dusk. Binks went out to Mrs Beattie in the kitchen to be given dinner.

Wallace sat down at his desk, to write a letter which must be done and sent tonight. Grimly, he paused, considered opening phrases, but then began to write and they came fluently—as though they'd been waiting their time.

Later, from his portico, he watched Binks go off along the gas-lit street on his errand. The die was cast, though, the matter could only be properly dealt with face-to-face. After this letter, he hoped she would still give him that chance.

37

The leading valuators of those days should have gone to prison.

The leaders of the boom were mostly extremely pious men and almost invariably they were teetotallers.
George D. Meudell, The Pleasant Career of a Spendthrift

Tears of Autumn

THE LETTER DELIVERED overnight was handed to Susan as she left for the store. The maid had been surprised to find it in the post-box. A weighty epistle. The Lancashire woman didn't recognize the handwriting, but immediately guessed the writer. She hesitated; she would take it with her. Today the Bargain Basement was opening, and everything would be at sixes and sevens.

She had given Hanna an edited version of the meeting at the Federal Coffee Palace—had been vague in describing that interlude because, in her own mind, it was nebulous. The bookseller had been disappointed to hear a similar report when she'd returned last night from the gardens. That expedition had been charged with a certain expectation, but another anti-climax!

However, here was a letter. She hurried to catch her tram.

Lady Adams could not believe her eyes. They were skimming the print at an accelerating rate, until she wasn't comprehending it. She stopped, dazed. Wait!—she instructed herself. She quickly regained her equilibrium, her eyes cleared, were back to their most penetrative.

'This will interest you, John,' she said drily, but with a hint of excitement.

The knight glanced at her, put aside his own paper, and frowned at the article she pointed out in the *Melbourne Punch*. He read it. His face, habitually in a self-absorbed expression these days, didn't change.

'Well, what do you think of it?'

Sir John reached for a cigar. His reaction contrasted to his wife's. The town was always awash with scandal of one kind or another. And this paper was an organ specializing in attacks on opponents of the conservatives. The fellow's rather active libido wasn't news in male circles—nor, he imagined, in a rather more circumscribed female one. He wasn't on his own there. Still, a family stashed away in the suburbs.

'The fellow's always been a bit of a mystery.'

Lady Adams looked at him pityingly, thought: This business has dulled him. He's showing signs of brain-fag. She said, 'I trust you see it might help you.'

The knight nodded slowly. 'It might give Chadwick more ammunition. I'll be seeing him this afternoon—about these charges.' Wallace's laying of the criminal information featured in both papers on the breakfast table.

Lady Adams gazed at her sun-filled breakfast room, and beyond. The dappled lawns, immaculate as ever, were fresh from overnight showers. The tears of autumn, her grandmother had called this season's rain; in her head, she heard the faint voice across the years. But the criminal information, given in at the Central Police Station, lay across her heart like an iron bar.

She said, 'This is *scandalous*. In one fell swoop, his character is exposed. I wonder what Hilda will say?'

———◆———

Hilda Wilberforce did not take that 'parliamentarians' rag', so it was not brought to her attention until mid-morning when a friend called, bringing a copy. After the lady had gone, she'd wondered how many other such public-spirited calls she would make. Though relatively few read this paper, it wouldn't take long for the news to percolate through the upper and middle reaches of Melbourne society. In these matters, the velocity matched the degree of the sensation.

Why are men such fools? It was a question she had asked herself many times. But in this case, it was merely the first in a number which rose in her mind. What motives would impel a man to take such drastic measures? Did filial feelings play no part in his make-up? How on earth could he have expected to get away with it? These, and others, tripped in her mind.

His father had been a dear friend. From her breadth of experience, she had inclined to be tolerant of reports, doubtless exaggerated, of his amorous career. All of that had a different complexion now. She looked at it again. *It appears that the gay bachelor around town has certainly put one over ladies of his acquaintance…* She frowned. Whatever stage the relationship with Susan Fairfax had reached, it would be killed stone-dead. No woman would be able to take this.

Who was responsible for this venomous action? Whoever it was, had hit a bull's-eye. Damage had been inflicted, how much they'd soon find out. She sighed. Everything seemed as obscure as the heart of a Mallee dust-storm. One thing, Laura would see it through different eyes. The accuser was now also the accused!

Sounds of an arrival in the hall. Judge Mountain had come for luncheon. The judge might have some inside information—if it could be extracted from him.

Otto Rudd had been watching the house at Prahran for two days. He'd seen the woman and the youngsters come out each day. They didn't suspect his presence. He had the knack of standing beside a tree, say on a shadowy corner, and all anyone saw was the tree. They'd gone to the shops at nearby Chapel Street, or to play in the Victoria Gardens while the woman watched from a bench, and the detective from another, more distant.

Now this house and its occupants had fallen into place. Up to a point. His avid readership of the Melbourne press—which kept him abreast of the local milieu, as he called it—had paid a dividend. He'd seen the *Melbourne Punch* at half-past ten at a corner shop. He was not unduly surprised by what he found out in the course of an investigation. In this case, he'd cleared up at a stroke what he'd begun to suspect, and, opened up a new line of inquiry.

His musing was interrupted by the approach of a man who came from the direction of the hotel about two hundred yards away. A tall, rake-thin individual in a flashy, worse-for-wear checked suit; hair sandy-coloured and too long; walking with his head tilted to one side, his gaze fixed on the footpath. He had an air about him and the detective identified it: public bar, the bookmakers' circle at Flemington Racecourse. He could've placed him in several other similar locales. And, yes, deeply immersed in his affairs.

He entered the gate of the house, walked up the path, knocked on the door, and a moment later was admitted by the woman.

'Hullo,' Rudd said softly. The twists, and turns. He'd had one of his sudden convictions, that this case had taken one or the other.

38

To you 'tis wild and dark;
  No light, no guide, no ark,
For travellers lost on moor and lea,
And ship-wrecked mariners at sea.
                        Ada Cambridge,
                    'What Of The Night'

Sandbanks

THREE MILES FROM where the indefatigable Rudd was on duty, Susan was reading the six sheets of letter-paper. Reading with an appalled fascination, her very breathing seeming suspended. Each sentence rolled on its way under her eyes to build up a picture totally beyond her expectation—or, experience.

She had turned pale. So pale that each tiny bluish vein on her face and throat was suddenly evident. Her blonde, fine hair had fallen over her brow. The fingers of her left hand rested against her face—as if they'd flown there in dismay, been forgotten.

At last, audibly, she exhaled a breath.

In the past few days, her feelings about this man had been steadily changing in tone and density. In a sense, it might've even been connected to the onset of autumn. It was definitely not a spring-like impulse. What had been at first virtually a curiosity, had become something else. However, even if this sea-change had not happened, she would've found the contents of his letter amazing. She let the last page fall to the desk.

She felt drained. How could a man write this, then go out about his business, as she presumed he had? It seemed unnatural—but the whole tenor of the communication was that! Unaware of doing it, she was slowly shaking her head. Her ideas, and half-formed expectations, seemed to have collapsed as swiftly as a sandbank under the waves.

In the adjoining room, William had finished reading the *Melbourne Punch* article which Isaacs, with his long-faced, Jewish look, had laid before him ten minutes before. At first, he'd thought of a customer's bankruptcy. But the headline, the opening paragraph, had instantly plunged him into the midst of a disaster of another kind. His eyes had widened.

Unbelievable! How had he managed to keep them all in the dark? However, he supposed that few friendships were rigidly continuous—gaps occurred. He'd spent a year in Europe, Wallace had, likewise… Even so!

A question struck him: Was it true? A moment's reflection on his friend's character didn't reassure him. But something of *this* nature? What had got into the man? He rose from his chair, and paced the room. He stopped in mid-stride.

'Good God!' he breathed. She mustn't find out by accident.

He had paid some attention to the evolving relationship between Wallace and Susan. He'd overheard it discussed by the women, up to a point had observed what was going on. He realized he'd felt a vague disquiet. It had his full concentration now. A protective spirit arose in his breast. For weeks, they'd been working side-by-side in an arduous common endeavour. He'd come to know her in a certain way. He took up the paper and headed for the door. He pulled up again. Blundering in could do acute harm. He didn't know how things were between them. It might be a small shock—or a large one.

Under his breath, he swore one of his rare curses. Hilda had asked him to talk to Larkin about Hanna, to bring Philip to his senses, but he'd turned her down flat. Personal relations were a minefield; Hilda seemed to have a misconceived idea that it was one of his roles in life…In this case, he had no choice.

Susan seemed to be gazing at the far wall as though it had de-materialized. He cleared his throat. She turned her clear eyes to him.

'Susan…I've something here which I think you should see. It concerns Angus Wallace. An article in this journal of a very personal nature…Of a most unpleasant nature…'

He advanced into the room. She had extended her hand. He put the journal into it. She turned her head down to the twin columns. Standing there, tensely, he guessed she read only half before putting it aside.

'It's kind of you, William. I do know of this.'

Thank God. But, he did not know what to say.

She smiled at him. 'Should we go to the basement? To see how our new venture is progressing?'

'Just the thing,' he said.

Sir John entered Chadwick's chambers in company with Barnaby. He remembered his previous visit all too well, thought of it as stepping back into a kind of Hades. Already, his handkerchief was in hand to filter the dust.

'Sir John, Barnaby,' Chadwick nodded. 'Things have been moving along, I see.'

His visitors nodded their agreement. Barnaby said, 'The summons is issued, the committal hearing's laid down to commence the 29th. You've had the other paraphernalia.'

'They're not wasting any time,' Chadwick commented. He smiled his wide-mouthed, embracing smile. 'Just as Wallace hasn't been in other directions. You've seen today's *Punch?*'

'We have,' Barnaby said.

'Clearly, someone doesn't love our diligent liquidator.'

'It could be put that way.'

'I wonder who that might be?'

The visitors were silent. The knight had his idea about it. He watched the two lawyers with eyes which had become slightly inflamed. 'Nerves,' Lady Adams had pronounced.

'Just as our liquidator doesn't love the defendants in this matter. He's after blood, you know. I watched him at the meeting. Like a damned crocodile on a sandbank waiting for someone to get in the water. He's always been a maverick—a bit of a crusader. And to take it on himself to lay charges...'

'Sometimes the knife can turn in your hand,' Barnaby suggested.

The Queen's Counsel nodded. 'Who's against us?'

'They've briefed Redmond for the committal.'

'Very well. Let's get down to tin tacks.'

And the QC did. For an hour, he and Barnaby criss-crossed the room with legal argument. Chadwick made it plain that he wished to separate Sir John from 'that parliamentary duo', to the maximum extent. The fact that Savage and Sandhurst had extra charges laid against them helped that process.

'They were pulling the wool over the eyes of Sir John in more ways than one, and that might be part of our case,' the QC said.

The knight considered this proposition in silence. It was in accord with his own thinking.

'With a modicum of luck we'll get it thrown out at the committal stage. There'll be no trial.'

'I hope so,' Sir John said, speaking for the first time.

The visitors left. The giant of a man and the small, neat, square-shaped solicitor with the terrible hat walked away in the shadow of the Law Court's dome. Sir John was blowing his nose.

'It beats me, the way these fellows talk,' he growled, mopping up. 'Crocodiles, and the like.'

'The colourful and telling phrase for a jury is what they trade in as much as anything,' Barnaby replied earnestly. 'You mustn't be put off. Metaphorically speaking, Chadwick's shot more than his share of crocodiles.'

Sir John grunted, and let it pass.

39

O what is life, if we must hold it thus
As wind-blown sparks hold momentary fire?
                    Ada Cambridge, *'Despair'*

Prisoners of Silence

AFTER THE INITIAL SHOCK, Susan appeared to coast through the remainder of the day with an equanimity which puzzled William. That evening, when he discussed it with Katherine, she understood perfectly. It was similar to the first days of some bereavements: the Lancashire woman had been more seriously involved than she'd guessed.

Sitting in Hanna's drawing-room, after dinner, there was no more 'coasting'. The breathing space she'd been allowing herself was over. She stared out the windows into the gardens with an intensity which seemed to seek out the individualistic features of each tree—to trace each yard of lighted path. Actually, she saw no detail.

In a restrained voice, she said, 'It's so strange. I'd determined to observe him in different situations. To build up a picture. The Lancashire detective on the case! That's why I went to the ball, met him at the Federal Coffee Palace, dragged you off to the bank's meeting. Each was a means to an end. To dispel the mystery, inch by inch. Suddenly, this! His past, his character exposed—as if the wind has blown mist off a mountain.'

Hanna looked thoughtful. She had read and laid aside the dramatic letter. Earlier, she'd read the *Punch* article. A short while ago she would have condemned him as much as anyone. Now she wasn't so sure. It looked very black—so black, she was suspicious. And, there'd been that little talk…She said, 'He asks for a meeting.'

Susan was silent. She'd not drunk her coffee.

Hanna tried again. 'At least, he's been honest with you.'

Susan continued to stare into the darkening trees. Here and there was a flash of russet: like a leaf or two, delicately embroidered on a velvet evening cloak. That penetrated her consciousness. She said: 'He hardly had another option. He must've known *that* was to be published.'

'What enemies he must have,' Hanna mused.

At the same instant, each of them wondered about that. What hidden enmity had brought it to light? And why, at this particular time? His letter had been silent on these aspects. Susan stood up and went to the window, her hands joined behind her back.

'*The unexpected consequence...* Those are his words. How lacking in any finer feeling. How heartless! He sends me a letter like this, what does he expect me to do? Only one response is possible from a woman who possesses *any* natural feelings.' She rounded on Hanna, suddenly looking as distraught—as beautiful—as her friend had ever seen. 'His own children—abandoned. One might, conceivably, overlook the woman, though that's hard in itself. But innocents—treated like this!'

She was shaking her head very deliberately, and her friend recognized the spark of anger always so carefully concealed in her. And, the deep disappointment.

Hanna said, 'He has supported them—apparently quite adequately.'

'Surely, you don't try to excuse it?'

'No. But, love, men have a different attitude towards their children than you or I might have. They pay them little enough attention—until they're of a certain age.'

'Not *disowning* them...keeping them hidden from the world. Prisoners of silence!' She tossed the fallen hair back from her eyes. 'That is unnatural.'

'Will you see him?'

'I don't know.'

'I think you should. I find gaps in this. I think there may be more to learn. More undisclosed history. I've a suspicion there might be...a mitigating factor.'

Susan sighed. A despairing sound which made Hanna look quickly at her. But she was not a person to break down. 'It's all beyond words. I won't see him. It would be of no use,' she said.

40

…The present Government appears to take pains to discourage the criminal prosecution of fraudulent landboomers. They refused a large proportion of the expenses incurred by Colonel Templeton (liquidator) in connection with the Premier Building Society frauds.

Table Talk, 26.8.1892

Whispers of Discord

ON THAT FATEFUL Friday night, Wallace slept fitfully. He had spent an agonized day. He kept starting into wakefulness, trying to visualize her reaction to his letter; reviewing what he'd written, questioning whether he should have sent it at all. It was a nightmarish mix-up in his mind. He didn't think beyond it to the article in *Melbourne Punch*. The letter seemed to be all that counted.

However, when he awoke on Saturday, each was dead-centre in his mind. In the pearly dawn light, the situation was absolutely clear-cut. One would have to be a super-optimist to think that his case would be anything but the blackest in *her* eyes. In the heat and haste of composition, he'd got *black* down on white, been strictly factual. Probably, a bad mistake. But it was done, and he could only wait, and hope, that she'd grant him a meeting.

He couldn't eat his breakfast and left immediately for the bank. He would throw himself into that.

Binks was drinking coffee from a flask when he arrived at the boardroom, and he accepted a cup. They sat in silence, sipping the beverage.

With a vengeance, Savage and Sandhurst had made good their threat. Those rotten partners in crime!

At ten, Philip Larkin came in bringing the barrister, Redmond. Both men regarded Wallace curiously. Philip was stiff and formal.

Wallace thought grimly: What else could he expect? Helena Spencer…His own convoluted situation, concealed from this old friend. Whether it was to be a permanent rift, time would tell. They got down to business. Redmond was to be their barrister at the committal hearings in the Police Court on the 29th. A brief had been prepared, and they went over it with him. They discussed the opposition—Chadwick QC for Sir John, and Mr Spearman for Savage, Sandhurst and Jamison Smith.

Following Katherine's note, Binks had been out to see Harbrace. He'd reported back that Savage's visit had shaken up the ex-chief accountant, though what the parliamentarian had said hadn't been extracted. Harbrace would still give his evidence. If he lasted long enough.

Wallace had decided to take a calculated risk. He wouldn't bring the sick man into the committal proceedings; he'd reserve him for the trial—assuming they got that far. Reluctantly, Larkin had accepted this strategy; another gamble.

The Government was ominously silent. The Attorney-General had not responded to Wallace's remonstrating letter, written following the Government's decision not to take over the case. However, overnight, whispers had filtered out indicating discord amongst the cabinet on the question. The men in the boardroom had no doubt this sudden perturbation was linked to the article in yesterday's *Table Talk* reporting Tuesday's meeting. It castigated the Premier for refusing to prosecute in the face of strong allegations, and evidence—a line the dailies hadn't taken up.

In the midst of his personal troubles, Wallace had smiled at Murdoch's headline: *The Premier Fiddles While the First Bank of Victoria Burns*, then down the column, *Government Closes Ranks to Protect its Own*. Despite Sandhurst's threat, no writ had been issued.

Larkin, Redmond and Binks left after twelve; Binks was going out to Prahran to check that there'd been no untoward developments following the *Punch* disclosures. The address of the house had not been given, but Savage and Sandhurst knew it. Larkin and Redmond had gone up Collins Street to their club for lunch.

Wallace returned to Albert Park to take a solitary lunch—which Mrs Beattie tried to enliven, as she served it, with local gossip. She'd been shaken by yesterday's news, though she'd had her suspicions. Her sympathies were steadfastly with her employer. She didn't understand the ins and outs of it, but had long since decided on his character.

After lunch, he decided to walk across to the lake. On another impulse, he came back into the house to pick up the stick.

The Panama hat—one of William's imports—shaded his eyes as

he gazed across the shimmering water towards a hazy St Kilda. Small waves driven by an afternoon breeze raced into the shore. A few sailboats were planing across the lake, tacking frequently in its tight dimensions. A number of conveyances were in motion on the 'Rotten Row' which roughly followed the shoreline. The cooler imprint of autumn was on the air, despite the bright sunlight. The afternoon had the tranquil pulse of perfection. He stirred gravel with the stick.

It was almost unbelievable that lives touching his could be in such an entangled, adversarial condition; that even as this afternoon breathed benignly, grim matters were being analysed, desperate remedies plotted. *Never* unbelievable. The normal condition. Today, the pulse might have dropped to a nullity, but it was an illusion.

A man was approaching. He was coming across the grass, directly towards him. Wallace turned his head, and squinted against the light. The approach was purposeful...the man was removing his hat.

'Mr Wallace, I wished to say that we're with you, sir. Right behind you.' It was the leader of the Camberwell group. 'The Government's a rotten fiasco. Take care, sir...I know we may not get a penny. But God bless you for trying. And, for doing your duty.'

He stalked off, as quickly as he'd arrived, leaving the liquidator, leaning on his stick, staring after him.

After lunch, Larkin and Redmond found high-backed wing chairs in a corner of the smoking-room, and sank into the old leather.

'An amazing business—yesterday's *Punch*,' Redmond said, throwing Larkin an oblique look. He produced a cigar, and fiddled with it. He knew Wallace and Larkin had been close for years. They'd avoided the subject during lunch.

Larkin let his eyes drift over the room. They appeared to have it to themselves. 'A big shock to me. He's played it close.'

'His business, I must say. Will it effect the case, though?'

Larkin had been thinking about this for the past two days. 'It's possible.' He thought it likely.

Redmond persisted: 'His altercation with Savage and Sandhurst, back in '88, is well known. What's a jury to make of that?'

'They might think it's time those two got their desserts.'

Redmond had his cigar alight. 'Perhaps. But now there's *this* business. It may not come up in the hearing, but it's going to be in the air.'

Larkin nodded. He understood Redmond's reservations. Probably he'd made a mistake in appointing Wallace as liquidator. That's how the cards seemed to be falling.

A member stood in the doorway, as though testing the air. A soft-looking, moon-faced, totally bald man. Suddenly he moved forward and with small feminine steps went to another corner. Larkin's attention had become riveted on him.

Sebastian Low! He hadn't seen him for years. The detective's recent report was instantly in mind. What business had Savage and Sandhurst with this man? He'd neglected to give it thought. Wallace's past? The thought came like an arrow. The mercantile agent rarely associated with, or spoke to, other members. He moved through the club like a shadow, drifting in its odd corners, merging into its dun-coloured background. Eccentric, some members thought. A few of the older brigade remembered events, and rumours from the past. A very few knew what a dangerous man he was. He sank from sight into a chair. He had certainly spotted the two lawyers.

Larkin had gone back four years to when Low had got his talons into William Boyd. Low should have gone to prison over that—but nothing had been done. Doubtless, he'd pulled strings behind the scenes in the Government to get it dropped. Probably, those papers were sealed up in perpetuity.

Seeing him had suddenly left a taste of brass in his mouth, tightened his nerves. Redmond was saying something about Wallace, but he hardly heard it. Was Low still plotting to settle that old score with William Boyd? Had he seen an opening in the liquidation to deal himself back into that vendetta? Or was there other game in his sights?

'He's going to be in the witness-box,' Redmond was saying, 'and we'll want him as quiet and correct as you please, no speeches, or comments on the perfidy he obviously sees all around him. Chadwick might try to get him going, but we can't have it…'

Larkin nodded absently, still thinking.

41

See those resplendent creatures, as they glide
  O'er scarlet carpet, between footmen tall,
  From sumptuous carriage to effulgent hall —
A dazzling vision in their pomp, and pride!
           Ada Cambridge, 'Fashion'

The Lady in the Lake

THREE, OR FOUR? Philip Larkin had lost count of the circuits Helena's equipage had made of the 'Rotten Row' around Albert Park Lake. They were going at a brisk clip, and he supposed the horses would soon tire. He hoped so; he was feeling ridiculous being whirled around and around like this to no particular destination, amid the strident odours of horse-sweat, polish and leather. He smiled to himself: The undulating motion reminded him of being in her majestic, well-sprung bed.

On this Sunday afternoon, a variegated traffic was out, and Helena's barouche with its fifteen-coats of shimmering paintwork, hand-rubbed between each coat, its gleaming harness, and its matched pair of sixteen-hand bay geldings, caught the eye.

They were the survivors, Larkin reflected. In the late '80s, it would've been a traffic jam; today, numerous second-hand equipages were abandoned on allotments, and he'd heard the famous coach-builder Pickles' had sacked hundreds.

The hats and parasols of the human survivors fluttered in the breeze. *En passant*, cries of acknowledgment were made. Here was the equestrian equivalent of the Block's pedestrian parade. In the band-stand, Herr Plock's band sent their music across the glittering water, setting the tone for this social cut and thrust. Over the lake, following their own rituals, seagulls wheeled and squawked.

The breeze in her face, silk and ribbons flying, Helena Spencer loved the speed and the smooth-sprung rhythm of these outings—which her driver had nick-named 'the Sunday spin'—just as she loved her Thursday appearances and foot-promenades on the Block—circulating in the airy, Milan-inspired galleries of smart coffee houses, music shops and booksellers.

Vanity Fair, Larkin thought, uncritically…

Continuously, they were overtaking other vehicles; none of whose occupants were acknowledging them, but it didn't matter. The scene was much more animated than when Wallace had taken his stroll there yesterday…

Wallace! She was thinking of him, a pensive smile on her lips. On Friday evening, she'd roamed through the Parisian elegance of her house, champagne glass in hand, marvelling at the news—at the man. 'Wallace, you certainly had your reasons,' she'd repeated to herself several times, shaking her head. 'You certainly did!' It was exciting to get to the bottom of such a mystery. She wondered which way he would go now. To his ruination? She detested that idea.

Larkin had removed his hat to his lap. He was giving himself a rest from the liquidation—and the liquidator. His normally pleasant countenance had a restrained, even depressed air. Like the liquidator, he was showing the strain. Apart from the cares of the liquidation, he had a busy practice to run. He'd cast critical eyes over Helena's affairs, had concluded that they were soundly constituted, wished all his clients were so well placed.

For the past week, she had excluded him from her bed. It was not the usual reason. She had said nothing, but there was a new atmosphere between them—a hint of expectation in the air. Larkin wasn't obtuse. He knew that he'd been given a taste of honey, and now a declaration was expected. It was a watershed, and he felt as if he were gazing down a slippery, reverse slope into deep water. Murky water!

'Why so glum, Philip?' She cast him an amused look.

'Do you think we might stop soon?'

'This is good for you. Taking the air, blowing all those legal tangles out of your head. Enjoy it, my dear.'

He inclined his head slightly, settled resignedly into the leather upholstery, and squinted against the refracted light from the lake. Did she need that tiger-skin rug?

They had never discussed Wallace, not even this recent imbroglio. She appeared to have shut the door, irrevocably, on that interlude…What a lovely woman she was. He glanced at the classic profile, the slightest of aquiline noses, the green, summing-up eyes, the delicious movement of the abundant bosom. And, here was an intellect, which, day-by-day, seemed to be de-constructing his own.

He now understood, perfectly well, Wallace's motives in attempting to advise him. In his state of infatuation it had been a shock to be spoken to thus. He gazed ahead.

A carriage wheel was spinning away towards the lake of its own volition. He watched it go its solitary way—as if with an academic eye. Seconds later:

'Good God!' he exclaimed.

The victoria ahead was upright but wavering, then it was tilting, the wheel-minus side hit the tan and it slewed towards the lake gouging out earth, spraying it skywards...

A woman was screaming. Helena had gripped his arm.

'Stop!' he was shouting to the driver.

With a great splash, the victoria went into the lake.

Rearing and squealing, still on the shore, the two horses, hopelessly entangled, were anchored by the conveyance which was half in the water. The driver was lying motionless on the grass...

The passenger? He'd noticed her, vaguely, a minute or so before. Now she was nowhere in sight. People were shouting, carriages being pulled up.

Larkin dropped to the ground before their own had stopped, staggered, regained his balance, ran the ten paces to the lake-side, leapt in. He didn't feel the shock of the water—immediately up to his chest. The near side was too high for him. He waded fast around the rear; he could get in this side. He couldn't see her. God! Was she under the water? The victoria was slipping off the embankment. He flung back the door. She was lying on the floor, arms stretched over her head.

When he waded to the shore, other men leaned down to take her from his arms. She was small and light as a feather. A woman in her late thirties. Two men in top hats were holding the horses. Several women took his hands and helped him out of the lake, the water draining from him, squelching in his shoes.

Two gentlemen's cutaway coats had been laid on the grass and the inert woman on top of them. Women were kneeling beside her.

'Is she alive?'—someone asked.

A man hurried up from the lake-side walk. A tall, rangy man in black suit and a wide-brimmed black hat...A white face, with dense black side-whiskers shot with some grey. He'd tossed away a cheroot. 'Stand back, I'm a doctor,' he said.

He knelt down, took her pulse, laid his head against her breast, listened. He took a small bottle from his pocket, pulled out its stopper, placed if under her nose. Immediately, her eye-lids fluttered. 'Be calm, you are all right,' he said. He began to examine for broken bones.

Feeling like a bystander, Philip watched. The doctor was named Blackstone—a medical man, but an alienist. He'd not seen him for years.

'It's Mrs Chadwick,' a woman said. 'We will take her home. Doctor…?'

Helena was by his side. 'Come, we must get you home and dried,' she said. 'There's nothing more we can do.'

They left the scene and the circuit, headed for St Kilda and his house. Dr Blackstone had been attending to the driver, who was complaining of a headache. Not the usual type of headache Blackstone looked after, Larkin thought drily. He was flooding the floor of Helena's equipage.

She was looking at him intensely, he realized. A new kind of look. 'You are going to be everyone's hero over this,' she said.

'I was in no danger.'

'No matter, you are certainly mine.'

42

Without hail or tempest,
Blue sword or flame,
Love came so lightly
I knew not that he came.
Shaw Neilson,
'Love's Coming'

Tactics of the Heart

HIS IMMERSION in Albert Park Lake had not done Philip Larkin any harm. In fact, it could be said that it had done him some good. In the days following the incident, friends and acquaintances had congratulated him on his quick thinking—even bravery—in coming to the aid of Mrs Chadwick. The Queen's Counsel wrote: *Dear Larkin, Mrs Chadwick and I are greatly indebted to you for your prompt and courageous act on Sunday. We shall not forget it. Mrs Chadwick is quite recovered, I am glad to say. Yours ever, Richard Chadwick.*

This brought a blush to Larkin's cheeks. He meditated on how remarkably interweaved lives were in this metropolis—in '89, he'd retained Chadwick to defend William in the case involving Sebastian Low; now Chadwick was against them, defending Sir John; the QC's wife had come out of the lake in his arms! Dr Blackstone, who he hadn't set eyes on for years, had materialized at the scene! It's a village, Hilda Wilberforce had pronounced, and she was right.

Certainly, it had done him some good with Helena. He knew she'd seen something new in him. That this was the outcome of such a minor incident, he found slightly ridiculous—similar to the interminable circuits of the lake. While the vivacious and worldly widow had previously seen certain qualities in him, she had been looking for something extra; she'd found it. Now, she was satisfied.

'You are my hero,' she'd exclaimed lightly, with a flash of those eyes which disguised the serious impact it had had on her. Thus, the adroit pressure of her personality, of her sex, was brought to bear even more forcibly on him; she now anticipated a blessed event, to be consummated in St Paul's Cathedral.

'What in damnation should I do?' he muttered to himself. He felt no lessening of his passion. But he was beginning to feel trapped. It was quite clear that a decision was waiting to be made—and he was finding it devilishly hard to make it.

On the Thursday morning, the announcement that Hanna Dewhurst was waiting to see him jolted him out of the glassy stare he'd fixed on the turgid deed on his blotter. In a moment, he felt back in the past.

Hanna swept in from the ante-room, as though she were racing to the back of her store to get a book for a customer in a hurry. She was dressed in an autumn walking dress—a russet tweed, bell-shaped affair. Her hair, in a narrow coiffure, had set upon it a small cavalier hat with green feathers. The brisk air in her walk up Collins Street had tinted her cheeks with a rosy glow. She exuded good health and good humour, and the modish costume accentuated the generous curves of her hips and bosom. In part, it was a facade beneath which she was inwardly shaking. The pace of her arrival was an excuse for her breathlessness.

Larkin had got to his feet—seemed to have been struck dumb.

'Philip! Everyone's talking about how you saved Mrs Chadwick. What a wonder!' He was pulling a chair around for her. At a glance, she took in his worn and wary appearance.

'I hope you're all right?' She sat down, sitting slightly forward. She dropped her gaze to her hands folded tensely on her lap.

He flushed with embarrassment. 'A little wading in the Albert Park Lake isn't going to hurt me.'

He was back behind his desk, wondering…uneasily… Hanna had never come to his office before. Surely she wouldn't have come for *that*?

She lifted her head, smiled brightly, concealing her nerves. 'I did wish to make sure you were all right, to congratulate you, but I must admit, I've come also to seek your advice on a business matter.'

Larkin's relief was perceptible.

'The insurance on my store expires on the 31st March. Here's the existing policy. Half of Melbourne's businesses seem to be going up in flames! I'm not so comfortable with my present arrangements. What would you advise?'

He took the policy which she'd removed from a small valise and glanced through it. 'Will the value of stock remain the same?'

'Yes.'

'Hmm. The replacement cost of the building, fixtures and fittings, shouldn't need alteration.'

'No.'

He hesitated. He couldn't see anything wrong with this insurer. However...'I'd recommend Liverpool and Lancashire. I know them well. I could arrange for them to take over the cover.'

'Would you? I'd be so grateful.'

'I'll attend to it.'

A long, silent moment. He felt that images of all the dances at the club's ball might be in motion in her mind. That scene was uncomfortably in his own. She was frowning slightly, looking towards the window, nonetheless he felt under an acute observation.

'We don't see much of you these days. I hope it's only temporary.' She couldn't resist this.

His hands fidgeted on the blotter. 'I'm run over with work. This liquidation business.'

'And, what a business it is.' She rose to her feet. 'Susan and I were at the meeting. I trust Angus Wallace is bearing up?'

Larkin considered this. 'He is.'

She was offering her hand. Having made a tactical advance, she made a tactical withdrawal. Until the previous evening, she had been quite happy with the performance of her existing insurers. She hoped they wouldn't be too hurt. It was amazing what was lying close to hand for use when you needed it.

And—he did *not* have the appearance of the love-lorn swain. Her impression was that he was a man in a tight corner. With Angus Wallace's remarks held like a talisman in her mind, her heart rejoiced as she walked up Bourke Street.

43

Victoria Gardens were dedicated in 1885...construction of the sunken oval, symmetrical paths, forested mount and formal garden beds took another two years. The layout, by...William Sangster, was complemented by the magnificent gift of a renaissance fountain, statue of Victory and terracotta vases by a former mayor, George Taylor. The gardens were named in honour of his wife.

The Age, Melbourne's Great Outdoors Parks,
Waterways and Trails

Midnight's the Hour

IN THE WEEK following the *Punch* revelations, Wallace threw himself into preparing for the committal hearing. It hadn't been proof against his downheartedness. Each night, he'd eagerly inspected the post on the hall table. Each night, he'd been disappointed. He imagined an implacable silence had descended on the house at Carlton Gardens; that conversations were being held in hushed voices, as though there'd been a fatal accident; that his name was unmentionable. This only slightly resembled the reality.

On Wednesday night he was in bed, had drifted into an uneasy sleep when he was awoken by a tremendous banging on the front door. He sat up. Midnight? He threw on a dressing-gown and went downstairs. All the gas-lights had been turned off. Mrs Beattie, white nightgowned, appeared in the hallway, an oil-lamp in hand.

'What is it, Mrs Beattie?' he said. The banging had stopped. It hadn't been the knocker, he realized.

'How should I know.'

He slip-slapped across the hall in his slippers, drew back the bolt, cautiously opened the door—on an empty portico. He stepped outside and looked up and down the street. Deserted. A breeze flicked at his hair. The street-lights glowed eerily. Across the way, the moon cast a white riband on the oil-black lake. A kind of mockery came at him.

'No-one,' he said over his shoulder. But he'd seen the paper nailed to the door. He turned and plucked it off, tried to get the nail out but couldn't. He went inside and closed the door. 'This,' he said to his housekeeper. She looked amazed.

'What in Heaven's name?...'

He brought it to the lamp, already knowing its nature. He stared at the irregular, pasted-on letters...Mrs Beattie's face, in the oil-lamp, had a bronzed sheen—seemed cast in intensity and mystification.

'What is it, Mr Wallace?' She put her hand over her breast, abruptly conscious of them standing together in their night-clothes.

'Nothing to worry about. Someone's queer idea of delivering a message. One would have thought the post-box might have sufficed.'

She was not reassured. Beneath her night-gown, her shapely knees, which no-one but she ever saw, were aching with rheumatism. The faint odour of Solomon's Solution drifted in the hall. It wasn't working. Everything seemed at sixes and sevens.

The next morning he tossed it down on the board table. 'Here we go again,' he said. 'Nailed to my front door last night around midnight. No sign of anyone when I came down.'

'Nailed?' Binks read:

THE WAGES OF SIN IS DEATH.

Wallace stood watching his clerk. 'What's that detective up to?...Better get him in. I think what we have here is someone playing games, and I'm deuced tired of it.'

Binks cogitated: A reasonable reaction.

The caretaker knocked on the door and brought in a letter. Wallace opened it. He laughed quietly. 'The Attorney-General acknowledges my letter, wants to see me.'

'Took his time,' Binks said, and thought: What's next?

Which was precisely the question in Wallace's mind as he was ushered into the Attorney's room. Nothing had changed here—except Crown Prosecutor Danby stood by the ex-Premier's desk.

'There you are, Wallace. You know Danby, of course.'

Wallace shook hands with them. And the big, round-shouldered man waved them to the leather chairs.

'That letter of yours. I haven't come back to you on it for several reasons. Pressure of business is one...'

But the least pertinent, the liquidator thought, though the parliament had been locked till midnight in debate over a rather noxious Bill this past week. They sat down.

'So, you've begun this ill-advised prosecution.'

Wallace let 'ill-advised' go by.

'You won't get very far, you know. It'll be thrown out at the committal hearings. Killed stone-dead.'

'How do you know?' Wallace said levelly. He'd observed Danby's face flinch at the Attorney's assertion.

'My dear fellow, I've read a summary of the evidence you sent…Weak stuff, for a magistrate and a bench of justices of the peace in this city. Against people of the reputation you're trying to impugn.'

'Oh? That's an interesting conclusion. The evidence's iron-clad,' the liquidator said coolly.

The Attorney opened and closed his large, white hands in the air, ignored the remark. 'Not to mention the *possibility* of an ulterior motive. The bench will know of your stand-off with Savage and Sandhurst. Thinking men put weight on that kind of thing.'

'I find the proposition insulting.'

The Attorney shrugged. 'Wallace, I'm giving you the views of the Premier—and the cabinet. Commonsense views.'

Wallace thought: Not *all* the cabinet, if the rumours are right.

'And something else has come up. Certain shareholders have approached the Government…questioning your use of the bank's limited funds…for a purpose…which won't recover one brass razoo for the liquidation…' He beat his soft hand softly on to the armrest, emphasizing each phrase. Amid the glittering spray of diamonds on his fingers a solitary ruby glowed potently.

'Expense I'm incurring, because the Government's failing in its duty. I've a contrary view on what might be recovered.'

Danby was sitting like a statue.

'"Failing in its duty". Now *that's* insulting. You want to be a bit careful, Wallace.' The Attorney glowered at the liquidator.

Theatrics, he doesn't give a damn about the remark, Wallace thought.

'These people say that every extra day the liquidation spins out, another ten pounds goes in your pocket. They want it finished up.'

Wallace stared at the ex-Premier, didn't respond.

'Vexatious, hopeless and wrong-headed. You'd be best advised to drop it. Get on with the liquidation proper. Do your duty, man!'

He studied the liquidator from under his prolific and ragged eyebrows. 'Remember the old adage: People in glass houses shouldn't throw stones.' He was referring to the disclosures in *Punch*. The propagandist organ of his party and of the conservative upper house. He was a blunt man, his fixed ideas mainly revolving around the interests of himself and colleagues. But he was also cunning and ruthless.

'Is that all you wish to discuss?'

'It's enough, isn't it?'

'I'll bid you good day then.'

Wallace heaved himself up and walked out leaving the two men staring after him. When he was in Spring Street, he wondered if Danby had told the Attorney of his approach to him. He suspected that he hadn't, otherwise the parliamentarian would have thrown that in, too. The Crown Prosecutor had sat there like the Sphinx awaiting the next sand-storm.

At a few minutes to four o'clock, Detective Rudd arrived at the bank. Before ringing the bell at the side-entrance, he reinstated the high-polish of his brown boots' toecaps with a small cloth he carried, then brushed flecks of lint from his bowler. You had to be on your mettle when reporting to clients. He rang the bell, and was admitted by the caretaker. As he followed the man into the dusty twilight, he thought about what he was going to say. He was now convinced that he was looking in the right direction—an incident had persuaded him so.

On Friday, it had been a long wait. What had happened was this: the check-suited man, who looked like an *habitué* of the racecourse and public bar, stayed inside the house until nearly midnight. It was as black as the ace of spades when he re-appeared and slipped away in the direction of the Victoria Gardens. He picked up a bit of pace and the detective wondered if he'd been spotted. The man entered the gardens, and vanished amongst the tree trunks.

Rudd knew there was only one exit—in High Street—and he cut across the grass in that direction. The place seemed deserted, was coolish. Leaves drifted down into his face, alighted on his shoulders.

The next thing that hit him was not soft. Right across the back of the neck. With a bone-shaking impact. The ground came up at him, lights were flashing before his eyes.

He came to—after several minutes—with his face in a patch of damp turf; with a quite remarkable headache. He stood up unsteadily. Beside him the dark, bronze statue of Victory loomed up. He put his hand on it for support.

'You've been pole-axed, Rudd,' he advised himself. He felt for his watch, his purse, both were present. He leaned on the statue massaging the back of his neck. Otto Rudd had a short, thick neck. On an occasion like this, his forebears deserved a vote of thanks.

It seemed the five acres of Victoria Gardens had been abandoned by humanity—including his attacker. The trees sighed in a breeze. The sunken garden resembled the black waters of a lake. The leaves from the planes girdling it continued their silent descent. With his cross-grained humour, it struck him that the gardens had imposed a non-committal atmosphere—were denying liability on behalf of the municipality. He continued to rub the back of his neck.

He had no way of telling whether his assailant was the check-suited man, or another—which was fairly unsatisfactory. In most parks, homeless men were sleeping under bushes...But if another, to what purpose? He still had his valuables.

In the days following, he kept watch on the house but saw no-one coming or going. The occupants didn't come out at all while he was watching. He'd gone and read *The Age* files covering a few weeks in '88 when his client had been locked in combat in the courts with the two land-booming politicians. He'd done that because he was thorough. He hadn't had much hope of it. However, he felt he'd confirmed his instinct that it was the wrong track. An ex-Government Minister of the stripe of his client, a barrister in the courts specializing in controversial cases, must have enemies. But people who sent messages of this kind were a special breed. This affair was close to home. The check-suited man's the key, he'd told himself...

'Wait here,' the caretaker said.

Rudd took off his bowler, and again massaged the back of his neck. It was going to be a difficult interview.

'Well, Mr Rudd,' Wallace said, when the detective was seated at the board table, 'Mr Larkin's given us good reports of your work...What have you been able to do for us?'

The detective looked unblinkingly at the liquidator. 'I've been watching the house at Douglas Street, Prahran.'

Wallace and Binks glanced at each other. 'Go on,' the liquidator said.

'I've come round to thinking that these communications are close to home...'

'Close to home? How did you reach that conclusion?'

Rudd's hands were calmly joined on the dusty table which he'd observed needed a polish. He wasn't going to explain his rather instinctive mental processes. There's a gent—no, not a gent—who I've seen going into that house ...' He described the check-suited man in detail. 'And he's set my fire-bell ringing. Maybe you know him?'

Wallace's analytical brown eyes regarded the detective. So, he'd turned up again. This was a surprise. He pondered, his face expressionless. A line of thinking had opened up.

'I do. His name's Julian Ellis. He's the brother of the lady living there.'

Aha, Rudd thought. He said: 'Do you know where *he* lives?'

'No. He's been away for years—in Queensland.'

Rudd waited for more, but the liquidator appeared immersed in his thoughts. Suddenly, he pushed last night's communication across the table at the detective.

'This was nailed to my front door last night.'

Rudd read it. 'A reader of *Table Talk*,' he said. Again the capitals matched the typography of that journal. Wallace and Binks looked surprised.

The liquidator said, 'I don't know whether I'm dealing with a madman, a prankster, or a religious crank. Whether to take account of it, or not. I'd be obliged if you could sort it out. Expeditiously.'

The detective nodded. 'Someone struck me on the back of the neck the other night…laid me out. It might've been this Ellis.'

Wallace absorbed this. 'Unlikely, he's an individual not given to such violence. A weak man.'

None of: 'I hope you're recovered. No ill effects, I trust.' Rudd was amusing himself. All in a day's work for a detective.

'Nothing weak about that blow. Does his turning up ring any bells?' Obviously it had, the detective concluded.

'You might talk to him,' Wallace said. 'I'd be interested to know what he's up to…why he's back.' He looked at Binks. 'Of course, we could ask her…Maybe not. As for him being connected to *these* damn things. I doubt it.'

Binks showed the detective out.

'Not Savage and Sandhurst?' the clerk inquired in the corridor.

'Not their way. I'd be looking for something more direct and dangerous from that pair, if I was you.'

The detective sauntered off into the autumn evening. He was sure he was on the right track now—weak man or not. Yes, close to home. Always the first place to look. He was close to Bourke Street, and there was an open-air coffee stall where they served it hot and strong—loaded with the chicory and burnt sugar he favoured. He'd look in there for a bit. *The Leader* was in his pocket. He was looking forward to reading an item on the Panama scandal. The chief of the Paris detective force had resigned in the face of allegations. Juicy stuff!

44

The unemployed seem now to be always with us. They appear in our streets…in battalions. Not, as in the old country, making importunate and impossible demands—not incurring ridicule by their bizarre appearance and protestations, but in manly, honest and respectable…style, endeavouring to move the Government to action…

Illustrated Australian News, 1.5.1893

Labyrinth

'WHAT WILL YOU DO?' Hanna stared at Susan across the breakfast table. No need to be specific as to subject; in the household, one had predominated since that issue of *Punch*.

The Lancashire woman glanced at her friend, glanced towards the windows. The foliage in the gardens was quite tinted now. She found comfort in the notion of the city's seasonal rhythms continuing, heedless of human affairs, her own life.

'I've not decided.' Despite the apparent finality of her remark on Saturday night, it was still an open question.

Hanna's gaze had not deviated from Susan's face. 'He'll be waiting for a reply. Whatever you decide to do, is it fair to let him wait so long without a word?'

'Fair?…I don't wish to be vindictive, but is fairness a quality which he's applied to his…family?'

Hanna was silent.

'Who knows what the children—the woman—feel in their hearts?'

'You cannot know, unless you go closer.'

Susan became calmer. 'In his letter, he didn't explain all. For instance, is he married to this unfortunate woman, or not? What kind of a situation am I looking at?'

'That's why you should see him. I surmise he'll make a clean breast of it. Then, you can decide. You can imagine the haste in which he wrote that letter.'

Susan's instinct was to end it. But she was deep in an entangle-ment of conflicting emotions—and curiosity wasn't the least of them. It was a knot in her brain teasing to be untied. A labyrinth. A facile metaphor, but she wasn't her usual decisive or pragmatic self.

Hanna shook her head. 'I think there's more to it.'

Susan smiled sadly, perplexedly. 'I hope you're right, otherwise my judgment has been totally astray, though it's hard to believe anything could outweigh the gravest breach of duty.' She thought: But is that all I'm concerned about?

Hanna, was thinking of her own dilemma, her call on Philip. She said, 'Hardy wrote: "The paths of love are rougher/ Than thorough-fares of stones." You should be ready for twists and turns. That will be the way of it.'

Susan took the bookseller's last words with her on the tram. When she walked into the store, she put them aside. The entrance to Boyd & Montrose had been transformed. Miss Pettifer's elegant Flemish laces, Italian black-stitched kid gloves, delicate ivory-sticked fans, no longer greeted the customer in the premier show-cases. Miss Pettifer had herself gone into retirement at bay-side Mentone. Instead, plainer trimmings in brocade and velvet from the Midlands were displayed.

On the ground-floor, marble steps, previously blocked off and concealed, descended to the basement. A decorative arch had been constructed by their window-dresser, above which *Bargain Basement* was inscribed in gold paint. 'The entrance to golden opportunities,' the advertisement in *The Age* had announced. And, old and new cus-tomers were passing beneath this portal. For the month of March to date, sales were up twenty per cent. Much dead or slow-moving stock had been converted to cash—albeit at a book loss. However, that wasn't the sole source of stock for the basement.

At ten o'clock, Isaacs appeared in her door, an unusual excite-ment about him. 'Miss Fairfax, one of the delivery men reports a large fire at Raymonds in Richmond—the towel-makers. Might be an opportunity?'

Susan stood up. 'Thanks, Mr Isaacs, I'll see Mr Boyd.'

She had given instructions for the delivery men, as they went about the suburbs, to keep a lookout for fires. Already, she'd twice secured slightly damaged goods at knockdown prices for profitable dis-posal in the basement. This had stimulated Isaacs. He was keeping his own lookout. He'd smiled at her and said, 'Cases of Jewish lightning, eh?'

She hurried into William's room.

They left ten minutes later in a hansom. It took fifteen minutes to reach the factory at Richmond. Fire appliances from the Central Brigade were in attendance. The fire was out, though a black streamer of smoke still curled above the suburb. The building was intact, except the roof at the rear had fallen in. A crowd was disbursing.

'Could have been worse,' a Raymond son said, shaking hands with William and acknowledging the commiserations. He knew why they'd come. 'Most of the machines were saved, and we're insured, though not for enough. Have a look around, but be careful—especially you, miss.'

In a corner they found stacks of cotton towels, liberally sprinkled with cinders, damp from water.

'The cinders are superficial, only on the top layer. The water-spoiling minimal. Most will be all right. We can sell them at 1s 6d a piece.' She walked around, pulling out bundles, examining the condition. She estimated the quantity.

William went off to talk to young Raymond, made him an offer. The son went to see the father who was busy in another part of the factory. A counter-offer was made, accepted, and William wrote out a cheque. 'Our dray'll be here within the hour,' he said. They went back to town.

'Mr Robertson was our driver who reported it,' Susan said.

'I'll see he has an extra pound in his pay packet.'

William looked at the line of shipping along the river wharfs as they clattered down Flinders Street, weaving in an out of the drays drawn by heavy-duty horses. He looked the other way towards the seamen's eateries, unclean public houses, chandlery places, pawnbrokers. He saw none of it, was thinking about the changes Susan had brought in.

The first shipments from England of low- and medium-cost drapery had arrived, were on their floors. The Grocery Department had been closed—after a massive sale—and he'd found a buyer for the liquor licence. Credit sales had been discontinued—which had put a burden of explanation and liaison on his shoulders with old customers—and they were advertising cheaper prices for cash, and free deliveries to the suburbs.

The basement...and a host of other changes. It was early days, but it seemed to be working. For the first time in twelve months, cash in was exceeding cash out, and they were working well within the Commercial Bank's limit. Meeting the wages bill each Thursday wasn't the nightmare it had been.

We're hanging on by the skin of our teeth, he thought.

But perhaps not. The overdraft of £7,500 called up by the First Bank of Victoria still hung in the balance. He'd taken legal advice, sought a postponement, but it'd have to be settled by the end of the month. It'd given him a queer feeling to see the demand under Angus's and Philip's signatures. But business was business, and the law was the law. They'd reached no conclusion on what to do. They were facing things day to day.

Since he'd laid that wretched edition of *Punch* before her, they'd not exchanged a word concerning Angus Wallace. He had a shrewd idea that the matter hadn't been resolved. He'd been making up his mind to say something. Now seemed like an ideal opportunity. He looked at her.

'This business with Angus Wallace has shocked and mystified his friends. Regardless of it, I consider him a sound and honourable man. And a stout friend.'

He'd faced back to the front, but was conscious that she was now looking at him. Was that a sigh?

'Thank you, William. One should stand up for old friends.' Now she was gazing out the window at the passing squalor.

45

Count Leon Tolstoi is engaged on a new novel…Guy de Maupassant has so far recovered his mental health to leave the lunatic asylum…has seen his publisher with a view to a forthcoming volume of short stories…Zola has got three books on the stocks; first, Dr Pascal…

Literary Gossip, The Leader, 11.2.1893

Sticky Wicket

HELENA SPENCER entered Dewhurst's book shop with two clear objects in mind. The subordinate one was to buy a copy of a book which had been recently advertised. Behind her, the revolving brass-framed glass door continued to revolve with a subtle swish-swish-swish, as if hinting at literary delights in store.

Eleven o'clock on a Friday, not many customers. She swept up the main aisle dressed in a high-waisted, reddish-brown walking costume, a waistcoat of white silk brocaded with coloured flowers, black gloves, black buckskin rounded-toe shoes, a charming russet cavalier hat fixed with a large black buckle. A delicate umbrella was carried against showers. The whole effect was of autumn personified. She exuded self-assurance, patronage, and good humour. She drew quick and admiring looks from the assistants. At the central four-sided counter, she asked for Miss Dewhurst.

The book shop, one of Melbourne's finest, possibly only surpassed by Coles' Book Arcade with its million books, was organized as follows: each side of that well-known door, two bow windows fronted the street (displaying on this day, cricket bats of dark-varnished English willow, cherry-red stitched leather balls, and a selection of cricketing books, to mark the Intercolonial match with West Australia). The main aisle was flanked by tables of new books. These ended at the before-mentioned counter. In this vicinity were set out a dozen crimson velvet chairs for the comfort of customers.

Beyond this space, very high oak shelves in close rows gave to the imaginative the idea of a forest of tall-timber, penetrated by half a dozen glades. At the rear was a receiving and dispatch room, and beside it the large room, previously occupied by Hanna's father, now occupied by her. Mrs Spencer was shown in.

In what could only be described as an unguarded moment, Philip had mentioned Hanna's visit to his office. Helena Spencer had received this information without comment. She knew at once the reason for it. Previous to this 'incident', though she'd not used words, she'd made it crystal clear to him what she expected. She'd observed his consequent irresolution and nerves. She could manage that.

'My dear Miss Dewhurst,' she said smiling, 'what a marvellous establishment! And here you are, in full control, at the *centre* of management.'

Hanna was taken aback at her rival's manifestation before her eyes. How else could she regard her? Though they were hardly on equal terms; she had little doubt that Mrs Spencer and Philip were sexually intimate. She thought, grimly: What on earth does she want? However, the bookseller was no novice to the cut and thrust of the business life, and that had overlapping qualities.

She said, 'Centre of management's a little grand.'

'But you're so good at *trade*.'

Hanna gave the widow-about-town a look. 'One tries to do something useful.'

Mrs Spencer's brilliant, green-eyed gaze surveyed the thirty-year-old woman. She had never paid her attention before. Her instant verdict: Attractive—in a simple, fresh-complexioned way. A certain briskness of manner, clearly efficient. But not *interesting*. Yet, had she sown unlikely seeds in Philip? Naturally, desperate for a husband. She divined the pent-up passion in that shapely, abundant body. The spinster's fate.

Under this searching gaze, Hanna thought: This is intolerable. God, don't let me colour up.

Mrs Spencer smiled. 'I would like a copy of Mr Deakin's *Temple and Tomb in India* which you've advertised.'

'Of course.' Hanna rang a bell on her desk.

She thought: She's thirty-eight if she's a day. Three years older than Philip.

Mrs Spencer maintained her gaze, her white-gloved hands resting on the handle of her umbrella. The pose of the superior woman addressing the inferior, Hanna thought. She had not coloured. She felt quite cool and collected. It was a situation made for a cool head. She knew now, precisely, why Mrs Spencer was here. An assistant came in, received the instruction.

Helena Spencer got down to it. 'I've been re-reading Miss Austen's *Emma*.' This was a lie but it was a convenient ploy. 'What a romantic tangle! Poor Emma, so deluded. Frank Churchill paying her attention but it's all a sham. Secretly, he's courting, is engaged to, Jane *Fairfax*—your friend's namesake, I think?'

Hanna listened to this, trying to take the meaning. She guessed there was a message in it. She frowned, projected her mind to the fictional sphere Mrs Spencer seemed bent on. 'Frank Churchill wasn't a straightforward man.'

'My dear Miss Dewhurst, it's the way men are! They keep their clandestine affairs under wraps. Say one thing, mean another. Recently, we've had a blatant example in our midst.'

With a small shock, the bookseller realized she was speaking of Angus Wallace.

'And—Emma was jealous when she found out…but he wasn't the man for her.'

Hanna shrugged slightly, still puzzled.

Mrs Spencer's eyes were amused. 'It's fascinating. I think all this novel-reading we women of the leisured class do, is grist to the mills of our own lives.'

Hanna remained silent. She wasn't of the leisured class, didn't agree with that.

Mrs Spencer's lips teased into the slightest smile. 'So many lessons. But you'd know so much better than I.' She paused, changed direction. 'Fortunate Mrs Chadwick, coming out of the lake in *his* arms.'

Hanna stared at this. 'I hope she's recovered.' Suddenly, she had worked it out.

'Quite. A letter from Chadwick said so. Naturally, they're most grateful to Philip. As we all are for his attentions.' She paused again, and inspected her finely stitched gloves, came back on course—if she'd ever been off it. 'It's so wonderful to find one's soul-mate. One feels—so uplifted.'

Swish-swish-swish, Helena Spencer, parcel in hand, went out into Collins Street to be greeted by the chilly tail-end of a passing shower. The elegant umbrella was opened in an instant. She headed downhill to lunch alone in the dining-room reserved for ladies at Parer's Crystal Cafe, in Elizabeth Street, thinking that Miss Dewhurst might be a harder nut to crack than she'd anticipated, but not disquieted by the thought one bit.

Hanna sat down. She had never had to deal with anything like this before. However, the fact that Helena Spencer had thought it necessary to come to her in this way *must* mean she wasn't so certain of Philip. It added substance to the euphoric feeling she'd had as she'd left his office. She smiled brightly. Fancy, *Emma* as a metaphor for her situation!

Shaking her head, she went out to the counter. She rather fancied that in going to see Philip, she'd gone into bat on a sticky wicket—as the cricketers said. That was a metaphor with a bit more grit to it.

46

*The bolt of justice has fallen on five banking criminals, and the law
has thus avenged itself on the three directors, the manager and the
auditor of the Anglo-Australian Bank.*

The Age, 9.3.1893

Out of the World

'CALL ANGUS ALEXANDER WALLACE.'

At twenty past eleven, on the 29th March, the liquidator entered
the witness-box in the City Police Court, rested his hands lightly on
the railing and looked around. The gallery was packed. People stood
at the back, overflowed into the corridor, voices, coughs and stirring
coalesced into an inharmonious pot-pourri. He gave these observers
and bystanders only a cursory look. They were anonymous to him. His
mind was concentrated on the evidence he was to give, on the main
participants. He took a deep breath.

The bar table had been extended and around it barristers manoeuvred for elbow room; a similar party of solicitors were ranked behind
them, Philip Larkin among them.

There had been a sensation already. Jamison Smith had not
answered the summons. His counsel had reported that inquiries over
recent days elicited that he and his family had sailed for England a
month since. Reluctantly, the magistrate had issued a bench-warrant
for his arrest.

Stupid man, Wallace had thought, catching Binks' eye.

Skedaddled, the clerk thought.

Sitting in their places, Savage and Sandhurst had heard this—
Sandhurst, with a smooth, uninvolved demeanour, Savage, with a
trace of self-satisfaction. Argument had taken place on it between the
opposing counsel, Chadwick had wanted an adjournment, but it was
denied.

Sir John Adams stared into space. Is he acting? Wallace wondered. To the liquidator, this 'other-worldly' detachment from the man

of affairs seemed counterfeit.

Up in the gallery, in the midst of that anonymity, Lady Adams, gazing at her husband, her thin lips compressed, was almost as much at a loss on the knight's mental processes. Pale, but quite in control, she was noting each detail. Delicately, she held a posy of violets which a well-wisher had presented to her.

'Why won't they get on with it?' she said in her distinct voice to Hilda Wilberforce.

'Hush, they are.' The East Melbourne matron hated this life-denying, joyless environment. She'd sat several days in a court in '89, in William's case. How did Edgar stand being cooped up in these places? However, there was nothing she wouldn't go through on Laura's behalf. 'Are you all right, my dear?'

'Quite.'

Redmond was on his feet. Already, the first charge had been read. Under section 159 of the Crimes Act, the defendants, etc., were charged on the first count, etc., with signing and publishing a false and fraudulent balance sheet, etc.; on the second, with altering and falsifying certain books and papers, etc...

The tip of the iceberg, Wallace had thought grimly.

Redmond said, 'If your worships please, I appear for the prosecution. I will trace the figures back to show what has been done...' He threw a glance at the liquidator, consulted his brief.

And Wallace had been called. He wore a grey suit, the same as he'd put on to see Susan Fairfax on that breezy Sunday at Carlton Gardens. It set a lighter note than the prevailing black of the lawyers—and he did wish to differentiate himself from them.

Savage and Sandhurst were not away in another world. He felt their iron-hard stares. But he watched the prosecutor. And like eagles in an eyrie, the magistrate and the four justices of the peace peered down at him. A man in the public eye, in more ways than one. In fact, a notorious man.

At Redmond's invitation, he began his evidence related to the first charge. For over an hour he spoke clearly, calmly, and concisely. He worked back from the last issued balance sheet, giving details of a string of transactions. Redmond guided his evidence with a minimum of questions.

The bench was silent.

The details rolled on, giving chapter and verse of: interest booked though not collected, bad and doubtful loans not recognized or provided for; profits struck when there'd been none; dividends declared from these 'profits'; the extreme difficulties of balancing the books; questions still not answered. Finally, balance sheets for two nominated dates—prepared, signed and distributed—which were indisputably false.

He and Binks had laboured to reduce his evidence to the essentials, to make it as clear as possible to the bench. Nonetheless, it was technical and complex and the gallery fidgeted.

He continued after lunch. For another hour, he heard his voice going on and on…detailing the write-offs of directors' loans two days before the bank had suspended payment.

Redmond said: 'I want to make this point very clear. Exactly four weeks after the balance sheet as at the 30th September last was settled, the defendants saw fit to recognize advances *in their own names* aggregating £412,000, as bad, and accordingly wrote them off. In effect, eight loans for eight different projects which were good on the 30th September, were bad four weeks later!'

Wallace: 'Yes, that is what was done.'

He was not cross-examined. Chadwick for Sir John, and Spearman for the others, declined the opportunity. This caused a stir. He and Redmond exchanged looks. Neither had they interrupted his evidence with any objections.

Then it was Binks' turn. In response to Redmond's request, he stated his accountancy qualifications and experience. He gave details of the accounting entries and the mechanics of the balance sheet and profit and loss account on the dates in question. This took another hour.

Then Redmond took him through the circumstances of the expunged No. 2 Accounts in Savage's and Sandhurst's names. Carefully the facts were put before the court. A deeper silence settled on the chamber.

Again, no cross-examination. It seemed almost as though the defending counsel were unconcerned about the outcome. Larkin couldn't believe it.

It was after four, the light was failing and the court was becoming decidedly murky. Spearman complained to the bench that he was having trouble writing notes. Redmond said he was not—suggested that his learned friend put on spectacles, and asked that the next witness be called. It was to be Murdoch of *Table Talk*.

The magistrate consulted the justices of the peace, and decided that the court would adjourn till ten tomorrow.

Susan Fairfax was seated ten paces from Lady Adams and Mrs Wilberforce. The young Lancashire woman had been drawn to the court as she had been to the meeting at the Athenaeum Hall. This is ridiculous, she'd told herself. What good can it do? It was really another step following on from that earlier one. However, on that occasion there had been some point to it. It had pre-dated his letter, the revelations in *Punch*. Now, what was the point? It was all ashes.

The point was, that she was under sway of an impelling force to know more of the subterranean workings of this mysterious affair. To discover how a man of his apparent character could behave like *that*.

Staring down into the well of the court she had no eyes for anyone but him. No interest in the proceedings beyond how he conducted himself. Yet, she did feel the strangeness of it all. The lawyers hunched around that bar table, sifting paper, whispering, crow-black in their robes, be-wigged, reminded her of black magicians concocting incantations.

Had all present stepped out of the real world?

She had come away with a continuing sense of his steadiness of purpose, had travelled home by tram, the eyes of her fellow travellers drawn to her beautiful, lost-in-thought face.

But steadiness of purpose, impartiality, was something of a disguise Wallace had put on. He had screwed down the enmity and contempt he felt for these men. His own party had been giving him enough hints that he should.

What was worrying him was the atmosphere coming from the silent bench. He didn't like it one bit, and the Attorney-General's prediction hovered in his mind like a black cloud.

47

THE LIQUIDATOR OF THE MERCANTILE BANK
Mr Ducker made an admirable witness, cool, collected and imper-
turbable, and successfully steered his way through the labyrinth of
entries, cross entries…balance sheets and similar records which he
was called upon to unravel.

Illustrated Australian News, *1.5.1893*

Cold Birmingham Steel

'WHY DIDN'T THEY cross-examine?' Larkin asked. He looked tense.

'It is something of a mystery,' Redmond replied, 'though, I think, a couple of possibilities. Wallace gave his evidence in a very competent, straightforward and factual fashion. A bit hard to challenge. It might look like nit-picking. More important—I got the impression they're waiting on some development.'

Larkin nodded in agreement. 'Anything else?'

'Oh, we'll hear from Chadwick at some stage. He gets his effects, his wins, by playing on a jury. I've always thought he treats 'em like one of his operatic audiences.'

'In this case, he's got the bench for that,' Wallace interposed.

'Yes…and when I look at them, they worry me,' Redmond said.

The liquidator didn't disclose his own concern about this. He ruminated that some, at least, of those justices of the peace had been caught up in the land boom at its zenith. It was conceivable that they saw outcomes such as the bank's collapse as primarily due to the inexplicable failure of economic principles, to acts of fate beyond the control of human beings. Each Sunday, a prominent minister of religion continued to preach that line.

The three men sat at a corner table in Parer's, downstairs from where Helena Spencer had lunched the previous Friday. They'd carried out a post-mortem on some beef-steaks, were now doing one on the day's proceedings, concurrently investigating a second bottle of hermitage from the Goulburn Valley's Chateau Tahbilk.

Wallace thought Larkin looked exhausted, supposed his own face showed the same strain. He gazed across the room, caught a party at a nearby table looking at him. The women appeared both curious and hostile. They turned their backs quickly, burst into fierce conversation. Such is fame, he thought.

'Waiting for what?' he asked quietly.

Redmond shrugged. 'That's the question.'

However, they didn't have to wait long for an answer. Binks was threading his way through the tables towards them. The clerk's face, never expressive, tonight had a sitting-in-a-Temperance-hotel-lounge-on-a-wet-Sunday look. Wallace recognized it. What's up now? he wondered, turning in his chair.

The clerk glanced sceptically around the room where he'd never dined, drew up a chair, sat down and leaned forward. 'I've just seen Murdoch. Around the traps he's picked up that Wilfred Johnson, the stockbroker, saw counsel this afternoon. The word is, he's to seek an injunction from the Supreme Court restraining the liquidator from using the bank's funds to defray legal costs.'

Larkin had started—at Johnson's name. He remembered another occasion when that man had intervened in a case, that he was an associate of Sebastian Low. A picture of Low treading through the club's smoking-room a fortnight ago came back.

They absorbed the news. The Attorney-General's prediction was what came back to Wallace.

'When will it be heard?' Redmond asked.

'Tomorrow.'

The barrister sipped his wine. 'Once it gets into the Supreme Court—if it does—our bench will adjourn.'

'It's a race to get a committal,' Wallace said with a calmness which belied his new tension.

'If they get the injunction, you're looking down the barrel of three or four hundred guineas a day on your own head,' Redmond said.

'This has been in the wind,' Larkin said.

'I fear you're right.' Redmond smiled. 'But we always knew they weren't going to lie down.'

'Can we get it finished tomorrow morning?' Wallace asked.

'If they'll let us. We'll put our best foot forward.'

Immersed in this development Wallace took his hat and stick, and walked down Swanston Street. He turned into Flinders Lane to take a short-cut. They'd have to slice the prosecution case back to the minimum. Or, those men might slip through the net. If they cut it too much—they might slip through anyway.

He was hardly aware of his surroundings, of where he was going. He looked up. He was passing the uncompromising facade of Bible House. It looked as dark and empty as the cosmos. He smiled cynically, felt the pressure of the two turgid messages from the Old Testament, one from the New.

He would pick up a hansom in Elizabeth Street. The gas-lamps were few, and thus far apart in this minor conduit. Two hundred yards ahead, like an inhabited island seen from shipboard, glimmered brighter lights of an electrified section of Elizabeth Street.

Footsteps behind? Suddenly, he was fully alert. What..? He turned his head, searched the pavements, the doorways. Two moving shadows—suggestions of human forms—against the thick, stationary dark. He quickened his pace, slipped the catch off the handle of the ebony-topped stick. Click!

Running!

Two of them! Apart, but out in the centre of the lane. Each holding something...He stopped, turned quickly to face them, put his back to a doorway. They slowed to a walk, separated further, were coming at him—one pretty straight, the other in an arc. Dammit! He'd let his guard down.

The Birmingham blade came out in a long steely whisper.

He found himself at the *en garde*. Had fenced, years ago.

One of the men swore. The other hawked and spat as though clearing the decks. Wallace said nothing, watched them both. The point of steel traced marginally through air from one to the other. He moved his feet, put his back to Elizabeth Street, gave himself space.

The man coming straight leapt forward, his weapon up-raised behind his head. Wallace sprang back, avoiding the deadly blow which came singing through the air. He lunged at the torso. His thrust went home. Fast and clean. In—like into butter—out, as easily.

The man screamed. The next instant an iron bar clanged on the blue-stone pitchers.

Something hard hit Wallace a glancing blow on the head, sent him staggering, seeing stars in the dark firmament of Flinders Lane.

He shook his head. The wounded man was reeling back...retreating, supported by his companion, swearing, groaning.

Wallace became aware of the blade still in his hand, went after them. But he was dizzy, couldn't see. Blood was streaming down into his eyes, down his face, splattering on his shirt-front.

Back in the lighted aperture of Elizabeth Street was the silhouette of a constable, blowing away at a whistle.

At the Central Police Station a doctor had come and dressed the abrasion. An inspector had taken his report. The police reporter from *The Age*, following a tip-off, had arrived, an eager glint in his eye. The men had escaped. The second must've flung his steel bar, Wallace concluded. He went home alone in a hansom, declining the offer of a constable to accompany him.

In his hall, Mrs Beattie spasmodically drew in her breath. 'So!' She took his hat and the stick, peering at the bandage, at his blood-soaked clothing.

'I'm all right,' he said. 'A slight altercation in Flinders Lane where I was foolish enough to walk.'

His head was throbbing. Almost absently, he took the stick back from her, unlatched it, and withdrew the blade. He drew it almost tenderly through a handkerchief. It left a faint smear of red.

'My God!' she said.

He smiled. 'It's had its airing.'

He was suddenly aware of her look. 'I'm sorry to alarm you.'

Collecting herself, she said, 'I'll bring coffee and aspirin. Take off those clothes.'

———————

Susan sat at a writing-table in her room. A blank sheet of note-paper lay within a circle of light thrown by the shaded gas-lamp. 'Write to him,' Hanna had pleaded as they'd said goodnight. 'Meet him—at least hear what he has to say.'

And be dragged in further? The small faces of the abandoned children…all right, semi-abandoned…kept appearing in her mind's eye. A cold monument seemed to stand there also—a stone obelisk to an unfeeling heart.

Perhaps she was over-dramatizing the situation. But her instincts, her judgments of people, were usually reliable. Hanna considered there might be redeeming factors. She visualized him in the court giving his evidence in a reasonable, straightforward, impressive manner. Was that *also* his character?

What to do? She laid her pen aside…The idea had come like a beam of light. She considered its ramifications. If she'd brought her usual clear-eyed gaze on it, she might have seen it as covert and underhand. But tonight, she did not.

48

And, all thro' the year,
  The fierce seas run
  From sun to sun
Across the face of a vacant world!
    Henry Kendall, 'Euroclydon'

The Dissenter

AT TEN O'CLOCK the next morning, the committal hearing resumed. Immediately, Wallace noted that the dressing on his face was attracting great interest. It seemed to add a new, vibrating note of tension. Ironically, he recalled the equally curious looks yesterday, based on another press report.

The court reporter from *The Age* had made a meal of the incident: *Liquidator of First Bank of Victoria Attacked in Street.* The headline was prominent beside a lengthy report of yesterday's hearing.

In the gallery, Lady Adams stared at him and his injury in puzzlement. Beside her Mrs Wilberforce, tight-lipped, thought: So we *have* come to this.

The gallery was again full to overflowing. The case had been described in the papers as the 'sensation of the month'. Savage gazed at the liquidator. He turned slightly to Sandhurst, said softly, 'Slash and burn.' His colleague was leisuredly examining each justice of the peace as though they were political opponents on the hustings. Savage switched his hot gaze back to Wallace.

'Come on, get it started,' the liquidator muttered.

They'd decided not to call Binks again—or Murdoch. Binks, the trained accountant, was to have given additional evidence on the writing-off in the books of the loans to Sir John's companies; Murdoch, details of the secretive voluntary liquidations of the same companies. The cause and effect.

They'd decided, also, not to call the auditor, Moore, from whom Wallace expected interesting evidence could be extracted. These witnesses would be kept for the trial—together with the desperately ill Harbrace.

If a trial eventuated!

'I believe we've shown enough cause to persuade a reasonable bench to commit,' Redmond said into Larkin's ear. Larkin looked doubtful. Worry was gnawing in him. And they *were* gambling. He'd no doubt that the moment an application was filed in the Supreme Court for that injunction restraining Wallace, this bench would adjourn with alacrity. They were racing against time.

The magistrate and the justices of the peace entered and took their places. The previous day's evidence was read over by the clerk of the court. Sir John's eyes flicked to Chadwick who sat relaxed, that semi-smile on his face. He supposed he was going to hear from the Queen's Counsel today.

With a dispatch which clearly surprised the defence—and the bench—Redmond finished off the case for the prosecution.

Long, well-crafted statements from Sir John, Savage, and Sandhurst, were then read to the court in turn by their counsel. Each was cut from the same cloth. 'Directors had no hand in the preparation of the profit and loss figures'…'books of account never brought before the board'…'these proceedings won't yield the shareholders and depositors a brass farthing', etc. These and like phrases fell into a restless court, now impatient for the outcome.

'Weak as water!' a man shouted from the gallery. The magistrate stared, couldn't identify the perpetrator.

Chadwick QC rose to address the bench. He looked both serene and serious—as though he were about to sing on the stage at the South Yarra Musical Society. He bowed to the bench; the lower the court the more respect he showed.

Wallace and Larkin consulted their watches. It was plain they'd not finish before lunch.

Chadwick reckoned himself on solid ground with this bench, though nothing should be taken for granted. Ignoring any matters inconvenient to Sir John's case, he put weight on the 'semi-insane' events surrounding the collapse of the land boom; on their unpredictable nature and the devastating impact on the fortunes of banks, on business affairs such as Sir John was engaged in.

He said: 'Acts of God! One could quite properly term them thus. Beyond the abilities and faculties of human beings to cope with! No writer of *fiction* could have pictured what has occurred. How could this situation before us be prudently committed to trial before a jury unschooled in business, not knowledgable of the deepest intricacies of those times?

'Sir John hasn't a dishonest bone in his body, it is *ridiculous* to suggest he has. He's a man of proven character and reputation. A generous benefactor of good causes...'

'Yes—very generous. With our money!' The same voice.

'Who spoke?'—the magistrate demanded of the court officials. They didn't know, and the gallery sat silent.

'Go on.'

'He is a diligent, public-spirited man caught up in a maelstrom beyond his control...I do not intend to suggest the situation of this bank isn't disastrous. It is. But my client has nothing to answer for in the charge laid against him. The chief manager should've been the one to throw some light on this matter. Should've been the one called to account for the alleged deficiencies in the balance sheet. To give the chapter and verse of it. But he's not here! No doubt your worships will have reflected on *why* he's not been brought here by the prosecution. Other witnesses we understood were to appear, haven't been called. What is going on?

'Finally, I submit that the gaps in the prosecution's case mean there is no prima facie case against my client. It is clearly appropriate and just that the charges be dismissed. I leave it all to the good sense of your worships.'

Chadwick sat down with an air that quite enough had been said.

Wallace glanced at Redmond, who raised his eyebrows. The QC seemed to have been merely going through his paces, marking time. At least, he'd given Larkin a friendly nod.

Spearman had a harder task. He looked at his watch and proceeded to take his time. He followed much the same route as Chadwick. In connection with the additional charges against Savage and Sandhurst, he said: 'We've been shown a few cheques unearthed by this rather rash liquidator, and a list purporting to show loans in each of my clients' names mysteriously excluded from the books. The liquidator's given a rather convoluted explanation of it. But as my learned friend has already remarked, the chief manager's not here, the chief accountant's not here, nor, unfortunately, is the head cashier...Officials of the bank, who could've given explanations on this point. This is a very incomplete story. One, I submit, no jury could reasonably be expected to convict on. Therefore, the charges against my clients should be completely dismissed.'

The court adjourned to two o'clock.

Susan's heart had turned to ice when Hanna came around the break-fast table and showed her the headline in *The Age*.

'It's one thing after another with him,' she said in her shock. 'How bad is…?'

'Only a slight wound,' Hanna said quickly, still reading. 'The attackers escaped.'

Susan took the paper and stared at the half-column. The colour had left her face. What kind of a place was this Melbourne? She'd felt she'd been getting its measure, yet, almost daily another dimension was emerging. However, her disquiet and uncertainty were to do with her personal dilemma. It was putting everything off the bias.

Hanna said, 'It might be connected with the case. "Touched by something hard." Remember that?'

Susan had already thought of it.

'Are you going to the court today?'

The Lancashire woman frowned. No. She looked up at Hanna, and asked her advice on the plan which had come to her late last night. The bookseller was surprised.

'Probably, Philip would know. I might ask him. But, love, is this wise?'

'I think it's what I must do,' Susan said.

Wallace, Redmond, Larkin and Binks were huddled around a table in a hotel nearby the court.

'How do you read it?' the liquidator asked Redmond.

'It's going to be a close-run thing.'

'Even if this bench gets to a verdict,' Larkin said grimly. He looked at Wallace. Sir John's statement had said a trial wouldn't yield the liquidation 'a brass farthing', which was precisely his own fear. He brooded afresh on Wallace's determination to bring the directors to book. Obsessional.

However, in another vein, he considered again Wallace's motive in speaking to him about Helena. No doubt it had been well-intentioned. Though it still rankled. The future of that relationship was another obscurity on his horizon.

The liquidator had given them a brief account of the affray in the street, which they listened to in a thoughtful silence. They'd not analysed the possibilities.

Larkin's clerk stepped into the bar, looked around, spotted them. He'd been up at the Supreme Court. He shook his head. Nothing. But he'd made inquiries of contacts: the application was expected early afternoon. He returned to wait.

Redmond pulled out his watch. 'Back to court.'

Hullo, something's been going on, Wallace thought as the bench filed in. The faces of the magistrate and the justices of the peace were disharmonious—nervy, even angry. Except in one case. A small, aging JP, by the name of Welsh, appeared calm and inscrutable—impervious to the irritated, side-long glances his colleagues were casting at him.

'This looks interesting,' Redmond whispered.

The gallery stirred, became very quiet.

The magistrate said: 'I and the bench—with one exception—are agreed that the charges against all the defendants should be dis-missed…'

A justice of the peace named Williams, a land boomer and par-liamentarian in the upper house, leaned in to Welsh and said forcibly, but in a low voice, 'If you persist in committing them to trial, I, for one, will never speak to you again.'

On his other side, a bearded JP informed Welsh that he'd better keep clear of their club after this.

Welsh ignored these remarks, stared at the defendants, listened to the magistrate spelling out his reasons…

'…I have not heard enough to persuade me that a prima facie case has been made out against the defendants. I'm of the opinion that there may be more on these questions to be said, but it's not been said here. It would have been helpful to have heard from officials of the bank…To try to lift these events out of the context of their time, serves only to muddy the waters…I would deplore the fate of the defendants at the hands of a jury without business education…'

Mr Williams JP made some impassioned remarks, concluding with: 'In my opinion, a verdict for committal would not improve the present calamitous situation—would not regain any funds.'

Welsh smoothed papers with his hand, then looking straight at the defendants, spoke in a matter-of-fact voice with no frills as to phraseology. 'When the public hear the names of the magistrates who've addressed the court, I think they will make up their minds quite easily on this matter. Though it has given me a good deal of trouble, there's no doubt in my mind that a prima facie case for committal to trial *has* been made out.

'Mr Wallace gave very clear evidence. He was never asked a question by the prosecutor which he wasn't in a position to answer. And the answers came straight from the books of the bank. Why wasn't he cross-questioned by the defence? I can only conclude that it did not *suit* the defence to do so. I have listened to the wealth of detail provided by Mr Wallace—to the figures…The absence of officials of the bank, or other witnesses, does not change this one jot. I find for committal.'

A long exhalation sighed across the court.

'Hear! Hear!'—that voice again.

A spattering of applause, instantly dying out. In the dock, Savage swore audibly and smashed his fist down on wood. Sandhurst looked out under hooded eyes at Mr Welsh. Sir John showed no emotion, nor much attention.

In the gallery, Mrs Wilberforce looked anxiously into Lady Adams' face: she was dead-pale, but calm.

The magistrate, stern-faced, and three of the justices of the peace, variously agitated, left the bench. Mr Welsh JP was left to continue alone. He showed an air of righteousness—and obviously did not care who saw it. He named each defendant and committed each to trial at the Sessions on the 11th April. The matter of bail was then argued, was fixed at £1,000 for each defendant.

'Far too high,' Mr Spearman objected. 'If your worship pleases…'

'One thousand pounds,' Mr Welsh repeated calmly, and adjourned.

A few minutes later, as the court was clearing, Binks hurried in from the Supreme Court. The application for an injunction against Wallace had been filed at three o'clock, was to be heard the next day.

'By God! That was close,' Redmond said.

Larkin was slumped in his seat. 'Now, it's up to the Government. There's only ten days to prepare for the trial.' He didn't look like the man who had jumped in Albert Park Lake to effect a rescue.

But Wallace had a triumphant and determined look. 'I'll call on Danby immediately. With some authority on this occasion, I think.'

49

London, 16th March
The Financial News, commenting on the result of the Anglo-
Australian Bank trials in Melbourne expresses the opinion that the
sentence of 5 years' penal servitude passed on Staples, the manag-
ing director, will prove a salutary lesson to fraudulent financiers.
                                          The Leader, 18.3.1893

Dance Like a Butterfly, Sting Like a…

OTTO RUDD HAD SPENT several days going around public bars and billiard saloons. With his calm eyes, he'd peered through drifting banks
of tobacco smoke at the men with glasses or cues in hand; examined
their green-hued faces. The previous Saturday he'd haunted the bookmakers' ring at Flemington Racecourse. He'd not sighted the check-
suited man.

Each evening, he'd scrutinized the crowds thronging the Eastern
Market as they shopped under brilliant blue, electric light. He'd taken
a snack at Tom and Bill's Oyster Saloon nearby in Exhibition Street,
and kept up his watch. This last was his home away from home;
people came looking for him there.

He'd drawn another blank. The man had dropped from sight as
abruptly as he'd appeared—or re-appeared—according to the client.
His itinerant watch on the Prahran house had yielded nothing further.
Nonetheless, unless the flashy individual had left town he was confident that he'd find him. However, the client wanted quick results.

So the detective had made a cast in another direction: he'd turned
up at the Police Court on each day of the committal hearings—to
scrutinize the public gallery, the court environs.

On the final day, at about three o'clock, standing at the rear of the
gallery, he drew in his breath sharply.

'Got you!' he intoned.

The man had entered the gallery not ten paces from the detective,
had taken off his hat to reveal the long, sandy hair, turned his florid

face down to the proceedings. It was the very moment that the defendants were being committed for trial. Rudd was not distracted, which was fortunate, for, the man having heard the result, left immediately. He'd not been there more than a minute.

Nice timing, the detective thought. He was able to stay close as the man slipped through the mass of humanity with a practised ease, took the tram down to Flinders Street Station. Thank God for a check-suit! It seemed to dance through the crowd like a butterfly going through a cabbage-field. Out to Prahran Station they went, up High Street, through the Victoria Gardens.

The detective, once he was confident of the destination, dropped back two hundred yards or so. As he passed the spot in the gardens where he'd been attacked last Friday night, he speculated whether this man had been his assailant. He'd not carried a stick that night, as he wasn't today.

'Bit of a mystery that is, Rudd,' he told himself. Then: 'He's going to report. Is that what you're up to, Mr Ellis?'

This was a short visit. He came out of the house after a half-hour, and instead of returning via the gardens, walked in the opposite direction and entered the side-door of a hotel which closed off the end of the street.

Aha, Rudd thought. This might be the opportunity he'd been looking for. Even if the man had been his attacker, it had been pitch black that night, and he might not be recognized. Anyway, opportunity or not, at some point on this little outing he was going to accost this fella.

He checked the hotel's exits, waited for a minute or so, before entering—sighed to himself. Ellis sat in the saloon bar at a table with a glass of beer already in front of him; he'd spread out a newspaper and was hunched over it. Except for the barman, they had the place to themselves. A wood fire had been lit.

Rudd bought a beer, moved to a table, unfolded his own paper. The man had only glanced up briefly. So far so good, the detective thought. Nothing happened for several minutes; the newspapers rustled, the fire crackled.

Suddenly, Rudd gave a low chuckle—as though intrigued. He seemed fascinated by what he was reading. The other looked up and their eyes met. The detective found himself looking into almost colourless eyes, rimmed with pink. Extremely wary orbs.

Rudd tapped a stubby finger on the paper. 'This Victoria Bank business stinks like bad fish. I hope those directors go for trial.'

Ellis regarded the detective thoughtfully, took a sip of his beer. 'Committed for trial this afternoon,' he said.

'Ah, that's good. How do you know?'

'I was there.' He straightened in his chair, laid his hands on the table. 'As were you.'

Hullo, Rudd thought.

The hands had closed to fists. 'What's your game?'

The detective brought out his pipe and tobacco pouch. Deliberately, calmly, he began to pack the pipe. He said, 'I might ask the same.'

The man laughed roughly. 'You've been following me around— and I don't like it.'

Rudd glanced up sympathetically—as if this were perfectly understandable. However, he was slightly miffed: the fella must have eyes in the back of his head. He thought: You slipped up, Rudd. But he would've *lost* Otto Berliner. His namesake as to 'Otto' was Melbourne's best known private detective. Rudd thought himself the better operator.

'So, you gave me a bit of smack on the neck the other night.'

Ellis moved his checked shoulders aggressively, but looked puzzled. Interesting, Rudd thought.

'Who am I talking to?' Ellis demanded.

The detective scratched a match alight, applied it to the bowl of the pipe. 'Rudd's the name. Private detective.' He drew on the pipe.

Ellis started, stared. 'Ah…Bookmakers?'

'No, that ain't the way of it.'

'Well then?'

Rudd considered his options. Not front on…He glanced down at his paper. 'The liquidator in this bank case. Wallace. I've read something else about him recently. Seems he's got a wife—in a manner of speaking—and two kiddies, hidden away from the world…now that's interesting. Curious, even. Why would a man do that? An honourable man, who seems to be doing his best to put a few wrongs right.'

'God damn you, Rudd, what are you after?'

The detective smiled.

Ellis suddenly took a long draught of beer. The left fist had opened, the fingers were tapping nervously on the table, the florid face had changed to beetroot. '"Wife"—don't make me laugh,' he sneered. 'If *that's* what you're after, take a ride out to St Kilda Cemetery. Take a look at a gravestone in the name of Ellis, fifty yards in from the south gate on the left.' He laughed bitterly.

The detective, pipe in mouth, observed him in silence.

He stopped laughing. 'Honourable man! God Almighty!' He pounded his fist on the table, making the glass jump.

Rudd, watching him, knocked out his pipe, stowed it away. Out of the corner of his eye he noted the barman had them under observation. Good.

'Reader of *Table Talk* are you?' he said.

Ellis looked at him. The colourless eyes now were flecked with red. The detective brooded on this. Blood? Or, firelight?

'And, the Bible?'

Swiftly Ellis reached in his pocket and brought out a large pocket-knife. With a dirty finger-nail, he easily extracted the largest of the steel blades. He laid it on the table.

'See that, Rudd?'

The detective nodded. The barman was reaching under the counter.

'I don't use sticks, or blunt instruments. I don't want to see you again. If I turn around, and find you there behind me…Get it?'

The detective did. He stood up. He nodded again, and ambled out the side-door into the coolish evening. Smoke from the thickly ranked neighbourhood chimneys drifted up, staining the night-sky, but the stars still glittered with promises of tomorrow.

He stood under the sign of the Flying Duck and thought of boiled pig's trotters crusty with salt at a stall in Chapel Street. Another day's work under the belt, and another supper coming up.

50

Quietly as rosebuds
Talk to the thin air
Love came so lightly
I knew not he was there.
　　Shaw Neilson, 'Love's Coming'

Lonely as a Dream

THE NEXT MORNING Otto Rudd visited the St Kilda Cemetery. The detective was in no hurry. He'd come here on the information given yesterday by the aggressive, nervy Ellis—mainly out of curiosity—but also to write an appropriate conclusion to the case of 'The Biblical Threats'. He'd noted his file thus. He was meticulous with paper work, and the case was at an end.

He found the gravestone without difficulty. He took off his bowler and gazed around. No-one else here...above ground that is, he corrected. A nice piece of polished, white black-veined marble, chiselled with black script. He read it without any change in his expression. The story was as he'd suspected this past week or so; in this trade you developed a nose for matters like this. He contemplated that story.

'So there we are, Rudd,' he said, his voice sounding unnaturally loud in the drowsy sunlight, amid the sleeping community. 'It's a lonely business. A one-way ticket.'

He replaced his bowler, and headed back to town.

Hanna had undertaken this commission reluctantly. However, it *was* a further opportunity. She smiled to herself wryly—balancing her concern for Susan, with this selfish motive. Susan could be taking a large step in the wrong direction—but, she was determined to take it. In the end, the bookseller had given one of her expressive shrugs, and come straight out from business to St Kilda on the tram.

At half-past six, she walked up the front steps of the house on the Esplanade, rang the bell, and turned to look back over the bay which, in the failing light, seemed bleak, solitary, and stand-offish. An omen? Her heart was beating hard, and she was quite breathless. Would he be here? If not, perhaps she could wait. Looking for a thought to lighten the moment, she wondered if she should have the telephone put on. But then most of her friends didn't have it; they'd all have to make a pact! Though something like this was a face-to-face task.

'Why, Miss Dewhurst!'

It was a maid Hanna hadn't seen for over a year.

'How are you, Julie?…Is Mr Larkin at home?'

Philip came out to the hall. He looked surprised. He'd been reading papers connected to the case in his study while he waited for dinner. Then the doorbell had rung.

Hanna got in first. 'I'm sorry to keep tracking you down, Philip, but could you spare me a few moments?'

He had removed his coat, was suddenly conscious of this. He gazed at her, perceived her seriousness—and embarrassment. In a flash, he regretted this old friend should feel like that. However, an embarrassment did lie between them.

'Of course, come into my study.' She left her umbrella with the maid, kept on her hat. He showed her to a chair, put on his coat. A wood fire burned in the grate. They hadn't begun fires yet at Carlton Gardens.

She smoothed her skirt. 'I've come to ask *another* favour. It's a little delicate…' She paused, re-thinking how to manage it. 'It concerns Angus Wallace—and Susan.'

He watched her, wondering what was coming. Wallace had become a dominating force in their lives—at various levels. A perplexing figure, upon which incidents and innuendo were breaking like waves, as he forged relentlessly ahead. A sword-stick! Who would have thought it! As for that family! It was hard to keep the lid on it all when you were dealing with him day to day.

Hanna's eyes were on his. 'There's something between him and Susan. You know that…After that poisonous piece in *Punch*, you might guess her feelings. He wants to meet, I suppose, to explain. She won't agree. I think she's determined to find out more for herself, to make a judgment independent of his influence. Perhaps, doesn't trust herself. She's profoundly shocked by the children's situation.'

'*Obviously*, her feelings are engaged.'

Hanna had spoken gravely, evenly. Now she dropped her eyes,

thought: Perhaps even as much as mine are bound to you. She said, 'She wishes to talk to the woman, see the children, their circumstances. The address is needed.'

Larkin was startled. He rose, and paced across the room, stopped, and turned, rubbing his jaw. From the indefatigable Rudd, he knew the address.

'Hanna, is this wise? One can imagine Wallace's reaction. Specially if it's done behind his back.'

Hanna shrugged. 'Those are my feelings. On the other hand, I think Susan is *so* engaged that she's compelled to do it. She can see no other way forward.'

Larkin remained still, lost in thought. In the light of his present relations with Wallace, if he released this information…Damnation! These personal affairs were trickier than a summer breeze on Port Phillip Bay.

Sympathetically, Hanna watched this inner struggle. She said, 'You may know more than I, but a sixth sense tells me that something may be found out favourable to Angus's case.'

'I know nothing. I'm in the dark,' he muttered.

She smiled. Yes, that was it. Past, present and future.

He shook his head. 'This is devilishly hard—but I'll do it. I'll have to tell him, of course.' He smiled grimly. 'And, wear the consequences.'

He turned abruptly to his desk, wrote on a piece of paper. She had removed her gloves. For the briefest moment their hands touched as she took the note.

'Will you stay to dinner?' He was looking at her keenly, the preoccupation of Wallace and Susan cleared away. The intensity of it startled her.

She thought: Is that the kind of look he gives Helena Spencer?

'Thank you, no.' An instinct told her to be gone. 'But thank you for this.'

Julie was sent out to get a hansom.

He took her to the door, past the huge chromo-lithographs of windswept Highland scenes which had belonged to his father. Why did these men live steeped in the ambience created by their fathers—adding so little themselves? It was sad that his late wife appeared to have left no visible trace of her few years residence.

Helena Spencer, champagne glass in hand, in a dream, floated through her Parisian rooms. She was not going out tonight, but nonetheless looked majestic in a black velvet gown sumptuously trimmed with airy pink silk, her dark hair splendidly coiffured. In a few minutes, she would sit down to dinner—alone. She would eat in solitary state. As lonely as a dream.

Tonight, she wasn't expecting Philip, either, was allowing him a little leeway. He'd told her that Wallace was driving them all hard on this case, that he'd be working into the early hours. So his note had said. In most liaisons, communications became a trifle ambiguous at some point. Did this one have a hint of that?

Is your ardour fading a little, my love? She smiled tightly—as though picturing the question winging its way to St Kilda. Are you beginning to think: This troublesome woman?...Helena, you must keep your nerve. You are a wonderful catch for a partner of discernment! His ardour in the boudoir certainly hasn't faded—if anything has quickened. The malignant gossip of the society ladies, with their tea-shattered constitutions, won't come to *his* ears. All will be well.

Her thoughts *went further*...to Angus Wallace. Her heart, also, had turned to ice as she'd read of the attack in yesterday's paper. But he was all right, she'd found out. She was still marvelling over the disclosure of that hidden part of his life, which had so overwhelmingly confirmed the mystery she'd felt existed. Ah, my poor Angus. Why didn't you speak out? Like a man.

Went on...to Hanna Dewhurst. The competitor. The bookseller should not be under-rated; she was like an unfancied filly in the Oaks at Flemington: capable of slipping through on the rails in an eye-blink to take the prize.

She whirled around in the mirrors of the room. Don't blink, Helena!

The maid was standing in the door of the salon:

'Dinner is served, ma'am,' she said.

Sweet and Sour

SOMEONE WAS BANGING on the front door. Wallace flung off his bed-clothes, was out of bed in one movement. The last such time was instantly in his mind. It was half-past six, Saturday morning. He beat Mrs Beattie into the hall. Binks stood in the portico, a copy of *The Age* in his hands. The clerk was grinning out of his blood, cuts and paper patches. Behind him was a coolish morning, a white skim of mist over the lake.

'Good news! At last!' He held the paper open at page three. In his dressing-gown, on the door-step, Wallace read:

First Bank of Victoria Directors Committed For Trial.
Supreme Court Issues Injunction Against Liquidator.
Crown to Take Up the Prosecution.

Thank God for Mr Welsh JP! Wallace breathed.

The final headline was the development he'd been sweating on. He'd not called on Crown Prosecutor Danby. He'd decided to wait until Monday morning, hoping that what was 'in the air' might crystallize by then. And it had! He scanned the column which included a letter from the Crown Solicitor.

…I have been desired by the Attorney-General to make a state-ment…intention of the Crown to intervene in this case and the Crown Solicitor to take up the prosecution…interests of the public, and of the defendants whose characters are at stake…

The editor pithily commented that the committal for trial had forced the Government's 'reluctant hand'; that Mr Wallace's abilities as a tactician were to be admired.

'Come in, come in,' he said to his clerk. 'We'll have breakfast.'

As he went upstairs to wash and dress, a penetrative thought came. They'd gone over one hurdle, but just what instructions would the Attorney-General be issuing to the Crown law officers on the prosecution? This was as sobering as Mrs Beattie's hot, black coffee.

He and Binks called on Danby at ten and were shown straight into the Crown Prosecutor's room. The slight man with the lined brown face was smiling. He looked critically at the large bruise on Wallace's face.

'Well, Wallace, you've got what you were after.' He wasn't referring to the abrasion.

'I hope I have.'

There's a way to go yet, Binks thought, standing back. Before his shaving mirror that morning, the clerk might've attempted to cut his throat: an unsavoury sight, which had made Wallace flinch on his door-step.

'It's been put into my hands,' Danby said.

It was Wallace's turn to smile. They sat down around a table and the liquidator unpacked the brief, the files they'd brought. In a column of sunlight, dust motes writhed.

'There's a lot more here than we brought to bear at the committal,' he said. 'A lot more to get your teeth into.'

The Crown Prosecutor placed his hands flat on the table and eyed the papers. 'This is going to be an interesting trial on several levels.'

Wallace regarded him.

'I'll be up against Chadwick—again. I'm overdue for a win there, but he's a sharp opponent.'

'What else?' The liquidator knew Danby would pull out all the stops.

'The last thing the *Premier* wants, is a guilty verdict.'

Ah, yes…Wallace nodded his understanding. Well, they'd got this far.

———◆———

Wallace had been too self-absorbed to take in the other main news, though he soon caught up with it. News which, at half-past ten, sent William and Susan hastening out to East Melbourne, after receiving a note from Hilda Wilberforce. The Commercial Bank of Australia had suspended payment.

Since nine, Hilda had been on the move in her house, ostensibly directing her servants on a series of tasks, but mentally absorbed in reviewing her financial situation. Ten thousand pounds! In moments of crisis, both her physical and mental energy soared.

She embraced William and Susan on the stairs, and took them to her morning room. At least the sun was out there; downstairs it was chilly. As they sat down she said, 'I didn't think it would come to this.'

'There've been rumours, but the city's full of rumours. That's the problem,' William said.

'We thought we could trust Mr Turner,' Mrs Wilberforce said drily, speaking of the Commercial's general manager. 'It seems my £10,000 will be frozen indefinitely.'

Susan watched them. She guessed Mrs Wilberforce was worried about more than her fixed deposit. But, she went on about it: 'In February, even *Table Talk* said it was well trimmed to weather the severest financial gale. And here we are!' She smiled ironically. 'I haven't been as prudent as I thought.'

William said, 'It's very bad luck, Hilda, but they're reconstructing. There's a good chance you'll have the money back in time.'

'I hope so…'

She looked at him keenly. 'However, the main worry is the store's overdraft, isn't it? What will they do about that?'

William stood up and looked down at her. 'I think, nothing—so long as we meet our arrangements.'

Susan nodded. 'They'll want to—must—keep their good customers going.'

Hilda turned her eyes on the Lancashire woman. She'd had the idea of getting the young woman into the store, but Hanna had acted first. That was something which had worked out.

'Well, that's a relief.'

'I'll see Stevens at the bank to make sure of it,' William said.

She nodded, rang for tea. With this action, she often signalled a change of direction, as now. 'Susan, I hear from William you've been working wonders. I'm so glad—and so grateful.'

Susan smiled. She knew William had come here last week to report. Mrs Wilberforce's dark eyes lingered on the young woman. Not quite so fresh as before. A hint of strain—or was it sadness? That fiasco in *Punch*—now the attack in the street. And, Wallace seemed set for even more storms. She wondered how far it had got. It was a nasty mess to land in a young woman's lap. Even one as competent, and impenetrable, as this. But clues were beginning to fall out. Yesterday, some information had come to her, which pointed in a particular direction. She wondered if Laura had heard from Manchester yet.

Susan wondered what the East Melbourne matron would make of the expedition she was to undertake this afternoon. Already, the nerves were churning in her stomach.

Hilda Wilberforce noted the counter-scrutiny, smiled slightly. She turned away as the tea was wheeled in. 'Life must be made to go on, you know, whatever comes down on us. This is what Melbourne is finding out—and all of us, being swept along with her. Now, buck up, you two.'

52

The prosecutions in connection with fraudulent boom companies
are still the bête noire of the Government.

Table Talk, *18.11.1892*

Douglas Street and Spring Street

LATE THAT AFTERNOON, Susan took the train to Prahran into new territory. Building facades, denoting solid commerciality, thronged Chapel Street. Several sizeable emporia, one behind grand Corinthian columns, were lined up like battle-ships at anchor. This surprised her professional eye, though she'd heard of it. Her thoughts re-concentrated on the mission ahead.

At five o'clock, she stood in Douglas Street, gazing at the house. A whisp of blonde hair adrift in the slight breeze, a tall woman with an effortless, straight-as-a-die persona, dressed in a simple, tailored, olive-green, Newmarket coat, a narrow skirt with pleats let into the back, a small velvet hat trimmed with green feathers, she was quite alone. If a poetic mind had passed by, seeing her in the mellowing light, it might've speculated about visions, Grecian goddesses, etc.; nonesuch did.

This was *extremely* difficult. Her heart was beating as it had the day she'd gone on board ship at Tilbury. I must walk up that path and knock on the door. I must do it—now! And she did, and the brass knocker reverberated in the interior. She listened to the sounds fading into emptiness, then, her own breathing. O God! It would be too hard to do this a second time. And why would she? For a lost cause, a forlorn hope? She turned to face the street. Not a person in sight to ask.

Voices!—coming from the right. A woman and two small children appeared, the children chatting gaily, skipping ahead. Her heart seemed to stop. Her gloved hand went to her throat. Three pairs of eyes were on her. She stepped from the porch on to the path. She was smiling the smile that had broken hearts, charmed customers. The children—a boy and a girl—were obviously twins. A major surprise.

About five years old. The woman was slender, perhaps forty, well-dressed, carrying a light umbrella. Dark-haired, cinnamon-brown eyes—quite striking—and an intelligent, inquiring look. Another surprise...

'My name is Susan Fairfax. I'm a friend of Mr Wallace, I wonder could I impose on you for a few words.'

The woman's face changed instantly to assessing and cautious, yet not hostile.

'I would consider it a great favour, Mrs...Ellis?'

'Miss,' the woman said with a faint smile.

Susan absorbed this.

It would have gone against the grain for a lady as beautiful, as well-groomed and dressed as Susan, for that smile, to have been turned away at the door-step. They sat in the front parlour, the room with which Binks was very familiar. She'd surveyed the children—black hair, brown eyes, small white faces, suddenly quiet—met their curious, puzzled scrutiny. Now they were somewhere else in the house.

The woman was watching, her lips continuing to form that slight smile. One you could easily miss—or dismiss as a trick of light. But a pleasant look—of sympathy, of understanding? An educated woman, up to a point, Susan thought. She straightened her gloves on the polished table; all the furniture in the room, the hall, shone, smelt of polish. She gathered her thoughts. A clock ticked loudly, magnifying the silence.

'Miss Ellis, Mr Wallace does not know I've come. You should know that.'

The woman nodded. A delicate, waiting, movement.

'I've come about the article in the *Melbourne Punch*. It was a great shock to me. Beyond anything I'd thought of. It put me into great difficulty. A quandary...'

Susan looked into those yellowish-brown eyes seeking clues. She was assuming a degree of comprehension of her situation. The woman's watching-waiting-hint-of-sympathy expression hadn't changed. Susan compressed her lips. There was no oblique approach she could take. The only way was to be completely frank; sink or swim.

'I'm in a situation where I must know more than I do now. Mr Wallace wishes to meet me, no doubt would tell me more. Perhaps, explain. However, what may be at stake impels me to seek another reference—perhaps the closest.'

They were silent, heard faintly the children's voices. Susan smoothed her gloves again, suddenly thought of this woman's feelings.

By innuendo, the paper had inferred her situation, and she hadn't an alternative view. What was the truth?

'I hope my coming here isn't too unwelcome, this kind of talk too painful.'

'It's not painful.'

Miss Ellis sat with her hands quietly folded on the table. Her wariness hadn't decreased. The last sun coming in seemed to fleck her eyes with tiny golden lights. 'Miss Fairfax, what do you wish to know?'

Susan sat back slowly. She perceived that this woman, whatever her part in the mystery, unexpectedly had an undoubted air of efficiency, of independence. Suddenly, her hopes were on the rise.

───────

Wallace and Larkin had dined together early at their club. It was after seven, and those members not still dining had drifted away to the card-room, the reading-room, gone home, or elsewhere. Both men were weary. The liquidator had spent most of the day closeted with Danby, briefing the Crown Prosecutor, and the Crown Solicitor who had been called in. Larkin, who had his practice to run, had been absent from these discussions; he'd made his major contribution in the brief which Wallace had left with Danby.

They sat in the smoking-room, cigars alight. The room always seemed as dark as a dungeon to Larkin, and they were alone except for an animated group of town-visiting graziers, large-jointed men with big, rough hands twinkling with diamond rings, who were about to go on to the theatre—and then to an establishment run by Madame Brussells. At this moment, that lady's flash house was on their lips as though it bespoke a favoured and smart health resort.

'So Danby's cautious?' Philip said. 'That isn't encouraging.'

Wallace considered the smoky canvases on the wall opposite. It was difficult to distinguish between trees, pasture, and sky. Obscure as the outcome of this case, he thought.

'Danby'll do a good job. He's always cautious.'

'What's his view on getting their secret compositions re-opened; getting hold of their personal assets?'

Wallace laid his head back and exhaled smoke. Philip was airing his preoccupation: getting funds into the kitty. And fair enough. *He* wanted the directors nailed *and* their personal assets.

'It's going to depend on the judge. If we get a guilty verdict he might make an order—that's what we'll be after. If not, there's an alternative…' They discussed the legalities of that for a minute or two. Briefly, Wallace smiled. 'There's no love lost between Danby and Chadwick. I don't think Danby can wait to get into court. He's taken the high ground in a few cases touching on the land boom—had a couple of wins. But when Chadwick's been the opposition, he's lost. It rankles. He sees Chadwick as an opportunist—a specialist in finding ways out for a gang of rogues.'

'Danby shouldn't be in the law if he's that sensitive,' Larkin said. The dripping figure of Mrs Chadwick, light-as-air in his arms, as he'd waded to the Albert Park Lake shore, had flashed into his mind. He put down his cigar and leaned forward. Throughout dinner he'd been worrying about Hanna's request. He'd put it out of his mind during the day. He must bite that bullet.

'Listen, old man, you're not going to like this, but I can't help that. I've done what I thought was right. There's a matter *I* didn't like being raised by you—but I've got over it.' He smiled tightly—trying to lighten the moment. 'After this, it could be considered we're quits.'

Wallace's attention was engaged; he laid down his own cigar, turned his gaze on his friend and colleague.

'Susan Fairfax wishes to call on the lady—the family—at Prahran. Hanna asked me for the address—and I gave it. You'll know far better than I, why she would wish to go there.'

He leaned back, had nothing more to say. They stared at each other. Wallace's eyes gleamed in the smoky gloom. He was nodding slowly, as if some long-held conviction had been confirmed.

'You did quite the right thing, old man,' he said.

———•———

And, if she *was* to achieve that objective, there was no time or space for delicacy. Susan straightened her shoulders, looked this woman—Miss Ellis—in the eye.

'Is Mr Wallace the father of the children?'

A slight pause. 'He is.'

'And you?'

'I am their aunt—their dear mother's sister.'

Susan's eyes widened, and the woman smiled again that faint, enigmatic smile.

'She died in child-birth. Five years ago this 1st May.'

'Were they…married?'

'No.'

A silence. 'Why not, in Heaven's name?'—Susan burst out.

The woman's hands remained one in the other, still as a wood-carving. 'That's a question you'll have to ask him. I never have.'

Susan said in a very quiet voice: 'I don't understand—cannot comprehend—why he has separated himself from the children in the way he has.'

For the first time, the aunt–guardian–bereaved sister revealed a hint of emotion, dropped her gaze to the table's burnished surface. Her burnishing. 'Ah....,' she breathed—as though one of the mysteries of her existence suddenly had been laid there. After a few moments, she looked up at the Lancashire woman, who had arrived unexpectedly in her parlour to ask the questions which had long been in her own mind. Of course, the arrival of such an emissary from the outside world, had always been only a question of time.

'He sees them on special occasions. He has taken legal steps to legitimize their birth. He provides adequately for us. All else...is locked in his own mind.'

Unconsciously, Susan was drawing fingers down her cheek, more a smoothing of her mind. 'I see,' she said, but had not penetrated those mists.

'It *might* be possible for him to explain.'

Yes, it might. If she was to allow him that opportunity. To explain, persuade her, or finally, damn himself in her eyes. But she continued to distrust the danger of it—to *her*.

She had found out certain amazing facts, though the woman opposite was not telling all of it; she felt sure of that. And why should she?

A few minutes later she walked back along the street, at first in a daze. As night fell, her thoughts cleared. Something Hanna had mentioned after Philip Larkin's incident at Albert Park Lake came back. Her experienced, analytical mind grasped at it. Something else to wonder at...to go towards, like a night-traveller heading for a lonely light.

The Solicitor-General was seething, though only a few knew him well enough to pick it. Some of his colleagues around the table in the cabinet room had; they'd noted the fractional movements of his shoulders, the tilt of his head, the finger tapping briefly on some papers.

The room was full of eddies and banks of cigar smoke in which the heads and shoulders of the Ministers were ranked like promontories standing along a foggy coast. They had dined, and this late-night session had caused several of those heads to droop. Until a minute or two ago, when the exchange between the Colony's two most senior law officials had begun.

The Attorney-General, his large, rounded shoulders hunched forward, his great head supported by hands under the chin, gave his colleague across the table a taunting look.

He said, 'I wasn't at all keen for the Government to take over this prosecution.'

'We know that, but you had no choice,' the Solicitor-General said.

'You've had my views on it…'

'Public opinion—the press—forced your hand. Apart from the fact that they've been committed to trial.' The Solicitor-General looked at the Premier. 'If the Colony is ever to recover its good name, cases like this must be prosecuted with energy.'

The Attorney smiled. 'We've heard your views on *that*.'

'They're not original. For the British investor—for the world— we've got to get rid of the notion that the Colony's a paradise for rogues, that here Rafferty's Rules are the thing.'

The Premier, at the head of the table, watched this exchange broodingly—sick of it all. For the past week they'd been embroiled in the Mallee Bill, Government retrenchments.

'Oh? We believe in the marketplace, market forces—the cut and thrust of commerce. This isn't a place for the hot-house flower,' the Attorney said pointedly. He spun his cigar in his big white fingers, darting sparks of light from his diamonds.

'Like the Commercial Bank?'

'It'll be all right.'

'Really? You think so?'

The Attorney-General smiled again. 'However, I've a mind to alter the first indictment against the directors…from issuing a false balance sheet to *conspiring* to issue…'

The Solicitor-General laughed in amazement, and their colleagues stirred. 'Well, that'll certainly get them acquitted!' He turned to the Premier. 'Do you agree with that? Conspiracy is as hard to prove as getting blood out of a stone. And—it's not the charge they were committed to trial on.'

The Premier did not appear disposed to reply.

The Solicitor-General turned back to the Attorney. 'If you do that, I may have to intervene to reinstate the proper charge…'

'I'd think very carefully about that. I'm the senior law officer in the Colony. You might find it hard to get any instructions you issue, carried out.'

'We are equal in powers.'

'I disagree.'

With his open hand, the Premier thumped the table, slowly, heavily, once. 'Now gentlemen, I want a united front. Personally, I don't see what good it does to bring men like Sir John Adams—or our colleagues—before the courts. My view's that it cuts up the social fabric. But if we do, they've got to get a fair shake. So we'll adjourn, and consider it again tomorrow—with cooler heads.

The Solicitor-General was left seething. His cabinet colleagues went out into a Spring Street whose glassy surface was awash with refracted light—an impressionistic creation by a sudden, needle-sharp shower: something from the brush of Signor Girolamo Nerli, William Boyd might have thought, if he'd been there.

This evening Melbourne had been displaying the rich variety of its autumnal weather. Almost a conjurer's bag of tricks. At first, mellow late-afternoon sunshine had soothed minds, picked out the myriad 'turning' leaves to splendid advantage, then, sharpish, quick-silver showers had swept in, and now a pregnant, moist-aired stillness had settled over all.

Chadwick gazed into the dark garden on the heights of Kew. He stood at the window, hands joined behind his back. The Queen's Counsel recalled that four or five years ago he'd sung arias in the drawing-room next door in aid of a charity…The sixty-foot room, where Lady Adams was presently seated in solitary state, playing endless games of patience, thinking: John's now an enigma to me, and, I suspect, to himself. She looked up, as though at a sound. Only that whispery rain. Or the echo of voices? The shadows of the thousands of visitors who'd paraded through this room seemed to haunt it; all the entertainments they'd had here, the balls in the ball-room, the dinners in the dining-room; glittering, splendid occasions with no expense spared. Did anyone remember those nights? At all? Or, had it been one long dream?

Sir John sat at his desk before a cliff-face of volumes. The electric light irradiated his face, burnished leather. Barnaby sat nearby. The knight was brooding on the past in a more concentrated way: a land deal he'd done in '88 in partnership with a politician. East Brighton. They'd sliced a nice profit out of that one…

Chadwick turned back from the darkness. 'I think we'll be all right. The separate charge has distanced you from our friends Savage and Sandhurst.'

'Of course, Sir John had no notion of what it's alleged they were up to,' Barnaby said.

'Quite.'

The QC did not resume his seat, contemplated the knight's face. 'Also, I fancy there's something going on in the Government which may help us even further. I think we'll hear about it shortly.'

Barnaby turned his head to the barrister, but refrained from asking a question.

'Wheels within wheels,' Sir John said, nearly the first words he'd spoken in the half-hour. It was the kind of thing he was very familiar with. What he was counting on. He was grateful that Chadwick had come here. He couldn't face that hell-hole of chambers again.

'Something like that,' Chadwick smiled.

53

The Melbourne Club is the most exclusive, and the Australian the best in Melbourne, though the Athenaeum is comfortable, and the Commercial Travellers' Club superior in its building and appointments.

George D. Meudell, The Pleasant Career of a Spendthrift

Clarke's The Burglar's Horror
The New Patent Safety Night Light.
Advertisement, Table Talk, 1893

Inferno

THE FIRST TELEPHONE CALL came through to the superintendent at the Head Fire Station at twenty-seven minutes after six that evening. At twenty-eight past, he sounded a general emergency. Thirty-seven firemen, the two steam-operated engines, hose-carts, ladder carriages and salvage vans turned out from the Head, the No. 2, the North Melbourne, and Carlton stations.

The straining horses hauling the engines from the Head station hurtled through the streets. The rush hour was nearly over. At twenty-nine minutes to seven, as they turned the corner of Collins and Elizabeth streets, a blood-red glow stained the sky over the city's east end.

At sixteen minutes to seven, as the first engines arrived at the scene, the bow windows of Dewhurst's Book Shop and those on the three floors above, blew out. This was succeeded by a high-pitched sonata of tinkling glass. In an eye-blink, a vast sheet of flame, fuelled by the ingress of air, engulfed the entire facade. The crowd still assembling on the opposite pavement went diving for cover.

At the back of the dining-room of the Melbourne Club, Philip Larkin looked up from his plate. A strange, general murmur had arisen. Then, as if the signal for a time-honoured club ritual had sounded, members on all sides were putting down their cutlery and glasses, clutching serviettes, rising from tables and moving towards the Collins Street windows which, suddenly, unaccountably, were lit with a vulgar red glare.

He put down his knife and fork and joined them.

'My God!' a member ahead of him said, a split-second before a chorus of other, startled exclamations rang out.

He reached the windows as the first fire-engines arrived and the stricken building's windows blew out. He had it in a glance, seventy yards or so down the hill, on the other side. He left the dining-room and ran down the stairs. He seized one of the porters, took him aside, quickly wrote an address on a card, gave it to the man with instructions and two pounds and sent him on his way.

He followed the man into the street. Pandemonium had broken out. The police were rushing to set up barriers, other fire-engines were rattling over the tramlines, people were rushing away from the heat. Suddenly, the steamers came into action, shooting great streams of water at the building. He pushed his way through the crowd; all around him faces had a coppery look.

A curtain of soaring flames now enclosed the building. Behind it, with a thunderous roar, a floor fell in sending a new cloud of cinders and sparks boiling skywards. He could not get closer than fifty yards. A crowd of a thousand or so were being held back. Fat hoses coiled in the street, leaking sprays of water. At each new explosion the crowd shouted. He held a handkerchief over his nose and mouth...

It was consumed with astonishing speed. Nothing to be saved. Poor Hanna! What a cruel blow! Twenty-five years snuffed out like that. Thank God, they'd been closed when it started.

With a sound like a thunder-clap the roof fell in, and the flaming deadweight of rafters crashed down into the street. Fortunately the heat had driven the firemen well back. Six engines were pouring out water now in Collins Street. The South Melbourne Brigade had arrived and were working at the rear in Flinders Lane trying to save adjoining buildings.

He glanced back up Collins Street. Every balcony, verandah and window was occupied by spectators. In the club windows, the watching members were silhouetted. They were being served with brandy and cigars. The pulsating red glare had obliterated the club's comprehensive electric lighting from three hundred Edison bulbs. His eyes were streaming...

Hanna and Susan arrived at the club at half-past seven. He'd returned there to wait. He stepped forward as he saw their faces emerge from the crowd. At that moment, in one piece, the building's facade fell into the street, revealing a vast hill of embers over which licked wicked tongues of flame, but not the slightest sign of Hanna Dewhurst's sixty-thousand volumes.

'Hanna, I'm so terribly sorry.' He took her hand. She was dead-pale, but seemed otherwise composed. He could see that she expected the worst.

'All gone…?'

'I'm afraid so.'

'How could it have started?'

'There'll be an investigation.'

Susan had taken her arm, he took the other. The heat was abating, and they went to see. From across the street, they stared at the ruin. The fires in the adjoining buildings had been brought under control. The crowd was beginning to drift away. Faces were passing by, staring curiously at the doom-struck group.

'My father's, my life—in ashes,' she murmured.

Susan caught it. 'Hanna, you can re-build, re-stock within twelve months. Surely the insurance will cover it.'

'Yes, Philip has taken care of that,' she said quietly.

Larkin's mind had suddenly jumped like a belt on a machine missing a notch. The insurance…He was remembering, trying to remember more. An inspector of police approached him, had a few words. A man had been seen running from the building, seconds before the first flames were noticed…He barely took this in.

He could hardly speak as he took them home in a hansom. But the two women were silent, staggered by the calamitous event, by this turn of fortune. What a day this has been! Susan thought.

A terrible dread had fallen on him. He dropped them at Carlton Gardens, pleaded other urgent business, said he would return in an hour, and instructed the cabby to go out to an address in Parkville as quickly as he could.

Twenty minutes later he hurried up the garden path of Smithson, his clerk. He was perspiring freely. Smithson opened the door himself, was astonished to see his employer.

'Mr Larkin…?'

'Smithson, good evening, do you remember the insurance policy for Dewhurst's Book Shop? What did we do?'

He'd almost gabbled the questions. His clerk stared at him, alarmed at his obvious agitation. He'd never seen him like this.

'We cancelled the old policy, took out a new one with Liverpool and Lancashire for the same amount, paid the premium.'

Philip slumped back against the door-jamb. Smithson's face mirrored his concern. 'Are you all right, Mr Larkin?'

Philip straightened up, gave a crooked, sad smile. 'I am now. The premises burned down tonight, and I remembered we were to do something about the insurance—but I couldn't remember whether we had.'

He went slowly back to town in the superannuated hansom—as to driver, horse and vehicle—and it, and its pace, suited his frame of mind perfectly. He stared out the window with glazed eyes, and thought grimly: Things can't go on like this. Get your life sorted out.

54

Mr James Munro late Premier of Victoria, and who resigned his position as Agent-General last month, filed his schedule in the Insolvency Court on Wednesday…

Table Talk, 3.2.1893

Mr Gillies has declined the Agent-Generalship…A Victorian politician who does not grab the first opportunity of drawing a salary of £2,500 a year is certainly to be ranked amongst statesmen.

Table Talk, 24.3.1893

Barbed Wire

'WELL, ARE THEY going to slip through the net?' Wallace asked Binks. 'Get clear at the eleventh hour? What d'you think?'

From his seat at the board table, the clerk studied his employer. Behind his unruffled demeanour the liquidator was deadly angry. But we expected something like this, the clerk thought. He said, 'Makes it harder.' Much harder.

The liquidator scanned the morning papers again. *Attorney-General Alters Charge in First Bank of Victoria Trial*, trumpeted *The Age*; below that, another headline: *Solicitor-General Resigns*. Yesterday morning it had reported the conflagration in Collins Street. He thought: Poor Hanna! It seems calamities are stalking us on all sides.

And, yesterday, they had learnt a good deal of the battle going on in cabinet. The Solicitor-General had gone to the Crown Law Office to give instructions to reinstate the original indictment, but the Attorney-General had beaten him to it: the Crown Law officers had declined to take his instructions. He'd appealed to the Premier who had done his best to pour oil on the troubled waters, but had stopped short of intervening.

The Solicitor-General had resigned and written to *The Age*

setting out his reasons, describing the ethical and moral quagmire which the Government—in this case, and in general—was stuck in.

'The public's behind him,' Wallace said, 'and behind us. He's forcing a by-election for his seat. He'll win and he'll be back, a real thorn in the Government's side.'

Binks agreed it was highly probable.

'Though, maybe they'll offer him the Agent-Generalship in London,' Wallace said sardonically.

Binks thought it probable, but improbable that he'd accept it.

'The Attorney's got a barbed-wire mind. Every spike on it is pernicious.'

On that point, Binks was agreeable.

'I'll see Danby this morning. He'll be furious.'

Furious was not a state Binks could imagine the Crown Prosecutor being in—sarcastic, perhaps.

This development, disastrous though it was, at least was a distraction from the thoughts which Wallace had carried home from the club on Monday evening, after Larkin's revelation. He'd found a message from Prahran informing him that Susan had, indeed, carried out her intention.

His first impulse had been to go to Carlton Gardens. To find out the impact on her of that interview. To make his further explanation and plea. Instead, he'd roamed through his house, room by room, while Mrs Beattie listened as she darned his socks. He'd pulled up in the drawing-room which Hilda Wilberforce had found so drab. She must make the move! His best hope was for her to do this—for it to come naturally out of her investigations, her considerations. Then he could speak. He'd roamed on, pulled up again. Though—was he being too cold-blooded, too logical?

These matters had twisted in his mind until he'd lain down on his bed, fully clothed, and fallen asleep not to wake till dawn.

⸻

Susan was *not* ready to see him. Nothing had changed about that. His instinct had been well-founded. The next morning when she arrived at Boyd & Montrose, she had considered fully the 'next step'—the idea which had come at Prahran; had determined to act on it—if William would help.

However, that was to wait for several hours. As she went to a conference in his room, she told herself: I am *not* obsessed.

248

The others were waiting. William in the cracked leather chair, Maybury and Issacs on bentwoods, another of which was positioned for her in a spot which had become customary. They stood up. She thought: Another crisis.

William had been unable to obtain an appointment with Stevens at the Commercial Bank. That institution was in turmoil, totally taken up with the reconstruction meetings. Whether the store's overdraft facility was safe, was an open question. The rumours were that they had begun to call up overdrafts.

But the problem of overwhelming urgency was the £7,500 owing to the First Bank of Victoria. A second and final demand for payment had arrived. 'We're in a better position,' he said, 'but not safe enough, I think, to repay it.'

The store had made a profit in March. More significant to its survival, increased cash had been coming in due to the store-wide sales and the bargain basement. A new range of stock—mainly sponsored by Susan—would be on their floors for winter and spring. But it was going to be a close-run thing. The repayment of one overdraft, the continuance of the other, were vital.

Isaacs gave a forecast of the cash position at the month's end, canvassed each and every prospect of improving it. Expenses were cut to the bone, sales and income aspects gone over. His opinion was that they might meet half of the £7,500 but that was the very best that might be done. He spoke in his slow, lisping voice. Susan felt they were all exhausted, mentally, and physically.

Slumped in his chair, William mused aloud on whether he might speak to Wallace. They watched him in silence. He straightened up, dismissed the notion as unworthy—and impracticable. Wallace couldn't hand out special favours. The meeting concluded, predictably, with no decision taken.

Susan had hardly spoken a word. She had put in place all that she could to get the store going forward—this was a problem William must find the solution to. That thought did not make it easier for her to ask for his assistance now. She had remained when the others had left. She did offer one piece of advice: 'I think the only finance obtainable will be from a private source.'

He nodded, and looked at her acutely. 'Is there something else?'

'Yes…This isn't the right moment, but I wish to ask you a favour. I believe you've had occasion to consult Dr Blackstone…Would you introduce me to him?'

William gazed at her. He sat back. After a moment, he said: 'I hope you…' He stopped. 'You know, he's not in general practice. He's a specialist in mental disease.'

'Yes, I know.'

He thought: What is going on here?

'Of course. I'll write to him immediately.'

When Susan had left the room he sat, immobile. Memories of his own association with the alienist had returned to him. He shrugged, as though to shed them, concentrated on Susan. Was this to do with Wallace—or had some other grave difficulty arisen? He could only think of Blackstone in that context.

<hr>

If Wallace could have had an inkling of the move which Susan was now planning, he would have been flabbergasted. However, Otto Rudd, spick-and-span as always for a meeting with a client, has entered the boardroom and the liquidator waves him to a seat. Binks watches sceptically from the side-line, though he has come to respect the detective's work. It's the multiplying layers of the situation surrounding them which is getting under his skin.

Wallace smiled. 'Good morning, Rudd. I hope you bring us good news. We could use some.'

The detective shrugged marginally. Good or bad, hard to say. He took the three pasted-up messages and arranged them on the table.

'Julian Ellis,' he said.

Wallace drew in his breath.

'Well, well.' He seemed bemused. 'Did you confront him with it?'

'I did. No doubt about it. He's the one.'

The liquidator continued to absorb this. 'The poor foolish man. Weak as water. About as harmless a fellow as one could find.'

Rudd had his own idea about this. Unobtrusively, he eyed the healing abrasion on his client's head. Hard knocks could come from surprising sources.

'What did he think he'd achieve?' The liquidator didn't expect an answer, and the detective didn't intend supplying one. It was a case where a lot of water had gone under the bridge—most of which he would never know about. 'Is it at an end?'

'I reckon so.'

'Very well. We'll rule it off.' He dwelt on it for a few moments, then glanced at Binks. 'We've got another job for you, Rudd. Mr Harbrace's house. We'd like you to keep a watch there. Make sure Mr

Harbrace and his family aren't disturbed. Do you take my meaning?'

Otto Rudd nodded. He'd struck a good vein of work here. 'Keep him out of harm's way?'

'That's the score.'

'Body-guarding,' Binks intervened concisely. 'Twenty-four hours a day, till further notice. So you'll need to make arrangements.'

Rudd was considering an assistant. An ex-Carlton ruckman came to the fore. 'Any particular point of danger to watch for?'

'Try Savage and Sandhurst for size,' Binks growled.

But the detective knew that.

55

Nine-tenths of the doctors established in Melbourne before 1880 were immigrants trained usually in the great London and Scottish hospitals. The doyens of the profession—men like T. M. Girdlestone...the gossipy litterateur James Nield and the surgical virtuoso Thomas Fitzgerald—had generally learned their medicine and ethics in the bad old days before the advent of antiseptic surgery and the 1858 Medical Act.

Graeme Davison, The Rise and Fall of Marvellous
Melbourne

A Hypothetical Case

THE INSURANCE ASSESSOR had been working methodically among the charred timbers, rubble and sodden ash for over an hour. Waiting in Collins Street, Hanna wondered what he found that so absorbed him—what method could be applied amid such total destruction. A few walls remained standing, but her stock, fixtures and fittings, had vanished.

She stood in a dream. On a sparkling autumn morning, it was hard to believe this black reality. At her back, the sounds of life, commerce, went on. One flourishing unit had been subtracted; not a ripple remained marking its active existence. Why would it leave one? In this city, major institutions were falling like dominoes, leaving only consequences. Yet, she heard a faint persistent echo: the swish-swish-swish of the brass-framed revolving door...still revolving in her head.

This wouldn't do. Philip had been consulting with the assessor. He came back, hat in hand, his shoes and trousers dusted with ash, a black smear on his forehead. She turned her face to him, expectantly. He walked slowly, eyes down.

Something had happened to him. The fire had pulled him up: the impact when he first saw it, his sense of shock concerning the insurance policy; a catalyst. Suddenly, he'd seen Hanna's life—their long association—in numerous flashed-back images. He'd found himself standing off, taking a measuring look at her, at himself, at the future.

It had been an intense, sobering experience—becoming more and more so as he'd considered it.

Gazing at her now in Collins Street, he was remembering her visit to his house on her mission for Susan, how he'd thought of her later that night.

With a conscious effort, he lifted himself out of this. 'No-one has any idea how it started, though witnesses pin-pointed that man running from the building. At any rate, the insurance claim will go through.'

He had lodged the claim. By great good fortune, all the account books, even stock lists, had been with her accountant. The past two evenings he'd been at Carlton Gardens working with her on it.

Hanna felt this new current coming from him; firmly, she ascribed it to the emergency: the man of affairs stepping into the breach to aid a friend; would not permit herself to read more into it. The fire seemed to have killed off those earlier flickers of optimism.

But the Phoenix *will* rise from the ashes, she'd told Susan grimly. 'A new start,' she'd said.

Susan, amid her own troubles, had smiled at that.

'I'll re-build,' she said to him.

'Of course. The first thing is to arrange demolition and clearance. No-one likes the look of those walls. In the meantime, we should consult an architect. I've asked an estate agent to look for temporary premises...shouldn't be a problem.' He turned to gaze at the ruins. His tone had been earnest and involved.

She glanced up at the azure sky, at the ruin, down a coolish, thinly populated Collins Street—a quick kaleidoscope; her eyes came to rest on his face in profile. What should she say?

'Philip, you've given me too much of your time. I do so appreciate it. And, the moral support. You have this court case, and Heaven knows what else...'

'Don't say any more. *This* is much closer to home.'

He turned and smiled at her with determination. At that moment, from standpoints which did not differ that much, they were each thinking of Helena Spencer.

A quarter-mile up Collins Street from where Hanna and Philip stood together, unconscious of their similar thought, Susan entered a high, narrow building, the foyer of which was floored with marble, and chilly when you stepped into its dusk from the sunshine. She shivered in a brief spasm. Brass plates notified the public that here was a bastion of medical science.

She had noted only one name, and now she noted it again—gilded on a frosted glass door. William's letter had been sent, and a note had come back confirming the appointment.

In her appearance—especially her face, but also her light-boned, wonderfully proportioned figure—Susan had been compared by certain admirers to a rare and beautiful piece of porcelain. These snap judgments were, of course, ridiculous flights of fancy by star-struck persons grappling to get on terms with what they saw. Such persons didn't know her in her line of business, hadn't seen her intent on a mission. In that manifestation, her steady blue gaze seemed to probe your inner sanctum, made notions of 'delicacy' redundant.

She was not nervous, though some did enter this building with trepidation, and, almost fawning respect. Others would have been daunted by the speciality of the man whose rooms she was about to enter. Susan belonged to neither class. She needed information, and would track it down by the most pragmatic means to hand. However, these days, she knew that she had a slightly out-of-control momentum.

She compressed her lips. If he's any good, and can consult in these terms…who knows?

Dr Blackstone, graduate of Heidelberg University, former student of the famous Emil Kraepelin, held his gaze on the young woman for a few silent moments after the introductions. Then, in a mannerism, looked above her head as if gazing into the far distance—or the future. He thought: A remarkably beautiful woman. And remarkably composed, though nuances of 'pressure'.

She thought: About forty. Those eyes: rounded, staring, almost black. Like Mrs Wilberforce's. Dark complexion, brusque manner. A deep baritone of a voice. He must speak German. A careless, patronizing air? Is *this* the kind of man who might help me?

An antiseptic odour, tinged with tobacco smoke, permeated the room. 'Well, Miss Fairfax, how can I help?'

Susan stripped off her gloves, laid them precisely on his desk, regarded them. Her lips were compressed again, flickered slightly as though connected to her thoughts. The serious eyes came up to his; she wore a blue silk scarf and it made them strikingly blue. 'Doctor, you may find my request unusual, even frivolous. Though it's not to me.'

'Much I hear within these walls is unusual in its way. Don't feel constrained.' He waited.

A sympathetic tone? A slight shifting of his ground?

'I seek your opinion on the character of a man. On his involvement in a circumstance which I find...inexplicable. A situation, which logic tells me, I should abandon. I'm not an idealist. I've not led the sheltered life of many of my sex and class. I've seen black conduct—know it flourishes in our midst. Yet, in this case, I cannot understand how a man with other admirable qualities, could be so deficient in a matter of natural human feelings. Is it an ugly flaw in the glass—or, is there a deeper explanation? Am I making my dilemma clear?'

The faintest of smiles touched his lips. 'You might speak of Everyman.'

She frowned.

'You wish me to consider a hypothetical case? Give you an opinion?'

'It is an *actual* case.'

'Of course. But it seems I'm not to interview the person in question?'

She nodded. 'That's impossible.'

'Well, you had better tell me more about it.'

So, for the next fifteen minutes, Susan, in her matter-of-fact Lancashire accents outlined the case so far as she knew it, giving no names.

Ah, Wallace, Blackstone thought. It was interesting how events, connections, floated around society, slow-waltzed through the newspapers, sometimes through the courts—sometimes into his rooms—revealing new aspects. He listened without questions, once or twice his hand went to a box of cheroots, but didn't take one.

'His own children...' she said, finally finishing where, in her mind, it had all begun.

Blackstone meditated on the beautiful face, then on the long-distance. He knew Wallace by sight, had given slight attention to the events reported in the press. What was she doing at Boyd & Montrose? She said she'd been 'in the world' and certainly her talk and manner supported it. But, not enough to eradicate blind-spots such as this.

He said, 'You see his conduct in relation to his children—in relation to the whole affair—as reprehensible, as a flaw in his character?'

'As cold-hearted.'

'Quite. Yet you search for an explanation—a redeeming one—it seems.'

'If such exists.'

Blackstone moved his hand again, and this time it came back with a cheroot. 'Do you mind?'

'At least to understand…'

'You haven't allowed him the opportunity to cover the ground himself. That might've been—might still be—the most useful course.'

She shook her head. 'I've considered it a hundred times.'

'You've not trusted yourself?'

'I know the basic facts. A meeting might lead to my persuasion. My nature is independent. I fear a mistake. I *must* understand the possibilities.'

Blackstone lit the cheroot. She'd been oblivious to his polite inquiry. 'You might understand them already.'

What did he mean? Now, she was watching him and waiting.

He puffed on the cheroot. 'I would caution you, the processes of the mind are deeply mysterious. Despite the steady advance of science, I surmise, will always be so. Observation of patterns of behaviour, case histories, may throw light. Frequently, we don't find an answer.

'The case you describe…doubtless, will have several levels. On one, it might be quite simply explained. It's common that men of this class don't take much interest in their children—as infants. Aren't much involved in their up-bringing. It's the same here as it is in England. The nurse, the nursery, the governess, the boarding-school, etc.

'Keeping the existence of a family—children—secret, is a more complicated zone.'

He glanced at the cheroot in his fingers.

'Here, a motive might be found in the so-called moralities of our society, in the drawbacks to challenging them. Men are ambitious animals—sometimes blinded to all but that climb up the ladder—to whatever goals they've shaped in their minds. Some are driven by obsessions—such as a quest for justice, by a passion to sweep away what they find repugnant. They see themselves as *agents* of change. All else pales into insignificance.'

He smiled with a hint of cynicism. 'It's all part of the rich pageant of human frailty, Miss Fairfax, and there are infinite variations.

'In this case, another zone could be considered. More on the clinical side, one could say. The woman died in child-birth. The children survived. In his grief, the father more or less rejects what he sees as the cause of his grievous loss. It's a refusal to assimilate or accept. A type of enduring melancholia. It's not a process of the intellect.'

The smooth baritone fades away. He has laid aside his cheroot, and glances at her. While he talks his eyes have been either on her face, or on that patch of wall. Has that almost translucent complexion become more so? The wall is unchanged.

'If that hypothesis is relevant, the implication follows: the man was very much in love with the woman.'

Susan has listened—sitting perfectly still, almost tranquillized by that voice. Yet, her mind has been ranging beyond the information he's been assembling for her—much of which she's worked out for herself. It is this last which holds her.

'Why didn't he marry her?'

Blackstone lifts his hands, lets them fall with a soft thud, palm-down on the desk. 'The realm of speculation. If you want the answer to that, there's only one source to ask.'

Susan has received no illuminating flash of light, but the matter has been turned over in her mind. When she is alone, she will go over it. Blackstone has not given her as much as she expected when she'd approached William—but, more than she'd thought to have at the outset of the consultation.

She wonders if black eyes, and *that* kind of voice, are requisites for his profession. She takes up the gloves, draws them through her hand. He does not seem disposed to say more, but suddenly he does.

'You either meet him to seek information, or you turn your back on it and walk away. Aren't those your options? Whichever you choose—I wouldn't delay any longer.'

'Thank you. I do appreciate the trouble you've taken. Your fee?

'An account will be posted.'

She nods, rises, the rustle of her skirt seeming abnormally loud. He is still thinking. He says, almost with an air of upturning a delicate vase and inspecting its maker's mark: 'Sometimes the doubts we have, the answers we seek, are really to *other* questions lying deep within our own nature.'

She looks at him closely, shakes his hand and leaves.

What a strange life the man must lead, sitting in that room listening, peering into the mists of minds like a mariner searching the night for a light-house. Of course, he knows it's Wallace.

With that thought, she descends the stairs, but it is his last remark which is the one which, finally, stands in her mind. She knows, without a doubt, that it's the salient information.

Hilda Wilberforce looked up sharply at what Judge Mountain had said. He repeated it. 'I'm to try the First Bank of Victoria case which starts next week.'

She couldn't conceal her surprise. 'But you *know* John.'

'I'm acquainted with him—mainly through your splendid dinner parties. There wouldn't be a judge in Melbourne who doesn't know Sir John.'

'Well, I have very mixed feelings about this.'

The judge's eyes gleamed acutely in the flaccidity of his face. 'It's out of our hands, Hilda. I'll hear the evidence, and instruct the jury— just as any one of my brothers would.'

'You don't mean to say you're all stamped precisely out of the same mould?'

Judge Mountain smiled. 'Now Hilda…'

He continued to smile, thinking of something else. 'My dear, you are looking beautiful today.'

'Good God, Edgar! Yesterday I might've looked beautiful, today I look ordinary. We females are not in a static state, you know. We ebb and flow like the tides.'

The judge considered this.

With an irritated look, she rose from her chair and walked across the room to adjust the Paris silk tassels on her yellow damask curtains. 'I don't know, I used to think the connectiveness of people, events, in our city was interesting. I'm coming around to thinking that it's claustrophobic—and malignant.'

The judge didn't reply, but he knew what she meant.

56

The eyes of the LORD *are in every place beholding the evil and the good.*

Proverbs, 15 (3)

Shocks

MURDOCH WAS DEAD.

The liquidator was stunned. For a few moments, he stood in the boardroom as if converted to stone. But an image of the busy, earnest, perfectly turned-out press-man, with his bright button-holes, his carefully researched articles, honed, scathing sentences, danced in his brain.

Dead, in a nondescript hall. Friday. Half-past seven in the morning. Four days before the trial.

Binks had had the news from the *Table Talk* office—had rushed with it to Wallace. The journalist's body with its broken neck had been found at the foot of the steep stairs in his residential building. According to the medical officer summoned, he'd been dead for several hours.

Now, standing with his employer, chillingly, the clerk remembered the morning when they'd heard of ex-head cashier Hubble's body being taken from the Yarra.

Wallace sat down suddenly, shaking his head. 'The poor fellow. Are there any details?'

Binks cleared his throat. 'Not many. Dead for hours, the medico says...Found by another resident. The stairs are steep, but Murdoch was a small man, light on his feet and used to them.'

Wallace stared. 'What are you saying?'

'It *might've* been an accident.'

'Good God,' Wallace said softly.

They communed on this. Murdoch had had many in his sights, and some of his articles had cut deep. And, in the case in front of them, he'd cut as deep as any. Binks eyed his employer. 'Violence and threats have been coming out of the woodwork. Take yourself, take Rudd—take Hubble. I reckon this smells deadly, too.'

Wallace stood up, began to pace the room. 'The police and the Coroner'll investigate.' He looked at his clerk. He'd caught a whiff of brandy.

'Wouldn't expect much. Open and shut—unless a witness to the contrary is turned up.'

'Harbrace?'

'Rudd and his man are on watch.'

'All right…'

With an effort, Wallace switched his thinking to the future. 'Better break it to Mr Larkin, ask him to meet us at Danby's office. We've got some re-shaping to do.'

<hr />

While Judge Mountain, with the cool detachment which he habitually displayed (even in his exciting wine cellar), was moving towards his duty at ten o'clock on Tuesday, at the Criminal Court, other lawyers were engaged in a last flurry of preparation. With the tenacity of the stump jump plough invented in 1876 in the Mallee, these legal minds were re-ploughing and turning over the evidence.

Whether by accident, or design, Murdoch's story on the secretive liquidations of Sir John's companies, on the secret compositions entered into by each of the defendants, had been sliced from the case.

And Danby's natural pessimism had increased. The alteration of the indictment to *conspiring* to issue etc., had hit the prosecution a blow beneath the belt. In an editorial, *Table Talk* had chastised and mocked the Government over it, but that changed nothing.

However, Wallace suspected that the Crown Prosecutor, when at his most pessimistic, might be at his most effective. They had discussed the assignment of Judge Mountain to the trial. 'Is he up to it?' Wallace had mused. 'I've never been before him.'

'He'll do as well as most. Though if Judge Molesworth could be got out of the Insolvency Court, he'd be the man for us.' The Crown Prosecutor released a rare smile. 'This isn't a complicated case. What we've got to watch out for is that Chadwick QC don't twist it into a Gordian knot that the jury can't untie. He was remarkably silent at the committal. Holding his fire was one reason, I'd think. He's in his element in these big trials.'

'It's time he was cut down to size.'

Danby smiled briefly. It had crossed his mind.

An impromptu wake for Murdoch was held at the All Nations Hotel. The Coroner was going to have the body a few days. Wallace and Binks went out there for a half-hour.

Maurice Brodzky, seated in the side bar, was the centre of proceedings. The editor of *Table Talk*, cigar in hand, a short, broad, darkly handsome man, fortyish, with a soup-strainer moustache, acknowledged the stream of men who kept coming in, then stood around drinking beer with their hats on. Murdoch had had no relatives in the Colony.

Wallace had never met Brodzky, though he'd seen him about town. He'd heard somewhere that he'd been in the Franco-Prussian War, had a medal from the French Government.

'Pleased to shake your hand, Mr Wallace.'

'And yours, Mr Brodzky.'

Binks standing aside, grinned to himself: He'd had a notion of Livingstone and Stanley meeting in darkest Africa.

'A bad business, this,' Wallace said.

The editor let an inch of ash go to the floor. 'My men are trying to get a line on it. You know as well as I, appearances can't be trusted in this city.'

'Mr Murdoch was more than helpful. We're grateful. Will there be a fund for relatives, a testimonial?'

'No fund, no relatives. His testimonial, well, that's buried in our pages. Fifty or more unsigned articles for the public benefit. And, for posterity. Those that come after are going to be able to see how things were done here, what was what. No-one's got down to bedrock like we have.'

Wallace nodded, took the beer that was passed to him.

Brodzky studied him. 'We're still behind you. And others might be, so watch your back. But you know about that. Good luck.'

The editor turned away to greet new arrivals, and soon after Wallace and Binks returned to the bank.

A letter had been delivered to Wallace's house that afternoon. The envelope was addressed in a flowing feminine hand which Mrs Beattie had seen once before. However, it was to wait unseen on his desk amongst the other post. The pace for the liquidator was accelerating. The trial was now drawing the participants to it with the force of a tidal race.

Katherine arrived at the Harbraces' cottage about four o'clock, accompanied by young Tom who had come out by himself to Fitzroy with a message from his mother. The small boy, standing on her doorstep, cap in hand, had shocked her.

'Jean is sick,' he'd said.

Katherine stood beside the mother, staring down at the small pale face, the large eyes, the slight smile, the rag-doll held under her throat. Silent Jean. She felt the child's brow. She stood staring down, thinking.

Harbrace coughed from the next room where he was propped up in his bed. The baby lay, listless, on Mrs Harbrace's hip. She turned to face the woman, examined the exhausted face. 'Would you let me take Jean home, and I'll call a doctor. I'll take Tom, too. More illness is too much for you to manage here.'

'Yes, Mrs Boyd,' she said quietly. 'Would you do that for us? You've done so much…'

'Of course, let's wrap her up, and we'll get a cab.'

'But not Tom,' the woman said. 'He helps me so much.'

Otto Rudd, in position in a doorway opposite the Collingwood cottage, said out of the corner of his mouth to the six-foot-four, youngish man beside him: 'That's Mrs Boyd from the Ladies' Benevolent Society who's helping the family out.'

'A do-gooder,' the ex-Carlton ruckman said.

The detective shot him a look. Despite his broken nose, and a long-ago torn ear, the ex-footballer had a calm and reflective face. 'Well, Ambrose, thank God for it. The Government isn't showing willing.'

The man from Carlton stared at the door which had now closed. He hadn't had a job in a month, and this was a godsend.

Rudd said, 'I'm going off now. You know what to do.'

The giant nodded. He does, the detective thought, adjusted his bowler, and went off to an early tea—there was a street stall in Smith Street, where he could get a sixpenny dish of oysters sprinkled with pepper and vinegar. His heart warmed at the prospect. Then he'd get some sleep.

57

FASHIONABLE EVENING DRESS
The season is about to commence, not-withstanding bank failures,
scares and general depression, and evening dress demands atten-
tion...Charming gowns may be made at very moderate expense in
velveteen...Satin has quite come in again...
Illustrated Australian News, 1.6.1893

The Blue Horizon

WILLIAM LEFT the Commercial Bank vastly relieved: a hole at one end of the ship was plugged. At last, Stevens had been able to spare him a few minutes. Both men had stood for the brief interview. The manager had aged ten years since mid-February. William was taken aback. Though why? On all sides, battered men were stalking through the city, human flotsam and jetsam from the '80s.

'We are calling up some overdrafts,' the banker said, 'but Boyd & Montrose isn't on the list. We'll be reviewing your situation mid-May as arranged. But don't for Heaven's sake present cheques which would overdraw your limit. That'd put the cat amongst the pigeons.'

Boyd had nodded, shaken hands, and left. Electricity seemed to crackle in the air as he strode from the banking chamber. The first reconstruction meeting was to be held tomorrow. He thought: This'll be a weight off Hilda's shoulders. As it was off his own. His worry now focused on the leak at the other end.

Isaacs waited at the door to his office. His face was set and pale.

O God!—that same crackle of electricity. The small black-suited man said quickly in one lisping breath, 'I've just heard from Larkins'. A receiver's coming in tomorrow morning.'

In Edinburgh Gardens the leaves sailed down. Today, the fall seemed at its zenith, a glinting, red-gold rain descending to commune with the grass, earth, in an end-of-season, death-bed sigh. So thought Katherine, gazing across the street from her drawing-room window.

Behind her, a slight sound made her turn. The three-year-old girl was peeping around the corner of the door, the rag-doll held to her cheek; a hesitant but trusting smile slowly appeared. Silent Jean. Almost so—a few words were now coming at memorable moments. She had spent yesterday in bed; the doctor had pronounced a slight cold. Today, she had been going as quiet as a kitten through each room, as though she was discovering the wide-world.

Katherine smiled brightly, went to her, impulsively swept her up in her arms. 'Dearest, let's go and see what Mary is doing.'

Mrs Wilberforce received William's note at noon. Absorbing the devastating news, she went to her small drawing-room windows, and much as Katherine had done, gazed on the even richer leaf-fall in progress in the venerable Fitzroy Gardens. But it was a blur. Financial calculations were running through her brain, reflected in her dark eyes. A receiver! The demand facing Boyd & Montrose was for £7,900 in total. William said they could raise only £2,500.

It seemed the end. The entry of a receiver would force the Commercial Bank's hand; the store's financial underpinning would collapse like a house of cards. Even if her funds had not been locked up in the damaged banks, it would have been imprudent, out of character, for her to have sunk in more. But she probably would have...A mortgage on this beloved house? Not by tomorrow. She thought of Judge Mountain—of other friends. It was an impossibility to ask them to take on such a risk. For the first time in her life where finance was involved, she felt helpless.

Her eyes cleared. Abruptly, grimly, she was regarding the season bleeding to death before her eyes. She thought: All things run to their end.

'I feel so sorry for William,' Susan said in a depressed voice. 'He's fought so hard. Of course, sorry for everyone.' Including myself, she thought.

The dinner table had been cleared. She and Hanna sat with their coffee. The Lancashire woman had told Hanna of the catastrophic blow which had fallen that day, of what probably lay ahead. 'It seems Tom Montrose's ship must go down.'

Hanna was silent. After a moment she said, 'Won't the receiver keep it going?'

'In my experience, the receiver's closely followed by the liquidator. The Commercial Bank will step in to protect themselves.'

Hanna nodded thoughtfully. They moved into the drawing-room, each preoccupied. Susan began to leaf through a journal. She had had no time today to think of the letter which she'd written to Angus Wallace, but now she did. She recalled each phrase, weighed it. She'd fancied that Dr Blackstone might have been watching over her shoulder as she'd written them.

Hanna stood up abruptly. Susan stared at her.

'What is it?'

The bookseller was gazing at the dark silhouette of the Exhibition Building, as though she'd just seen an unexpected light.

'Hanna?'

'Susan, I know what can be done. I must see Philip immediately.'

She rushed from the room and ran downstairs calling for the maid, her coat. From the hall, she gave an excited wave to her friend who had come on to the first-floor landing, and went out to the street where the maid was already looking for a hansom. There had been a note of triumph in that final wave.

Philip Larkin was not home, but he was expected before half-past eight. It was now half-past seven. Hanna had ridden across town and heard the General Post Office and Town Hall clocks chime seven o'clock. She asked to wait, and was shown to a seat by the fire in his study. The reception rooms were all dark, except for the dining-room, where she noted two places were set—apparently for dinner. What did that signify?

She sat staring into the flames with time now to reflect on the idea she'd had, the decision she'd taken. She was not having second thoughts. On the contrary, she was impatient to get matters moving— there wasn't much time. And anxious. A tiny splinter of ice had lodged in her breast. But she put that aside. How long was it since she'd been here on Susan's behalf—six days? It seemed an age. The house was as silent as a tomb; only the crackling of the fire.

Sonia—Philip's late wife—had not been her friend, though she'd known her quite well. An intense, serious person, dedicated to her work in women's hospitals. She'd had no time for frippery. Much like

Katherine, except more uncompromising. But not without a sense of humour. She remembered that Philip's social banter had seemed light relief against his wife's amused pessimism. They'd been very much in love.

As they'd stood before the ruin of her book shop, she'd resisted the intimation coming to her. Had she imagined it? The impact had blurred. Just as the intervening few days had faded her earlier spontaneous optimism concerning the status quo with Helena Spencer. In the aftermath of the fire, she'd been off-balance. And this fire's flames seemed to be mesmerizing her. What *was* his situation with Helena Spencer?

The muffled sound of a female voice in the hall broke into these thoughts. She looked up sharply—towards the door. At this hour, who could this be? Good God!...Not *her*!

The door opened, and Mrs Wilberforce swept into the room.

'Hanna!' She pulled up short. 'What a pleasant surprise!'

Hanna rose, and they embraced. Hilda Wilberforce, dressed in a plum-coloured velvet gown, trimmed with tinsel braid, a matching mantle on her shoulders, seemed more regal, more in command than ever—despite the disaster they were facing. But she was extremely surprised. Two days ago she'd called on Hanna with commiserations...What was going on? Had she missed a few beats? She removed her mantle in an extravagant gesture, masking these thoughts behind her warm smile.

'Have you come for supper, too?'

Hanna shook her head. 'I'm not expected.'

'But very welcome. You'll stay...?' Philip had entered, an expectant look on his face.

Hanna stared at the black circles under his eyes, took in the extremity of his strain. She was thinking quickly. There was nothing she wished to say to him that couldn't be said in front of Hilda. In fact, she was at the heart of it.

They were regarding her curiously, clearly at a loss. She drew in her breath.

'Susan's told me. Told me £5,000 is required. Philip, the insurance money. I wish to make it available. How can it be done?' She has spoken rapidly, her breast rising, falling.

Mrs Wilberforce and Philip stared, dumb-founded. She looked from one to the other. Hilda Wilberforce recovered first. 'Good Heavens! My dear girl. You don't know the *risk*. There's no certainty that amount of money will save it. It could all be lost.' She raised her hand—to stop a dangerous idea in its tracks.

'That isn't news to me. I know of the fight for survival.' Susan has given her a running report.

'Philip?' Mrs Wilberforce commanded.

'Of course, out of the question. A noble offer…'

'Which I insist be carried through,'—said with a flat determination.

'Hanna—why put at risk a good business for one so imperilled?' Hilda Wilberforce had transformed to her most formidable. She smiled, to lighten the moment. She thought: It's like the Charge of the Light Brigade: magnificent, but not war. 'You must consider yourself, your staff—your customers.'

Larkin said, 'I agree. The funds are going to be needed very shortly to re-build. Hanna, it's out of the question.' Professional reason weighted his voice.

Hanna looked at him for a long moment. 'It's not, you know. There'll still be enough funds to clear the site, to acquire temporary premises, order new stock, a good portion of which can be got on credit. Rent is cheap. The re-building can wait—indefinitely.'

'It might wait forever.'

'It doesn't seem to me that it's a fatal step.'

Mrs Wilberforce watched the two younger people in this face-to-face confrontation with a rising expectation—which had begun when she'd come through the door. Again, she thought: *Have* I missed a few beats?

Up against this obstinacy, Larkin strokes his chin, lowers his head to regard the turkey carpet. He feels himself in a corner, feels a conflict of interest. Hilda has come here tonight at short notice to discuss the crisis—at her request. As the legal adviser to the liquidator, it has put him in an invidious position. He and Wallace were pulling the rug out from under the store…But what else could they have done? They have their legal obligations—are under pressure, and scrutiny. Nonetheless, in a convoluted way, he is an architect of this damned perturbation!

Hanna watches, waits. She can guess the rough line of his thinking. Incestuous is not a word usually in her vocabulary, but she thinks of it now. It aptly describes the situation they are all interlocked in.

Hilda Wilberforce's thoughts had moved on. If the die *was* to be cast in this way, then she would have to step in at the end; take Hanna out of her risky exposure. The possibilities of borrowing against her frozen bank deposits, of raising a mortgage on her house, were now active in her mind. Her lips had tightened pragmatically.

Hanna broke the silence. 'My mind is made up.'

Larkin unlocked his gaze from the carpet, had had an earth-shaking realization.

Decisively, he said, 'Very well. You and I will do it. In partnership. You'll put in half, I'll do the same. I'll not permit you to go it alone.' How he might have prevented her wasn't obvious—but he appeared to be under a new nervous pressure which was hurrying his speech, constricting his breathing. His right hand, held in front of him, was shaking slightly. In fact, he had progressed beyond this vexed matter.

The two women stared at him with concern. Hanna said, 'Philip? Are you all right?'

Mrs Wilberforce moved forward slightly. The expectant force in her was on the rise, like milk on the boil.

He gazed at each woman in turn, cleared his throat. 'Quite. Hanna, I hope you'll forgive me the circumstances. In the presence of our oldest and dearest friend...'—his voice had faded to a low tone, yet was absolutely clear—'would you do me the great honour of becoming my wife?'

In her shock, Hanna froze, turned dead-pale. All the vigour she'd been deploying was gone in an instant. But, suddenly, points of colour flamed on her cheeks. Mrs Wilberforce's dark eyes had widened in a blink. In another, tears sprang into Hanna's.

'I've long hoped to hear those words.' Her voice is as quiet in the room as a draught of air. He steps forward, out of his agitation, takes her in his arms and kisses her. It is a confused moment, but one they will both, in its essence, always remember. Then Hilda is embracing her—and him—in a flurry of arms.

The East Melbourne matron was jubilant. She had come here with one situation in her sights, and seen that crystallized; now had seen another—in which she (and Laura) had laid out survey-lines—miraculously connected in one of those mysterious, climactic outcomes which she's had faith in all her life. She said, for at least the third time, 'Good Heavens! How wonderful!' Then, 'We must take *all* this news out to William and Katherine—immediately!'

Larkin hurried out, calling to his cook. 'Mrs Wilson! Cancel supper! My apologies!'

William had spent the afternoon—into the early evening—closeted with the store's solicitor, who was dead set in his opinion that every-thing had been done to postpone payment of the demand. The money was now required. In its absence, tomorrow morning the receiver would be sitting in the old leather chair, and William in the visitor's.

Before their late dinner, he'd told Katherine every detail. She'd come to stand beside him, her hand on his arm, the blue Irish eyes turned up to his.

'I've let everyone down. You. Hilda. The staff.'

'No-one could have worked harder, given up so much.' She could not help thinking of the mortgage on their house. It appeared inevitable that events would now run out of control. During dinner, which they could hardly eat, she tried to brighten him up with anec-dotes of the child's activities, the latest news of the Harbraces. In this she had an ulterior motive: so many were so much worse off than they would be.

It only turned him to another, vague, sense of anxiety. He'd been worried about her health—but there was a new blush in her cheeks, a light in her eye—and, paradoxically, it brought this fresh worry. Several times each night she rose to check on the child's breathing. The child's welfare, naturally enough, was pre-eminent in the house-hold's affairs. She was a lovely little girl...But where was it leading? Katherine was the most sensible of women, yet, in this matter?

She had gone upstairs, he was pacing the drawing-room, unable to look at the morning paper. Beyond the windows, the gardens infused a distinctly wintry atmosphere into the house. He glanced at the fire-place, no fire set. He stopped, listening: a vehicle arriving. He con-sulted his watch, and walked into the hall. Katherine had heard it also and was coming down the stairs. He opened the front door as Mrs Wilberforce came up the steps, closely followed by Hanna and Philip. Behind them lights swung in an arc as her carriage turned.

'What's happened?'—the first thing that struck him was that something had.

Hilda embraced him without a word and went in.

Larkin said, 'The receiver won't be coming in, old man. We've fixed it up.'

Incomprehension on his face, he followed them, waited while they greeted Katherine. Then, Larkin, standing in the middle of the room, explained concisely what had been decided. In a daze, William heard it. Katherine, not in a daze, listened to each word, her eyes never leaving Philip's face.

'There you are, William. And it's no good trying to talk Hanna—

or me—out of it. We've been through all that.'

Rooted to the spot, William gazed at them all. If Hilda, as half-owner of the store, who knew the risk, had accepted it, it wasn't his place to oppose it. Susan had said: It will have to be private funds. He'd known that.

They were giving him time. There had been shocks all round tonight. 'I hardly know what to say…Thank you both.'

'Thank Hanna,' Larkin said gaily.

Mrs Wilberforce's laugh broke the tension. 'There's another wonderful thing to tell you of,' she said smiling directly at Katherine. 'Philip?'

There was an exuberance—an excitement—in Larkin, which Katherine had noticed immediately. An atmosphere about him she hadn't seen for years. He went and took Hanna's hand, and Katherine knew. She rose from her chair, her lips parted.

'I've proposed to Hanna…'

'And I've accepted him,' the bookseller said smiling joyously as Katherine came to her.

Everyone was talking and smiling, and William went to fetch champagne and glasses. Later, he was to reflect how Hanna's father had called on him four years ago with an offer of funds, no doubt sponsored by her, when he'd been entrapped in the criminal trial. He'd not taken up that offer; now the wheel had turned again.

Quietly, in a corner, over the rim of her champagne glass, Hilda said to him: 'I'll find a way to re-pay them shortly. Don't worry about that.'

She turned back to the others. 'I must admit, I'd almost given up hope. But Philip you've become quite gallant. That heroic incident with Mrs Chadwick…dear Mrs Chadwick!…seems to have got you started.'

She sipped champagne. Perhaps, it was something else. Helena Spencer came winging into her mind. But it wasn't the night to worry about that, though she supposed it remained to be dealt with—a cloud on this day's blue horizon.

58

Sweet Autumn with her gypsy face
Stands in the gardens splashed from heels to thigh
With spinning-vine blood...

Henry Kendall

The Holy Sabbath

KATHERINE WAS KEYED-UP from last night's developments. Miraculously, the world had revolved from its grim prospect to one illuminated with Hanna's and Philip's happiness—and their own great relief. Hilda and Laura would be basking in a triumph. Perhaps not Laura...the trial began on Tuesday. Even this didn't dampen her mood, as she put a tortoise-shell comb into her hair.

In bed, this morning, she'd thought of her childhood in Mayo. She'd been two when she'd gone to live with her aunt. A year younger than little Jean; a similar introduction to a mysterious house with a new existence to comprehend. She felt it between them like a silken cord.

At seven o'clock, when she went to the child's bedroom, the world turned dark again.

It was a quarter past eight when Dr MacKenzie arrived, and made his examination while she and William stood at the bedside, and Mary waited at the door. He pulled up the covers and turned, frowning, professionally grave.

'I'm very much afraid it's the typhoid.' He was a Scot and his accents, though hushed, sounded ominously foreign to Katherine. 'I strongly recommend calling in a specialist.'

Katherine had become as still as the autumn morning. Her hands were locked under her chin, the knuckles showing white. She gazed dazedly down at the small malignantly flushed face on the pillow.

'Who do your recommend?' William was saying in a voice which sounded equally foreign.

Her voice came: 'O God, who is the best?'

The child's tiny chest was rising and falling, her face and brow so hot. Her eyes were fixed on Katherine.

'Dawson's a sound reputation.'

William knew Dawson. He had attended Sonia Larkin in her last days. Had failed.

'Who else?'

'Dr Langham's a good man.'

'Call them both in. And we'll need a trained nurse.' He was remembering Sonia's case.

'Have you the telephone? No? I'll send notes to them immediately.'

Katherine had run to the bathroom, returned with a cold flannel with which she was lightly bathing the child's brow, talking softly to her, smiling, achingly smiling. Mary showed the doctor downstairs to a writing table.

'Oh William,' Katherine said from the bedside in a voice he'd never heard before.

He went and held her free hand. 'Steady on, old girl. We'll have the very best.'

But he felt as chilled, every nerve as deadened, as he had that night he'd waited outside Sonia's bedroom—nearly paralysed as he'd contemplated what was coming, how to deal with it…And Sonia, a strong, grown woman. He thought: When the specialists arrive, I must go and bring her mother. And take Mary to look after the others.

He gazed down at his wife's pinned-up, dark-auburn hair, at the amber-coloured comb in it. One step at a time, he told himself. Mary had been silently tearful when she'd taken the doctor downstairs. The women of this city were close to the bone, knew what these things meant. The men just sleep-walked through it. He was determined he would not do that.

———•———

Binks, at Collingwood, was also engaged in a medical conference. He had spoken to Harbrace, the doctor had examined him, and now they stood at the front door with Mrs Harbrace. Binks looked serious. 'He's set on doing it, but can he? And, do you agree, Mrs Harbrace?'

The doctor shook his head. 'I can't advise it. He might be able to, but it would exhaust him. The consequences…'

'His heart's set on it,' his wife said flatly. 'He must try or he'll have no peace of mind.'

Binks looked at the doctor who shrugged. The clerk said, 'It'll be the second day. Wednesday next. The Criminal Court. We've arranged a private room for him to rest in—and a nurse. A wheelchair. We'll have transport laid on.'

'Very well,' the doctor said. 'I'll be there, what time?'

In the street, Otto Rudd stepped into the doorway they'd made their own these past days. It was a bankrupt, closed-up butcher's shop. 'Mornin' Ambrose, on the ball as usual,' the detective said, eyeing the street, the houses, the hansom waiting outside the Harbraces'. Weary after the night-shift, the big man grinned. On the ball was where you found a good ruckman. He appreciated the detective's dual commendation of his reliability.

'What's going on?' the detective said, inclining his bowler at the hansom.

'It's the doc and that fella Binks. Been inside 'alf-hour or more.'

'Mmm,' Rudd said. 'Anything else to report?'

'Yeah. About midnight—a 'ansom come past. Slow. Two men in it. But they kept back in the shadow. Come past a second time. Suspicious-like.'

'See you?'

'I reckon.'

'Mmm.' The detective contemplated this. 'Well, Ambie, better get off to a meal and some shut-eye.'

The ruckman nodded, handed over the knobbed, blackened hawthorn stick like a badge of office, and went off in his peculiar, rolling gait.

Across the city, church bells, one by one, began to thunk chimes into the sultry air like an axe cutting into a sap-springy forest gum; Rudd grinned as he listened to the disharmony swell, thought: That Sunday Liberation Society, with its libertine ideas of opening museums etc., on the Holy Sabbath, had better think again. He'd been following that guerrilla warfare in the papers with interest. He chuckled as he thought of it: Prospect of blood in the streets.

59

The past is gone. We must believe
It has no power to change our lives.
Yet still our constant hearts rejoice
Because the past survives.
   Lesbia Harford, 'Lovers Parted'

'Ah, My Dear...'

AT WORK IN HER OFFICE, Susan wondered why William was absent...Over breakfast, Hanna had told her why she had rushed off—of the outcome—and of the visit to the Boyds.

'I would've come with you,' she'd said, slightly piqued. Wasn't she directly involved in the fight to save the store?

'I know, love. But I wished to see him alone. Hilda being there was a great surprise, but it couldn't have turned out better.'

Then she smiled, and with a kind of shy restraint, told her best friend that she was to be married. Susan had sprung out of her chair in delight, hastened to embrace the bookseller. 'How wonderful! You see? Fate is always weaving its mysterious pattern!'

Not always in the desired pattern, she reflected, gazing at the mail-order catalogue which had arrived from Manchester. A solution to her predicament seemed to be drifting beyond her reach, like a bottle with a corked-up secret going out on the tide.

No reply had come to her letter. Was he so occupied that he couldn't spare a moment to write a line, fit in the meeting which he'd been so eager to have? It was re-settling her negative ideas about him: Fickle, and cold-hearted. What would Dr Blackstone make of *this* silence? She had no intention of consulting the doctor again. Deliberately, she turned to her work.

These evenings his house was even more submerged in shadows,

Wallace thought, as he entered the hall, took off hat and coat and stowed them with his father's stick on the Gothic hall-stand. It was the night before the trial and he'd decided that a proper dinner and an early night was the prescription. Drily, he trusted they wouldn't be too much of a shock for his system.

And Mrs Beattie had turned on roast beef, roast potatoes, Yorkshire pudding, and small peas—one of his favourite meals. He'd gone down to fossick in his wine cellar and found a bottle of '87 cabernet, a vintage year—from Yering in the Upper Yarra—though he would only take two glasses. He appeared disposed to relax and talk, so Mrs Beattie lingered in the dining-room while he ate. Tonight she had put on a simple amber-coloured gown from Foy & Gibson's in Smith Street, Collingwood.

Like the soldiers around their camp-fires on the eve of a battle, she thought. In the past, she'd been through several similar tense preludes with him: when he'd been fighting in parliament; the libel case. She was praying for a better outcome this time.

He'd not said a word about the revelations in *Punch*. She had pondered it, and come to a conclusion, nearer the heart of it than Susan Fairfax had been able to reach.

'There are letters on your desk which need looking into, I suspect,' she said. 'Shall I bring your coffee in?'

Instantly, he was back in the midst of that other dimension of his life. The intonation in her voice sent him, unerringly, to a letter. He tore open the envelope.

She would meet him!

He stared at her handwriting, frowned perplexedly. The next few days he would be plunged into the trial. He must find time—perhaps in the evening. He reached for note-paper, but did not take up his pen. No more correspondence! He must state his case in person.

State his case... He began to pace the room, suddenly ill at ease, the momentary 'lift' gone. Mrs Beattie entered with the coffee. With a glance, she put down the tray and went silently out. State his case! He had to search his heart; find a way through that labyrinth to a comprehension which would stand the light of day.

Impulsively, he went to the hall, opened the front door and stepped out. The tomb-like silence of the suburb set his nerves on edge. The moon had come up. It was cool. His hair lifted in the slightest of breezes. He felt the closing-in presence of the lake, smelled it.

As reliable as the South Melbourne Town Hall clock, Mrs Hammond began to play. What was the woman thinking, as she played her lonely nocturnal pieces? Uncannily, they were often a subtle undersong to his mood.

Earlier that evening he'd walked past the statue of Sir Redmond Barry standing before the Public Library. He'd felt queer, seeing it; in a flash, had remembered an appearance as a junior barrister before the Chief Justice; a cultured considerate man, a special breed. He could hear the inflexions of his voice summing up that case. Yes, queer seeing him up there in bronze, mute and massive...

His perceptions were sharp tonight. With a tinge of bitterness he thought: But, not in that crucial direction. He went inside—turning his back on the night, the lake, and Mrs Hammond's tinkling sonata.

———•———

Philip Larkin, less than a mile from where Wallace had shut his door on a somnolent Albert Park, walked briskly along a South Melbourne street. He was walking the last half-mile from St Kilda Road to Helena Spencer's house. He was resolute—which hadn't often been his situation when he'd come here.

An occasional vehicle drifted past emitting quiet voices. The lines of gas-lights cast their yellowish pools along the margins of the super-wide streets. Barking dogs made canine communications. He wasn't conscious of any of this, nor that the city, in the late autumn cool, seemed to be sighing with relief.

The portico and steps of the house in Cecil Street confronted him. The bell clanged in the interior. The door opened, and the maid smiled. He followed her light-footed, whispering-skirted progress to the salon. The dinner-hour was over, though he'd not dined. He was announced, and walked in.

Helena had been waiting for him. Eight days had gone by without them meeting. With a mock imperiousness, she had granted him freedom to attend to his pressing duties, and it had stretched into this absence. She was an expert at interpreting this kind of situation; knew that there was no 'blue sky' in it for her. But she knew, also, that he would come—impelled by his sentiment, by his personal code.

That afternoon, she'd had herself driven down to the Vienna Café and had German cakes and pastries. 'You need a treat, Helena,' she'd told herself. And she'd given herself one...And here he was.

She sat at a card table, the cards laid out. She wore one of her green gowns—this one an evening creation from Patou of Paris. The emerald necklace sparkled, and tonight an emerald ring as well. Her dark hair, swept up and immaculate, pinned with a gold ornament, contrasted with her creamy arms, neck, and breathtaking *décolletage*. To him, her face in the first instant appeared half-pensive, half-absorbed in the cards.

She looked magnificent and Philip's breath *was* taken. He walked across the parquet floor, aware of himself advancing on several fronts, seeing *her* magnificence, repeated in the mirrors. Resplendent in them. The familiar perfume wafted at him. She rose from her French Louis chair and came to meet him, took his hands in her own. One look at his face told her where she stood. She laughed softly, almost gaily, one might have thought. 'Well, Philip, here you are.'

He smiled uneasily.

'Champagne? Or something else?'

'No, thank you.'

The maid withdrew, closing the door quietly.

She led him to a sofa, gazing at him all the while.

'I fear it's more than your duties that've been keeping you away.'

Seated stiffly on the elegant but uncomfortable sofa, he tried to interpret her mood. She was almost always forthright—no difference there. She knew the nature of his visit—that was plain. Wonderingly, it came to him that she might not intend to make it difficult for him. They were still finding out things about each other—and in her case, he'd thought of it as an infinite prospect. But he was resolved.

'Yes.'

The green eyes seemed to be penetrating his soul.

She sighed lightly. 'Ah, my dear…'

'This is quite unfair, I know, but I cannot continue…'

She waited, but he had dried up.

'Cannot continue our loving relationship?'

He nodded. His resolution, in an eye-blink, had become fragile.

'And, it has been a loving one, has it not?'

'It has.'

The Parisian room was fixated with elegance, nonetheless had a mobile spirit which, perhaps, was pre-eminently her spirit—or a fusion of what she and the room had exchanged. He felt something like that.

'Don't be concerned, I am not going to make a scene.'

He found himself almost wishing the contrary. He said, 'I'm cast down about it.'

'And so you should…' She touched his hand. 'But don't be.'

He stared narrowly at the line of three chandeliers marching away, as he always did when here.

'Of course, there's another. Is it—the bookseller?'

He nodded.

'The incendiary event,' she mused aloud. 'I can guess what has transpired. Are you sure in your mind about it?'

This time he gave an almost imperceptible nod.

She said gently, 'I hope you are right. Although I might want something very much, I'm a woman who never gives second chances. A rather perverse pride, I'm afraid.'

She smiled slightly, sadly; her eyes seemed to skim the floor to come to rest on the intricate and rich pattern of a turkey rug. How did these inexplicable twists and turns occur? Always a mystery.

'Your investments,' he said.

'I trust you'll continue to act for me. Why not? I'm a civilized woman—though, in a certain place you might not've thought so.'

He blushed. She laughed—her softest laugh. 'It's the way of the world, my dear. And I must confess I'm getting a little tired of it. Tired of men who are so irresolute in questions of the heart. Who do not know where they stand, or where they might stand. Who are haunted with burdens and secret connections and go through their personal lives like sleep-walkers. Who one moment rush to the aid of a lady in danger, and the next, rush round in circles. It's all so contradictory and tiresome, don't you think? Far too much trouble.'

Larkin accepted this in silence; would have found it impossible to comment; would have taken much more.

She was smiling affectionately at his stricken face.

'Don't concern yourself, I'm not about to weep. You should know, my sex tends to weep very easily—be on your guard.'

Face-to-face, they addressed each other, and kissed on the lips.

As he quit Cecil Street, suddenly he wondered how it had finished with Angus Wallace. Had his own bitter-sweet experience duplicated another? She was still with him, consuming him: the sound of her voice; the slightly bitter, slightly mordant humour; the air of knowing him better than he knew himself; the smell of perfume, her body; and, the lambency of the green eyes.

Regret had tightened around his heart. But a great sense of release was flowing through him. He was amazed that it was possible to have both, simultaneously.

Helena Spencer sat again before the cards. She regarded them like the old friends they were. She was a skilled bridge-player. It was true, there wasn't a single tear in her beautiful green eyes, but in her heart—that was an entirely different matter.

60

*In the shadow of our trouble we must go
to other lands,
And the flowers we have fostered will be
left to other hands.*

Henry Kendall, 'Araluen'

Rose and Thorns

IT WAS A QUARTER TO SEVEN in the morning, and the skeletal elms in the Edinburgh Gardens emerged from the mist, like morning-walkers. Streaks of pale blue sky promised a perfect day. Beyond Richmond, as though no longer earthbound, the towers of the land boomers' mansions thrust above the rolling white sea which covered the Yarra's southern slopes. Detached from reality, some might have said...

And the three-year-old girl's body was fighting with all its tiny strength to stay in the world.

Katherine strained after each small breath, took turns with the nurse to sponge her, fiercely concentrating her mind on each moment, each small task. But, finally, there was nothing to do but sit and wait, and then the thoughts couldn't be kept back, and the prayer which she repeated over and over became an incoherent babble of unfinished sentences in her head.

Yesterday, the specialists had arrived at noon, made their examinations, consulted each other and Dr MacKenzie, and immediately begun a treatment of cold baths. Brandy was given in small quantities. At two in the afternoon, they'd commenced a 'bran bath'. The child had been sewn up in a sheet spread with the hot bran, covered with blankets.

At four o'clock, Dr Dawson had left, and Dr Langham had remained to speak to William and Katherine and Mrs Harbrace. Gravely, he'd told them there was slim hope, but they should keep up the cold baths during the night. He feared the child was too young, too weak to survive the rigours of the fever. He'd stayed until ten, said he would return at eight in the morning; Dr MacKenzie had remained until midnight.

'I'll be back at seven,' MacKenzie had said. 'The crisis will come tomorrow.'

William came in, already dressed, and stood with his hand on Katherine's shoulder. He thought: Nothing to be said. Just remain close. He must get a message to Hilda.

———— ✦ ————

It seemed to Mrs Wilberforce that minute by minute the component parts of the trial, soon to commence in Court Three, were being assembled with the workman-like precision of a tiler laying out the blue–brown–gold tiles of a tessellated floor. The barristers had come in and sat down at the bar table; the solicitors and their clerks had taken up positions behind them; the public gallery had filled up in a discreet rush (she and Lady Adams had been an hour early to be sure of places); the press men had ambled in, gazed at faces, and settled down in their paddock; Judge Mountain, robed and wigged, his demeanour identical to that with which he graced her dining-table, had materialized on the bench. It all had the stamp of long and practised routine.

She abhorred it.

The defendants were brought in, causing a buzz. At that point, Laura Adams stiffened and leaned forward, scrutinizing her husband's face. Hilda touched her friend's arm lightly. She wondered what they'd found to say to each other as they'd driven in from Kew.

An hour later, and the jury was empanelled. The charges were read out—the defendants gave their pleas. 'Not guilty!'... 'Not guilty!'... 'Not guilty!'

As if to emphasize the three resounding negatives, the sun came out brilliantly, flooded through the court's murky east-facing windows, found the axe-sharp face of Crown Prosecutor Danby, tense, world-weary, beneath his prissy wig, as he rose to his feet. He leaned on his extended arms, gave the jury a searching look. Here I am, it seemed to say—a man about to undertake a job of work; if I look weighed down, ascribe it to the weight of crime on my back each and every day.

'If your honour pleases...Gentlemen of the jury, I am the Crown Prosecutor. You have heard the charges against the accused. Charges rooted in that unfortunate institution, the First Bank of Victoria, now in liquidation—of which they were directors...

'I don't need to describe to you the tragic consequences of that bank's fall—to its depositors, its shareholders, and their families! Victims, in the full sense of that word! A bank impelled, manoeuvred, into that calamitous fall by the accused—there, in the dock.

'It will be my painful duty to put before you evidence which will substantiate the charges beyond any reasonable doubt. I will take you back through the books of this institution—chapter and verse—to show you what has been done…In respect of the second charge—against the defendants Savage and Sandhurst—I will show you, quite clearly, how a loan in each of their names was made to disappear from the bank's books.

'Gentlemen of the jury, we've had enough of doom and disaster in this Colony. Enough of men who've manipulated and crushed the lives of innocent citizens. Enough of men who've hidden from their creditors, dodged their obligations behind secret compositions…who too often have walked away scot-free from the disasters they've set in train…

'If the Colony is ever to recover its good name in the eyes of the British investor, of the British public—of the world—these messes *must* be cleaned up. The perpetrators *must* be dealt with. Justice *must* be seen to be done.

'One more word. In the dock stands a knight of the realm, and two members of the Legislative Assembly.' He paused. 'What a terrible thing that is. How could such men fail us all? But I warn you, be alert to that. Don't be hoodwinked by their illustrious positions. It is a *grievous* fact that men in high places, men held out as paragons of virtue and responsibility, are being exposed time and time again as *tin* men who've been painted as iron—and worse. When *such* men transgress—isn't the offence the more heinous, shouldn't the punishment say so?'

Danby sat down, and smoothed his brief with a fist as though he might refer to it at some point; he hadn't in his opening speech.

Chadwick QC bowed to the judge, smiled at the jury. He looked like a man who hadn't a care in the world about the result of this case. He'd begun to wear spectacles, and they glinted in the sun's rays. His amazingly fluid walk was exhibited to the jury—a constrained few paces forward, a few back. Smooth and decisive. The walk of a man who cut through fat to get to red meat.

Wallace leaned close to Larkin. 'Look at it. Reminds me of a fellow parading on a Widow's Walk.'

Larkin, following the QC, didn't respond.

What makes him tick? Wallace thought. A keen legal brain.

281

Histrionics as an advocate, as a singer. What else?

Chadwick began quietly in his perfectly modulated voice. 'Gentlemen of the jury. I've the honour to represent Sir John Adams—one of the finest men in the Colony. A public benefactor extraordinaire. A man whose honesty is beyond challenge. But I won't go into that now. You're twelve good men, stout and true.' (All juries were 'stout and true' to Chadwick.) 'I'd be surprised if you put up with any nonsense which might come your way in these proceedings.

'So, I'm not going to beat your ears like my learned friend has. This is a very simple case. Against my client, it's alleged he was part of a conspiracy; no conspiracy existed—not a shred of one, and we'll show that. In the same breath, it's alleged that the balance sheet of this unfortunate bank was incorrect at certain dates. *If* it was, my client was unaware of it. Whatever Sir John has done, has been done honestly—as you and I would expect.

'Remember this, we are not here to punish a business failure, even imprudence—in the unlikely event it existed.

'The Crown Prosecutor spoke of victims. My client is one of them—a victim of events beyond his control—and, of an overzealous prosecution unable to see the wood for the trees. Suffice to say, Sir John feels this slur on his name most grievously, and welcomes the opportunity to remove it. He is innocent of these charges.'

Chadwick glided the few paces back to his chair.

Mr Spearman rose to his feet, advised the jury that he was here for Messrs Savage and Sandhurst, covered similar ground to Chadwick. Said he was not a word-smith, just a plain-speaker as were his clients. That was borne out by their conduct on the floor of parliament. The truth was going to come out and it would not be to the detriment of his clients. Finally, letting his plain-speaking persona drop a stitch, he said, in a confidential, dramatic tone:

'There are motives underpinning this action against my clients which are *base*. They will be brought to the surface. You will see them for yourselves.'

He nodded at the jury, and sat down amid the sudden stir.

Larkin and Danby exchanged a glance.

Judge Mountain looked at the advocates, much as he would have eyed the label of a flashy new vintage. 'Can we get on with the evidence? Call your first witness, Mr Danby.'

'*Call Angus Alexander Wallace.*'

Susan had got into the public gallery and into a seat with the aid of an usher, and an obliging gentleman who was willing to squeeze along.

'You are the liquidator of the First Bank of Victoria?' Danby was asking.

'I am,' Wallace was answering, as she settled and gazed at his face. She had come, she knew, like a moth to the flame.

For the next two hours, Danby led Wallace through his evidence. It was close to the evidence which he'd given at the committal proceedings. They'd spent days cutting, re-shaping, and simplifying it into a form which a jury might digest.

The jury heard of the convoluted situation which the liquidator had discovered. Danby, with his quiet, reasoned intercessions, Wallace with his firm, concise, factual statements, built up a picture of a jerry-built balance sheet and profit and loss account—which any trained businessman, any half-competent director, should have been able to see through. Yet, these men had signed and distributed these indisputably false and fraudulent documents!

Danby spoke with bitter amusement, showed an aggrieved, pondering face to the jury, suddenly turned back to Wallace.

'Did the accused know individually, and amongst themselves, of that falsity?'

'It's unbelievable reasonable men should not have known.'

'Unless they were the most incompetent fools who ever sat on a company's board?'

'They are intelligent men.'

'Men who have reached the highest positions?'

'Yes.'

Danby nodded slowly, dropped his eyes to his brief. 'Did an event occur in the bank's boardroom, exactly four weeks after the date of that last false balance sheet?'

'Yes, the board resolved to write off eight loans totalling £412,000 as bad debts, and did so.'

'Who were the borrowers of these loans?'

'Six loans amounting to £322,000 were to companies either owned or controlled by Sir John Adams, one to Mr Savage for £57,000 and one to Mr Sandhurst for £33,000.'

'Were loans to any *other* borrowers provided for or written off?'

'None at all.'

Danby raised his slim hand to cup his chin—as though trying to fathom the unfathomable. 'So, in the eyes of these directors—the accused—what was perfectly safe and sound on the 30th September,

1892, was absolutely failed and lost on 26th October, 1892. Eight loans for separate purposes or projects had gone down at one blow?'

'Yes.'

'What effect did this have on the position certified to in the balance sheet that brief time before?'

'It played havoc with it.'

'Was it a write-off to which each one of them was agreed?'

'Yes. The board minutes confirm that.'

'What was your conclusion about this event?'

'I concluded that it was a remarkable reversal of business fortunes, over multiple cases, in such a short interval.'

'And what happened two days later?'

'They closed the bank—on the 28th.'

Judge Mountain consulted his watch. 'I think this is an appropriate juncture to adjourn for luncheon. The court will sit again at two o'clock.'

Hilda Wilberforce, Lady Adams, and Susan, had joined up. They went to a tea-shop in Queen Street. The older women had been surprised to see the young Lancashire woman in the gallery, but each had quickly come to a conclusion, which created a slight awkwardness. Hilda cast back to her earlier review of that relationship. Something must *still* be in the wind. How strange…Lady Adams gave Susan a sharp, considering look.

Hilda said, 'Is John going into the witness-box, Laura?'

'No. Mr Chadwick believes it unnecessary. Apparently, he has some surprises which will destroy the case against John. I hope he can be relied on,' she added grimly.

Susan, eyes lowered, stirred her tea, had nothing to say. She left the tea-shop alone, and Lady Adams watched her go.

'Hilda, I've had a letter from my cousin in Manchester.' She paused. 'As we suspected, that young woman has "a past". I think you should read this.' She brought out and gave the letter to her friend, with the air of a person handling the explosive product of a continental anarchist.

61

The City of Melbourne Bank...It was latterly a badly managed concern with a Board of elderly directors. Old men who want to sleep in the afternoon and do not watch the general manager and the overdraft lists sharply are a menace.

George D. Meudell, The Pleasant Career of a Spendthrift

Something Sinister

THE COURT RESUMED at two o'clock. Chadwick QC rose to cross-examine Wallace, and paused, head held to one side, as if listening for a chord. No accompanist here, my learned friend, Danby thought with a flash of malignant humour.

'Mr Wallace, I've listened to what you've said—and one question immediately occurs to me: Where is Mr Jamison Smith the bank's chief manager?'

Chadwick knew that he was twelve thousand miles away—and tucked well out of sight.

'A bench warrant's been issued for his arrest. He's not been found.'

'How inconvenient. Without his evidence, we're scarcely going to get the full story of these events, are we? Or, perhaps that's *convenient* to the prosecution?'

Chadwick knew that the opposite was the case. Wallace and Danby would have given their right arms to have Jamison Smith in the witness-box; were still on the back foot from the shock of his absconding. But Chadwick could be relied on to play his games—if the judge let him, and Judge Mountain wasn't shaping up as an interventionist.

Danby did intervene. 'Your honour, it was the desire of the prosecution that he be here. The fact of the matter is, the *British police* have not found him.'

Chadwick smiled at the jury. 'Tell me, Mr Wallace, isn't it true that a bank employs accountants to attend to the books, chief managers, and auditors, to make sure they're correct?'

'Those officers are part of the process.'

'The main part, I'd suggest. Isn't it customary for the directors to rely on the work of those officials when forming their own opinions, when signing-off the balance sheet, etc.?'

'A competent director will keep a weather-eye out for what might be going on beneath the surface. He'll be watching the chief manager, and the overdraft list.'

Chadwick smiled to himself. Yes, a crocodile...He said, 'Beneath the surface? But surely, it would be totally impracticable for the directors to check the accounting entries? To check the compiling of the balance sheet? Not their job at all?'

'Not impracticable for them to know the condition of the bank's major loans. It's the point of greatest risk.'

'But, isn't it true a director might not know a great deal of what is going on in a bank—yet still be an honest man, acting in good faith?'

'There are degrees to that proposition. Commonsense, basic prudence, is expected of any director. The context and circumstances should be looked at.'

'Ah, degrees...context...circumstances. The jury must find this all somewhat confusing? I'm afraid I do. As I see it, directors have no option but to depend very much on their officials. I ask again, in this case, where is the chief manager to enlighten us?'

Danby interposed irritably, 'You know where he is.'

'I don't at all. It appears you might.'

'Get on with it,' Judge Mountain said flatly.

Chadwick shrugged elegantly, turned in a wide arc to this 'wild notion' of conspiracy—as he termed it. 'Now, Mr Wallace. These three directors sat down to sign the balance sheets and accounts, having relied on their officers, the auditor, to do a proper job. Hey presto! We have a conspiracy! And, you want to send 'em to gaol for it! Aren't you being one-eyed?'

Wallace regarded him calmly. 'No. The state of the books, the situation the bank was in, were obvious. Only complete numbskulls could have failed to know it. Or, men who chose to ignore it for their own reasons.'

Judge Mountain fixed Chadwick with a cold look. 'Mr Chadwick, I don't much like this line of questioning—or, answers along those lines. Will you get to the point with more dispatch and keep to it.'

'If your honour pleases.'

Wallace gave the judge a re-appraising look.

'We come to the bad debt write-offs on the 26th October.

Obviously, you saw something sinister in this, Mr Wallace?'

'Yes. Sinister is your word—not a bad one. My suspicions of that day's work go beyond the present charge.'

Chadwick's head jerked up, he slapped his brief down on the desk, glared indignantly at the witness. 'Shame on you! You're seeking to further unjustly blacken my client's name by innuendo. The prosecution's brought no other charges against him—isn't that right?'

'Yes.'

'Are you an inordinately suspicious man, Mr Wallace? I submit you have a reputation for finding conspiracies. I suggest if you looked under your bed you would find one.'

'That is a new name for what he might find there,' the judge said drily. (Laughter.)

Danby was on his feet. 'Objection, your honour. The witness is a liquidator with a *duty* to look into matters. It's my learned friend who casts the innuendo.'

Chadwick took a few paces towards the jury. 'Very well. I suggest to you, Mr Wallace, that in one way or another the loans written off were related to land development projects. That given the dramatic collapse in land prices, it's not surprising at all that the demise of those projects was virtually simultaneous. Quite natural that the realization of their failure fell upon the directors at that point in time. How do you answer that?'

'I don't believe it. The money wasn't lost as if hit by a single flash of lightning on that day. In my view, those projects had died at different times throughout 1891, and 1892.'

Chadwick folded his arms. 'Your view? I'm afraid I don't find your views very practical. And, I suspect the jury don't either.'

'Mr Chadwick!' the judge censured.

The Queen's Counsel bowed to the bench, said, 'Could there not be legitimately different views as to what caused those projects to expire?'

'I stand by what I've said about it.'

Chadwick sat down, pursed his lips.

Larkin gazed across the courtroom. Wallace's comment on his wider suspicions had been ill-advised. Chadwick was muddying the waters for the jury, and that had helped.

The judge said, 'Mr Spearman...?'

The barrister glanced at Chadwick. 'No questions your honour.'

Wallace thought: Thus far, those two are on the same horse. But not for much longer, I'll warrant. He wouldn't have taken anything back from his answers.

In the dock, Sir John sat, heavy, and quite still, gazing at the gilded coat of arms as though it were a kind of Buddhist mantra. His eyes were reddened. Otherwise, he showed no emotion, gave no clue to his thoughts.

From the gallery, Lady Adams wondered if he had any. Beside him, Sandhurst leaned back, also inert, his eyes hooded, his face bland. No-one could have thought that his mind wasn't working.

Savage was the counterpoint. He twitched, moved, scowled here and there. Occasionally, his teeth flashed in that dense black beard— a mannerism, not a smile. His eyes smouldered, shifted. Only when Wallace was in the witness-box had they become concentrated. The liquidator hadn't spared him a glance.

Susan had. A frightening individual. A prime candidate for Dr Blackstone's profession, she decided. Then her eyes had returned to Wallace, again seated beside Philip Larkin.

Thomas Moore, the bank's auditor, was in the witness-box. He was sworn and settled himself. He'd foregone his bright waistcoat for the court, looked diminished to Wallace; also, exceedingly nervous. It was late afternoon. Danby identified him for the jury, sized him up.

'Did you certify that the bank's balance sheet as at the 30th September, 1892, was correct in every particular?'

'Yes.'

'On the draft balance sheet, the certificate was amended by twice crossing out the words "in every particular"—after "correct", and twice reinstating them. Why was that?'

Moore frowned. His lips worked over his teeth for a full half-minute while he considered his answer.

'I cannot recall.' He watched the Crown Prosecutor, eyes blinking rapidly.

'Did it reflect the struggle you were having in your mind?…After all, as the evidence we've heard shows, there was plenty to set up such a struggle in the mind of any auditor. Your answer?'

'I cannot recall what was in my mind.'

'Oh? How much of the audit work did you do yourself?'

'My chief clerk did most of it.'

'Did he prepare the certificate?'

'Yes.'

'And your signature is on it?'

'Yes.'

'Did someone prevail upon you to reinstate those important words?'

'No.'

With his nervy eyes, the auditor watched the prosecutor. Danby looked at the jury, raised his eyebrows, and sat down. Judge Mountain wrote a note, then adjourned the court to the following morning.

Throughout the day's proceedings, Susan's attention had been mainly concentrated on observing Angus Wallace: his demeanour, his voice inflexions, his gestures (which had been few). The courtroom had become stifling. Beside her, Hilda Wilberforce was waving a fan she'd produced. Lady Adams sat like a statue. Susan was so absorbed that she'd forgotten the existence of the two women.

As the lawyers got up to leave, his eyes came up to the emptying gallery, and he saw her and stopped dead. He stared up, hesitantly raised a hand. Then Larkin took his arm to have a word about the case, and the connection was broken. When he looked back, she had gone.

62

On the twenty-seventh day of July, at the hour of twenty minutes to two o'clock in the morning, a hansom cab drove up to the police station in Grey Street, St Kilda, and the driver made the startling statement that his cab contained the body of a man who he had reason to believe had been murdered.

Fergus W. Hume, The Mystery of a Hansom Cab (1886)

Witness Protection

'HULLO, WHAT'S THIS, Ambie?' Otto Rudd said to the Carlton ruckman. A hansom cab had appeared under the solitary gas-light at the end of the street, and halted.

'Same as the other night,' the ruckman muttered.

It was near to midnight. The detective had joined his assistant at nine. Impelled by a stab of intuition, he'd decided to stand guard with the ruckman tonight. It wasn't just that. The ubiquitous Binks had turned up, said with a knowing nod that Harbrace was to give his evidence tomorrow.

A chilly breeze fretted in the bluestone conduit. The neighbourhood's deep silence seemed magnified by the amorphous sounds of the sleeping city. They were dark, immobile figures in the ex-butchery doorway, the only give-away the occasional flash of skin from face or hand.

The cab started up again. Its lights were unlit. They watched it come. Abruptly, the driver, a hunched, top-hatted silhouette, flicked the ribbons, flicked his whip, and the horse broke into a trot and went past them. They could see nothing of its passengers, then Rudd realized the blind was down. For a second, he'd thought to challenge the driver, but didn't. It went to the end of the street, merged into the darkness.

'These 'ansoms are no good,' Ambie growled. 'Can't get a clear sight of no-one.'

Nasty things have happened in 'em, Rudd thought. Then they

heard it coming back. It loomed out of the darkness again at a trot, went past, and halted fifty yards away.

'What's their game?' the ruckman said staring hard, hefting the knobbed piece of hawthorn.

'Wait on,' Rudd said. He held a similar 'decider'.

Movement, quick and blurred to the right. Running on toes—but now distinct: leather slapping on stone.

'Ambie! Watch out! To the right,' Rudd hissed.

Figures launched from the darkness splitting to left and right. One at the ruckman, one at the detective. More running coming from the left...

A glinting, swinging arc in the air above a dark torso.

Holding his stick like a battering ram, the ruckman drove at it. The attacker grunted, staggered aside, iron clanged on bluestone.

'Missed, you bugger!' Ambie grated, taking a fast look aside for his employer.

A scuffling shimmy was going on there; the detective was doing intricate things with his stick between the legs of a shadowy figure— which suddenly tripped up, launched itself backwards, crashed on its back. As fast as a snake's head striking, the brown boot went in once, twice, to the recumbent's privates.

Squeal like a stuck pig.

Wacko! Eyes front! The ruckman measured off the winded figure reeling at his front, this time, with a two-handed swing to the side of the head, batted him away.

An iron bar crashed down on his shoulder. The crack of collarbone sounded like a gunshot; the excruciating pain seared the shoulder, ran to his armpit like fire. 'You bugger!' he yelled. One-handed he swung his club in a round-house that reached maximum momentum as it smashed into the new arrival's face. The figure went down with a thump, out cold. They stood in undisputed possession of the Collingwood street.

'They got you, Ambie, I heard it,' Rudd said.

'Just a busted collar-bone,' the ruckman gritted. 'My oath, you kicked a good goal there, Mr Rudd, right between the sticks. But what's it all about?'

But the detective was blasting away at the police whistle, and the eerie pay-attention sound was waking up dogs as far away as Victoria Parade.

...poor Constance, who was fighting through the last hard two
minutes of her life, trying to breathe, while something clutched at
her breast and strangled her. She was sitting in a large arm-
chair...gasping for air, but otherwise making no sound, while her
husband held her up in his arms and howled—no other word could
describe the noise—howled...not loudly, but with a concentrated
force of savage anguish...The poor woman...looked up at her hus-
band with a pathetic helplessness and consciousness of their mutu-
al agony... As [Sue] ran through the long room...she saw the end
of the struggle. Constance lifted her arms to her faithful mate...and
he caught her up bodily, carried her a step or two, rocking her as
he went...As he laid her down she gently sank out of his arms,
sank back upon the pillows, limp and still; her delicate head rolled
a little to one side, and there rested...her pretty hands fell open,
palm uppermost. They smoothed her white gown over her placid
form, and Richard, looking at her, ceased to howl, for he saw that
she had ceased to suffer.

Ada Cambridge, A Marked Man (1890)

The Way of the World

JEAN HAD SURVIVED Tuesday—and Tuesday night. The dreaded crisis
Dr MacKenzie had predicted had not come. The doctors had conferred and continued with cold baths and another 'bran bath'. They'd
shaken their heads, confounded by the child's stamina. However, they
were not in doubt about the outcome. This they confided to William.

Katherine had not slept for two nights. William did not go to the
store during the three days. He hovered outside the sick-room, fetched
items that were required, watched Katherine. He was deeply concerned for her—as well as the child. Great bruises had appeared under
her eyes; her face had set into sharp planes; every tiny blemish in her
complexion stood out. Her gaze had become fixated on the small head
on the pillow. Looking into his wife's eyes, he saw they had faded to

the colour of lead. He doubted if she saw him. But it was the suppression of her desperation which frightened him.

She refused to listen to the doctors now, just kept the vigil with Mrs Harbrace, speaking softly to the mother—a few words only—assisting the nurse as needed. Tears had streamed down Mrs Harbrace's face earlier, now she was dry-eyed.

He felt a dark force abroad; an implacability in the atmosphere. He tightened his lips, squared his shoulders.

Dr MacKenzie had arrived at seven. Then Dr Langham, at half-past eleven. When the doctors left the sick-room, Katherine went and tucked the rag-doll beside the small, livid face. The delirious child murmured softly—in the few words she had, would ever have. The anguish of that struck into Katherine's heart.

'I'm afraid it won't be long now, Boyd,' Langham said quietly. 'Her pulse is a mere flutter.'

William went downstairs, at last, sent his message to Hilda.

Binks had been in the witness-box for over an hour. Danby had painstakingly taken him through the overdrafts in Savage's and Sandhurst's names, mysteriously expunged from the books. The cheques drawn on the No. 2 Accounts had been exhibited to judge and jury, as had the teller's sheet where their encashment was recorded. The ledger had been man-handled around, the tell-tale residue of two torn-out pages each in sequence behind the defendants' ordinary accounts, pointed out. Abstracts of overdrafts at the 30th September last, further evidencing the No. 2 Accounts had been produced—and, at the liquidator's appointment, wherein they no longer appeared…etc., etc.

Danby sat down.

Binks had looked in his shaving mirror with more care this morning; a single nick on his chin testified to it. Now he looked as carefully at Spearman's prize-fighter face, as the barrister for the parliamentarians rose to cross-examine.

'A dab hand at looking into accounts are you, Mr Binks?'

'I'm a trained accountant.'

'Ah—does that mean you can add up a bit faster than the usual fella—especially when working out your fees?'

A titter of amusement. So far, Spearman had been kept on a tight leash by agreement between the defence counsel. Now he'd come on to his ground.

'Couldn't keep up with your profession in that respect.'

(Laughter.)

Judge Mountain frowned.

'My clients, of course, *know* about those accounts. The disappearance of 'em from the books is as much a mystery to them as to anyone else. Far as they're concerned, accounts should still exist. They owe the money.'

Tight-lipped, Larkin thought: This is novel. Did they appear in the sworn statements to their creditors?

Spearman smiled at the jury. 'We've been hearing of conspiracies, bit of a conspiracy here don't you think, Mr Binks?'

'Is that a question?' Judge Mountain asked.

'It is, your honour.'

'I don't understand,' Binks said, but he did.

'Let me put it this way. Mr Wallace tried once before to bring charges against my clients—in 1889. Defamed them in parliament, defamed them in the press. The charges were found false, thrown out of parliament—as was Mr Wallace. Then, in court, he had a judgment go against him for that defamation. Result: rather painful damages.

'No politician likes to be a loser—and he took a bad fall. The average man might reasonably think that Mr Wallace's attitude to my clients would be unfriendly—to say the least. That he might harbour a vendetta. In fact, that he might've seen a Heaven-sent opportunity to exact revenge.'

Danby sprang to his feet. 'That is a monstrous accusation! I trust your honour will stop this vile line of questioning.'

Spearman smoothed his moustache, said mildly: 'I'm not making an accusation, your honour. However, I believe the jury should be aware of these facts.'

From the bar table, Chadwick interposed, 'I suspect they are, already. It was well publicized in the press.'

'Get on with it,' Judge Mountain said.

Wallace stared at Spearman calmly, conscious of the hundreds of eyes which had turned on him. Spearman was going to get a well-deserved shock when the next witness was called.

'Now, Mr Binks, a lot of people would've had access to that ledger. Anyone could've extracted those sheets, could they not?'

'Why would they?'

'Mr Binks, I will ask the questions. Your answer?'

'Anything is possible.'

Danby scowled, but said nothing.

Spearman wore red braces beneath his robe, and he stuck his hands behind them, thwacked them softly. '..."Monstrous", my learned friend said. But doesn't the liquidator's conduct in his private life, recently brought to public notice, better fit that description? Throw into question his judgment, his character?'

Danby was up again, visibly angry. Taking a leaf from Chadwick's book, he slapped his brief down. 'Your honour, this is infamous! I've not heard worse from a member of this bar. He's making assertions— loosely disguised as questions. And none of it's relevant to the case!'

'I disagree, your honour, these facts touch on the case, on its underpinning.'

Danby was on his feet again. 'On what grounds?'

'If you sit down and keep quiet, you will find out,' Spearman suggested.

'You are an obstructionist from beginning to end,' Danby said acidly.

Spearman smiled, fingered his braces.

'Strike out the last question—if it can be so described,' the judge instructed the recorder. 'Mr Spearman?'

'Your honour, my learned friend appears to be super sensitive to these hard facts...'

Danby bobbed up. 'We are having to put up with a lot of impertinence.'

'We are having to put up with a lot of malice.'

Judge Mountain stared at each barrister in turn. 'Will you get on? I won't warn you again.'

Spearman bowed to the bench. 'No more questions.'

'Call James Harbrace.' Spearman whipped around in his chair to his solicitor, Billings, and both turned questioning eyes to Savage and Sandhurst. This man wasn't going to be available to give evidence— why is he here?—they seemed to say. But the duo of stony faces was heedless of their lawyers.

In the public gallery, astir like a theatre audience during a change of scenery, a messenger entered and looked over the seated observers. He worked along a row, a note in his hand.

'Mrs Wilberforce?'

'Yes?' She showed her surprise.

'For you.'

She looked at the paper in her hand, at the man going out. She opened the single sheet which had been folded and sealed. *Little Jean Harbrace very grave. Specialists have no hope. Katherine desperate...Could you come? William.*

'What is it, Hilda?' Lady Adams asked in a low voice.

'This.' Hilda said grimly.

Lady Adams read it.

'I'm sorry, Laura, I must go out to Edinburgh Gardens.'

Lady Adams' grey eyes surveyed her friend, and then gazed down at her husband. The only movement about him was the steady blinking of his eyes, and she couldn't see that. 'We'll go out together.'

Not sitting with them today, Susan watched them leave, and wondered what was up.

They were bringing Harbrace in. He'd been waiting in a special room in which a bed had been placed, his doctor, a nurse, Larkin's clerk, Smithson—and Otto Rudd—in attendance. Heads craned to see the pale, mortally ill man propped up in the wheel-chair. They'd brushed his soft, white hair. A restrained, sympathetic sigh arose.

Wallace watched him enter. A minute before, he'd been brooding on his lost witnesses: Hubble, Murdoch, Jamison Smith. But they'd got Harbrace. The question was whether he had the strength for it.

The bank's ex-chief accountant took the oath, his voice weak. Danby approached him gently as if to avoid the slightest vibration of a floor-board. Assembling his remaining strength, Harbrace watched him come.

'Mr Harbrace, I'm sure we're all concerned to see you in this condition. Admire your fortitude in coming here. I won't keep you long...Until December last, were you the chief accountant of the First Bank of Victoria?'

'Yes.'

'Do you recall the No. 2 overdraft accounts the defendants, and former directors, Messrs Savage and Sandhurst had?'

'Yes.'

'Are you aware that the records of those accounts have disappeared from the bank's books?'

'Yes.'

'How do you know that?'

A long pause.

'I removed the ledger sheets myself.'

A murmur of astonishment...Danby waited for it to subside. 'Would you tell the jury *why* you did that?'

It was immediately plain how difficult it was for Harbrace to get out more than a monosyllabic response. He tried once, and failed.

'Take your time.'

The voice came at last, like one man's prayer in an empty cathedral. 'Mr Savage, Mr Sandhurst called me in…instructed me to do it. Put fifty pounds on the table…Said the ship was sinking, every man for himself…'

'You liar!' Savage was on his feet, eyes blazing, hands gripping the dock. A constable tapped him on the shoulder.

'Silence!' Judge Mountain said incisively.

'…I tore out the pages from the loans ledger…the paperwork from their files…handed them over.'

'Were they satisfied with this? What about the other evidence— the cheques, etc.'

'Everything was at…sixes and sevens…A mad rush…They left any details to me…'

'And you did nothing else?'

'I chose…not to.'

Wallace and Larkin looked at each other, and the liquidator nodded slowly, having plucked each quiet word out of the air.

Spearman approached the witness, his head cocked, as though he was seeing an oddity. 'Mr Harbrace, my clients are sorry to see you in this state, have instructed me to keep it short…' This was a lie.

'Nonetheless, it's my duty to put this to you: isn't what you've just told the court a complete fabrication. Not to mince words: a barefaced lie?'

'No.'

'No? If it were the truth, then that'd make you guilty of a very grave offence yourself, wouldn't it?'

Harbrace nodded. 'Yes.'

'I don't know what you perceive my clients to have done to you…but I mentioned the word "malice". Seems that's what is at rock-bottom of this whole affair.'

Danby was on his feet. 'Your honour, he's up to it again! It seems we must give my learned friend a medal for creativity—and obfuscation! What is the question?'

'Your honour, the question is simply this…' He turned back to Harbrace whose deathly pale face appeared to be melting into the pillow… 'Mr Harbrace, are you a trifle confused? Was the fifty pounds you mentioned, really paid over by the liquidator, Mr Wallace, for your presence here today?'

The court took in its breath—and held it.

'Shame!' someone shouted from the gallery.

Spearman, holding his braces again, rocking on his heels, had no doubt it was meant for him, but he was concentrating on the witness's face as if fearful it would decompose before he had his answer.

'No'—came the whisper.

'Sit down, you viper!'—again from the gallery.

'Silence!'—from Judge Mountain. 'Constable, get that man out.'

But Otto Rudd was already, calmly, going out the door.

'Mr Spearman? Is there anything *concrete* to put?'

'Your honour, I make the observation that a man in *this* condition has nothing to fear from this court.'

'Thank you for that wisdom. I trust it concludes your ministrations to this witness?'

Spearman bowed, and sat down. Danby was shaking his head.

The child was dying. Dr MacKenzie was doing something, his hands moving quickly near her head. Her eyes had half opened. William had his right arm around Katherine's shoulders, with his left was holding her left arm; they were shaking in a rigour—as one. Katherine's eyes were wild in powerless agony.

Over and over she was breathing 'O God! Don't let her suffer so!'

Not Katherine's voice, he was thinking dazedly.

The tiny face, like her father's, was melting into the pillow...

Katherine had broken off, brokenly, rapidly was saying: 'Our Father, who art in Heaven...'

Dr MacKenzie was whispering: 'She's gone, it's over.'

'...hallowed be Thy name, Thy kingdom come...'

Give us strength, William was intoning in his head.

Hilda Wilberforce and Lady Adams arrived at Edinburgh Gardens a few minutes after one. Two buggies waited in the street, their drivers yarning, casting glances at the house. The door stood open. Nothing could be heard from within. They looked at each other. Too often in each of their lives they had entered a house in these circumstances.

'I've never known a more sensible girl,' Mrs Wilberforce said firmly. 'One who *always* thinks of others first.'

'Nonetheless,' Lady Adams said. They went into the hall. William was descending the stairs; they saw that he could hardly control his facial muscles.

'William…?'

'She's gone,' he said. 'Ten minutes ago. Everything was done…We had the best men.'

Abruptly, he stopped this sad futility, halted on the stairs. 'Dr MacKenzie is with Mrs Harbrace. But Katherine…'

Hilda went past him and up the stairs. She found Katherine sitting in her bedroom gazing that gaze out the window.

'My dearest girl…' The Irishwoman turned her face.

'I can't cry, Hilda, but I don't think I can stand it.'

At a point in that sad, confused afternoon, Mrs Harbrace came in and took Katherine's hand. In her quiet, flat voice she said, 'Don't fret so, Mrs Boyd. We loved her, and we'll miss her, but it's the way of the world. She's in the best care now.' This was the third child she'd lost in infancy; no-one there knew that.

William, Hilda, Lady Adams, and Dr MacKenzie heard the softly spoken statement, but no-one could tell whether Katherine had—except the speaker, who felt the gentle pressure on her hand.

At about the time Judge Mountain returned to the bench, William sent another urgent message on its way by hansom. Hilda was upstairs sitting with Katherine. She'd come out to the landing to speak to him, which had resulted in his dashing off that message. Dr MacKenzie had taken Mrs Harbrace back to her family—to break the news to her husband when he returned from court. Lady Adams was proving quite capable of making pots of tea and buttering bread.

William moved through the house, fear had settled around his heart. A fear which had gripped it once before. Four years ago, there had been another woman, another tragedy.

———◆———

Maurice Brodzky was in the witness-box. The editor of *Table Talk* had come for his deceased reporter, bringing with him purloined documents certifying to Sir John Adams' secret composition with his creditors, the hole-in-a-corner liquidations of his companies—orchestrated to dodge his obligations, while maintaining his reputation.

While Danby was feeding this, piece-by-piece, into the record, Sir John's solicitor, Barnaby, had turned the colour of beetroot. Sir John had gazed at an illuminated patch on the floorboards made by a column of sunlight from a high window.

Chadwick had objected to this evidence, but had been overruled. Now he sized up the editor. He needed to tread carefully here—the man had considerable public support. Nonetheless…He glided a few paces, cast his embracing look at the jury.

'Mr Brodzky, how did you obtain these documents?'

'From an informant.'

Chadwick smiled. 'From the gutter? The way you get much of the mud you rake up?'

'Not from there. What we publish is factual. Subsequent court proceedings have vindicated it.'

'Oh? It's been a bonanza for you. I believe *Table Talk* made the substantial profit of £4,000 in '88, alone. Is that so?'

Brodzky looked narrowly at the QC. 'Near enough.'

'And even better since, I imagine. A pretty good line of business—this trading on the misfortunes of others, I suggest?'

'The public knows what newspapers are for.'

'Really? An informant you said? I'm sure his honour and the jury would like to hear the name of this informant. But I suppose you're going to tell us your sources can't be revealed?'

'On the contrary. His name is Thomas Windrush, former clerk in the Insolvency Court.'

Chadwick was silent. He turned to the judge. 'Your honour, it seems we are getting second-hand what we should have at first-hand.' He turned to Danby. 'Why isn't *this* man in the witness-box?'

Danby got up. 'If your honour pleases, Thomas Windrush is recently deceased. The documents before the court are sworn in the proper way for the evidence of deceased persons, and his signature is attested to, as you've seen.'

'This won't do!' Chadwick said, slapping down his brief on the bar table. 'Your honour, I must object to this.'

Judge Mountain was getting tired. He looked at his watch. A few glasses of claret would assist him consider the objection. He adjourned the court till the following morning.

———

Dr Blackstone strode into the house as the Fitzroy Town Hall clock struck five, tossed his wide-brimmed hat on to a chair. He shook hands peremptorily with William.

'Thank God, they found you…It's my wife.'

In a low, agitated voice, William explained as they went upstairs the events of the day—the sad, brief odyssey of the child and Katherine. The doctor said nothing, staring down at each brassrodded riser as they climbed.

Hilda came out of the bedroom, looking grim. Dr Blackstone went in and shut the door and they heard faintly his baritone voice.

The scream stopped all their hearts. It went through the house, out of it, shot across the gardens like a steel-tipped arrow. William had frozen in horror. Hilda Wilberforce and Lady Adams put down their tea-cups with a clatter and ran up the stairs as quickly as their long skirts would allow. Blackstone came out, nodded to the two women who hurried into the room from which now came the sound of uncontrolled weeping.

Blackstone touched William on the arm. For some reason, they went to the conservatory.

'She'll be all right, Boyd—your wife is a strong woman. Anybody has a breaking strain. She's had a terrible shock. Her own childless state…It's vital that they do break. In a healthy woman like her, time is the healer.'

He glanced with suspicion at the plants surrounding them, took out and lit a cheroot. His eyes rested on the elaborate gilded cage, somewhat tarnished, which was suspended amongst the shiny leafed foliage. He frowned, remembered it from another existence.

'It's a different case from that other…So put your mind to rest.'

William exhaled a long, tremulous breath. The woman referred to had died two years ago in an institution at Kew. Blackstone meditated on it. A happy release. He, also, had been in love with her, though no-one had known that.

———◆———

At seven o'clock, Judge Mountain sat down in Mrs Wilberforce's dining-room to a very pleasant hot dinner—and a bottle of All Saints' red. He dined alone. A message had come from the Boyds that she was needed there. Yet another sad event. Their lives seemed to be accompanied by twists and turns—with always, in the end, a sad destination.

He took up his glass and eyed the colour of the wine with appreciation. Even little Wahgunyah beauties like this had their day.

He turned his mind to the case before him—and that last point. Twists and turns—it was the flavour of his day-to-day work. It didn't surprise him at all that Wallace was being transformed from hunter to hunted. They'd see the outcome of it tomorrow. He studied the fluted mahogany legs, the carved claws of the massive dining-table. Even the furniture seemed to pose a threat in today's world.

64

The past month has been prolific of financial disaster. With the rapidity and certainty of a fatal epidemic the greater number of the associated banks have followed in the wake of the Federal and the Commercial, temporarily suspending payment...and then going in for reconstruction. One surprise has followed another, and each catastrophe seemed to be more and more serious...threatening to bring down a general collapse of business.

Illustrated Australian News, *1.6.1893*

A Brave Performance

WALLACE LOOKED across the courtroom into the eyes of Jonathan Savage. The eyes of a crook, he thought. Were they also those of a murderer? This morning they had a yellowish, sickish tinge as they brooded on the scene. Mad? Deadly, at any rate.

The final day. The minute hand of the clock was a shade before ten. Danby and Chadwick, seated a few feet apart, ignored each other; none of the collegiate banter of the bar table. Danby, gazing grimly at his brief, though he would not refer to it during his final address, thought: Make or break.

Philip Larkin glanced at the Queen's Counsel, specially debonair today, wondered how the delicate Mrs Chadwick was. Chadwick gave him a friendly nod. At that moment, Smithson hurried to his side with a cablegram. He read it, abruptly straightened up, passed it to Wallace. The liquidator read: *Reported in London press that Jamison Smith arrested yesterday took his own life in the cells at Bow Street.*

Wallace and Larkin exchanged glances. Then Danby was reading it. Without a change of expression he passed it along to Chadwick who read it, lifted his hands: What could one do?

'Mr Chadwick?' Judge Mountain said.

Seamlessly, the QC renewed his objection to the evidence submitted yesterday by Maurice Brodzky. With equal dispatch and fluidity, Judge Mountain dismissed the objection.

Mr Spearman sought leave to call a witness. The judge frowned. 'At this stage?' But agreed.

'*Call Julian Ellis.*'

Larkin looked quickly at Wallace, but the liquidator ignored him and watched the check-suited Ellis come into the witness-box bringing his disreputable air like a whiff of pungent tobacco.

Danby looked down at his hands. This fellow, Spearman, would try anything.

Spearman gently stroked his braces, and measured off the witness. He would need to be quick—and lucky. He took a breath.

'You are the uncle to your sister's two children fathered by Angus Wallace out of wedlock and hidden away in the suburbs,' he said, rapid-fire.

Danby was up in a flash—but too late. 'Your honour! Scandalous! Yet again, my learned friend attempts to hoodwink the court.'

The judge said, 'I'm glad you said "attempts". Mr Spearman, what is *this* about?'

'Your honour, we know of the bad blood between Mr Wallace and my clients. I seek to put before the jury evidence as to the flawed character of the Crown's main witness. To show that such a man is *quite capable* of fabricating this case against my clients.'

'They've read about it in the *Melbourne Punch*,' Chadwick interposed helpfully.

The judge frowned at the QC, looked at Spearman. 'It won't wash, Mr Spearman. The jury will disregard the question. The witness will stand down.'

Julian Ellis, having not spoken except to take the oath and state his name, left the court a puzzled and angry man, and Spearman sat down, not unhappy with his achievement.

At noon, the Crown Prosecutor faced the jury. His lined face was serious and earnest. Pay attention please, this is the most crucial day of your life, it seemed to say.

'If your honour pleases…'

Susan, her left hand lightly against her cheek, held her gaze on Wallace. For much of the trial, he'd been in the witness-box. His evidence, his response to questions, had been absolutely calm, concise, reasonable. He'd been like a rock amid the posturing, pirouetting, histrionics of the defending barristers. Admirable! She'd not paid attention to the unfolding of the case, only to him. Certainly, he'd been a man on a mission, and that had come through, but an eminently reasonable man. And, a man mindful of the human cost...

Single-mindedly, she had entered this interior monologue, semi-conscious of the Crown Prosecutor's words falling into the court.

'...*without a scintilla of doubt... balance sheet at the 30th September, 1892...false...directors signed and published it...*'

She felt guilty at being absent from the store with William also absent. This terrible event which had come down on Katherine and William. How could it be borne? How could they be best supported?...

'...*beyond belief, these businessmen...men of the world...did not know...agreed amongst themselves, and signed it...if that isn't conspiracy...*'

His eyes were down, listening intently, mentally linked to the phrases being articulated. Calm and steady, but it had taken its toll. The cast of his face, the set of his shoulders. If he were to lose?...

'...*a fact that the bank was insolvent...if the board had done its duty...dealt with the massive bad debts...four weeks later they had...only those connected to themselves...all in that together, too...*'

How to make sense of it? The answers were there...waiting to be uncovered. This unfinished business between them must be finished. No more postponements...Otherwise, her nerve was going to crack like the pod of a cassia tree underfoot.

'...*consequences were...new depositors made deposits... old customers kept their money in...shareholders kept their shares...their obligations to pay in more capital...ignorant of its rotten foundations...*'

She looked around, Lady Adams had come in alone. Someone found her a place. They exchanged looks, nods. This morning he'd not looked up at the gallery once...

Danby was well set. He'd not taken his eyes off the jury. Hadn't referred to his brief. Had hardly drawn breath...

'Why did these directors carry out this fraudulent deception? Maintain this false illusion? One has only to look at the nature of the bank, the composition of its loan portfolio for the answer. The First Bank of Victoria was conducted for the benefit of the directors—not for its shareholders, depositors, customers or staff. The defendants saw it as a personal slush-fund.

'We're all familiar with that expression. They had a vested interest in keeping it afloat—at least until they could write off *their* loan obligations.'

He nodded at the jury, enjoining them in this scenario.

'My learned friend claims that it's the collapse of business conditions which is responsible; or, that these directors relied on the work of officials—that it's the failure of these others which is the root cause of this débâcle. But, it goes well beyond that…'

He went on, laying out what that 'beyond' was, making his statements concise—ignoring some points to emphasize others, playing his brand of Russian roulette.

'It's clear, Sir John Adams has been a most careless and profligate land boomer—heedless of those who've entrusted funds to his enterprises, who've relied on his name. He embarked on a string of voluntary liquidations of his companies—a cloak and dagger affair—to avoid public scrutiny. He's made his secret composition—to pay one shilling in the pound! One can only wonder at the motives of the creditors who've let him get away with it. All in all—a sordid business.

'And, in a varying degree, the defendants, Savage and Sandhurst, are tarred with the same brush. But we'll get to them shortly. At the end of the day, the honest citizen, the widows with their small savings, are the ones who've gone down. We all know of the abject misery amongst us. Whichever way we look, the action of the defendants is all of a piece: to deceive, defraud and cover up.

'And, they seek to glide above all that, to keep their reputations, and their mansions—but I'm confident you will not permit it. The balance sheet was false. They knew it. They conspired in it.'

He poured himself a glass of water; the court drank every drop with him.

'Now I turn to the second charge—against the defendants Savage and Sandhurst—and I do so reluctantly—because it's a nasty direction to turn in…'

Implacably, he re-stated the evidence, drew out points to the detriment of the parliamentarians' case; reminded the jury of the 'frivolous attempts' of their counsel to attest that their presence in the dock was due to 'malice'. But, the evidence told a different story. He was confident that common sense would prevail in the minds of the jury, that they'd bring in the proper verdict of guilty.

He sat down.

Judge Mountain writing away, without looking up, said: Mr Chadwick?'

'If your honour pleases.'

'Widow's walk again,' Wallace muttered to Larkin.

And the QC did put in a final smooth performance—this time manifesting the weight of his thoughts.

'Gentlemen of the jury. As I said before, so far as my client is concerned this is a very simple case. I will remind you, as no doubt his honour will, that there are two parts to this charge and unless you find for *both*, you cannot convict. You can't have one without the other.

'One, is this fanciful notion of *conspiracy*. The prosecution has produced no witness to any discussion or agreement between the defendants; there's no correspondence between them on it. The prosecution merely takes the inference that there must have been, because they sat down to sign the balance sheet put before them by the chief manager and the bank's external auditor—as any reasonable men might have done! There's been no wrong-doing within the terms of the Companies Act.'

He pounded on the bar table. 'The chief manager, who might've thrown light on these matters, hasn't been brought to court. Gentlemen, this is not good enough!

'My learned friend has painted an emotional picture of the times we live in...the consequences of failure...again inferring this is the direct handiwork of my client. He is very handy at inferences and innuendo. But look around you...banks and financial institutions have been failing since '89; forty-seven building societies alone have gone down with a thud. It's an unmitigated disaster! An act of God! Market forces have run through us like a plague. The best business brains haven't been able to stand against it. Mistakes have been made, it should be admitted. This case may not be exempt from that. There may've been imprudence—but if there was, it was honestly done.

'The Crown has made a second charge against Messrs Savage and Sandhurst. *If* there is anything in this, my client knew nothing about it—and the Crown has not alleged that he did. It has nothing to do with him.

'Sir John is an honest and well-intentioned man, unluckily caught in this web of events. I ask that you acquit him—and give him back his good name.'

Chadwick, having by sleight of hand begged a lot of questions, delivered these last words with some emotion—not unlike the last notes of a romantic aria—then sat down.

Lady Adams' face had become rigid. Yet, an impressive face, someone noted. She thought the QC might have done well enough. The past months, her reflections had brought her to a state of near indifference as to the verdict. The damage was done. Her thoughts turned back to yesterday's events at Edinburgh Gardens. The real world of women's affairs.

Judge Mountain: 'Mr Spearman?'

The barrister brought his pleasant, pugilistic face into the jury's range. He wasn't going to say much. Didn't need to. He leant back, took hold of his braces, and fronted them fair and square. He represented an honest man, representing honest men. He covered similar ground to Chadwick, then diverged, with a thwack of the braces, to address the second charge.

Watching closely, Larkin reflected that there were many tales about Spearman. One was that each night when he took his dinner at a hotel, he was accompanied by the disreputable leg-man who did his odd jobs. This individual sat opposite the barrister who, when he was done with a dish, pushed it across to the leg-man to finish off. A perk of office.

'My clients have never denied the existence of the No. 2 Accounts...'

Behind the bar table, Wallace thought: I'll wager they didn't appear in the liabilities shown in their secret compositions.

'...they are mystified at this charge. And what does it amount to? The word of an ex-bank accountant against two long-serving parliamentarians? And, with malice aforethought—a good old English law which we all know about. Despite the Crown Prosecutor's haste to dismiss it, is there anything more likely on the horizon?

'The liquidator has had a long-running vendetta with my clients. It's a matter of public record. And—in his private life—he's been discredited as an absolutely immoral, ruthless and unreliable man.'

Blank-faced, Wallace gazed past Spearman to the intent, amorphous faces of the jury. Ruthless? Against these blackmailing criminals? With Hubble dead in the river, Murdoch dead at the bottom of those stairs, his own affray in the street. Were they acts of God, too? He'd been feeling the case slipping away from him, hour by hour. Grimly, he contemplated the future.

'...against this background alone, it would be *dangerous* to convict my clients.'

He sat down, and Judge Mountain adjourned for lunch.

At two o'clock the judge began to sum up. For over and hour he addressed the jury reviewing the evidence, only occasionally letting go one of his astringent phrases. He did point out the aspect of 'conspiracy', as Chadwick had predicted. He said also: 'There's no room in your considerations for passion. *No-one* here is on trial for morals or ethics. You must consider only the evidence which has been put to you.'

The jury retired at a quarter past three.

Susan, present for her own motives, was at last caught up in the trial. Twice since the lunch adjournment he had looked up at the gallery, and seen her. What was he thinking? She put this aside and turned to Sir John and Lady Adams, who, physically divided in that courtroom, seemed to her to be absolutely spiritually detached as well. There'd been no glances, signals or reassuring smiles.

If the verdict went against *him*, how would he react? With compressed lips, a determined neutrality, she'd listened to the aspersions thrown on him. Hard words...but nothing *Punch* hadn't printed.

She had made her decision. Throughout this day it had, finally, been formulating in her mind. Some things were so deep in her she was hardly in touch with them. Dr Blackstone had divined that. But, in touch enough to know what she must do.

Danby, Wallace and Larkin had conferred quietly, hardly more than a few monosyllables. Wallace had withdrawn from it, but did not look up at the gallery again. What must she think now? Was her presence a sign for hope? Or, curiosity to observe the monster at bay?! He could feel her gaze burning into his back. He would have chosen a different ground—but what would be, would be. As with the case.

Chadwick had gone to speak to Sir John, and now sat beside Spearman. They laughed together over something. And the QC turned an ironic gaze to the ceiling.

At half-past four a message came that the jury was returning, and Judge Mountain reappeared in a flurry of robes and standing up. In the hush, the foreman swayed on his feet.

'How find you, on the first charge against the defendants etc., etc.?'

'*Not* guilty!'

A communal gasp went across the court. With surprising vigour, Judge Mountain rapped with his gavel for silence.

'Sir John, you may step down and leave the court. You are discharged from these proceedings without a stain on your character.'

The knight, his eyes blinking quickly, was led out by an usher.

In the gallery, despite her coolness, Lady Adams' hand had gone to her heart.

Danby, Wallace and Larkin did not move, might have been converted to stone. Chadwick was smiling slightly.

'How find you, on the second charge, etc., against the defendants...?'

'Guilty!'

A much greater stir arose which grew into a commotion. Savage was on his feet pounding the dock, shouting, sending spittle flying. Sandhurst sat back with his hooded eyes on the foreman's face as though he saw him revolving on a fiery spit. Judge Mountain again was at work with his gavel. The constables were going to Savage.

'It was Harbrace who did it,' Larkin said to Wallace. 'A brave performance.'

A man in the gallery crowed: 'They'll soon have that beard off you in prison, Savage.'

Wallace looked up. Was it the man from Camberwell? Judge Mountain, white-lipped, continued to pound away.

65

The inclusion of women into the domain of political activity con-
tradicts all human experience as to the fitness of things and runs
counter to all our intuitive perceptions of the proper relations
between the sexes and their respective spheres of work...
Advertiser, *27.8.1891*
Quoted in Kirsten Lees, Votes for Women:
The Australian Story *(1995)*

Then came the bitter, sudden change,
The fastened lips the dumb despair:
The first few weeks were very strange,
And long, and sad, and hard to bear.
Henry Kendall, 'Rose Lorraine'

Fire and Ice

THE PROTAGONISTS stepped from the court precincts into an azure, coolish evening in which gas-lights were flaring dustily like late-blooming sunflowers. With relief, they turned their backs on the over-charged atmosphere, inserted themselves back into the world.

So Susan theorized, as she waited where an usher had suggested, her nerves strung tight. Moving between the 'real' and 'unreal' sectors of their lives, was akin to playing hop-scotch in the dusk.

The General Post Office clock, striking five, made her start. She listened to the carillon of its twelve bells cross the city's heart, quiver into silence. Nearby, someone was locking up. Sharply, behind a door—the sound of voices, footsteps. It opened, and Wallace appeared with Philip Larkin. They both halted and stared at the female figure in the murky corridor light.

A white, questing face (that was how Larkin described it to Hanna), white throat, white hands, illuminated in the dusk against the dark dress; only a flash of colour from a single peacock's feather above the small, darkish hat. Like a watching eye. Startling—at that hour, in that dismal place—he reported. Hanna had a precise mental picture of her friend.

'Susan!'—Wallace exclaimed, as though their last conversation had been an hour ago—not four weeks hence. Larkin bowed, and slipped away, his eyes down discreetly, his own problem of this nature settled.

The liquidator's face was haggard; shadows blacked-out one side. Decidedly thinner; his hair streaked finer, his lips compressed, a bruise beneath the one visible eye. From the gallery, she'd not seen this detail. Not the face of a victor, she thought. 'You're exhausted,' she said quietly.

'It's over now. For the present.'

What did that mean? she wondered.

'I've been here for much of it.'

He nodded.

'My congratulations…'

He shrugged dismissively, smiled thinly. 'I'm afraid a pyrrhic victory.'

He glanced back to the spot where Larkin had vanished. 'There's a room where we could talk…'

She nodded. He led her to the small room where Harbrace had been accommodated. The bed was still there. She stared at it, puzzled. He put down his brief case, his hat, frowned at the floor. He was finding it hard to grasp that this moment had arrived. He cleared his throat, had been calmer in the witness-box.

'I'd almost given up on a meeting. I'd hoped for one much earlier. For a response to my letter. I've speculated…all manner of things. Then it came, but the case blacked it out.'

She studied him, smiled sadly. 'I was remiss, yet couldn't do otherwise.'

Their eyes met, flicked away, re-joined. He felt an immense pressure to seize this moment. She thought: So hard, and complicated. How can I tell him?

He'd thought deeply of how he would put *this* case. Figuratively, he felt himself running a finger down a brief to find a place. The GPO clock did a merry job with the quarter hour. He found it.

'At the Federal Coffee Palace, I declared my feelings. It was…the first step to another declaration. That's the simple situation, but of course, not simple.' He smiled—a quick grimace. 'The newspapers, this trial, the innuendo have spoken for that. My letter gave an outline…which I'd intended as the base for a fuller account…But, perhaps we've gone past that.' He dropped his gaze, it was the last thing he wanted to think.

She said, conscious of his stare again, 'I've been deeply troubled…Perhaps, it's a woman's idea of the way of the world. But it *is* my idea. I've thought and thought and I *still* can't understand. It was—is—so heartless.'

She had come to her decision in the courtroom, had not meant to say any of this. It was immaterial. Until this afternoon, it had *seemed* that she had a choice. A deception against herself, as much as him. The words she'd spoken were true, yet not the fullest picture. A veil had been pulled aside. Blackstone had known.

His face seemed to shrink back on its bones. But his eyes hadn't left hers. He felt as empty as this building with its eerie draughts. Up against an immovable force. How could he explain in terms that she'd accept, what he could not fully understand himself?! At that moment, it was beyond his powers to perceive that the case ran deeper.

'That strikes home,' he murmured. With sudden energy, he raised his voice. 'We didn't marry. The reasons are hard to understand—now. Real enough at the time. A quagmire of them. Religion… This vice of religion and prejudice we must exist in. The damage to my parliamentary career—as it was then. My financial predicament.'

She had raised a hand. He took that in, but was going to say it. The levee bank had broken.

'We loved each other. The discovery that she was in *that* way was a shock. The outcome, a devastation. I can't recall much…Don't remember the doctors, the funeral. It's been wiped out.

'Her family kept it quiet—though there wasn't unanimity among them about that. I, too, wished it done with. There was plenty to attend to. Cases to fight. But, it remained a nightmare. And, of course, the remorse.'

He gave a tight, self-deprecating smile. 'The children. I knew nothing of children. I'd been an only child—motherless since infancy. My father always absent…It could be said, had no benchmarks. Heartless? Inhumane—even? You may be right. A natural feeling may be absent. Or, shocked into dormancy. I'd prefer to think that. The past year or so there's been a change.'

She was half-listening. His voice had become quiet and earnest—not the tones of bombast she'd been listening to that afternoon. Without knowing it, she was shaking her head sadly.

His arms were rigid at his sides. 'I don't think the *Punch* article was fair.'

'It was vile.'

He acknowledged her sympathy with a nod. 'They spoke of the ladies. I'm afraid there's no getting around some of it.'

He didn't mention the blackmail attempt—his defiance of it. He felt unutterably weary. For a few minutes, he'd felt buoyed up. 'This trial…I'm not out for revenge. It's a question of trying to extract a modicum of justice from the system. It's pitiful, really. Against the miles of rottenness, one makes a stand of inches.'

'I believe you. I've found your principles—admirable.'

He glanced at her. Yes. But it won't wash, he thought. His own flash of the future had come. As though clouds had opened and light had penetrated—he saw in her the kind of idealistic nature which would not, could not, compromise. It brought a sharp pain to his heart. He almost put his hand there. Could any man, with the baggage that men had, meet that standard?

His realization was accurate, yet, there was another dimension to it, and he'd missed that.

'My brother died,' she said almost to herself. Straining towards her, his turn to wonder what something meant…He must make one last effort.

'Do you have feelings for me?' The hollowest words of all.

Slowly she comes back from where she had drifted to. This stubbornness, this perversity against herself? An almost insane intolerance? A self-deception, or even an artifice, a barrier, behind which she is formulating her position for the future. Making the real plan. Sir Joshua had spoken to her just once on a personal plane. Fire and ice, he'd said thoughtfully, his eyes perceptive under the heavy brow…What explanation could she give him?

None was needed. He was reading the subtle flashes on her face: the shallows, if not the depths. 'I do not believe this,' he said almost to himself.

Her face was shadowed with sympathy, but she did not reply.

His body was frozen. But not his mind. *By God! It had never been a possibility*. He was remembering remarks, nuances, observations, raw clues: suffragettism, the Dugdale woman—which until now had not connected in his brain. For a brief period, the hiatus *between* Manchester and Boyd & Montrose, she'd been in limbo. Now she was back on course. She wasn't for any man!

Whether he was right in that catastrophic judgment was debatable, but it was his absolute conviction of that moment.

The solitary peacock feather winked in a trinket of light.

Somehow, after what interval he didn't know, he said, 'I will see you to a hansom.'

'I'll go by tram.'

They left the airless court building and walked into an evening breeze, already separated in their thoughts. The Town Hall clock struck the half.

He stood on a corner in Bourke Street, oblivious to the push of humanity going like a moth to the flame of the night's entertainment.

'I'm truly sorry,' she'd said. And, there it was.

66

And we—no longer actors of the stage
  We cumber now—maybe
  With other eyes shall see
This wasted chance, and with celestial rage
  Cry 'O what fools were we!'
    Ada Cambridge, 'The Future Verdict'

M. Lean Bros & Rigg Ltd,
107–118 Elizabeth-street.
Sportsmen are Cordially Invited to Call and
Inspect our Immense Stock of Guns
—Revolvers, Webley, Smith and Wesson, Colts…
    Advertisment, The Leader, 4.3.1893

The Colt

'WELL, YOU'VE SEEN THEM OFF,' Lady Adams said drily, casting the knight a look which was difficult to interpret.

It was a week since the trial had concluded. There had been no celebration on their part, nor even the sketchiest of post-mortems. He had spent the period closeted in his study. 'Catching up on paperwork,' he'd muttered. Hilda Wilberforce had come and gone on several occasions, supporting her friend in the aftermath. And support had been needed. To the East Melbourne matron, Laura Adams had become as preoccupied as her husband. Hilda could guess the nature of her thoughts.

The newspaper reports, the day after the trial, had been damning: Sir John was a very lucky man—as all the world could see. On the Friday, *Table Talk* had made it abundantly clear. The headline was branded on Lady Adams' mind:
      Knight Acquitted Without a Stain on His Character.
      Bank Shareholders and Depositors Left to Lament.
'I have,' the knight said.

'I see your secret composition might be re-opened.' It had been canvassed in that morning's *Argus*.

'It might.' They'd never before discussed this subject, but as he'd appeared from his study and stood, massive, before her chair with an attitude of lingering, she said this almost as small-talk. Nothing much mattered now. Daily, in the past week, she had pictured him sitting in his study staring out the window. Entering the room once, she'd seen no sign of paperwork.

'Are you feeling quite well, John?'

'I am, Laura.'

'Hilda is coming shortly.'

Sir John nodded slowly. 'I can see she's been a tower of strength to you.'

Lady Adams was surprised. For months, she had scarcely had a conversation with her husband at this level of intimacy. He still lingered. And now, she was waiting.

'I've come to an important decision, Laura.' He had joined his hands behind the tails of his coat—a gesture of resolution. 'One that'll be hard on you—on us both.'

She watched him with level eyes.

'I've been acquitted of the charge—which should be an end to it. But these things are never at an end. And, perhaps they shouldn't be. "Without a stain on his character."' The thick lips twisted in a bitter smile. She noticed that his clothes were a trifle looser on him.

'You know the principles I've lived by. I've been for Progress. She's turned out to be a rather tricky mistress.'

Lady Adams maintained her gaze. Inch by inch, it seemed a new facet of her husband was being revealed to her.

'I intend to put this house and its contents on the market for the benefit of the bank's creditors. It's the only asset of any substance which remains to us. The estate agent'll be here this morning.'

He spoke with the heaviness of one of his former boardroom pronouncements, presented one hand to straighten his gold watch-chain.

Laura Adams withdrew her gaze. 'I see.'

'You'll have your income from your father's estate.'

What will you have? she thought. It would be an end to their life in the Colony, but it was over anyway. 'I'm glad you've decided this,' she said.

Hilda Wilberforce arrived at eleven, by which time Sir John was re-closeted in his study with the auctioneer. She said as she whirled into the drawing-room, her face bright, 'How is he, Laura? More to the point—how are you?'

'Well enough, my dear.' Lady Adams took her friend's hands spontaneously.

Lady Adams' spirits had revived as she'd listened to her husband state his intentions. She'd felt a weight come off her heart. She told Hilda of the momentous decision. At which point, Hilda Wilberforce's mood turned, full circle, to the sombre. She saw their future clearly now.

Several days later three wagons appeared in their drive. They were packed with furniture which Sir John had taken on approval from a dealer. He informed his wife that he proposed to send their own valuable antiques into store—and substitute this consignment of inferior pieces for the auction.

She had stared at him, amazed. She supposed he could not help himself. One step forward, two steps back. She had shaken her head and fixed him with that gaze.

'John, you will send these wagons away immediately. Everything here is to go to auction. Including my family silver. You will keep to the arrangement.'

And he did her bidding, without a word.

———•———

A curse on the politicians and the aldermen, Otto Rudd thought. His normally pacific features had taken on a grim cast. Bowler in his hands, he was watching the tail-end of a funeral, its tiny coffin, disappear up Collins Street, remembering the one he'd attended last week, standing at the back, inconspicuously paying his respects. Each day, these black-garbed processions, small coffins, weaved insidious patterns on the metropolis. He'd read in the *Illustrated Sydney News*: 'It is the children, the little children which are being borne so thickly to the grave…In what city (except Melbourne) could such havoc of the very young and the wholly helpless take place without exciting an universal cry of agony…?'

He turned back into the hurrying crowd.

———•———

Later that week, Lady Adams went to Hilda Wilberforce's for dinner. She left Sir John in the cavernous mansion to eat alone. These days, the servants passed silently through the house like ghosts. They knew drastic changes were coming.

After a meal of his favourite boiled mutton, each mouthful of which he appeared to savour and meditate on, the knight retired to his study, and on a seeming impulse, pulled down a handsome leather volume of *Australian Representative Men*. He turned the pages slowly, reacquainting himself with the biographies of both friends and enemies. He did not turn to his own entry; he had that page of dense print by heart.

The clocks in the house chimed eight o'clock, pretty much together. He returned the volume to its place, and took out notepaper. He wrote a letter and sealed it in an envelope, and rang for the butler. The man came in, and took it and his instructions. As he went out, he gave the knight a look.

Sir John wrote another letter over which he took more trouble, sealed it in an envelope and left it on the blotter. He looked towards the dark windows, could not see out to the garden. Rain had begun to fall—whispery, wintry.

He removed his shoes, and padded out into the hall, furnished with aspidistra in brass pots, decorated with vast chromo-lithographs of Highland cattle and sheep in wild landscape. And, *The Stag...*

For an instant, the electric light flickered. He went into the great hall and stared up at the intricately carved wooden ceiling: the facsimile of the one in a nearby church which, on Sundays, he'd gazed at for years.

He moved on, a big man padding along in stockinged feet—a strange sight—into the dining-room with its delicately executed murals of Ancient Greece. He inspected them. Finally, he entered the billiard room, rolled a white ball across the expansive green baize of the Alcock table, to click against another...

He consulted his watch, padded back to the hall, and climbed the majestic sweep of the stairs, running his big hand up the curve of the mahogany banister, re-living the pleasure he'd taken from this simple act each night since they'd come here in '86.

The servants had been dismissed to their quarters.

The Colt revolver was kept in his bed-side drawer. He retrieved it, examined the mechanism, the bullets in the chamber, almost with curiosity—.476 calibre, Model P. He removed his coat and tie. He took off his diamond rings and watch and laid them, neatly, on his chest of drawers. They glittered on the mahogany. He padded along the corridor to the bath-room, engrossed in the procedure, a big, heavy man being as quiet as a cat.

The bath-room was huge with expansive marble surfaces, the bath a monster on clawed feet. He wrapped a white bath-towel around his neck and the back of his head, and with deliberation, climbed into the bath, slipping slightly, steadying himself on its sides.

William came to the door himself. He recognized the Adams' outside man waiting on the portico. A carriage, its horses restive, waited in the street. Rain hissed into the Edinburgh Gardens, drifted a glacial mist into his face.

'Mr Boyd. A letter from Sir John.'

William took it to the gas-light in the hall, tore it open. Katherine had come up beside him. He read the half-dozen lines of the knight's scrawled writing and his body jumped as though a nerve had been hit. He said nothing, read it again.

'What is it, William?'

He turned to Katherine. 'I'm afraid something might've happened at the Adams'. He folded the letter and put it in his pocket. I must go there. I'll pick up the doctor on the way.'

'O God!' she said.

'We mustn't think the worst.' He looked at her anxiously. Her face was pale, taut. He called Mary to her, and left.

Bound for Kew with Dr MacKenzie, and the Adams' man, he couldn't picture what he might find there. The muscles in his throat had tightened, and he swallowed quickly a few times. Thank Heavens, Laura was absent, but she'd be returning—pray God, he'd get there first. He'd no hope that the other could be averted.

En route, they stopped to hire a hansom and sent it post haste to St Kilda with a note he'd dashed off to Philip. He settled back. He recalled the night Tom Montrose had died and Sir John had driven in from Kew to make the arrangements.

The Kew mansion was ablaze with light at the end of its drive. Fredericks, fully dressed, stood in the hall with all the servants. The women had been weeping, the men looked shocked.

'The bath-room, sir,' the butler murmured in a choking voice.

'Her ladyship?'

'Not yet home.'

'Quite dead,' Dr MacKenzie said, looking back to where William stood like a statue in the doorway. 'Better go out and sit down for a moment. Always, rather nasty, though he's done it neatly enough.'

William did go out. The horror seemed to follow him down the stairs. The waxed ends of the knight's moustache had survived, inviolate, in the ghastly mess. He took some deep breaths, pulled himself together, questioned Fredericks. Lady Adams was expected home after eleven. He went back and spoke to MacKenzie. He would go to Hilda Wilberforce's. There was time enough to head-off Laura from returning home.

Philip Larkin arrived at a quarter-past ten as he was about to leave. When William told him, the solicitor staggered, clutched at the balustrade which Sir John's hand had earlier given his touch of approbation.

'I'll break the news to Laura. Should I miss her, you'll have to do it. Dr MacKenzie is upstairs.'

He left Larkin at the front door.

The hansom, going at its best pace, took thirty minutes to reach the Italianate mansion at East Melbourne. Here, the rain, even-handed tonight in the city, drifted into the Fitzroy Gardens.

William took more deep breaths as he went up the front steps, found himself shaking. This wouldn't do. He stopped, shrugged his shoulders several times. Nonetheless, he felt impelled to press on without delay—as though the tragic news might beat him there by some back-door route.

Hilda's maid took one look at his face, and showed him immediately to the small drawing-room where the two women had gone after dinner. He was in the room before she had time to announce him. Hilda looked at him sharply and rose to her feet with a soft exclamation.

Lady Adams remained seated, her head tilted up, an expression which manifested strain and expectation on her face. Tears had sprung into those glacial eyes, with instant understanding.

'My dear Laura,' he said, 'I have the saddest news.'

67

The great physician, Time, shall pacify
This parting anguish with another friend.
Your heart is broken now, but it will mend.
Though it is death, yet still you will not die.
Good-bye! Good-bye!
            Ada Cambridge, 'Good-bye'

The Saddest Day

HILDA WILBERFORCE thought this, as she looked into the eyes of her friend: The day, at the cusp of autumn and winter. The bay was flat-grey and lustreless as iron. Equally as sombre, the milky sky flowed to a seamless join: the horizon was a myth. The air was washed-out, chill-edged from the Southern Ocean.

Streamers were hurling from shore to ship, ship to shore. At any moment, they expected the announcement: 'All ashore that's going ashore.' The ship was concentrated with all the minutiae that attached to a departure on a 12,000-mile voyage. And, all the emotions.

They'd come in hansoms; Hilda had sold her carriage. Laura Adams had accepted this bohemian mode of transport without comment. Her trunks had been sent ahead. The others in their party—Katherine, William, Hanna, Philip, Judge Mountain—had stepped back.

'Write often,' Mrs Wilberforce said, holding Lady Adams' hand in a way she had never quite held it before.

'I will, my dear.'

Sir John had been buried six weeks, the Kew mansion and its contents had been auctioned. All the Adams' affairs were settled—so far as they could ever be. Along with the sensational reports of his death, the press had acknowledged his gesture towards the victims of the bank's collapse. In his two final acts, some claimed that the knight had wiped the slate clean. Laura Adams thought it possible. Her gaze had lost some of its acerbity.

Pensively, they dwelt on the friendship of thirty years—as if together they were lightly fingering a piece of rare Flemish lace.

'Thirty years in the Colony. They've gone by like a dream, Hilda. John seems like a ship which passed in the night. All that life—gone. Isn't it strange?' She said it wonderingly, for Hilda's ears only. In the years to come, back in Derbyshire in the bosom of her not-too-welcoming family, she was to wonder if her colonial life had been anything but a dream.

Hilda Wilberforce nodded. On one of very few occasions in her life, she could not trust her voice.

However, in the final week Laura had stayed at her house, and the things that each desired to say had been said.

Susan had not come to the ship; she'd known Lady Adams only briefly, and they'd found no common ground. The information contained in the letter from Manchester had reduced Lady Adams and Hilda to silence when they'd read it. And the two friends had made a pact to remain silent. If she had known this, Susan might have had a different idea of Laura Adams…

The Derbyshire woman would not return to the Colony; Hilda would not travel to England—for reasons which she found hard to determine. Perhaps it was because all her dear men were buried here.

In the background, forced gaiety…Lady Adams wore a sable collarette with the head and tail of the small animal intact. It encircled her soft, white throat, and looked alive.

Bizarre, Judge Mountain thought. He couldn't help staring at it. A soul-searing blast; the ship's horn went on and on and hundreds of hands were pressed to ears.

Lady Adams stood alone at the rail, another posy of violets in her hands, smiling sadly for the past, cautiously for the future—one might have guessed. But she was smiling for her friends. A tentative breeze arose, and the ostrich plumes in her hat danced.

Standing near the edge of the wharf, Hilda, who had been seeing people through things all her life, suddenly thought: Who is going to see me through this? Edgar was no good for that. Men didn't have the sensibility. There wasn't an atom of self-pity in this pondering—just a pragmatic appreciation of her situation.

Katherine, watching the ship turn slowly like the old lady she was to point at the thirty-five-mile-distant heads of Port Phillip Bay, couldn't divine the exact question, but with a glance at her mentor's sad profile, knew what was required of her. She had been reserving a piece of news for Hilda, which she anticipated was going to prove quite a distraction.

68

The fierce, disastrous flying fire
  That made the great caves ring,
And scarred the slope and broke the spire,
  Is a forgotten thing.
                    Henry Kendall, 'Orara'

Reprise of Bells

THE CITY'S AIRSPACE reverberated with the sounds of bells criss-cross-ing it from its plenitude of bluestone churches. To William, the quiv-ering resonance in his ears brought the visual image of a heat-haze shimmering along a desert horizon.

But heat and summer were memories. From the desolate reaches of the Southern Ocean, southerlies were driving up chilled air with the gusto of a carpenter banging in stops with a mallet. Few Melburnians ever thought of that lonesome, icy sphere, but it was as salient to their lives as the continent's arid heart.

Yes, a city of churches, he thought. Prayer and hymn books were being laid out by vergers, wafers and communion wine being readied; in its brief history, never had so many of its citizens embraced religion. Passengers on a stricken ship rushing for life-boats, was the metaphor being thundered triumphantly, each Sunday, from *one* pulpit.

Rugged up, he and Katherine walked across the gardens towards the tolling of St Luke's bells. The church wasn't a frequent destination for him, was for her. Today was special.

The tan from his summer transits of the city had already disap-peared. Her face, under the reddish tints of her hair, under shady hats, kept its pale translucency whatever the season.

And today, at last, she had an aura of peacefulness which made his heart rise. Had they come through? It was too fragile a hope to put much weight on yet. Beneath her overcoat, the prominence of her stomach was a miracle which he couldn't quite believe in yet, either.

Katherine's mind curved away above this city, going homewards.

She was thinking over the events of the past months. How could she ever have pictured having this life? What lies ahead? Whatever it was, would it all pass by to seem, in the end, like a dream? At the ship, she'd caught Laura's whispered remark to Hilda—had wondered if she'd been allowed a glimpse of her own future.

…It was out there, dancing under the trees. She'd felt it arrive. A small, silent spirit coming to her. She gazed to where she thought it might be, smiled. William didn't know…She whispered some words…

St Luke's bells were now setting up a formidable clangour; the portly, red-faced, bachelor verger would be swinging on his rope like an animated sand-bag. She glanced at William, held his arm a little tighter as they crossed St George's Street, wondered what he was thinking. He was smiling: yesterday she'd smelled of fish; the Metropolitan Fish Market had sent six baskets, fresh and gratis, to the Collingwood centre.

<hr>

Immaculate in his frock-coat, his face and cranium shining from soap, cold water, and a brisk towelling, Sebastian Low entered his study and, from a wall-safe, took a tin box which was obviously extremely heavy. With a key on his watch-chain, he unlocked it, threw back the lid.

En masse, the mint sovereigns gave off a fecund glow which underlit his throat, face and bald head; like a saint's sun-illumed fresco. This was as much a Sunday ritual as the opening of his hymn book in the front pew of the Scots' Church.

As he replaced it, other pleasantries came to him. Yesterday, he'd attended the boys' orphanage to supervise the Saturday baths. He loved seeing all that innocence splashing around. The round moons of their little bums were a source of pleasant meditation. Some men went to view fine paintings; didn't know what they were missing.

Alas, Boyd, Montrose & Co. was still extant. He'd once overheard an angler at the club say there was more satisfaction in playing a fish than landing it. He *could* see that side…

He'd been thinking about Brodzky. He'd picked up choice information on officials of the Commercial Bank. He hadn't decided how to approach the proprietor of *Table Talk*. Up to a point, they were in the same line of business. And, in this city, what a fertile line it was! Even in these straightened times. Profit, progress, ethics, morality— toss it like a french salad! These court cases were a temporary setback. It'd be muddied up again pretty soon; the demarcations again as obscure as a sea horizon on a pissing-down day. Marvellous! His brougham was at the door. The Scots' Church and its wonderful organ awaited!

Helena Spencer's barouche was making a third circuit of the Albert Park Lake, going at a good clip. Round and round like a bloody merry-go-round, her coachman thought, unhappy with Sunday duty. He was an artist with the ribbons, in favour of Sunday Observance. But soon, a long holiday…

The bells were pure and clear coming over the water. She took in the sound with the icy rush of air on her face. All last night she'd been thinking, and this morning tears as clear and sharp as diamonds did glitter in her green eyes. This breeze…

On the merry-go-round of the lonely life, she pronounced silently, suspended in her perfect equipage beneath her tiger-skin rug. Abruptly, she told herself, 'Helena, this is unlike you. Off to Paris we'll go, then we'll come back and we'll see.' Her trunks stood packed and ready in her hall. The ship was in the bay.

Philip and Hanna, arm-in-arm, walked up Collins Street laughing over something, behind them the book shop was rising from the ashes. Philip's smile died. In a sudden unexpected flight, his thoughts had gone back to the Sunday he'd come wading out of the lake, delicate Mrs Chadwick in his arms, Helena giving orders in the background. With a faint smile, the bookseller watched his abstraction.

Susan stood at the drawing-room window of Carlton Gardens, watching and listening. Her head inclined, a wisp of blonde hair seemed artful on her forehead. *Not* artful. Her beauty was most striking when she was at her most casual—and most reflective. She was closely inspecting the Exhibition Building in the greyish light.

She smiled at the abundance of church bells. Did it represent some kind of colonial bravado?…She had been stepping carefully through a maze: the deep labyrinth within herself. Sir Joshua, the autocratic protagonist of the strategic business plan, had given her his principles. Clear, undiluted—and portable. And, of course, there was that other banner…As much as any human being could, she now saw the way ahead. But always, whichever way one turned, were regrets.

———•———

Breakfast over, Wallace had climbed the tower and taken a steady look at the bay, then had turned to the lake—like a surveyor taking bearings. But he had no such idea in his mind. He lit a cigar. A breeze had chopped the lake into white flecks. Around its margin a few vehicles were in motion. It was too far for him to identify Helena's barouche.

Next door, Mrs Hammond was airing a new flag. In a moment or two, he supposed he would get the Sunday morning concert.

The liquidation had a way to go yet. It would be madness to sell off at current prices the properties they'd taken over. And, he had hopes of getting Savage's and Sandhurst's personal assets, of opening up their secret compositions like cans of sardines.

In certain quarters, he'd been blamed for Sir John's death. *Punch* had found qualities of martyrdom in the deceased knight. He was going to carry the scars. So be it. Brodzky had got in good thrusts at the Premier and the Attorney-General, though they soaked up such attacks like a sponge. However, he had some ideas on that for the future—and, an inch or two had been gained.

Had *he* the capacity to absorb setbacks and damage? He smiled grimly at a notion: the numerous wounds carried by some of Napoleon's generals after a lifetime of combat—Oudinot had thirty-four serious ones. What lives they were! He let the small fantasy go.

He laid his hands on the parapet. He believed he had got it clear in his mind: *her* essence. At least, close to it. His brain had laboured at it night after night. At first, it had horrified him. It amazed him still, how far off the mark he'd been. But for all of that it was merely a glimpse of an unknown landscape for which he, personally, had no map…*Terra incognita*. Nonetheless, he would have taken it all…

He narrowed his eyes. Life was a bit like that mosquito fleet out on the lake—tacking this way, that way—never giving up. Maybe he should consider Susan in that light…Yes, maybe. One thing *was* certain: his life had reached a turning-point. Certain things had been burned away…

His gaze was still fixed on the lake. Suddenly, it had received sunlight. His thinking died away as in a lull of wind.

In her kitchen, Mrs Beattie said—as though to the southern city at large: 'Oh, have I told you?…The children are coming home.'

Afterword

PUBLISHED HISTORIES, the La Trobe Library, and the Newspaper Section of the State Library of Victoria, are rich in material about Melbourne in the 1890s, and I have used these resources extensively in creating this fiction.

The following books were especially useful: *The Land Boomers* (which deals comprehensively with the personalities, frauds and manipulations in the finance sector, the related trials, insolvencies, etc. of the period), and *Life in the Cities Australia in the Victorian Age: 3*, both by Michael Cannon; *The Rise and Fall of Marvellous Melbourne*, by Graeme Davison; *The Rush to be Rich*, by Geoffrey Serle; *The Store on the Hill*, by Keith Dunstan; *The Pleasant Career of a Spendthrift*, by George D. Meudell; *Thirty Years in Australia*, by Ada Cambridge; *Gold and Paper*, by Geoffrey Blainey.

The following journals and newspapers were invaluable: *Table Talk*; *The Age*; *The Argus*; *Illustrated Australian News*; *The Leader*. The indefatigable editors and journalists of those days have left a treasure-trove of information in their reports of the financial scandals, bank collapses, and the numerous criminal trials.

I must express my gratitude to the Australian poets, authors, and unknown journalists whose work I quote as a preface to each chapter. They have all passed from the scene but their 'voices' remain to illuminate brilliantly our past.

The characters portrayed are the author's inventions—except in two cases where actual personages appear as themselves but in imaginary events. Also, certain public officials are identified by their titles of office; they are fictional counterparts of the incumbents of those offices at that time. The emporium, the bank, the liquidator's inquiry, and the criminal prosecutions described are the author's inventions. However, in pursuit of verisimilitude, I have 'lifted' several incidents from the plethora of such available, as I have several snatches of dialogue from the reports of trials and hearings.

My thanks to Keith Dunstan, once again, for reading the manuscript and generously commenting thereon, and to Ian Salmon for his comments, once again, on the trial scenes. The responsibility for the decisions ultimately taken is mine.

I am grateful to my mother for her memories of her grandfather, John Marshall, a land boomer in the 1880s, who as a director of the famous Melbourne store, Georges, and of the failed Dominion Bank, was in the thick of the historical events backgrounding my fiction. Finally, my heartfelt thanks to my wife for her ever-present support and practical assistance without which this fiction would not have been finished.